Francis Cowley Burnand, H. Savile Clarke and others

No Rose without a Thorn and other Tales

Francis Cowley Burnand, H. Savile Clarke and others

No Rose without a Thorn and other Tales

ISBN/EAN: 9783744728355

Printed in Europe, USA, Canada, Australia, Japan

Cover: Foto ©Andreas Hilbeck / pixelio.de

More available books at **www.hansebooks.com**

'I CANNOT—'I AM ENGAGED.'

NO ROSE WITHOUT A THORN

AND OTHER TALES

BY

F. C. BURNAND, H. SAVILE CLARKE, R. E. FRANCILLON,
JOSEPH HATTON, RICHARD JEFFERIES,
THE AUTHOR OF "A FRENCH HEIRESS IN HER
OWN CHATEAU," &c.

WITH ILLUSTRATIONS

By LINLEY SAMBOURNE, M. E. EDWARDS, ADELAIDE CLAXTON, A. CORBOULD,
M. KEARNS, DOWER WILSON, &c.

LONDON:

VIZETELLY & CO., 42, CATHERINE STREET, STRAND.
1886.

CONTENTS.

	PAGE
"No rose without a thorn"	1
An entr'acte	28
A story of a garden party	60
A social failure redeemed	73
Veni, vidi, vici	102
The fair face in the yellow chariot	120
Kiss and try	148
Miss Monkton's marriage	163
The story of a return-ticket	246
Kites and pigeons	264
How we got married	329

LIST OF PAGE ENGRAVINGS.

		PAGE
"I cannot, I am engaged"	Frontispiece.	
An unexpected meeting		35
A declaration rejected		57
A flirtation and its results		63
A quadrille and its consequences		65
A palm house tête-à-tête		98
May goes unwillingly to receive Sir Marmaduke		116
"Here were the hundred valentines"		159
"Stanny you're a big man; can't you push your way in the crowd?"		160
Letitia interrupts an interesting conversation		200
Letitia at Jack's Croft		229
The arrival of Lord Dash and his daughters		260
A new way of entering a drawing room		332

NO ROSE WITHOUT A THORN.

A Story of a Bayswater Bouquet.

By F. C. BURNAND.

ILLUSTRATED BY LINLEY SAMBOURNE.

I.

THE TWO NINETEENS.

OON after the first quarter-day of eighteen hundred and seventy-seven Mr. and Mrs. Blythe Byrton took formal possession of their new house, No. 19, Chetwick Gardens, Bayswater.

So far there was nothing particularly striking or mysterious about the event above recorded. The metaphysical mind will observe nothing either striking or mysterious in any ordinary-looking black hat, frock coat, and regulation gloves and boots; and yet that glossy hat may cover the nefarious schemes generating in the brain of a bank-note forger, those gloves may hide from view the hands of a mixer of subtle poisons, those boots—well, the boots couldn't conceal much except large feet, unless the scoundrel to whom they belonged had acquired the knack of committing forgeries with his toes as easily as the celebrated armless artist of Antwerp, who paints his copies of Peter Paul's works with his feet.

I do not say that there is no mystery, no deep plot, connected with No. 19; but all I wish to mention, at present, is, that Mr. Blythe Byrton was a handsome Italian-looking man, with dark, piercing eyes, and that his wife—no, I do not wish to make any mystery about it—she was his wife—I will admit *that* at once—his wife, I repeat, was as sweet-looking a lady as any that you or I have ever seen; which may be saying too much or too little, but which, in my opinion, is just enough, and no more, to enable the reader to conclude that Mr. and Mrs. Blythe Byrton were a remarkably good-looking couple.

But what are good looks without happiness? Were they unhappy, then? No, they were not. On the contrary, speaking in a general way, decidedly happy. They had not been long married, it is true, but quite long enough to have been miserable, had not their tempers been equal to their circumstances, which were, as the expression goes, " comfortable."

" But, don't tell me," as the lady at No. 18 said to her friend Miss Mitton, a severe spinster of forty-five, " don't tell me that a dark-looking man like that can be anything but jealous, and horridly jealous, too." So the lady at No. 18 kept on the watch for something to turn up which should prove the correctness of her theory as to Italian-looking men.

Weeks passed, and nothing happened.

Yes, something. Apparently of no sort of importance to anyone except the lynx-eyed matron of No. 18.

And this was it. Lynville Place lay exactly opposite Chetwick Gardens. If you walked up or down in front of the houses of Lynville Place, you were simply walking up or down in front of the houses of Chetwick Gardens, only on the opposite side of the way. It follows, therefore, that the numbering and the size and arrangement of the houses on both sides being the same, No. 19, Lynville Place, at all hours of the day and night faced No. 19, Chetwick Gardens. This being the situation, Lynville Place stared Chetwick Gardens out of countenance, and asserted itself in a sort of " I'm-as-good-as-you-any-day-of-the-week " kind of way; which was a barefaced falsehood, as the Chetwickers had gardens behind, to which the Lynvillers couldn't be admitted, and the Lynvillers had nothing at all, except twopenny-halfpenny back yards, which served as the happy linen-drying grounds by day, and were the playgrounds for squalling cats and the liveliest blackbeetles by night. The Lynvillers, too—much to the disgust of the Chetwickers, who had had several meetings on the subject, I believe—were mercenary, and let lodgings.

The ground floor of No. 19, Lynville Place, had been to let up to the 29th of March, when over the window-blind of the parlour, instead of the vulgar lodging-house card, there appeared a gentlemanly-looking, aristocratic face, with a pair of light moustachios under its nose. Further investigation on the part of Mrs. Lupscombe, of No. 18, opposite, with powerful opera-glasses, showed that this gentleman was in his dressing-gown, had just breakfasted, and was smoking a pipe.

Then he stood at his window watching something, or somebody, straight before him.

"He's got his eyes fixed on the drawing-room of next door," said Mrs. Lupscombe to herself, as she stood concealed behind her own window-curtains, focussing the unconscious lodger; "and I shouldn't be surprised if he isn't "—she paused; the idea was too good a one to be allowed voice all at once—" if he isn't watching Mrs. Blythe Byrton. From the expression of his right eye—dear me, I do wish one's breath wouldn't dim these glasses so." She was obliged to stop to wipe them. "Yes, his right eye *is*, I am certain of it, making signs; and I'm not sure that he isn't doing something with the dumb alphabet on his fingers. Putting this and that together," she said to herself, as she withdrew from her concealment, and deposited her

spy-glass on the table with the air of a Wellington who had taken a last decisive look at the enemy; "putting one and one together, I think there's something more than meets the eye in this."

She might have added, "and opera-glasses," seeing that they had been in constant use for the last few days.

But what were the "one" and the "one" which Mrs. Lupscombe had to put together? Up to this present time, simply nothing; but ere June was well over she had heard enough to warrant herself in dropping such hints and innuendos with which we have already seen her favouring her friend and gossip Miss Mitton, who herself was a Lynviller, and ready to exchange news.

Poor Blythe Byrtons! Eyes were upon them without. What was happening within you shall soon hear.

II.

ABOUT BAYSWATER — THE TWO EIGHTEENS MEET — THE BEAUTIFUL BOUQUET.

THE fashionable Londoner of the south-west, the Mid-Londoner, and the East-ender alike know very little, if anything, of Bayswater. Their acquaintance with this district is bounded by the Paddington Station; and the stockbroker and wine-merchant, whose business calls them to the east, and to the centre, of the metropolis, would find themselves in a strange land, were they suddenly put down in any one of the numerous thoroughfares which are crowded on either side with fresh-looking shops, for the supply of the surrounding terraces, squares, crescents, and villas.

Compared to this part of London, the retreat poetically named the Wood of St. John—and how pretty this would look in French, when, no doubt, were it a Parisian suburb, the qualifying epithet Little would be placed before St. John, just to give the Bois a colouring of rural simplicity and infantine innocence—I say, compared with Bayswater, the Wood of St. John is but a dingy imposture. Sooty leaves, grimy barks, and the most out-at-elbows, tumble-down, lath-and-plaster architecture—of some pretence, too, in parts—are among the characteristics of St. John's Wood. Its general appearance of

having been laid out for private lunatic asylums, and its per-
vading atmosphere of depression, cannot for one moment vie
with the positive marine aspect, bright colours, and bracing
ozonian climate which distinguish Bayswater. Here the air
seems so clear and fresh, and so strongly indicative of the
proximity of the boisterous sea, that were the stranger to come
suddenly, at the end of some newly-finished street, upon a
notice of " This way to the Bathing Machines," and were to
read some sumptuary regulations as to bathers, he would be
not only not in the least surprised, but would probably observe
to himself that it was nothing more than what he had expected
to find round the corner; and he would begin to wonder if
there were a steamer, and if so, whether it was about its time
to arrive ; and, finally, if he were a family man, whether, being
so convenient and handy for rail and omnibus, it wouldn't be
a most healthy place to take the children to.

Despite underground lines and subterranean stations, despite
increased communication with the other parts of London,
Bayswater keeps itself pretty much as usual to itself, and
knows comparatively little of the world outside. It has its
own society and its own organs, journalistic, as well as the
varieties played by distinguished Italian refugees in our streets.
It has its churches, chapels, assembly rooms, and halls.
Politics are superseded by polemics, and Ritualists, Anglicans,
Evangelicals, and all other shades of opinion within and without the Established Church, find no warmer adherents, no
more muddle-headed expositors of their own views, or more
violent denouncers of one another, than are to be met with,
before and after mid-day dinner on Sunday, and on the
evenings of week-days, gathered together in this thriving and
rising colony of Bayswater.

The houses look new; the streets look new; the people,
too, look so very new, that they might, but for their years,

have been born yesterday, or, at all events, have been ready-made by a special Providence for this particular purpose, and plumped down in this new settlement. One of these days, emigrants will give up Melbourne, and try Bayswater.

It is for pleasure, though, not business, this Bayswater. There is, as yet, no Exchange, and I have not come across, in the commercial column of *The Times*, or other newspaper, any quotations of prices at Bayswater. It takes very little longer to go to Brighton, by express, than to Bayswater by cab or omnibus. Of course you can reach it by the Underground, which is the dreariest, most choking, and most sneaking method of travelling ever invented. Who wants to be grubbing away underground?—except that celebrated historical character, Baron Trenck—or some such name—who was locked up in the dungeon of some fortress, and dug himself out of it, managing to scratch out a tunnel with his own hands, and coming up, alive and well, either in a drain in Germany, or in the sea at Holland—at least, so the impression, after many years, remains on my mind, mixed up, somehow with a picture representing a man with matted hair, in a strait-waistcoat and pantaloons, which I still fancy was intended for a correct likeness of the unfortunate, but mole-like, German nobleman.

The houses of Bayswater, like the maids of merry England, "how beautiful are they!" I am not in the pay of any Building Society, on my honour, and my admiration is as guileless as it is profound. The inhabitants have a community in gardens. They can walk in their own little eighth of an acre, or, passing through their own little iron gate, may suddenly step upon the comparatively boundless prairie, on which the sun, literally, never sets, as the garden, in the instance I mean, is on the wrong side of the house for that; and the sun won't alter its plans—which have been found to answer, on the whole, very well for the last five thousand years or so, there or thereabouts—even to oblige a denizen of Bayswater.

There is just one drawback to Bayswater—there is no shade. I can't call to mind any shade in the part I know; and for the part I don't know, of course I can't answer, nor would I do it an injustice, even in thought. I own to being ignorant of the boundaries of Bayswater, except where it impinges on the line of Westbourne Terrace; but as to the other three points of the compass, this deponent has nothing to say with certainty, and is above the rash hazard of a mere guess. But as far as I do know Bayswater—and so far only I can speak—I have so great an affection for the place, that if I were a poet and a musician, I would, in order to be presented with the freedom of Bayswater, compose a patriotic ballad, with exciting music and a thrilling refrain, and I would present it to the Colonel of the Bayswater Brigade; while my wife—if I had one—should work a banner, to be borne aloft by the standard-bearer of the same corps, on any occasion when it might be necessary to display their military force, rising as one man, either to defend their rights, or to avenge their wrongs.

If England has a thorn in her side in Ireland, let London beware of Bayswater. Bayswater, with its own private army, and its own navy floating upon the Water of the Bays, is a foe which might yet give the royal Ranger of Hyde Park some trouble, and to whose doings even the Lord Mayor himself, in the fancied security of his own Mansion House, could not afford to listen with the cold sneer of indifference.

There are fashions, too, there—not Parisian or Londonian, but purely Bayswaterian; and on a sunny morning in winter time, when walking is a necessity, the streets of the rising colony are alive with the brightest colours, and the freshest and prettiest possible faces. The shopkeepers, too, are sprightly, and not too mercenary. They are generally inclined for a chat with their customers, and business is conducted on the pleasantest terms possible. Ladies trip about, doing their shopping in perfect freedom, without attendance of any sort— just as you will see them at any watering-place, where a certain amount of conventionality can be dispensed with. They meet and gossip in the shops, especially at the pastrycooks', the florists', or the fruiterers'. Harmless gossip, no doubt; but gossip, for all that.

Bayswater has its mysteries, which have yet to be written : and I am going to write them. Let who will write laws for Bayswater—I'll write its ballads. The Ballads of Bayswater ! Stupendous ! The Legends of Bayswater, too; from the arrival of the first settler down to the present day. Comedies of the Crescent, without a Mahomedan in them; Tragedies of the Terraces ; Scandals of the Squares—these have to be written, besides a whole mass of scientific literature concerning the geological formation, the strata, and the different periods exhibited by the soil of this highly-favoured spot.

Mrs. Lupscombe, of No. 18, Chetwick Gardens, met Miss Mitton, of Lynville Place, one morning in June, at the fruiterer's. The former was paying a bill, and the latter came in to see her do it.

"No," says Mrs. Lupscombe to Miss Mitton, "I've not yet called on them, though they've been there since March ; and, really, I don't know whether I ought to, or not. Things will come to a crisis in that house, I'm certain. Even as a neighbour, one doesn't like to interfere. But if Mr. Byrton were at home less often than he is, I think I would call on her, as she seems to have no company."

"But you were saying, just now, that you had heard a great deal of crying, and the voice of a man in a passion ? " asked the other lady ; who, having listened to the story three times already within as many quarters of an hour, now wanted it to be repeated to her again, for the doubly charitable purpose of either catching her friend tripping in her narrative (which wouldn't prevent her repeating *her* own version of the story, oh dear no !), or of learning some further particulars, which should

add to the interest that the story had already created, and enable her to come to a certain decision as to the merits—or, rather, the demerits—of the subject of their conversation.

"He came in," answered Mrs. Lupscombe, "one evening, and he seemed to me to bang about, and use such language !— you know the walls are *not* very thick."

"And not only that," suggested Miss Mitton, "but the sounds will come down the chimneys, and you can't help it. I'm very cautious myself."

"Well, thank goodness, we haven't the necessity to be; for

no one would hear Mr. Lupscombe saying a word to me ; and indeed, for that matter, I only wish they could—for I don't myself—as he comes home tired from the City, always late. He once let out that he stayed after business hours to play billiards."

" They do, I know," said Miss Mitton, with kind consideration.

" I've no doubt of it," continued Mrs. Lupscombe ; " and when he *does* come home, he eats his dinner, without hardly a word, and then falls asleep in his chair. Ah ! "—here she sighed—" it's really very wearisome; unless when we've company, and then, of course, he's lively enough."

" It's just the same with them all," returned Miss Mitton, who was·not best pleased at her friend's digression, and was determined to bring her back to the subject again—" but what did you hear ? "

" Hear ? " said Mrs. Lupscombe, as if for a moment quite at a loss to arrive at the bearing of the question.

" Of these Byrtons, I mean."

" Oh ! " said Mrs. Lupscombe, who had now given herself time to consider how much she should tell, and how much she should reserve : " Oh yes ! Well, not much ; except that it seemed to me that they were having a really fearful quarrel ; and I couldn't help waking Mr. Lupscombe, and asking him if he didn't think he ought to interfere, in case murder might be committed."

" And did he ? "

" *Did he !* " replied Mrs. Lupscombe, with evidently supreme contempt for her sleeping partner's conduct on the occasion in question ; " Did he ! I should like to see him disturbing himself out of his first snoring, even if there were burglars at the bedside. No ; he only growled out that he couldn't bawl up the chimney to the man in the next house, and that every man had a right to do what he liked in his own castle—and beat his wife, too, if he pleased, as long as she didn't complain."

"And *was* he beating her?" inquired Miss Mitton, all italics and eagerness.

"Ah!" said Mrs. Lupscombe, who had artistically raised her listener's excitement to a high pitch, and was not going to gratify her curiosity: "*that* I don't know.   But I certainly heard a clattering of fire-irons.   Mr. Lupscombe said that it was only some one raking out the grate, and begged me not to bother him, as he had had enough worry during the day."

Miss Mitton sighed and pondered.   This was indeed a lame and impotent conclusion.

"You've not noticed anything on your side of the way?" asked Mrs. Lupscombe.

"No," answered Miss Mitton.   "I've seen him go out for a walk about the time *she* goes out."

"So have I," observed Mrs. Lupscombe, not to be outdone; "and I've met him when I've been shopping."

"Where?"

"At Mercer's."

"The florist's?"

"Yes."

Both ladies paused. Then Mrs. Lupscombe asked the fruiterer's boy—where, as I have intimated, this remarkable conversation had been taking place—if he'd given her her change, which, being an honest lad, and unwilling to err for want of caution, he immediately replied that he had, a quarter of an hour ago, whereupon the two friends left the shop, and continued their interesting conversation as they slowly walked towards their respective homes, stopping on the way to give an occasional order at a grocer's, a fishmonger's, or a baker's; and by the merest accident, of course, and because the fancy took them both at the same moment, they entered Mercer's, the florist's, to ask the price of a Mrs. Pollock geranium. A gentleman was quitting the shop as they were on the door-step. His last words to the elegant young woman in charge were, in answer, evidently, to some question of hers, " Oh, never mind that. You send it before the afternoon." To which she replied, " Very well," without adding, " sir,"—a familiarity on the part of this remarkably forward young person that made Miss Mitton eye Mrs. Lupscombe, who returned her glance by nodding her head in such a manner as seemed to convey " Well, this is a nice young woman, this is ! "

But as they had a purpose in view, the two ladies chose, for the moment, to blink any question of morals that might have arisen ; and, advancing boldly, they noticed, both at once, that a magnificent bouquet lay on the counter.

" Purchased by the gentleman just gone out ? Indeed ! How lovely ! "

" Isn't it ? " said the pert miss, putting it away in wool.

" And for whom ? " they wanted to know. The pert maiden was their match on this point, and they left the shop as wise as they had entered it—that is, as regarded the destination of the beautiful bouquet.

" I shouldn't be surprised——" began Mrs. Lupscombe.

" No more should I," said Miss Mitton.

They both meant the same, and knew it.

At that moment a gentleman, walking briskly towards London (I am throughout treating Bayswater as an independent colony), attracted their attention.

" It's Mr. Byrton," said Mrs. Lupscombe.

" Why don't you call this afternoon, while he's out ? " asked her friend. " You might do some good, and you can't do any harm."

Mrs. Lupscombe considered for a few seconds, and then

replied, " I will," as firmly as she had ever uttered those words in her life, not excepting the time when she took Augustus John for her husband, years since.

"Do," said Miss Mitton, shaking her heartily by the hand at parting; "*and come and see me afterwards, dear, do.*" As they parted company, the florist's boy passed them swiftly, carrying a basket on his left arm, and in his right, covered up in paper and wool, what might have been, to all appearances, a concealed cauliflower, but which was, no doubt, they both exclaimed at once, "*the* bouquet." Where was it going to ?

III.

THE GREEN-EYED—OUR GOSSIPS AGOG.

MR. BLYTHE BYRTON was jealous, excessively jealous. In the first place, of every male generally who happened to pay the slightest attention to his wife ; in the second place, particularly jealous of one Captain Downton, with whom Mrs. Byrton had danced several times at a Woolwich ball, and whose visits he had discouraged with so much asperity as to cause, on one occasion, a slight unpleasantness, as it is called in domestic circles, between this otherwise loving husband and wife.

On the first opportunity Mr. Blythe Byrton gave up the furnished house where he was then living, and, for the purpose, as he said, of gratifying his wife's desire for having their own abode, he had taken No. 19, Chetwick Gardens, to which quarters, after an interval of travelling, they repaired at the date already mentioned.

Not long after they had taken up their residence here, Mrs. Byrton's sister, Miss Grantham (Ellen was her Christian name), came to stay with them. She had usually been residing with her elder sister ever since her marriage; and it was greatly owing to this young lady's good sense, and the amiability of her disposition, that no serious outbreak of jealousy had, as yet, ever taken place.

As for Captain Downton, Mr. Byrton had not heard anything of him for months, and was beginning to forget his existence, when No. 19 was, as I have recorded, taken; and, as ill-luck would have it, Captain Downton was the new tenant.

"I won't see him! I won't have him here!" said Mr. Byrton, violently, but to himself, in his own dressing-room; and I have no doubt that it was the chimney of this apartment which had conveyed the sounds of strong language to the ears of the listener in No. 18. As to fire-irons rattling—well, they might have fallen down, as fire-irons, being of sympathetic turn, are apt to do, especially when the occupant of the room stamps about energetically, and dashes his boots into corners in order to relieve his feelings.

By the way, what mysterious articles of furniture are fire-irons. If anything could (and many things can) induce even an unimaginative person to believe in invisible imps of mischief, it is fire-irons. Isn't there something strangely human in the tongs, with its little head, its thin waist, its symmetrical hips, long, lanky legs, and its little Chinese feet that were never made to be stood upon? Then the shovel, with its long neck, little flat, buttony head (in some instances) and its petticoat finish below—quite the lady of the party. As for the poker, its rigid, inflexible, upright character is evidently that of the policeman on duty, and ready for active service at a moment's warning. What a romance might be written about them, wherein the tongs should be the Life Guardsman, enamoured of Miss Shovel, and having as his dangerous rival the cold and authoritative Policeman Poker! But this is a digression. Only, what does strike anyone who interests himself at all in fire-irons—not as a business, but in a speculative manner—is that they do fall about unaccountably, as if they had had quarrels among themselves, and had been kicking at one another, and that they are so obstinate sometimes, that not the greatest gentleness, not the utmost care, will induce them to remain in their places. Puck is behind the poker, and Moth, Grub, and Mustard-seed playing with the tongs and shovel.

These thoughts, however, didn't trouble Mr. Byrton: but many others did, of a far less agreeable character.

"Why should *he* come here?" he asked himself; and he couldn't have put the question to a worse person, for he immediately answered, "Why? Of course it is evident why. He watches at his window; I've seen him. Perhaps he'll speak to her out of doors—he's blackguard enough for any-thing. And then to tell me, as she did, that he's harmless! Harmless! As if I didn't know. What should he dog us like this for? And yet," here he confronted his own image in the glass, "my wife can't surely have given him any encourage-ment?" He meditated, frowning at the reflection of himself. "I do believe," he continued presently, "that he was at the opera the other night. I'll almost swear I saw him perpetually looking up at our box. If he had come up to see them while I was out, my wife would have told me—at least, I suppose she would have told me. Confound him!"

In this cheerful frame of mind he continued for several days; and to prove to himself that he was not jealous, but had the most profound confidence in his wife, he would go for long, objectless walks, all alone, and return home more suspicious than ever, having, as he flattered himself, walked off his ill-humour. This was the sort of constitutional in which he was engaged when Mrs. Lupscombe and her friend had seen him.

That afternoon the last-mentioned lady did make her long-intended call on Mrs. Byrton. Within an hour she was closeted with Miss Mitton.

“What *do* you think, my dear?” she began, perfectly swelling with the heat of her fresh-baked information.

“What?” asked Miss Mitton, putting down her cup.

“I called on Mrs. Byrton.”

“Yes.”

“And on her table——”

“Well.”

“Was the very bouquet we saw this morning at Mercer's.”

“No!”

Such a “No” was this of Miss Mitton's. Such an expletive of condensed incredulity, agitation, and curiosity. Talk of fire-irons falling, it is a wonder that they did not faint away in a heap in the fender at hearing this exclamation; and so they would have probably, had they not been on their best highly-polished drawing-room behaviour, lying down at full-length, and listening with a well-bred air of indifference to news which, after all, really didn't (as they probably said when they talked it over afterwards at night) concern them.

Mrs. Lupscombe took a cup of tea, and sat down.

“When I saw it,” she went on to say, “I was dumb-foundered. All my worst suspicions were confirmed. I don't understand the language of flowers, but if camellias mean any-thing, that bouquet could speak to the purpose.”

“Was she alone?” inquired Miss Mitton.

“Quite. Her sister, you know—a sly girl she is, I'm sure —left her the other day, but only to go not very far from here —to Heatherton Terrace, where her father and mother have recently taken a house; so, you see, we've got the whole family here now, and I expect there'll be a pretty scandal very soon."

"It seems like it," said Miss Mitton, thoughtfully.

"I'm sure of it," returned Mrs. Lupscombe. "Well, while I was there, in came Mr. Byrton."

This was most exciting. Miss Mitton sat with her eyes intently fixed on her friend. She wouldn't lose one word by even putting in an interpolation on her own account.

Mrs. Lupscombe continued, with her listener well in hand, "He was introduced to me, and turning towards the table, he said, 'What a lovely bouquet you have brought us.'"

"What did you say to that?" asked Miss Mitton, seeing that there was a pause in the narrative.

"Well," answered Mrs. Lupscombe, "I didn't know *what* to say. I thought I detected an imploring look in Mrs. Byrton's eyes, which begged me, as I imagined, to tell an untruth, to save her; which, of course, without knowing the circumstances of the case, I really could *not* do, even for my best friend."

"Of course not," put in the high-minded Miss Mitton.

"And so I simply spoke the truth, and told him that the present did *not* come from me. 'From whom, then?' he asked, turning to his wife. 'I thought,' she replied—but with hesitation, my dear—I couldn't help remarking *that*—'I thought that you had sent it.'"

"Meaning that *she* thought her husband had sent it?"

"Quite so," answered Mrs. Lupscombe, who didn't like being interrupted at this point. "Well—let me see—well— he said, angrily, 'Nonsense, Gwenny'—he's got some pet name for her like that, so I suppose her real one must be Gwendoline—'Nonsense, Gwenny; you might have been pretty certain that *I* didn't send it. Don't you know who *did ?'* She assured him that she hadn't got the slightest idea. Whereupon he walked to the window. That looked like a coming storm, so merely observing, quite pleasantly, that I dared say it was some admirer of Mrs. Byrton's, and that one had heard of such a thing in olden days, of a letter being concealed among flowers, I wished them good day, and came here."

"Poor man! it's a pity he's so blinded." Miss Mitton walked to her window; but No. 19 on the opposite side of the way showed no signs of life; and though they remained anxiously with the windows open, until Mr. Lupscombe sent over to say that he was tired of waiting any longer, and would his wife come in to dinner—yet, up to seven o'clock that evening, there was no report of fire-arms, and the neighbourhood was apparently at peace.

Later on, by the aid of the chimney, with the register up, and assisted by the thinness of the walls, Mrs. Lupscombe's curiosity was, to a certain extent, gratified. If Lupscombe had not snored louder than usual, she might have heard a good deal more.

What did reach her in detached sentences was sufficient to enable her to supply what escaped her, and so to render the connection perfect.

IV.

THROUGH THE CHIMNEY.

" You *must* know from whom the bouquet came," said Mr. Byrton, argumentatively.

" Indeed, I don't. I thought *you* had sent it," replied his wife.

Her husband evidently did not consider this a satisfactory explanation, as he went on in the same strain of sharp cross-examination. " Thought *I'd* sent it! Nonsense! You couldn't have thought *that*."

Such attention might have been unusual on his part, as he was not the man to waste his money on flowers. He never had done it, even in the most earnest days of his courtship.

" I did think so, because, when I said the other night at the opera how I wished I'd had a bouquet, you asked why I hadn't bought one."

This was a diversion, but not a happy one. It reminded him of the man whom he considered as his detested rival. He was about to say as much, when it suddenly flashed across him that the last person to be mentioned at this moment was *the* person with whom he was anxious, as it were, to confront his wife. He returned to the charge.

“ That,” he said, “ has nothing to do with it——”

“ Everything,” interposed Mrs. Byrton. She was clearly plucking up her courage. She was not to be bullied.

“ Nothing at all,” repeated her husband. Contradiction was flying to his head. He paced the room for a minute, with his hands in his trousers pockets, his wife watching his movements closely, but without any show of anxiety.

“ I come home,” he said, stopping suddenly, and facing her with the air of a man who was going to state hard facts, “ I come home, and I find a bouquet, left at the house for you, addressed to *you*——”

“ It was not addressed to me,” said the lady, quietly.

This sounded, to a jealous ear, uncommonly like a mere prevarication. His temper was rising and getting the better of him.

“ Addressed to you or not,” he continued angrily, “ it was left here for you—the man *said* it was for you——”

“ How do you know that ? ” asked his wife, quickly. She saw that she had him at a disadvantage. If he told her the means he had employed to obtain this information, he would at once confess a meanness. The simple fact was, that he had questioned the maid who had taken in the bouquet.

“ Never mind how I know it,” he replied, evading this point. “ It’s enough that I do know it.”

“ Quite enough,” returned the lady, with a sarcastic smile, at the same time taking up a book which she had been reading before this conversation commenced.

“ I must beg you to listen to me,” began Mr. Byrton, imperiously.

“ I can’t help *hearing* you,” replied his wife, without raising her eyes.

“ Once for all,” her husband continued, highly incensed,

"I won't have it." This was violent, but vague. "I won't have bouquets left here by people for you."

"People don't," was the concise reply.

"And that woman—what's her name?—Lupscombe" (she was absent, and therefore could be abused with impunity)—"what did she say about lovers, and notes in bouquets?"

"I don't remember, I'm sure," said Mrs. Byrton, carelessly, and turning over a page of the book. At that moment she could have jumped up and put her arms about her husband's neck, imploring him—but, no, the spirits of Pride and Jealousy were in the room that night, standing as seconds to the duel.

"Did she come with a message? Is she the go-between?" he demanded, loudly. ("What a suspicious wretch!" exclaimed the listener on the other side of the lath and plaster.) "I will know the whole truth. Was there a note in the bouquet?"

Mrs. Byrton smiled scornfully. "Did you find one?" she asked.

"That is no answer to my question. That bouquet came from Captain Downton—I know it!"

"Then why ask me?"

His reason for asking her was, of course, so evident that this question irritated him beyond measure.

"Why!" he thundered, "to hear what you'd say. To hear whether what I had long suspected was true. To have the admission from your own lips. I told you I would *not* allow his visits; I told you I would *not* have him here; and now I find him in the house opposite, and sending you the bouquet. What does it mean?"

No answer. He repeated fiercely, "Gwendoline! answer me! What does it mean? I *will* know! By——"

"Stop, Blythe! that will do." She had risen and thrown

down the book. Calmly she faced him as she said, "If you have ceased to trust, you have ceased to love me. I had better leave you until you can speak in a proper manner." With that she left the room, not turning back once to watch the effect of her words upon him.

For a second he stood clenching his fists and breathing hard. Then suddenly, "Gwendoline!" he called out, furiously, tearing open the door which she had just closed. "Come back! don't be——"

The street door below slammed. In another minute he was standing on the pavement in front of his house, shading his eyes from the gaslight, and peering into the gloom, to the right and to the left. Not a soul. Not a footfall.

Had she left him? Where had she gone? To whom? He stayed a few minutes outside. Then he returned, leaving the door ajar while he searched the rooms below. No. The conviction forced itself upon him that she had really gone—really left him. Then he closed the front door cautiously, hardening his heart against her, as he drew the bolts sharply to, as if placing an eternal barrier between them, shutting her out, thenceforth, from his home—from his heart.

Then he went to his room, and sitting down by the table, leant his burning head upon his clammy hand, and looked down upon the blank and cheerless hearth.

Soon after daybreak he was out, pacing up and down before Mercer's, the florist's.

"Why had he not thought of this before? Still he would be the first there. Yet his wife might have held communication last night with Mercer's!"

The man came to take down the shutters, and he interrogated him. The man's answer—when he had roused himself sufficiently to understand that he was being addressed (he lost a good deal of time in yawning, when his mouth might have been better employed—which was irritating)—his answer was clear and intelligible:

"Yes, he *had* left the bouquet at 19, Chetwick Gardens. Yes—yesterday."

"For the lady there?"

"Yes, undoubtedly, for the lady there—certainly not for the gentleman." Which idea so tickled him, that, in stopping a laugh with a yawn, or a yawn with a laugh, he was very nearly choked. On his recovery from this peril, he repeated his information.

"Who sent the bouquet? Ah! that he didn't know: he wasn't in the shop when it was ordered. The young person in the shop would know, of course."

"Could his questioner see her?"

"Oh, certainly—when she was there, not before."

His questioner—intimating that he had no particular wish to see her when she wasn't there—observed that he could wait.

"She don't live here," the man explained.

"So much the better," thought Mr. Byrton. "Then there is less chance of any communication having passed between them."

The young person at length arrived. Fresh as the roses; and as trim, neat, and captivating a young person, whether in or out of business hours, as you'd wish to see.

She coquettishly fenced some of the questions, and would have, evidently, rather enjoyed the novelty of an early morning flirtation, had not the serious demeanour of her visitor, and his anxious, weary face warned her that this was a customer not to be trifled with. So she quietly replied, that a gentleman, answering to the description given her by Mr. Byrton, *had* bought a bouquet, had ordered it to be sent to a lady, and had given the address.

"Would she mind telling him the name of the lady to whom it was sent?"

She demurred at first; but, on being pressed, she said that, as she had not got to keep it a secret—only that gentlemen didn't generally like those things known—she would gratify the inquirer's curiosity by referring to the order book. There it was—19, Heatherton Terrace.

"Eh?" exclaimed her visitor, scarcely able to believe his ears.

"Nineteen, Heatherton Terrace," replied the young person, decidedly. "You can see it yourself, if you like; and "—she added, handing him the book—" the lady's name is Grantham. That's all about it."

He examined the page throughout, and other pages, too. Not a single mention of Mrs. Byrton's name, except when she had ordered some flowers for herself.

Then the half-wakened sleeper was re-examined. In five minutes it came out—that yesterday he had stopped on his rounds (humbly begging the young person's pardon for so doing), and had ventured to slake his thirst with a friend at another friend's house (of a public character) in the neighbourhood. That, somehow or other (begging pardon again), he had lost the address, and had trusted to his memory; that he was unaware, until now, that he had also lost his memory, having rather prided himself upon it being a very good one up to this moment, and (begging pardon once more) that was how it came that he had left the bouquet at No. 19, Chetwick Gardens (knowing it was No. 19 somewhere about), instead of the same numeral in Heatherton Terrace. That was all.

Then Mr. Byrton ordered the very finest bouquet to be made up—full of flowers signifying love, peace, and devotion—and walked home.

His wife was in the dining-room.

"My own darling Gwenny!"——

That was his first and last fit of jealousy. Had not his eyes been blinded, he would have searched the downstair rooms before going out into the street, when she had taken the opportunity of coming out of her hiding-place and running upstairs to her own bedroom. Of course, she had never been out at all.

And to think that they had long ago told him that Captain Downton had only visited them on purpose to meet his wife's sister, Ellen Grantham—a story that he never would believe !

Mrs. Lupscombe—as may be imagined—never called again ; but she and Miss Mitton got most of the particulars here recorded from the florist ; and they had the melancholy satisfaction of witnessing the marriage of Captain Downton with Miss Grantham at their own parish church ; and the next day, " Apartments to Let " was up in No. 19, Lynville Place.

The Downtons and the Byrtons are the very best of friends, as brothers and sisters-in-law should be. And so, let us hope that the evil spirits of Jealousy and Discord have quitted the bright colony of Bayswater for ever and a day.

AN ENTR'ACTE.

I.

"' APARTMENTS to let!' I wonder if they would do?"

He who thus pondered was standing in the middle of the road, which a quarter of a mile further on became the High-street of Penmouth, a town on the western coast.

He was staring meditatively at a long white gate, on which was fastened a board, bearing the above-quoted inscription. The gate was set between a high hedge, white with hawthorn bloom; above it the laburnums shook their golden locks; and beyond it was a winding path, leading down between shrubberies to a house which, however, could not be seen from the road.

"I might as well try," was the conclusion arrived at by the individual before the gate; and, lifting the latch, he swung the wicket backward and entered the garden.

The path led downward between thickly-set syringas, already showing their flower-buds, and the dark-green arbutus and laurustinus. A sharp turn brought him suddenly in front of the house—a long rambling building of gray stone, which looked rather surprised at the neglected state of itself and its grounds, and sulky at the degrading announcement, again put forth in a front window, of there being "Apartments to let."

"What a nice old place!" thought the stranger, as he rang at the front door, and the rusty bell-wire creaked in orthodox romance fashion. "I wonder what has made it come down in the world?"

Romance, however, was dispelled by the appearance of the lady who opened the door—a stout red-faced dame of fifty, her countenance framed by tight rolls of dark hair and a miraculous cap.

The gentleman had come after the lodgings. How many rooms would he want? A bedroom and sitting-room, she supposed. As a rule, she preferred letting to families; but as this was not the busy time of the year, and as they had let part of the rooms to a lady, and as— Would the gentleman follow her? And Mrs. Watkins, mistress of old Horneck Manor-house, led the way up stairs, quite trembling with secret eagerness to secure a second lodger at a time of year when visitors to Penmouth were rare.

"You have a large old house," said the stranger, as he followed her along the hall up the wide staircase, and noted the quaint carving over the doors, the delicate moulding of the cornices.

"Yes, sir; we don't live on this side of the house at all ourselves. There's plenty of room for me and my master and the children on the other side, which used to be the servants' part in the old times. You don't know Penmouth, sir? This used to be Horneck Manor, and the lords of the manor used to have rights over the whole of Penmouth. But the people it belonged to went to rack and ruin, and so did the place."

"How?"

"Mines and drink," replied Mrs. Watkins tersely. "We

shouldn't have taken the house; but my husband he wanted to farm the land, and as we couldn't have it without the house, we thought we'd do the best we could by letting the rooms."

Her possible lodger could easily imagine this best to be not at all bad. The old house was by no means in good repair, and even a person not much learned in the value of house property could guess that a rather tumble-down dwelling in the extreme west of England, three hundred miles from London, did not command a very exorbitant rent.

Still, Horneck House was a singularly perfect specimen of its class. It had been built in 1603, as was still registered in stone over the back door, and had never been spoilt by additions. Poor old house! it was sadly maltreated now, with green-glass lustres surmounting the delicate grace of the carved-wood mantelpieces, and the walls of the staircase embellished by a many-coloured wall-paper, displaying, in a series of blotched scenes, the drama of domestic life in China.

Despite of this, the rooms that were to let took the visitor's fancy greatly. The sitting-room was on the first floor, and from the window could be seen in the distance the blue waters of the bay and the fretted line of coast; and nearer was the garden, a wide expanse of grass, that had once been lawn, in the midst of which was a patriarchal mulberry-tree.

The bedroom was quaint enough, and would not have been easy to match, telling eloquently, as it did, how the old house had fallen from its high estate. It was a very large room, leading by a door at the further end to another of equal size; but it was chiefly remarkable from the upper end of the room being raised two steps above the other, so as to form a dais or stage.

"I suppose this was built for masques," said the stranger musingly.

"That's just what people say, sir," said Mrs. Watkins.

"Something like acting, masks are, aren't they? I often tell Watkins we might let this room for a theatre; but he don't like the idea, sir, being a Wesleyan."

"I will take the rooms," said the visitor, who did not seem to have heard much of this speech. "I'm staying at the King's Hotel. Major Norman, that's my name; but as it means nothing to you, I suppose you would like a week's rent in advance."

Mrs. Watkins smiled blandly, and deprecatingly, and murmured something about "gentlemen being so much pleasanter to deal with than ladies; not but what the lady down-stairs——"

All preliminaries were satisfactorily arranged, and the next evening found Major Norman comfortably settled in his new quarters. Mrs. Watkins proved herself by no means a bad cook, and served her lodger for dinner with a spring chicken delicately roasted, fresh-cut asparagus, and a gooseberry-tart with clotted cream. A hamper of wine had arrived from London, Vincent Norman not being a man to trust himself in the matter of drinks to the tender mercies of the Penmouth wine-merchant.

"Fate cannot harm me, I have dined to-day," he murmured, as a neat-handed and bright-faced Phyllis retired, after clearing away the dinner things, and left him alone in his glory. "This is better than that confounded hotel. I believe I shall be able to work here. Shall I begin to-night? No; I'll have a smoke, and think over it—plan it out."

He filled his pipe slowly, drew up an armchair to the window, and leant back in the seat, enjoying the freshness of the air blown across the western sea.

Vincent Norman was a man of about thirty-five, tall, broad-shouldered, well knit, the ideal soldier in form, but with a face which, though not unsoldierlike, looked rather to belong to the man of thought than of action. He had a broad forehead, but with soft dark hair, musing gray eyes, lips that could be either sweet or stern, but which of late years had grown a little bitter in their smile, a little hard in their repose under the well-trimmed moustache ; a straight nose, not too thin ; a strong but not heavy jaw. He was good-looking, certainly— not quite handsome in the usual sense of the term, but it was not a face that one soon tired of.

It was a fair night ; the May moon rose softly over the distant sea, and touched the jutting-out edges of the coast with her clear light. In the cold brightness the blossom-laden hawthorns and pear-trees in the garden below Major Norman's sitting-room gleamed like snow, and the wide lawn was chequered by the dark shadows of the trees on the paler turf. There was evidently a stream somewhere beyond the dark belt of sleeping trees that shut in the end of the garden, for Vincent Norman could hear the low plash and ripple of running water.

A nightingale was singing among the branches with that passionate liquid tremble which stirs so strange a delight in us, and Vincent wondered vaguely how long it was since he had heard that bird's song amid the blossoming sweetness of an English May.

How long ? So long ago, that the memory awakened by those throbbing notes seemed to be part of another life. The song took him back out of his present self to an ardent dreaming boyhood, when all had seemed possible. He did not know when the bird ceased to sing ; but when he shook himself free from the thought of the dead years, all was silent, except the far-off ripple of the brook, and the low rustling of the breeze through the boughs. He rose, with something between a sigh and a yawn, and was looking for the day's paper, when he heard from below the tender quiver of a violin.

Was it fancy? Vincent leant out of his window and looked down, but he could see nothing; the window of the lower room was at right angles with his. He leant back again in his chair and listened to Schubert's serenade, released from silence by the touch of some one to whom music was life. The sound of the violin, unalloyed by any grosser music, rose through the night air with an infinite sadness and sweetness, telling, in that yearning cry of love, of the fulness of human melancholy, of joy too near akin to sorrow.

As the serenade died away in the stillness, Major Norman held his breath. Who was the musician? "The lady down-stairs?" Presently the violin sang again; this time a cavatina of Raff's, tender and passionate; then, after a pause, there came one of the wildest, gayest, and most mournful of Chopin's waltzes. That was the end; the silence was not again broken by the sound of the violin.

"Is it 'the lady down-stairs'?" thought Major Norman. "I wonder what she is like? Forty-eight and frightful, I suppose; or, more likely, it isn't she at all, but some visitor or relative of the music-master genus. Whoever it is, knows how to play. She can't be young and unmarried, or she wouldn't be here alone. How the deuce do I know she is alone? and what the devil does it matter to me? If she were the very spirit of romance,

> ' Be she fairer than the day,
> Or the flowery meads in May,'

I didn't come here to make a fool of myself, but to set to work in earnest."

II.

Major Norman got up late the next morning, and it was about one o'clock when he sauntered out of doors, and took the road down to the shore. The beach was deserted; the children and nursemaids who had populated it during the forenoon had departed to their mid-day dinners. One old gentleman in a bath-chair was being dragged slowly along the esplanade; three small boys were doing their best to commit suicide by hurling themselves violently down from the esplanade on to the sands below; and two coastguardsmen were sitting half in and half outside the lifeboat-house, ready for a chat with, or a tip from, any stranger. Major Norman was well acquainted with their habits, and, not feeling a desire for conversation, briefly replied to their original remark of " Fine morning, sir," by " Very," and, turning away from the esplanade, took the road that followed the line of the bay, past Penmouth and the little fishing village which nearly joins it. He walked along under hanging boughs, by apple orchards in which the trees were just past the full flush of their rosy bloom, and under gray stone walls over which the ivy clambered, and which a month before had been gilded by the primroses and purpled by the dog-violets, which grew in every mossy crevice and chink between the stones.

As he reached a place where the road branched off into two he hesitated for a moment which way he should choose. One, as he knew, still followed the line of the bay; the other was a narrow woody lane, with steep banks and overarched by trees. He turned down the latter path, and had gone a little way when he saw some one in front of him—a lady, standing high

AN UNEXPECTED MEETING.

on the steep bank, which she had climbed to gather some late-
blooming primroses.   Her face was turned from Major Norman,
and she did not perceive his approach till he was quite close,
and she caught sight of him as she sprang down from the bank.
Her look was one of half recognition, half doubt ; then a smile
flashed over her face as she exclaimed,

"Major Norman ! "

"Miss Duncombe ! "

She was a woman of twenty-eight or thirty, very graceful,
with gold-brown hair which caught the light, a beautiful forehead, and more beautiful eyes.   She wore a dress of dull olive-
green, and her hands were full of flowers she had gathered—
dark wild hyacinths, golden cowslips, a cluster of the apple-
bloom's mingled rose and snow, and the pale primroses.   A
vision of spring?   Hardly : rather a very gracious perfectly-
dressed woman.   In spite of her woodland surroundings, she
involuntarily reminded one of Piccadilly.   Her dress was very
quiet, but spoke eloquently of the mistress-hand that had made
it; her gloves, boots, hat, were all too perfect to be picturesque.
Nevertheless, she was a fair picture, and her face was charming
enough to make one forget her attire.

"Are you very much astonished to see me here ? " she
said.

"Well, yes, though it is always foolish to be surprised."

"You thought I was bound to be in London, and at my toil
of amusing the British public.   No; I am on sick-leave, and
came down here to recruit.   The doctors won't let me sing for
another month yet : I have been ill.   But you can't be more
surprised to see me than I am to see you.   I did not know
there was another London exile besides myself at Penmouth."

"Did you fancy you had the monopoly of the place ? " he
said dryly.

She laughed ; her laugh was wonderfully sweet.

"I feel my sovereignty to be disturbed," she said; "and I daresay you do the same."

"What is to be done?" said Major Norman. "Shall I abdicate, pack up, and return to-night to Paddington? or shall we agree to reign together?"

Miss Duncombe shook her head.

"I can't determine at once," she said. "I don't know whether your claim is better or worse than mine."

"How is that to be decided? By priority of arrival?"

"I think, rather, by the strength of one's reason for being here."

"In that case," he said, "I yield. I have no reason for coming here. Any place that is quiet and pretty will do as well for me. Shall I leave?"

"You know I can't say yes without being rude," she replied. "I think you will find the place very dull."

"There is no fear of that now, unless you tell me that I bore you."

It was the conventional compliment conventionally spoken, but for once it expressed truth. After a week spent in his own companionship, Vincent Norman felt quite a sudden pleasure at meeting a graceful and sympathetic woman, with whom he had sufficient acquaintance to entitle him to try and better it. He had met Miss Duncombe once or twice at crowded London receptions, had taken her down to supper, had talked to her in the Park. Of course he knew her well, as did the rest of the world, as Miss Clement, a famous singer and actress, as Marguerite and Ophelia and Elsa; but his knowledge of her as Miss Duncombe was confined to what has been already stated.

Down here at Penmouth, however, where they both had felt themselves as social Alexander Selkirks, they had met almost as old friends. Vincent, as he strolled along the lane by Nora Duncombe's side, thought he had never known in London how beautiful a woman she really was, how sweet her voice was in speaking, how soft the curves and how rich the tints of her hair. Or, rather, he did not think this so much as feel it, as he felt the sunlight shining through the leaves above, flecking with light and shade the turf of the banks, the greenery of the hedges, and the tall masses of the feathery leaves and delicate white blossoms of the hemlock.

They walked along together, talking "Shakespeare, taste, and the musical glasses," the last new play, the Academy exhibition, which as yet neither had seen, the last artistic fads in room decoration. At length they reached the end of the lane, which had so turned and twisted that when they emerged they found themselves looking down from the brow of a hill on the sea, glorious in the sunlight.

"O!" said Miss Duncombe, drawing a breath of pleasure; then she burst out laughing. "What creatures of habit we are!" she said. "Here you and I have been talking, just as we might in a London drawing-room, of things we have no present interest in, and have never spoken one word of the beauty round us."

"Probably in London we should have discoursed eloquently on the beauties of Nature—or you would. I am never eloquent."

She looked up at him.

"Don't you think," she said, "that the good of such a place as this is that one's thoughts and feelings grow simpler and purer, and one forgets the Babel our lives are now?"

"If I must confess," he answered, "I love the sweet shady side of Pall Mall; and so would you, Miss Duncombe, if you had been grilling eight years in India, and were due on the gridiron again in five months."

"Are you going back to India?"

"Yes; I may be there as well as here. India is a better

place than England for a person who has no particular aim in life. There's less fuss made about living there than there is here."

"I think you are rather inconsistent."

She gave a little laugh.

"I am quite of your opinion. Are you consistent, Miss Duncombe?"

Her large soft eyes met his.

"I want to be," she said.

"Don't," he said, "don't wish to unhumanise yourself; you could not be a woman if you were—or a man."

"I don't want to be the last," she answered a little sharply. "Are you in jest or in earnest?"

"I can't tell you myself."

"Major Norman," she said suddenly, "I believe you have a very bad opinion of people. There is something cynical in your way of speaking."

"I am very sorry to hear it; there is nothing I hate as much as cheap cynicism, and mine would be very cheap indeed."

"But you think men and women are—"

"Men and women," he put in. "Ah!" with a sudden change of voice, "there is my favourite wild flower."

He sprang up the bank, and in a moment returned to her with a few of the frail and small white bells and tender green trefoil leaves of the wood-sorrel in his hand.

"I don't know it," Miss Duncombe said, as he gave them her. "Pretty thing; how lovely it is! It is like Shelley's harebell,

> 'At whose birth
> The soil scarce heaved.'

It is too delicate and small to put with the other flowers."

"Yes; and it will fade almost immediately."

Miss Duncombe produced a dainty note-book from her pocket, and placed the little flowers among its leaves.

" I can't bear," she said, " to throw a flower away till it is quite dead, or to watch it dying."

" So you embalm it, where it may die out of sight without paining any one. It is the way of the world."

" Did I not say you were cynical ? "

" If you choose to take every word I utter as spoken from the depths of an embittered heart, I may figure as a very Timon."

" Or Alceste ? "

" You do me too much honour. Alcestes are not as common as—" he suddenly remembered she might apply his words personally, and stopped.

" As Célimènes ; " she finished his sentence for him quite calmly. " No, she is natural enough ; poor Alceste ! "

" He would have been much more to be pitied if Célimène had taken him."

" But if she had been different ; there are other kinds of women."

She was speaking simply and earnestly ; simply and earnestly he answered her,

" I believe it."

But something in his look made her, actress and woman of the world as she was, flush rosy red, and a silence fell between them for a few moments. At last Miss Duncombe felt the need of making some casual remark to break it, and said,

" Are you staying at an hotel, or in lodgings ? "

" I was at the King's till yesterday ; now I am in lodgings."

" Are you well off now ? " asked Miss Duncombe.

" Yes, I have found rooms in a charming old place ; do you know it ? Horneck House."

" Horneck House ! why, we are fellow-lodgers ! So you

are 'the new gentleman' Mrs. Watkins told me of this morning!"

"And you are 'the lady downstairs!' I understand now, Miss Duncombe; it was you whom I heard playing the violin last night."

She blushed slightly.

"I should not have played if I had known anyone could hear; but they won't let me sing, and music I must have, so turned to my Guarnerius for comfort. I hope it did not annoy you."

"Do you think me 'fit for treasons, stratagems, and spoils?' But I never knew you played the violin."

"How should you?" she said; "I only play to myself. My father was an amateur, music was his great passion, and so he had me taught the violin when I was almost a baby, and made me keep on the study even after my other capabilities were discovered. I hated it then, but I am so glad of it now. I might lose my voice any day, but unless I were deaf or paralysed I should still have my music."

"It is a great blessing," said Major Norman, "to reflect, as a listener, that one enjoys the sweets without the bitters of music."

"But you don't know all the sweets," she answered quickly, "any more than one who looks at a picture knows the joy of an artist."

"No," he answered, "you are right; and yet, Miss Duncombe, you can never hear your own voice as we hear it."

"I wish I could," she said; "then I should learn my faults. But neither can you know what it is, not only to sing, but to sing in a great theatre, with the dramatic excitement to aid one."

"I suppose, to you, it is the only real life."

"Yes," she answered—"that is, at times; but then at other

times one feels such a poor thing : one's art is only for a day, only a rendering of other people's higher art. It passes away and is forgotten."

"But without it we could not appreciate the higher art in the same measure."

"I know; the singer and the player are simply the instruments through which the composer and the dramatist speak to men. It is not always a pleasant thought, if one loves art."

"I think what you say is only a half-truth; but it is no mean lot to be the priestess of Mozart. Is it not," he said, with real interest in his eyes, "that you are over-tired by the strain of work ? You will get rested here, and will see things more healthily."

"Yes," she said, "I am resting between the acts. I feel rather as if you and I had first met on the stage, and now were resting and talking behind the scenes."

"It is a pleasant rest," he said ; "but are you not longing to be back in the midst of your triumphs and your labours ?"

"No ; I am glad to breathe quietly, to have time to think and remember myself."

All this while they had been walking along the road that led to Horneck House, and now they were opposite the tree-embowered gate. Major Norman held it open for his companion to pass through, and then followed himself.

"Good-morning," Nora Duncombe said as they reached the front door. "I don't go in this way; I have my own door into the sitting-room round on the other side."

She held out her hand, then turned round by the side of the house, and Major Norman went up-stairs to his own rooms.

III.

The days went by like a quiet pleasant dream to the two people who had established themselves for a little while at Horneck House. Major Norman simply had come to Penmouth because he wanted some quiet place where he could meditate on a book he had wished to write for the last ten years on our Indian frontier. Nora Duncombe's reasons for visiting the pretty out-of-the-world seaside town have been already given.

Neither he nor she often spoke of returning to London; but if Miss Duncombe alluded to it, it was always with a certain regret that this lotus-eating calm must come to an end, and the curtain of her life-stage ring up again shortly.

Vincent and Miss Duncombe had seen a great deal of each other during this time, while the apple-bloom faded to brown and the syringa burst open its creamy waxy blossoms, thickly sweet. They had met in the garden, had walked together along the " umbered beach " and green lanes, and through the pleasant fields now golden with the buttercups.

This could not last long; it was but an *entr'acte*, as Nora had said, a dreamy melody, peaceful and tender, between the acts; but perhaps one of the two half unconsciously wished it could be the overture to a fuller and fairer life.

It was the first evening of June; the day had burnt itself away in the west, but the sky was still blue, deepening to the darkest hue of the sapphire tint. Major Norman had had letters to write for the Indian mail, and they had kept him in his rooms the whole day; but now, looking down to the garden, he saw there a tall and graceful figure in a dress of dim gray.

A quick thrill shot through him, such as of late had stirred his pulses whenever he had touched "the white wonder" of Nora Duncombe's hand. He mentally anathematised himself for a fool, sat down, and took up a French novel.

He read three-quarters of a page, then threw the book aside and left the room for the garden, where Nora Duncombe was walking in the twilight.

She looked up as he came towards her. It was not so dark but that he could catch the smile on her lips and the welcome of her eyes.

"I have not seen you before to-day," she said. "It was a pity if you stayed indoors, for it has been such a perfect day."

"And will be a perfect night," he said.

"The day grown pale. O, if June would but last!"

"How tired one would be of it!" Major Norman lazily observed.

"I don't think I should," said Nora. "This is the first June I have spent in the country since I have been a woman. June to me always means the season and the stage."

"And June roses, Covent Garden bouquets. This is a different side of the month."

"Yes," she said softly.

For a moment he seemed about to say something; but her face was turned away, and his words, whatever they were, remained unspoken.

They had wandered down to where the garden was bounded by a stream, flowing between banks of rushes and forget-me-nots, overshadowed by trees and shrubs.

They stood by the side of the stream at a little open space; the lingering light fell on Miss Duncombe's fair face, making it look pale, but showing the long sweep of her white throat, the full curve of the heavy eyelids, the beautiful mouth. It was one of those times when she was lovely, and contented the eye absolutely.

She was leaning by a syringa, plucking its white blossoms one by one, and casting them into the water as she spoke.

"Shall you remain at Penmouth much longer?" she asked.

"No," Vincent answered. "I am due at my brother's on the 14th; and you, I suppose, will soon be in the midst of that other June you know so well."

"Yes, my voice is quite strong again."

She spoke musingly. Major Norman could almost have fancied he heard a ring of regret in her voice.

"Would it be asking too much, I wonder," he said half jestingly, "if I asked you to let me judge of your recovery?"

She laughed.

"There is no accompaniment, except the brook."

"What does that matter? Your voice needs no support."

"Thank you," she answered; then she half turned away as though to pluck another syringa flower, and the low notes of her voice fell on Vincent Norman's ear, perfect in their tenderness and sweetness.

He had heard her sing in a great theatre, her voice put forth in all its strength; but her singing had never touched him as it did now. How could it? Then she was only an actress and singer to him, he but a unit of her audience; but now they were man and woman together under the silent stars, and each one of her notes vibrated in his heart and stirred to new life—what?

It was a strange song she sang, with a passion and sadness in the music that gave life to the words:

> "Was it for this I loved thee? Only this?
> O, bow thy head down once before we part;

So seal mine agony with one sad kiss ;
  Fear not, thou shalt not feel my salt tears' smart.
    No word of hope or comfort ere I go ?
    'Tis better so.

" Turn thou away ; be mine the grief alone !
  Thine eye shall keep its light, thy lip its red ;
Earth has enough of woe without thy moan ;
  Retain thy beauty though its soul be dead.
      'Twas not in thee Love's perfectness to know ;
      'Tis better so."

What strange contradiction in her nature was it that moved her to choose that song ? A song written by a man out of his heart's bitterness, and the words and music of which held a reproach for her, and for her alone.

Years ago she had been engaged to marry Cyril Elmore, a young man just rising into fame as a musician. She broke off the engagement in a moment's revulsion at the idea of losing her freedom, Cyril having wished her not to sign a contract for America for the winter after their proposed marriage. He left her without a word of reproach or reply ; and, in spite of her relief at once more being her own mistress, she was sorry for the loss of her boy-lover with the dark-gray eyes and beautiful sensitive face.

Shortly afterwards she heard that he was about to leave England for a long while, and then wrote to him asking one kind word of farewell and forgiveness. In reply she received no letter, only the MS. of the song of which the words are written above. A week later she learned that the ship in which Cyril Elmore had sailed had gone down with every soul on board.

Nora was sorry then ; perhaps her self-reproach never quite died away when she thought of the poor boy who had loved her so well, whom she had fancied she was fond of. She kept to herself his legacy of this his last song ; and no one but herself had ever heard it till this night, when she sang it to Vincent Norman.

She could not understand now what impulse had made her choose this song of all others, and was vexed with herself the next moment that she had done so.

She had the dramatic sympathy with the musician, which goes so far towards the making of a great singer; and she had sung this song, which told of the love which she had never understood or prized, as though she herself felt the pain from which the music had its birth.

And so Major Norman, looking at her, thought that here was a woman in whom a man might safely trust.

"Do you remember," she said, turning to him, "our talk that first day of Alceste and Célimène? My song agrees with your view of the matter."

"Yes; yet Alceste needed pity as it was."

"I thought that you held that Célimène was not worth the winning."

"Better care for some object unworthy love than not care for anyone."

Nora shrugged her shoulders.

"Very well," she said; "and in real life Alceste would have carried it out by marrying the first girl he met, and consoled himself for Célimène's weakness by being weaker himself."

Vincent turned quickly on her.

"You don't believe that!" he said. "Why should you say it?"

She laughed.

"I have only caught your own tone of talk. You should be glad to have so apt a pupil."

"My pupil! Heaven save you from such a master!" he answered bitterly; then in a gentler, though not less earnest, voice, he said, " That first day we met you reproved me for cheap cynicism, and you were right; though perhaps if you knew my life you would say I had some cause for despising myself, and so a poor cause—a very poor one, I own—for railing at the world."

Her eyes sought his pityingly and tenderly.

" There is no reason I should tell you this," he said, " except that, since I have known you, your freshness of heart and your faith in the world have been a constant lovely rebuke to me, making me feel my bitternesses and slight. I don't like to hear the echo of my own empty words from your lips. Don't speak so again."

" I never will," she said.

The low tremble of her voice made his pulses beat faster; but he constrained himself by an effort, and said,

" Thank you. You know in *Faust* it is the woman saves the man from the mocking devil of disbelief; the woman who draws him by her influence to the heaven of her own faith, to whom the charge of his soul is given; not the man who drags her down to be degraded with him by the sneering spirit who believes in nothing."

" That time is dead," she answered, in a sudden fierce impulse of honesty, alien to her usual mood. " Now we women are like you men ! We, too, have lost all you sought when you came to us ; so how can we tell you where to find them—those lost treasures of faith and hope ? "

" By a greater than these. By Charity, by Love; and through that, both will find what are lost. But you are speaking of other women, not of yourself. Do not be so bitter. You do not know how much you have taught me, or how different the world looks to me now. I believe in the ideal of womanhood I have learnt through you, even against yourself."

Her head drooped, her voice was sad and true, as she answered,

"I can do nothing. A worldly woman, leading a worldly life."

Against her own will, something moved her to speak the truth to this man; but it was hardly a truth he was likely to accept as such.

"Why will you slander yourself to-night?" he said. "'A worldly woman'! Well, if all worldly women were like you, the world would be very fair. Good-night."

He left her, afraid lest he had said too much; she stood motionless, with a look on her face of mingled joy and sadness, touched with self-reproach.

"If all men were like you," she thought, "there would be no worldly women. If I——"

A quick delicious shame, a sudden and intense ecstasy, made her cover her face with her hands, as though to hide it even from the night.

"He does love me, I am sure of it," she thought, when again she looked up at the brightening moon. "And I—yes, I do love him. I never knew before what it meant, but now— O, if he wished it, why did he not speak now? I should have yielded and been happy; and yet—— Could I really? I might regret. I should if I had to give up my artist life; and I have fancied poor Cyril was right in his song. No, I am not afraid; just now, I feel I would give up everything for love, the love I have wanted all my life. I know I should be happy."

She stood with her face raised to the stars, and full of a rapt sweetness it had never worn before. Now, in the very fulness of her womanhood, Love's mystic chrism was laid on her brow.

Was she worthy to receive this baptism into the world of

self-sacrifice and holiest duty, without which love is naught? to take up the burden which should be borne proudly as a crown for Love's dear sake, or never lifted at all?

Meanwhile Vincent Norman was passing across the fresh grass, hoary with dew, towards the house, with his whole heart passionate with a great love, an intense tenderness and longing to perfect the life of the woman he loved. He thought sometimes that a shadow of weariness and discontent troubled the fairness of her face, that she needed something. Was it love? and could he give her what she wanted? Would his love suffice? It was strong enough, if that were all.

Yet he feared himself—feared lest he should only be asking her to enter into a harder life in being his wife. Knowing how much she would be to him, he dreaded lest he should be but selfish in asking her. Marriage for a woman must always be renunciation of much of the ease and pleasantness of her life; he knew this, and wondered if he were sure love would make amends to her; sure that if Nora Duncombe trusted herself to him she would never repent it, or he have to feel he had dealt unjustly by her whom he loved so much.

He must put his fate to the touch, whether he won or lost it all. His heart pulsed still quicker as he thought of her loveliness and sweetness, of her soft eyes, so melancholy in their beauty. "A worldly woman!" He laughed to himself at the words. Even when he had met her in a London drawing-room he had fancied there was a deep tender nature under the careless charm of her outward seeming, and now he knew it. Whether she loved him or not, she would still be to him the one woman in the world.

IV.

STRANGELY, or rather naturally enough, Miss Duncombe avoided meeting Major Norman for one or two days after that evening.

> "Climb high, feel high, no matter; still
> Feet, feelings must descend the hill.
> An hour's perfection can't recur : "

And Nora felt very differently the morning that followed the night when she had stood by Vincent's side under the trees by the stream.   She had been moved out of herself by mingled influences, and had taken the reflection of Vincent Norman's strong passion for the same feeling in her own heart ; but the next day she had returned to herself, and half-wondered if she were the same woman who had lifted up her face to the sky in rapture and thankfulness for the great gift of love.

A strange shyness at the idea of meeting Major Norman overpowered her ; the truth was, she dreaded lest he should ask her the question to which she was not prepared to give an answer.

For she did love him.   If she gave herself up to her thought, she experienced a luxury of rest in the idea of his love and care, as in the dream of the shadow of a great rock in a weary land ; he suited her, too, better than any man she had ever met ; she knew she would not tire of him, but—— There were so many " buts."

She could not bear to give up her freedom, she said to herself, thus glibly sliding over the tangible and intangible objections, which, if fairly stated to herself, would have had a somewhat small and selfish aspect.   And if she gave up her freedom, she had always determined in her own mind, ever since poor Cyril Elmore's death, that it should be for something worth the exchange, a social position that should fitly crown her triumphs. She knew that such a position was ready to her hand if she chose to take with it a baronet of old name, large fortune, and musical and æsthetic tastes, with lank hair and a retreating chin ; but she would forfeit all chance of it if she married Major Norman.

Nevertheless this morning, the third since she had seen him, she was conscious of a longing for his presence, for the restrained warmth of his greeting, the sudden light in his brave eyes. She rose from the breakfast table, pushed away from her some music she had been studying, and, going to the tarnished glass let into the panelling of the room above the mantelpiece, she inspected the reflection of herself therein with a questioning gaze, as though seeking help.

"I am looking better," she thought, "than when I came down here."

The conclusion was right ; her face was fresher than it had been a month ago ; it seemed as though she might have been bathing it in the May dew which had lain thick of mornings on the grass. Her eyes just now were restless, but they shone darkly soft under the white line of her even brows, which had lost the weariness they had worn when she had first come to Penmouth. Her dress was dark chocolate cashmere, made very plainly, its only ornament a gold brooch, "Rome work," made "by Castellani's imitative craft," fastening the dress just below the narrow line of white collar. The bright waves of her hair were smooth and shining, closely coiled at the back of her head. She looked exquisitely fresh, that most potent charm in a woman to a man's eyes. She put on a round hat the same colour as her dress, with a jay's wing in front, then stood irresolutely by the window, as doubtful what to do.

"I think I'll go down to the shore," was her final determination.

Now it was just half-past ten, and Miss Duncombe might have remembered that Major Norman always returned after his morning swim and walk about this time, so that she was nearly certain to fall in with him on her way towards the sea. But as she would have indignantly scouted the idea that she had any thought of meeting him, it is but fair to suppose that this had escaped her memory.

She did meet him, after all. His face was graver than usual, and after they had said good morning, he added abruptly,

"I see you are going away."

"You saw yesterday's paper?"

"Yes, the advertisement of Miss Clement's appearance——"

"And consequent disappearance from Penmouth of Nora Duncombe."

"Our holiday is at an end."

She felt as though the "our" in his sentence had touched some responsive nerve in her, but only answered lightly,

"We shall meet in London, though?"

"Yes." He spoke hesitatingly, then looked at her, as though he would fain read her thoughts; but she had been an actress too long not to be able to conceal them when it pleased her, and it pleased her now. "When do you leave?" he asked at last.

He had turned back, and was walking with her towards the sea. She had the feeling of having been through all this before, of knowing the end.

"On Tuesday," she said.

Then they walked on in silence till they reached the esplanade. They leant over the railing and watched the tossing play of the waves, each touched with white, and laughing in the sunlight. The sea was shot with green and dark purple; but though the breeze was fresh, the sun shone royally, throwing the line of the coast out vividly, and showing each gray rock and patch of dry turf of a little island about a mile out in front of where Major Norman and Miss Duncombe were leaning over the rail.

"Do you know," Nora said at last, for the sake of saying something, "I have never yet been to that island."

"Neither have I," Vincent Norman answered; "I never thought about it. Is it a *sine quâ non* we should go out there and pay our respects to the gulls? If so, let's make the call in company."

"It wouldn't be etiquette, and I have no cards with me; still——"

"Would you like the row?" he asked. "If so, let's go now. I can get a boat in a minute."

"You really don't mind? If it wouldn't bore and tire you too much."

"And if you can dispense with cushions, shawls, &c. Well, then, it is settled. Have you sufficient confidence in my rowing powers to trust to them, or would you rather we took a boatman?"

She made a pretty gesture of dissent.

"Please not," she said; "they are so worrying and wearisome. But won't it be too much for you? I wish I knew how to row, and could help you."

Major Norman did not join in Nora's wish. When they were in the boat, and she was leaning back in the stern, with her own peculiar grace of attitude, a bright smile of enjoyment on her face, and her eyes meeting his, he realised how much he preferred seeing her thus, to watching her struggling with an oar, and growing heated by the work and the sun.

They soon reached the little island.   Vincent made the boat secure, and then helped his companion out of it across the slippery seaweed-covered rocks, to a smooth little stretch of turf, which was the highest point of the small cluster of rocks. They explored everything there was to explore with a minuteness worthy of the Swiss Family Robinson ; but as one rock pool is very like another rock pool, and one small patch of turf much resembles another small patch, their journey of discovery did not take them long, and they returned to the stretch of turf they had first come upon, with no greater result than the moulted feather of a gull, which Nora had found on a rock and fastened in her hat.

" There is not much to see here," Vincent said, as they sat down under the shade of a sloping rock.

" No; but I have enjoyed the row; I wish it were not the last."

She had meant to be on her guard, but, alone here with him and the sky and sea, she could not help being softer, gentler, and less cautious than she had intended.

" Who knows but the world may end to-night ? "

" I hope not.   What is that from, though ?   I know it."

" *The Last Ride Together.*"

For a moment she made no reply ; she plucked the pale blossom of a sea-pink, and held it up against the deep blue of the sky, seemingly engrossed by looking at it, as she said at last,

" If his wish had been fulfilled, they would both have grown very tired of that eternal ride."

She spoke quietly, trying to cheat herself into thinking she was doing best for him as for herself.

" Do you mean that ? " he said.

Her eyes dropped before his steady gaze, and her voice faltered as she stammered,

" I don't know."

She saw from his face that the moment she had steeled herself against had come, and she nerved herself to meet it, as his voice asked,

"Are you afraid to make the trial? Could you trust me enough to let our lives meet?"

He leant forward, waiting her answer, all the might of a man's love in his earnest face, his expectant eyes.

Nora Duncombe felt as though her brain were burning, her senses and will failing her in her longing to yield, to turn and give herself up to him, and so take the happiness she yearned for and yet feared. She clenched her hands tensely in this brief fierce struggle against her tenderer self, and forced herself to reply,

"I could not."

He could not guess all that was passing within her mind; he only heard the short cold answer, that sounded as though there were no hope that appeal or prayer would soften her. A low but very bitter sigh escaped him.

"I have been a fool," he said after a pause.

She felt a foolish sick pain in her heart at his sigh, and all the anguish it told; she could not bear his words, and it was more to comfort herself than him she said hurriedly,

"No, not that. Have I hurt you? You do not know how I hate to give you pain, how I hate myself for——O, why did you care for me?"

"Why?"

The question was sad, rather scornful. He did not echo her word as a reproach, but it fell as such on her ear.

She knew too well how she had caused him to yield to his love for her, how she had drawn him on, but why? Not even to herself could Nora answer the question.

She had called him cynical, but she knew all along that he was not; that he was simple, true, brave, holding faith in any man or woman unless he or she gave him proof of being unworthy belief. A thousand times simpler, truer, sweeter in his nature than she, who had rebuked him for bitterness, who had charmed him with her pretty enthusiasms, her seeming faith that the whole world and those who dwelt on it were very good.

For one moment she saw this clearly as in a lightning flash; it was not a pleasant self-revealing.

"I should never suit you," she said to him; and her voice was pleading, her eyes were imploring, in spite of herself. "We should not be happy."

"Say you would not," he answered, "and that is enough. To me the mere winning you would overbalance all the worth of life."

"You say so now, but in two years' time——"

"You hardly know me; I am not very changeable."

"And then you would want me to give up my art."

"I should want you to do nothing except your own will. You cannot think I should wish to tie your freedom."

"But you would like me to leave the stage," she said, with a perverse pleasure in trying to discover his nature.

"What does it matter," he asked, "since you have refused me? But you would have been free. I might have been glad if this had not been your life; but I cannot say even that, for I love you as you are, complete. I would never have cramped you, as it would cramp you, to sever you from your art."

"But how about your profession? It is as much to you as my work is to me. I could not have borne to think I had spoilt your life. Can you not see it would never do, even if——"

"That 'if' would have smoothed all; if you had loved me, the crooked would have been made straight and the rough places plain; as it is—— O my dearest, I could have loved you so well!"

A DECLARATION REJECTED

His words shook her resolve, but still she did not surrender. She knew there was a traitor, or one whom she deemed as such, within her gates—Love—who whispered to her that this man against whom she held her heart's citadel was her rightful king, at whose approach the gates should have been thrown open wide, not barred as against a foe; that, if she denied him entrance, she did so at her own peril, the peril of his scorn and of a desolate life.

Something of this may have shown itself in her face, for he bent forward and spoke eagerly:

"Nora, do you love me? Is it anything else that separates us? Tell me plainly once if you can care for me or not; do not say 'yes' if you cannot from your heart, but remember a lie either way will be a sin against your own soul. Do you love me?"

Her head swam; she felt as though all the world, the bright sky, the flashing green and purple sea were a dream, as if nothing were real but Vincent's voice; but she gathered up her whole strength, and looked at him unflinchingly as she said,

"No."

And all the while his words rang in her ears, as though they were a judgment: "A sin against her own soul;" she knew it only too well.

Silently he rose and turned aside, and a few moments afterwards, as with one accord, they went down to the boat; silently Vincent handed Nora in and took his own place; but now he never looked at her as she sat with bowed head and heavy eyelids, as though fearing again to meet his gaze.

They reached land at last, and walked along the beach till they came to a road which led up to Horneck House; then, as by a common impulse, they turned to say good-bye. A strange stricken look was on his face; but there was a wilder sadness in Nora's eyes as, holding out her hand, she whispered rather than said, "Forgive me."

Vincent felt a quick pity, he knew not why, in the midst of his own pain, for this woman through whom he suffered.   Did a suspicion of the truth cross his mind ?   If so, he made no attempt to alter her mind ; he knew it would be of no avail.

"Have I anything to forgive ? " he said gravely and gently. "If I have, Nora, forgive yourself ; I only love you, dear."

It was a quiet spot, and there was no one near ; she raised his hand to her lips, and kissed it twice ; then turned swiftly away from him down the road that led to the house.

V.

Miss Duncombe was engaged writing that evening in her own sitting-room at Horneck House.   She had delighted her maid by telling her that they should return to town on the morrow instead of waiting till Tuesday, and ordering her to set about packing up forthwith.   Then she wrote to the landlady at her London lodgings to tell her to get things ready, and to her dressmaker about a costume for a new part.

She finished her letters and gave them to her maid to post. The girl went out in the glimmering twilight, and Miss Duncombe leant back in her chair, wondering what Vincent Norman was doing in the room above.   Was he sitting there lonely and sad, thinking of her ?

A dim idea came to her of stealing up to his room, bending over him as he sat there in the dusk, and saying, " It was only a madness, darling ; I love you, and love is best of all."   How would he receive her if she did ?   She could fancy the gladness dawning on his face, the feeling of his arms round her, an utter rest and happiness such as she had never known.

She shook herself free at last from the dream, with an impatient anger at her own folly. She rose and looked about for the matches with which to light the candles, and so shut out the sad twilight of this long bitter day. In her search she came across something which struck her eye—her note-book.

She took it up listlessly, and opened it without any reason that she knew of. In it, between a letter from the *dilettante* baronet mentioned some way back, and a calculation of what her receipts would be from a foreign engagement, there lay the wood-sorrel blossoms Vincent had given her, faded and crushed to death between compliments and money calculations —poor little flowers that had been as the first tender breath of love's summer, the summer whose beauty Nora would never know.

With a quiver as of pain and a sharp sob, she shut the little book again and turned to light the candles.

The *Entr'acte* was over.

A STORY OF A GARDEN PARTY.

By H. SAVILE CLARKE.

THE possession of such a name as Bingo gives me, I think, some claim upon the commiseration of the public. Bingo is not a name which inspires respect. It does not tell of a long line of ancestors, some of whom took part in the Norman Conquest and the Crusades; nor does it call up before the reader's eye a vision of a man of knightly bearing,—rather may it be said, if it suggests anything, to remind people of a small and insignificant dog, and you may be sure that was made the most of during my school-days. When I say that as a boy I have been led about at the end of a string, with a piece of blue ribbon at my neck, and been addressed as " good doggie," you will see that I have suffered much from my unfortunate patronymic.

Nor has it been made any better by my sponsorial appellation. It pleased my godfathers and godmother, or more probably my parents, to call me Randolph. That is a name which was appropriate enough for a Border chieftain, a " Warden of the Marches" who had the run of Branksome Hall, if there was anything left to eat after the retainers had dined; for some gallant moss-trooper, who, after a life of daring, died on the congenial gibbet at " merry Carlisle; " but it was no name for me. It was bad enough to be called Bingo; it was positively revolting to be called Randolph Bingo. I had serious thoughts of changing my name at one time, but gave it up on a friend's remarking that it would be a Norfolk-Howardly thing to do; but I never signed my name in full—it was always R. Bingo; and you might make what you liked out of the " R."—it might stand for the harmless Robert, or even for Rhadamanthus—I never confessed to anything but the plain initial.

Existence, however, was not entirely clouded by my absurd name. I had compensations. I was not bad looking, as young men go nowadays, when there are a good many living proofs of Darwin's theories to be seen in any place of public resort; and I had a good income—rather over than under that received by the President of the Board of Trade in his official capacity. That I inherited from my father, who had been something—I never knew exactly what—in the West Indies, and I had nothing to do for it. I was, in fact, a young man about town, and, having no occupation, I naturally took up a hobby.

You will never guess what it was. I look upon chinamania as a delusion. I am not particularly fond of pictures. I hate insects, and I don't care about flowers. I am not averse to seeing other people make fools of themselves in private theatricals, but I would scorn to make an exhibition of myself. I have no æsthetic tastes, nor any leaning to science, and I think politics are an unutterable bore. But I have one mania, or rather I should say one peculiarity, and that is what may be medically described as chronic devotion to the fair sex. I am always in love. I am perpetually getting engaged, and as I never dream of being off with the old love before I am on with the new, things get a little mixed sometimes.

People talk about love at first sight; that is a slow and hesitating passion to that which animates me. The mere mention of a girl's name is enough ; I can fall in love with that, with a shadow on a blind, a specimen of handwriting, a flower, a photograph—with anything, in fact, that can call up the vision, however remote, of feminine loveliness. I can adore on provocation so slight that it would have no effect at all on other people. I fell in love once, for instance, because a young creature wore her hat low over her eyes, and looked *up* at me so bewitchingly from under it. Another enslaver used to climb a ladder in the paternal garden, and look *down* upon me from the fifth rung in such a way that I proposed on the spot. I fell in love with a soprano voice, and wrote it (the voice) warm letters, till I found out that it patronised 'buses and tram-cars, and flung the aspirate about with positively lavish profusion.

Of course this extreme susceptibility led me into an enormous number of scrapes. I don't think I broke many hearts—none of the little affairs lasted long enough for that—but I caused much consternation, and upset the equanimity of quiet families who had too confidingly received me as Jessie's or Ada's lover, as the case might be, and found out how soon I transferred my allegiance to another shrine.

When this artless narrative commences, I had just scrambled out of my twenty-third engagement. The word "scrambled" does not imply dignity, and it was in a by-no-means-dignified manner that I had evaded my responsibilities on the occasion. The object of my affections had professed herself deeply injured by the withdrawal of my proposal—it had really been hardly one at all—just a whisper about an hour long in the conservatory, and she snapped me up like an alligator ; and her brother had come and flourished a stick about, and been very hasty and absurd. He soon cooled down, however, while the young lady accepted a modest *solatium*, and married a curate two months afterwards.

Thus at the time of which I am speaking I was in what I

may call a comparatively disengaged condition. My mind was open, as it were, for any new impressions—though, by the way, a letter from an old flame, a cousin Annie, had made me feel very spoony on her again ; and I had a decided *penchant* for a young lady with divine hair I had been introduced to at a morning concert a day or two before. But still I was as open to further feminine influences as it was ever possible for me to be, and accordingly I accepted an invitation to go down to Sunnyford Hall with infinite alacrity.

Sunnyford deserved its name. It was the breeziest, brightest little village imaginable, and the Hall was worthy of it—a delightful old Elizabethan house, always full of pleasant company, which invariably included a number of the most fascinating girls to be found in the whole country-side.

I went down, therefore, with the liveliest anticipations of what the Americans call a "good time;" but had I known what was to befall me, I would as soon have packed my portmanteau for Pandemonium as for Sunnyford. I must not anticipate, however, as they say in novels; let me state, then, that I arrived at Sunnyford Hall, and there I found what the local newspaper, describing our archery meeting, called a "perfect galaxy of beauty" assembled. I am not exaggerating when I say that I would willingly have led to the altar any one unmarried girl in the house who would have had me; and the difficulty of singling out one special object of devotion was really immense.

At last I settled upon a most piquant little lady who rejoiced in the name of Georgina Barstow, who also seemed to have a real genius for flirtation, and to her I devoted myself as assiduously as a newly-elected member for a Radical constituency given to deputations devotes himself to the House. I am betraying no confidence when I say that Miss

Barstow, like the immortal Barkis, was exceedingly " willing."
Other swains hovered round her, for, like Mr. Locker's
heroine, she was

> " An angel in a frock,
>   With a fascinating cock
>   To her nose ; "

but Georgie seemed to prefer your humble servant.

I proposed to her at a garden party. We had been driven
in by the rain, and were having afternoon tea in the house,
and I was standing with Georgie at one of the French windows
opening on to the lawn, when I made the plunge. She
balanced her teacup thoughtfully for a moment, and then, to
carry out the aquatic metaphor, she jumped in with me. For
the twenty-fourth time in my life I was an engaged man, and
upon my word I breathed more freely after it. I was so used
to it, you see, that I felt quite uncomfortable without a young
woman attached, as it were, to my fortunes.

Georgie and I had one brief bright hour of bliss—that is to
say, of engaged bliss. We had experienced unengaged bliss
to any extent previously, but we only had an hour after the
fatal words were spoken ; for an old aunt with whom she was
staying carried her off at the end of that time, and left me dis-
consolate. However, I had no time to mope, as we were due
at a ball that night some dozen miles off ; and though I knew
I should not meet Georgie there, I felt in excellent trim for
the festivities. Who knows, I thought, but that I may meet
some congenial spirit who will cheer the forlorn lover during
his lady's absence ! And egad the forlorn lover was cheered
with a vengeance, as you shall see.

I went to the ball. The rule laid down by that excellent
and easy-going poet Mr. Thomas Moore concerning the lips
that are near when we are far from those we love, has been
mine through life. On this occasion, the lips that were near

A FLIRTATION AND ITS RESULTS.

A QUADRILLE AND ITS CONSEQUENCES.

I. 65.

were those of a young thing whose dancing was of the most sylph-like character, and whose conversation was so beautifully besprinkled with scraps of poetry that I had hard work to keep myself up to her level. The Barstow was blonde, *petite*, and prosaic ; my new friend was a brunette, rather over the average size, poetic and romantic—a complete contrast, in fact, in every way. Under such influences I became poetic and romantic myself ; and as I engaged Miss Leland—for that was her name—for dance after dance, I need not tell you how my susceptible heart comforted itself ; and how, after two quadrilles, two waltzes, and a galop, I was hopelessly in love.

It happened in the conservatory. I have always been peculiarly susceptible to the influence of conservatories, and the moment we sat down amongst the camellias I knew what would happen. Miss Leland had been quoting *Hyperion ;* and what could I do but, like Paul Fleming, tell her that the student Hieronymus was lying at her feet ? I did not *quite* mean to propose, you know, but she took me up directly ; and instead of playing the *rôle* of Mary Ashburton, she reclined her head gently on my shoulder (I ought to have said my arm was round her waist) ; and for the twenty-fifth time I was an engaged man. Of course I never remembered Georgie Barstow ; but my thoughts went back to her with a sudden shock when I discovered that Miss Leland's name was also "Georgina," and that she, too, expected to be called "Georgie." It then occurred to me also, for the first time, that I had carefully engaged myself to two ladies at once, and that the consequences might be a little awkward.

I went back to town next day with what I believe it is *de rigueur* to call "mingled feelings ; " and mine were certainly a good deal more mingled than was pleasant. Here were two charming girls both willing to be Mrs. Bingo,—I don't mean together, but separately,—and I really didn't know which to choose. Never surely was mortal man impaled on the horns of a livelier dilemma; and the more I looked at it the less I liked it.

The plot thickened next morning when the post brought me two letters. They had both written, bless their hearts; and in two different handwritings a little flutterer remained, at the end of a charming epistle, my "affectionate Georgie." At any rate, these letters must be answered while I made up my mind on the matter. So in a spirit of fairness, which I think deserves commendation, I despatched the same neat little letter to both, only altering the superscription. One Georgie should not crow over the other, if they ever compared notes, if I could prevent it.

In the meantime, I never felt more perplexed in my life. Frequently as I had been engaged before, there had been only one lady in each case, and now I had two on hand at once. A too susceptible heart was certainly a very dangerous organ. Nor could I consult any one. I mentioned my difficulty to one friend, hoping he would be touched by my position and give me some good advice, but he received the news with demoniac laughter, and persisted in calling me "Bingo the Bigamist," which he declared would make a capital title for a play.

The more I thought the matter over the more awkward it seemed; and in the meantime, of course, both engagements went on. Each of the dear creatures wrote every day, and I was kept at work answering them. The same letter would not do after the first, and I was always afraid of mixing up the letters and referring to the tender inquiries of Miss Barstow in an answer addressed to Miss Leland. The prosaic Georgie Number One clashed with the poetic Georgie Number Two in my mind in the most confusing manner, and it was all I could do to keep them distinct. I received two engagement rings, and duly returned two, both of precisely the same pattern; and lockets also, the jeweller grinning in a most aggravating manner when I ordered them. Both the Georgies sent photographs also; and altogether I was driven nearly wild.

At last there came a crisis. I received letters from their respective mothers. Number One hadn't a father, and Number Two's male parent didn't appear to trouble his head much about the matter; and they informed me they were both coming to town on the same day, arriving at the same station. I was in despair; the only comfort was, they were not coming by the same train. Miss B. was to arrive in the morning, and Miss L. in the afternoon. There was nothing for it but to pluck up courage and meet them both; and I did so. I met Georgie Barstow, and was received rapturously. I lunched with her and her mother at their hotel; and I tore myself away from her on the plea of a pressing engagement,—true enough, forsooth,—and flew to meet Georgie Leland and dine with her and Mrs. L. at *their* hotel.

Then began a state of things which is but feebly described as appalling. I had to dance attendance upon each lady every day; and after blissful moments—or rather moments which should have been blissful, but weren't—to invent excuses and fly off for ditto with the other. I was in perpetual fear, of course, of meeting Number One, after inventing a series of engagements, when escorting Number Two. London is large enough, no doubt; but there is no place in the world in which you so often meet the very people you wish to avoid. They were both charming girls singly, and I could have been devoted to one of them; but together they were too much for me. I felt my mind giving way under the strain of a double devotion, and my hair growing gray from the tax this dual existence made upon my energies.

It was really something frightful.   Neither of them had seen many of the sights of London, and I had to do all the show places *twice*. Judge if any human being could stand that ! And when I add that I visited Madame Tussaud's admirable exhibition in Baker-street twice in one day, with one Georgie in the morning and the other in the afternoon, with a short interval for lunch, and that the door-keeper evidently recognised me, and must have thought I had a relation in the Chamber of Horrors,—you will admit that even the two victims of my susceptibility would have pitied me had they known my position.

I rose each morning with a feeling that the climax might come on that particular day, and I went to rest at night like a man who had been sentenced to death and then reprieved.   No wonder I grew worn and gray, and showed my anxieties in my face.   Both my Georgies remarked it, bless their sympathetic little hearts, little knowing that they were the burden which was wearing me to a shadow.   One morning I rose with a peculiarly ominous feeling in my mind; and it was by no means relieved when I heard from Miss Leland that I should be expected to escort her with some friends to the Opera that night.   I agreed, however; and after luncheon I sped off to take Miss Barstow to a morning concert.   She was engaged for the evening—I did not ask how ; and after seeing her home I rushed to the club and dined, and then went to the Opera.   I shall never forget that awful evening.   It was the *début* of Zaré Thalberg.   She came out, as you remember, in *Don Giovanni*, and all eyes were centred on the Zerlina of the night.   I had neither eyes nor thoughts for singer or music, for the moment I took my place in a box on the O.P. side, in dutiful attendance on Miss Leland, I became conscious that in the box exactly opposite to us there was Miss Barstow and her mother; and though they would possibly resent the imputation, they glared at me.

Then Georgie Barstow, with cruel kindness, bowed to me with *empressement*.

"Dear me," said Miss Leland, "who is your friend, Randolph?"

Now I was prepared for such a position as this, and had the answer ready ; so I replied blandly and coolly, "O, my second cousin." Not "cousin," you will observe, "second cousin," which is more remote and more circumstantial. No one could doubt a statement about such a relative, or be jealous of her. So I thought, at least; but Miss Leland, said, with considerable *hauteur*—

"Indeed! She seems much surprised to see you. Hadn't you better go and speak to your *second cousin?* I am longing to be introduced."

"Jealousy," I said to myself; and then I said, as quietly as I could, "Well, perhaps I had better go round for a moment;" and hastened off to Number One.

I found Georgie Barstow in a similar frame of mind—that is, in a state of aggravated jealousy. She scorned to ask me any questions; but her mother begged to know who my friends on the other side of the house were, in a tone which would have frozen the Victoria Nyanza. Having found a second cousin rather a failure, I said mildly that it was my cousin's wife, whereat the old woman looked suspicious, and Georgie sniffed. I was evidently in hot water here also, and was just going to make my escape, when Mrs. Barstow said—

"Perhaps you will introduce us after the opera is over, Mr. Bingo. We have seen so few of your friends."

I could only bow and rush out and cool my burning head in the lobby, and try and collect my thoughts.

I dare not go back to either box, for I felt certain some one would come in, and I might be betrayed, as the lady with Miss Leland knew a good many people in town ; and I was, besides, in so excited a state I might commit myself. My head was whirling, and I hardly knew where I was.　At last, in desperation, I tore a couple of leaves out of my pocket-book and wrote two notes.　They were both alike, saving the necessary variation, and ran as follows :—

" Dearest Georgie,

"Very sorry.　A telegram has called me away, so I must put off introducing you to my $\left\{ \begin{array}{l} \text{second cousin} \\ \text{cousin's wife} \end{array} \right\}$.　See you to-morrow.

" Your own devoted
" RANDOLPH."

And I sent a man with them to each box.

That was all very well; but, after twisting up the notes, in my hurry and excitement I misdirected them, and Georgie Barstow received with astonishment my excuse about my " second cousin," while Georgie Leland heard with equal astonishment of my " cousin's wife."　Furthermore, they would see each other reading the notes, would divine at once that the latter had gone wrong, and, as a natural consequence, that I had two " dearest Georgies," and was the " own devoted Randolph " of my second cousin and my cousin's wife.　I say they would see all this, for I fled from the house and rushed home like a madman.　What took place afterwards at the theatre, I don't know; but I do know what happened next morning, and I am not likely to forget it while memory holds a seat in this bewildered brain.

In the first place, I received a letter early in the morning delivered by hand, which contained the following :—

" Sir,—We have met, and know all.

" GEORGINA BARSTOW.
" GEORGINA LELAND."

Prepared as I was, I was stunned when another letter came

to revive me, which informed me that Mrs. B. and Mrs. L. would call on me that morning, and also that they had instructed their respective solicitors to commence immediate actions against me for breach of promise of marriage. That was pleasant; but there was a more trying surprise than all to come next.

I had just finished my breakfast, and was vaguely wondering how I should face the situation, when the door opened, and my servant—the rascal was grinning, and had evidently been bribed—ushered in the two Georgies!

You have heard of people wishing the earth to swallow them; but if the Maëlstrom had yawned before me then I should have taken a header into it.

I started up and gasped; I could do nothing else.

Gazing at me sternly and in complete silence, they put down on the table together the rings, lockets, photographs, and other presents I had given them. Even in my agony I could have laughed to see how each little pile contained exactly the same articles, and my letters, including the two fatal notes I had sent the previous night. Then they slowly retired, all this time without saying a word, while I of course was speechless; but just as they were going out of the door Georgie Barstow—she was always an impulsive little thing, bless her heart!—found her feelings too much for her, and ejaculated the simple but all-sufficing word, " Wretch ! "   And then I was alone again.

I did not wait for the mothers or the solicitors. I fled. Before leaving the country, however, I wrote to the parents of the outraged damsels, saying that, as I was honestly willing to marry both of them did the laws of my country permit it, I would marry either of them if they chose to submit their claims to the arbitrament of the customary coin, or, in other words, toss up for me. Nothing, I'm sure, could be fairer;

but I received no reply, and to save them the trouble of proceeding against me I left the country.

I remained in foreign lands two years. I will not say where, though Sir George Nares, could tell, an he listed, how the name of Bingo was not unknown even on the verge of the Palæocrystic sea; and I did not return till my victims were happily married. But the story got wind, and my duplex matrimonial intentions afforded a theme for the scoffer; so that though I am innocent of the crime, I am known from China to Peru as "Bingo the Bigamist."

A SOCIAL FAILURE REDEEMED.

I.

IT is a disastrous thing for a man to be a social failure. Far worse, ladies, than for one of yourselves. Listen to my confession.

Three years had elapsed since I, a would-be gay thing of a bachelor, started in chambers in Mayfair, and there was no more blinking the truth. Society had jilted me cruelly—indefatigably though I continued to court her. Introductions, good family name, unblemished character, private means, excellent intentions, had all failed miserably to float me on the tantalising sea of pleasure, fashion, flirtation, that surged around me.

The fourth May came, bringing with its spring blossoms a magnificent crop of spring gaieties—but not for me, Johnny Anstruther. Thirteen posts passed my door daily, nor left me so much as a card for a ball. I had ceased even to dream of invitations to dinner. Why was I "dropped" thus? I bitterly inquired. Had I not invariably gone when invited, arrived punctually, and called within forty-eight hours? For society, ladies' society, young ladies' society, was to me the one sweet thing that made life worth living. To dally awhile in the "rosebud garden of girls," deliberately select thence the queen rosebud I should prefer—such was my heart's hope quenched, my youth's ideal unconditionally denied me.

My disappointment, which amounted to despair, broke out one day to my friend and fellow-lodger, Francis Barry, whose brilliant butterfly life wretched I had once aspired to emulate. The mere sight of his mirror stung me to frenzy. It was a maze of pretty notes and cards—my Lady This and the Hon. Mrs. That competing for his precious company at dinners, dances, fêtes, water-parties, and every conceivable variety of alluring entertainment. I saw names that sent a thrill to my bosom, and addresses—I would have forfeited a gold-mine for the right to enter those walls.

"Favourite of Fortune," I cried enviously, "what a heaven is earth for a Prince Charming like you!"

He is a fool who complains to a handsome and popular fellow that he is neither the one nor the other. But passionate longing bore down self-respect.

Francis twirled his black moustache, and asked, with affected surprise—

"What's wrong with you, Johnny?"

"I should like to know," I rejoined, with grim irony. "Whatever the cause, I'm a failure, Barry, a dismal failure, in the society to which I was born. If I were a convict or an idiot, or deformed, they couldn't give me up more unreservedly. Compare our lots" (pointing eloquently to the mantleshelf). "Yet are you not, like myself, a Government Office young man? Are not our families on a par?"

I spoke generously, for my father was colonel of a crack cavalry corps, Barry's but an officer of marines.

"Rank's not everything now-a-days," he reminded me. "All depends on—circumstances," leaning his tall spare figure back against the chimneypiece, his black hair and provokingly good features displayed in a becoming frame of invitations to dinner.

Circumstances? Ha, ha! He sang like a bird, did Barry;

acted like Charles Mathews *redivivus;* and decorated any room
he was in.   I could not sing, stammered intermittently in my
talk, and spoiled the only farce I ever played in by speaking
my part—"Dinner is on the table"—in an inaudible voice.
My shyness, intensified by repeated rebuffs, was like a de-
moniacal possession that seized me when in company.   I never
opened my lips now but to say the wrong thing—never made a
step without stumbling, or treading on some ones best gown.

"You look ready to cut your throat," remarked Barry,
laughing—the villain!

"I am.   Other fellows would fall back on low company.   I
sha'n't do that; but I'm tired to death of my own."

"Take my advice," he said.   "Cut Vanity Fair.   Try the
opposition shop—the ladies of intellect and learning, the camp
of the Amazons, the emancipated.   Don't make faces.   I knew
a man much in your predicament last year who now enjoys the
reputation of a lady-killer among the sisterhood."

"The shrieking sisterhood of suffrageous spinsters," I broke
in savagely.   "They will put up with blockheads like me
because fine fellows like you detest them."

"O, I'm told they've crowds of pretty and charming women
among them now, and that shy fellows like you get on there
like a house on fire," he pursued, chaffing on heartlessly.
"Here's the very thing for you—a ticket Lady Gay has sent
for the *conversazione* of the Ladies' Athenæum to-night at the
Cassandra Rooms, with a note—'I have promised to scatter
these cards.   Help me, if you have any old frumps of
friends . . . . to send to the Cassandra Rooms.   Don't
forget that you dine with me at eight.   The Duchess has
promised,' &c.   Well," tossing me the card, "How about
Cassandra?   Won't you go and see the land?"

"Confound Cassandra and her club!" I exclaimed, striding
out in a rage, and I heard the scoundrel laughing behind me.

That night, finishing my solitary chop at the club, I had a vision. I saw Francis Barry dining with a duchess, charming her by his empty talk, peeling a peach for her. My brow burned. As I drew out my handkerchief, a card fell on the floor. I read "Cassandra Rooms—Ladies' Athenæum." I had pocketed the hated thing unawares in my distraction.

"I'll go," I said madly. "If I stay here I shall cut my throat in good earnest."

I entered the Cassandra Rooms, my mind made up for a bad dream of plain women with cropped hair, neutral attire, and spectacles. But there was a lion in the path to be faced first, namely, a lady by the door, doing the honours. She glanced at my ticket—I had filled in my name—then at me.

Wretched experience has rendered me morbidly acute to the "first impression" I make. Was it possible that this, for once, was not unfavourable? I felt a strange soothing sensation. And she was not so uncomely a matron, and rather well dressed.

"You are a stranger here, I think, Mr. Anstruther?" she said kindly, but with no exasperating pity. "Let me introduce you to our secretary, Miss Priscilla Hale."

Introductions are my moments of supremest anguish. My stammer comes on, my brain evaporates. I rack the remains of it, but nor words nor ideas will come. A film crossed my eyes. Then a loud cheerful voice said—

"Are you in favour of ladies' clubs?" This was uttered in a bracing tone, and gave me nerve to articulate intelligibly—

"The ladies themselves are the best judges of them. What are your views Miss—— ?"

Confusion! There—I'd forgotten her name!

"Priscilla Hale," she supplied it calmly. "Well, I hold that if our clubs mostly fail it is because they are too mixed. Put butterflies with bees, and they will fight. The Ladies'

Athenæum admits workers only. This brilliant assemblage" (I stared) "is an auspicious inauguration. O, you're quite among the blue-stockings to-night, Mr. Anstruther. Shall we walk round? I can tell you who's who and what's what, if you care to know."

I did not object—I never can. Were a lady to say to me, "Shall we jump out of window?" I should acquiesce. As we paced the rooms she made good her word, and proved besides a most amusing cicerone.

"That angel-faced golden-haired creature is Mrs. Haller, the grand bulwark of female suffrage. The fat little old person, whose gray hair is coming down, is 'Zephyrine,' who writes such passionate romances. The pretty girl behind us is Janie Somers, a great Greek scholar, and the translator of *Agamemnon*. Those glass cases contain a collection of flying dragons, fossil fungi, and a gold beetle from Yucatan, said to attain a fabulous age. Here comes Professor Omnium, who is going to lecture us upon them by-and-by."

Here was my partner—dancing gentleman so to speak—piloting, protecting, instructing, entertaining me. I experienced a beneficial effect. My self-consciousness, my worst enemy, relaxed, and I began to "take notice." By Heaven, there was no lack of young and pretty girl-faces, and the men present were not of Barry's supercilious stamp. I hazarded a remark, then a joke or two—jewels that I grudged to Miss Hale, a stout spinster of forty-five, which was base ingratitude to this sister of mercy who first drew me out. I was answering her with a fluency I could not account for, when, half-way in a sentence, I broke off, coming to a dead stop. In reply to her look of inquiry, I faltered out—

"Miss Hale, who is the lady at the door?"

"Dr. Victoria Vivian, the very best authority on diseases of the brain."

" And the lady shaking hands with her—she who introduced us ? "

"Lady Crookshanks, President of the Ladies' Athenæum Committee."

" *Who is she now crossing the room !* "

This was a girl just come in, whose face fascinated my gaze, lover, hapless lover, of brilliant beauty that I am !   Her finely-shaped head, exquisite features in a frame of curiously-cut brown hair, and her large earnest eyes, thrilled me with a never yet experienced admiration.   Miss Hale replied simply,

" That is Beatrice Arne."

Arne ?   I knew the name—fashionable friends of Barry's.

" What is she doing here ? " I asked inadvertently.

Miss Hale stared.

" Ah," she said, " then you know about her, and how her family disapprove of her devotion to science.   They want to make a professional beauty of her, but she won't hear of it. See Professor Omnium rush up to her.   She is his pet pupil and private secretary.   Now she has come he will read his paper on the ' Ancestral Ant.'   But suppose we go to the refreshment-room for a cup of tea instead ? "

I acquiesced, though I was longing to stay and watch Beatrice Arne.

We found the refreshment-room empty—the tea cleared away, the ice just come in.   I supplied Miss Hale, and, at her bidding, myself.   At the first mouthful I barely restrained an interjection.   Trembling I watched her ; for I knew if she ate hers, I should not dare to hint at anything amiss with mine.   I should swallow the nauseous compound.

" Good heavens ! "   To my relief she laid down her spoon.

" What is this ? " she exclaimed.   " Salt ! "

Exactly.   Owing to accident or negligence in the freezing process the sweetstuff had been sent up saturated with brine.

"Horrible!" she pursued. "Take it away! But," with sudden consternation, "it is our staple refreshment to-night. The *soirée* is ruined. It will be all over London to-morrow that the Ladies' Athenæum gives salted ices! Our enemies will make us the laughing-stock of Society. It might be fatal to the club at its birth."

"Can I do nothing?" I stammered, touched by her distress.

She turned to me, and answered with decision,

"You can save us. Jump into a hansom—Graves', the confectioner's, is not far. Be back with a fresh supply of ice in a quarter of an hour, before the Professor has done. Then no one need ever know."

It was years since a lady had appealed to me, or given me a chance of distinguishing myself. Now if I can't originate, I can obey. In five minutes I was at the shop. An ice-man was just leaving with a supply for a ball. By an inspiration worthy of Francis Barry, I bribed him to take his load to the Cassandra Rooms by mistake. We arrived just as they were applauding the Professor up-stairs. Miss Hale, white with suspense, was on the look-out. At the sight of the ice-tins her face beamed. I was breathless, my tie untied, my boots splashed, my hair awry; but she shook both my hands, saying warmly,

"Thanks, a thousand times!"

I thought her beautiful for a moment. Now the company came trooping down-stairs. The ice was ready for them. The beauty came with the rest, on the old Professor's arm— thank Heaven, not a Barry's. He was talking to her earnestly, but all about the physiology of the nervous system of the cray-fish. I kept apart, a prey to a return of despondency, and should have slipped away, but Miss Hale detained me.

"Pray don't go. I must speak to you when the *soirée* is over," said she.

So I waited till all had dispersed but Miss Hale and the lady president, who had introduced me to Miss Hale, and to whom Miss Hale now reintroduced me as the saviour of the evening, with a lively account of the mishap I had helped to avert. Hope revived had worked miracles on me that night; but a reaction had now set in. I felt myself under criticism, and shook with a palsy of nervous awkwardness. I held on like grim death to a chair with one hand, clutching with the other at some papers on the table. I fumbled at one, and pored over it so fondly that Miss Hale, imagining I was interested in its contents, said—

"Would you be inclined to join? The subscription is only ten-and-six."

I awoke to the fact that I was perusing the prospectus of the Field Naturalists' Scientific Association and their periodical lecture meetings. The list of members was alphabetical, and headed by the name of Beatrice Arne.

"There is a lecture to-morrow night," said Miss Hale. "I can introduce you as a friend, and you can judge if you care to become a member."

I accepted with alacrity and withdrew. I felt like a country after the shock of revolution, like Columbus on sighting a new world. Was there then a world, new to me, outside the world of spoilt beauties, over-dressed dolls, and flippant coquettes, who, without having done anything all their lives but smile and look pretty, and ruin their male relatives by their dress-makers' bills, claim the notice, consideration, devotion of sensible men? A world where a shy, timid, modest, and un-assuming young gentleman like me is not instantly lynched— nay, in which his diffidence counts rather for than against him —and where my *début* had not been a complete *fiasco?*

And to this world belonged the loveliest girl I had ever seen —Beatrice Arne!

We met—'twas in a school, lent to the Society for their lectures. Deal benches, glaring gas-jets, and some thirty solemn-looking Field Naturalists' faces constituted the *mise en scène*.

I thought, with a pang, of the maze of fair smiling countenances, the flutter, dance-music, and flower-scents of the intoxicating atmosphere where the London man seeks his ideal. On the other hand, none of these people seemed thinking of attracting notice, or of cutting up their neighbours. Attention was monopolised by certain mysterious objects on the table—powerful microscopes, said Miss Hale, under which were the compound eye of a snail and the pro-leg of a caterpillar.

Suddenly Beatrice Arne, like a blaze of beauty, entered the room. She took her place in front of mine. My evil genius was on me now. I fidgeted till the bench creaked, my umbrella dropped on the floor with a loud noise, at which the Field Naturalists frowned ; for the lecturer had just begun to enlighten us on the interesting subject of " Snails and Slugs." He was a young man, with angular features and carroty hair. Beatrice's limpid eyes were fixed on him with an ardent expression that would have transported me to the skies. It did not affect him in the smallest degree. He was short-sighted, and his mind's eye was intent on his slugs. By and by a snail inside a glass cylinder was handed round, that we might admire its wonderful method of locomotion—passed from Beatrice's firm white hand to my nervous fingers.

" Beautiful ! " she murmured, looking earnestly at me.

" O, beautiful ! " I responded—she would think I meant the snail.

Of the lecture I heard no more. I had thought of a thousand brilliant things to say to Miss Hale for Miss Arne to overhear, of various ingenious ways of approaching the latter, and was far ahead in my imaginary courtship, when continuous applause announced that the lecture was over. Now was my opportunity; for Miss Hale and Beatrice were talking together. And I shrank away, and turned my back, and pretended to be studying the illuminated texts on the wall. When I mustered courage to look round, Beatrice was gone.

Miss Hale, who was returning to her home at Richmond, asked me to walk with her to the station. *En route* she rallied me playfully on my evident admiration in a certain quarter.

"Am I the first," I asked mournfully, "to discover her extraordinary beauty?"

"By no means. All the professors at X— College adore her; they say it is for her devotion to science, and the imaginative mind she brings to bear on the subject; but I think the eyes she brings have also some part in it. However, Miss Arne is charming in every respect. Why did you run away? I would have introduced you."

"Heaven forfend!" I cried energetically. "Fly what you admire, is the wisest maxim for a wretch like me. O Miss Hale, if you only knew!"

"Tell me," she suggested; and I told her all—my sad social history, my aspirations, and my woes, culminating in this monstrous malady of self-mistrust that clung like the garment of Nessus. Doomed to be ridiculed, depreciated, left out—and all for a luckless manner—to see the most idiotic Adonises, the most worthless sons of Mars, preferred before me. Miss Hale seemed to consider my modesty excessive. Then she remarked pertinently,

"Neither Adonis nor Mars would have any start with Miss Arne. They could have no sympathy with her favourite scientific studies."

"Nor I; they were omitted in my education," said I, in a mournful way.

"It is not shyness that hinders you from removing that barrier," she said.

A hint. If I could not lead a cotillon, act in a comedy, or sing sentimental songs, had I not other qualities à *faire valoir*? Next day I sent for a bushel of books—Darwin, Huxley, Wallace; all the newest and best works on science henceforth peopled my shelves. Novels and plays were ruthlessly ejected. I buried myself in the 'ologies, forsook theatres, paid no calls, forgot the way to the Park. The Museum became my lounge, the Royal Institution my Hurlingham. It is incredible the rapid progress you can make even with a serious study if you give your mind to it.

In Miss Hale I found my first lady friend, and under her wing stepped into new circles, where I took a fresh departure in ladies' society. She was a lady of good family, whom necessity had compelled to spend her youth in teaching. Later, a small inheritance had set her free to devote her middle age to her ruling passion for astronomy. She had a snug little house at Richmond, where she gave snug little dinners, and kept two large telescopes on the lawn, where she spent the summer nights sweeping for stars and calculating nebulæ. She was kindness itself to me; and here, in the company of Dr. Victoria Vivian, Mrs. Haller, and others, new social possibilities in myself were revealed to me.

I felt I was getting on; I stammered less, nearly got rid of a nervous twitch in my eye. I found out that my forehead had good points, and took care to display them; carried myself upright, and ventured again to look people in the face. Beatrice I only saw at the Society's lectures, where I held aloof, and solemnly forbade Miss Hale to introduce me. Meantime, what a mercy *not* to think of her as twirling round a ballroom in Barry's arms, a gazing-stock for supercilious fops! If she was looking lovingly at anything, it was at the lineaments of an innocent lizard or some exquisite gem of a spider ; if leaning on any one's arm, that of some wizen-faced professor, full of wisdom and years.

One lecture-night the lecturer made a grave mistake, as lecturers do sometimes, which passed unnoticed, as mistakes will, by the best-read audiences. He called the mistletoe a perfect parasite, the dodder an impefect one. It electrified me. Like a schoolboy before an examination, I had all my little knowledge at my fingers' ends. At the end of the lecture I ventured to rise and respectfully ask what he meant. Did not the mistletoe, by means of its own leaves, supply itself with carbon, whilst the leafless dodder sucked the sustenance for its flowers from the plant it clung to, and always killed? Sure of my ground, I spoke fluently, and elicited applause. The lecturer courteously admitted his error—a slip of the tongue or of memory. I saw at least a dozen ladies beholding me with respect and interest. Several members addressed questions and observations to me. I answered readily, and finally felt two dark-blue eyes fixed on me in eloquent approval.

"Now, Mr. Anstruther," said Miss Hale, " I really *must* introduce you to Miss Arne."

Such a favourable moment had never in my life turned up before. But, with all my newly acquired *aplomb*, I was diffident now, and dumb, till her low grave voice said,

" Are you going to Epping with us on Friday ? "

" Us " was the Field Naturalists. The excursion was to be headed by Professor Omnium, who would hold extempore lectures on common wayside objects.

" That I am," I returned promptly; and there our conversation ended. I went home, and dreamt of Friday next.

It was the Eton and Harrow match-day at Lord's. Barry had his choice of six drags to lunch on.

"Coming, old fellow?" he drawled, meeting me on the stairs.

"Engaged," said I.

"Eh?" incredulously.

"To Epping Forest."

"Epping fiddlesticks! Are you mad?"

"As a hatter," I returned, tripping past him down-stairs, Barry casting a mystified stare after the butterfly-net and collector's box I carried with me.

For I had become an ardent student. Once enter the "fairy-land of science," once dip into the mysteries of "Life and her children," from whatever motive, and you will soon grow as sincere an enthusiast as the veriest beetle-maniac and fungus-fanatic, as rapt and absorbed in their speculations as any poet or lover in the universe.

A score of us Field Naturalists met at the station. A number of ladies crowded round me, eager to learn the result of certain experiments they knew me to have been lately trying with ants. I suspect Sir John Lubbock of underrating the colour-sense of these insects, and, whilst testing it in novel ways, had made some interesting observations which I managed to impart to my fair hearers with lucidity, though Beatrice was listening. An advance. Only I despaired of ever venturing to accost her; my social accomplishments, after all, fell short of a great occasion. Crumbs of comfort there were. Among the gentlemen of our party was a young barrister I had met long ago in "Society." He was in love with a "sweet girl-graduate," studying for her natural-science examination, who was one of those most clamorous to hear about my recent investigations. He looked at me so jealously that I could have hugged him. No one had ever looked jealously at me before. The more he scowled the lighter my spirits. I never dreamt of trifling with his *innamorata*. I am no flirt. But what a relief to my strong sense of justice to be no longer doing myself injustice everlastingly, as of yore! You are changed, Johnny Anstruther, you are changed. Why, how, was a mystery; the fact was patent.

In the general conversation that followed I took my full share. Our talk, reader, was not of the Grosvenor, the French play, the last ball, or bit of club gossip, but of light and heat and magnetism, electricity, organic germs, atoms, molecules, comets, and skies. I won't say no flirtation went on; but Beatrice had nor part nor lot in this, and my most dangerous rival was certainly Professor Omnium. But what availed her fancy freedom, if, regenerated though I was, I let the hours go by without daring to snatch a word?

During our forest perambulations the Professor had successively lectured us on a Dead Nettle, a Newt, Cock-chafers, and the Skeleton of a Crow. We then got scattered, and wandered about, "evolutionists at large."

My eyes followed Beatrice. She had strayed down to a little pond, and stood bending over, Narcissus-like. Espying some rare aquatic plants, she tried to reach them. I flew to the spot; then, recalling a word Miss Hale had once said, refrained resolutely from assisting her, merely waiting ready to rescue her if she should slip. She did not, but secured the flowers, and, turning to me, said,

"Thank you for letting me get them myself."

"I felt sure you wanted to," I faltered, delighted. "Who cares much for specimens taken by other people?"

"Ah, but people never think of that. They are in such a hurry to show they are more expert than you," she said.

Her appreciation emboldened me to stay by her, contem-plating the pond, as she sat sorting her flowers. My sharp sight, formerly a source of torment—since no covert smile or sneer or jest at my expense ever escaped me—was invaluaable to Johnny Anstruther, Field Naturalist. It served him now.

"Miss Arne," I cried suddenly, "did you ever see a water-spider's nest?"

"Where—? where?"

Springing up, she came eagerly to look. I had to hold her hand to keep her from falling as she leaned over to scrutinize the silken cocoon under water I had been so fortunate as to discover. Only last night I had been reading up "Spiders," and I had quite a little lecture (which I took care to spin out) ready on my tongue about this curious insect that builds its nest in the water, and brings down supplies of air from the surface in bubbles with its hind legs, illustrating the principle of the diving-bell. And as we stood thus, hand in hand, I had a vision of Lord's. I saw Francis Barry flitting from drag to drag, smiled on by all the greatest beauties in London (all but one), and felt that not for worlds would I stand in his shoes.

"How much you know!" said Beatrice gravely. "Professor Omnium himself could not have explained it more clearly."

"O no," I disclaimed. "I have been looking up 'Spiders' lately; but my knowledge is the merest smattering. I despair of ever knowing all I wish."

"No life is long enough for that," she sighed gently.

"But Professor Omnium says all faithful and minute observation of Nature is valuable. We bring the bricks with which he builds the city."

"Yes, yes," she responded genially, "and I enjoy bringing the bricks. The world is so full of strange sights. I should like to travel—I should like to go to Surinam, like Madame de Merian, and see whether what she says of the fireflies is true —that you can read by their light."

And we talked of the wonders of the tropics—with their

butterflies larger than birds, flapping past on transparent wings of dazzling hues of blue and orange; of the golden-green beetles, the monster horns, and the spotted rose-chafers filling the air with the hum of their wings.

Then we came back to our English pond, and the dragon-flies darting over its surface.

" Look there," whispered Beatrice, pointing to a leaf far out, whereon lay a chrysalis, whence the lovely-winged insect was just going to emerge.

" You would like to watch it," I said, and vowed to secure it, mud and wet notwithstanding. I did so, and her glance of gratitude rewarded me for the ruin of my best clothes.

" Women of the world," though you rush through fire and water for them, will laugh at you the next minute, if you have got your hat battered, your hair singed, or your coat splashed, in the ordeal. Not so Beatrice Arne.

We bent over the plant I had plucked. The " demoiselle " crept out of its sheath slowly; then, clinging to the stalk, drank in the sunlight with its wings, spread them, and flitted away, leaving us the husk on the leaf.

Our eyes met, and we laughed irrelevantly; then remarked relevantly how different it is to read of a thing and to see it, and how only when seen it becomes a reality.

" What are you doing, you two? " cried the voice of Miss Hale from afar. " Here is the Professor delivering a delight-ful address on the ' Transformations of Tadpoles.' You will lose it all if you don't make haste."

" Let us go," said Beatrice, smiling divinely.

And I followed in her steps.

For months Barry and I had not met, except on the stairs. One night at a brilliant *soirée* at old Lord Crookshanks', given by electric light, the scientific principle of which I was busy explaining to some ladies, we suddenly confronted each other.

"How on earth did you get here?" he asked spontaneously.

"I should rather think you had come by mistake," I retorted; "you look so bored."

"I am," he owned. "I don't know any of these people."

One day he knocked at my room-door. Absorbed in an experiment, I did not hear. I had lately taken up "gnats," and, desirous of observing, by means of a powerful magnifier, what went on during a sting, was coaxing a mosquito to settle on my hand. They won't when you want them to. I was just about to receive the solicited wound, when Barry's entrance put the insect to flight.

"What the deuce are you doing?" he asked.

"What do you want?" I said, vexed at the interruption.

Sauntering carelessly forwards, he stumbled over an object in the path.

"Confound it, Anstruther! Why do you keep slop-pails standing about?"

"Slop-pails!" indignantly. It was a bucket of water I kept for observing the genesis of gnats. "Why don't you look where you tread?" I returned, peering in anxiously, to see that the larvæ had not been disturbed.

"I want to know if you'll come down the river to-morrow evening."

"Delighted, if"—taking out my engagement-book. "Sorry.

I dine to-morrow at Richmond. It's for the centenary of the discovery of the planet Uranus."

"Wednesday, then?"

"Wednesday, picnic at St. Albans with the Archæological. Thursday afternoon, Mrs. Haller's last ' At Home.' Dine there and go with them to the House. Friday, to the Zoo, with a party, to see an undescribed species of cassowary just arrived. Saturday, garden-party at Kew. Dine with Lady Crookshanks, and take her and her daughters to the *conversazione* at X— College."

"Well, upon my word!" he ejaculated. "How about to-night?"

"O, to-night," I blushed—a bad habit I retained—"I've a particular engagement—friends at home, as they say."

"Lady friends?" he asked banteringly. I retaliated,

"Exactly. Two from the ' opposition shop,' the ' Amazons' camp'—ladies of intellect and learning. Short hair, Barry, my boy "—Beatrice's hair *was* short. "Bloomer costume and spectacles." My altered manner piqued his curiosity.

"Have you been preparing your rooms for a reception?" he asked. "I don't know them again. What's the drawing there—where Adelina Patti's portrait used to hang?"

"That's a crocodilian jaw from the Coral Rag at Weymouth. It's no use you looking for the pictures of Gladiateur and Mdlle. Nadine. That, Barry, represents the inside of a star-fish; that, a fragment of bath-sponge magnified a hundred times; that, the ideal section of a prawn. Don't lift that glass, it contains a live pet wasp I'm keeping under observation. If it were to sting you it would die."

"You are a lunatic," he said; "I shall inform your relations."

"On the contrary. Last season I was a lunatic, pining for

the world of fashion. Now I'm a philosopher, and have re-nounced it, as you see."

My gaiety, alas! left him fatally inquisitive. I had let my spirits run away with me, for Beatrice had consented to come with Miss Hale and a few other friends to my room that evening, to see a valuable collection of leaf and stick insects, tropical beetles and spiders, made by my deceased grand-uncle in the West Indies and Malaccas, and which I had found con-signed to the lumber-room at my parents' home as rubbish! It brought Beatrice to my roof! My guests included some eminent men, who contributed a mint of information bearing on the treasures exposed. Beatrice enchanted wise and un-learned alike by her original comments, her imaginative speculations. She and Miss Hale lingered, and were the last to leave. Three minutes afterwards enter Francis Barry, dressed for a ball.

" I say, Anstruther, who's your friend ? "

"Miss Priscilla Hale, assistant astronomer to Sir John Ogle, F.R.S., &c."

"No, no ; not the elderly lady, *the other* ? "

"I thought you knew the Arnes," I said stiffly. "Her name is Beatrice."

"Beatrice Arne ! " he repeated, amazed. "So that's Beatrice—*the blue one !* She never appears, you know—never goes out. Good Heavens, Anstruther ! Her three sisters are all considered beauties ; but she leaves them nowhere."

"Well," said I provokingly ; "why don't you make haste to your ball ? Don't you wish to engage her for the first dance ? "

"Such a glorious creature as that to bury herself alive in dusty books and fossils ! Hang it all ! Some one should tell her to fling all that nonsense to the devil. I've a mind to myself."

"Hullo, Romeo!" said I; "what's this? Love at first sight?"

"Not exactly," he said. "I was in love with all her sisters in rotation; but I see now it was Beatrice I had in my fancy. Upon my life I never knew what blue eyes were before."

"Do you know?" I inquired. "A blue eye, as Miss Arne could tell you, is simply a turbid medium."

"Her complexion would kill all the reigning beauties with jealousy."

"The hue being caused by the extinction of some of the solar rays by the colouring matter of the cheek, the residual colour only being seen. O Francis Barry, I think I see you, with that brilliant whorl of abortive leaves common people call flowers in your buttonhole, listening whilst Professor Omnium explains how consciousness of love is associated with a right-handed motion of the molecules of the brain, of hate with a left-handed motion—"

"I don't," he said; "but I shall call on the Arnes to-morrow."

Words that fell on me like a *douche*. Now first I perceived I had ventured to hope. My best ground was a conviction that Beatrice was not in love with anyone else. But one reason for this might be that none of the swains around her ventured to aspire to the hand of one so rarely gifted; and here was Barry, the sort of fellow to adventure anything, and carry his point.

I went to my dinner at Richmond in the lowest spirits. Beatrice was not there. It was all I could do to sustain my rising reputation as an agreeable member of society. Miss Hale, struck by the languid interest I displayed in her discovery of a new comet, detained me, after her guests were gone, to ask what was the matter. I confessed,

"A friend of mine has seen Beatrice on the stairs, and

fallen in love with her, and I am in despair. For he is a dangerously good-looking fellow, and his name is Francis Barry."

"Barry," she repeated ; "doesn't he sing, or something ? "

" O, he sings, and plays and wins, and acts and dances and flirts. He is accounted irresistible, and means to compete with me for Beatrice's affections. Can you wonder, Miss Hale, that I am half wild ? Why do you smile ?"

" I am thinking," she said, "how last year you described yourself as a no-account man—out of the race altogether—and now we find you on the lists as a rival to one of the most brilliant figures in London society. Really, Mr. Anstruther, that ought almost to satisfy you, even should he carry off the prize in the end ! "

"It ought, I acknowledge. Last year no wanderer in the desert was more out of sight or mind of 'Society,' more shelved, than was I. Now I am *répandu*, befriended, invited, and my prospects brighten every week. But I have fallen in love by the way, and I feel that if Beatrice Arne accepts Francis Barry I shall be miserable for life !"

Miss Hale made me promise not to despair. I wrung her hand and departed. On my return home I met Barry whistling expressively on the stairs, with a look of complacency that rendered superfluous his statement that he had contrived to see Beatrice and get introduced.

Three weeks now ensued that I had looked forward to as to a spell of enchantment, seeing that they held out seven distinct opportunities of meeting Beatrice Arne, beginning with a rendezvous of the Field Naturalists at the Zoo, and ending with a grand dinner at Lord Crookshanks', in honour of a famous foreign botanist on a visit to our shores. Those twenty-one days proved a period of unremitting exercise for the most Spartan qualities of my nature.

When we Field Naturalists met at the gates of the Zoo, Beatrice joined us with three gaily-dressed girls she introduced as her sisters, and escorted by Barry. Never once did he leave her side, or relax his marked attentions. And I must bear it all, hear him pretend to be interested in the cassowary, and provoke her to laughter by his nonsensical jests. It was small consolation to reflect that last year I should have shrunk into the background and collapsed, whilst to-day I blazed out as a star among the rest of the ladies of the party, and created quite a sensation in the aquarium, by delivering off-hand a monograph on the Manifestations of Fear and Anger in Fishes. Barry would not allow Beatrice to listen ; he kept whispering jests to her and her sisters, to upset their gravity. Finally, when the time came to adjourn to the lecture-room, where Professor Omnium was to hold forth, Barry, to my discomfiture, announced that he and the Misses Arne meant to " cut " the lecture.

" I don't care for the subject," said Beatrice simply.

" I don't even know what it is," I let fall hastily ; whereupon Barry read out, with malicious emphasis,

" On the Geographical Distribution of Gulls."

I passed a bad night. Next day was the garden-party at Kew.

Beatrice came with Miss Hale. A blessed chance brought us on the lawn at the same moment. She was charming as ever, and eager to hear about an article I had been writing on the Shapes of Leaves, and which was shortly to appear in print. To account for my indifference about it, I complained of feeling tired and overworked.

" Will you come to tea at home on Saturday afternoon," she asked, " instead of working ? My sisters and I expect some friends."

I accepted with effusion. Even as I spoke, the figure of

Barry, lurking Mephistopheles-like among the trees, checked my spirits, and dashed my felicity. Up he came and drew Beatrice into conversation. I struck a critical attitude, listened to his brilliant superficial talk, and longing to cry out, " O, Beatrice Arne, that fellow is no better than an animated puppet ! " I would not stay to be shunted, but devoted myself to Lady Crookshanks and her daughters, solacing myself with dreams of Beatrice's birthday. It would be my first visit to her house.

I had my birthday-gift ready. Hearing Beatrice express a wish to examine that marvel of brute architecture, a squirrel's nest, I had rushed down to my home in the country, sixty miles off, to procure the desired object, and all but broken my neck in the effort to secure it intact from a fir-top. It was a splendid specimen.

I arrived punctually, but Barry was beforehand with me. It was well I had brought no bouquet, as his would certainly have outshone it ; well, too, I had left my little gift in the hall, as the moment was unfavourable for its bestowal. Barry engrossed Beatrice, leaving me to entertain her sisters, who bored me, as I may have bored them, for with one ear and a half I was straining to catch the dialogue of the other two. By and by came a pause in our tittle-tattle. Very distinctly Barry was heard to say, in tones of entreaty,

" Now you will come, won't you ? "

" Well," said Beatrice ingenuously, " I will."

" Where, where ? " cried the Misses Arne and I, in a chorus of curiosity.

" To Ascot," said Barry triumphantly ; adding, for my separate benefit, " The Misses Arne are going down for the race-week, and Miss Beatrice has graciously yielded to my suggestion that she should accompany them, to ascertain if it is as delightful as I tell her."

That was a broadsider for me, as he saw. The sisters laughed, and congratulated him on his victory over the obdurate girl-student.

He had the impudence to ask if he should not see me down there. I replied I was too busy. Withal that my notes on the Shapes of Leaves were passing through the press, I had a wild notion of being true to my colours, and making Beatrice ashamed of her desertion. Nor should I have bettered my position by turning renegade, in imitation. But Barry's star was in the ascendant. I left, taking my squirrel's nest away with me, and feeling as if a great gap had sprung suddenly between Beatrice and myself. Most probably it had been there all along, and I was a fool. So the spell was broken, and Beatrice would become a professional beauty after all. My bitter feelings broke out to Miss Hale.

" Barry hasn't the slightest faith in women caring for anything serious seriously; and no wonder. When has he not found them yield to his flattery and persuasion ? How well he is playing his game, which is to win Beatrice by storm ! He is a fellow who charms the universe at first sight. Let him secure her hand before she has had time to find out that Prince Charming's charms will never grow—on the contrary ; and that he is deficient in the sterling solid qualities—"

" Of a Johnny Anstruther," she put in pointedly.

I groaned, conscience-stricken.

" I deserve it. Savage jealousy makes me unjust, and I am savagely jealous."

Ascot week began. Absence, under the circumstances, was torture. To drown thought I went incessantly into society. Excitement stimulated my newly-developed social faculties, and I had to defend myself against the flattering attentions of æsthetic heroines and sprightly Girtonians. I spent afternoons reading Greek poetry with Miss Janie Somers, and translated a love-song of hers into Latin. I fear I flirted shamefully with pretty Mrs. Haller, whom young ladies, as a rule, did not like, and thought too advanced. My social success was becoming emphatic, and with it my misery of soul.

The third week was one of despair. Beatrice had returned home radiant. We met at two or three *soirées*, Barry invariably at her elbow. A coldness had arisen between Miss Arne and me. I was steeling my mind for what I felt was impending. Hollow for consolation proved the blandishments showered upon me by an increasing number of fair acquaintances. Mothers with daughters had now discovered I was an eligible *parti*, and I had invitations to country houses to last me all through the summer. I scarcely looked forward beyond the dinner at Lord Crookshanks', in honour of the illustrious French *savant*, where, perhaps for the last time this season, I should meet Beatrice Arne. It was a brilliant affair ; to conclude with a large evening-party, at which Royalty, it was whispered, would be represented. But the compliment of the invitation was spoilt for me, since Barry, Heaven knows how, had contrived to get invited too.

" Que diable allait-il faire dans cette galère ? " I muttered beforehand. I was answered when I came in, and saw him standing by her side with the complacent look of an accepted lover. Little he recked of the distinguished scientific guest, treating him with the patronising amiability which young sparks of his school display to the greatest worthies of art and literature, if less polished than themselves. It was Barry, of course, who sat by Beatrice at dinner. I was opposite with Mrs. Haller ; and whilst pretending to devote myself to my fair neighbour, had the full benefit of his insinuating conversation.

My triumph, which came after the ladies left the room, I

found insipid, as Beatrice was not there to behold it. The illustrious foreigner desired to be introduced to me. He had seen my paper on the "Shapes of Leaves," and been pleased with it. He kept me in conversation then and in the drawing-room, talked while Barry was singing (which I did not mind), talked on and on. Here was Johnny Anstruther monopolising the lion's attention, the envied of all observers! It would have been delightful at any other time; but I had seen Barry, with Beatrice on his arm, wander into the palm-house; the garden was thrown open, and I was fiercely impatient to go wandering there after them. At last I was released. Several charming eyes were raised to mine encouragingly. I cursed my ambition, cursed my fastidiousness, that drove me to turn away, regardlessly, to see if Barry and Beatrice were in the palm-house still. They were, and alone. Beatrice sat, leaning back; her beauty, framed in the wonderful ferns and creepers of the tropics, was as rich and strange as they. Barry, who occupied a chair by her side, was playing with her fan, and looking so much more serious than usual that I needed not to play spy on him another moment.

I hurried into the garden, where it took me a quarter of an hour to recover my senses. My determination was taken on the spot—to cut my country engagements and leave Europe for a time. Feeling calmer, I then went indoors to take leave of my hosts. I passed the palm-house with a firm step, and cast a steady glance towards that bench. Beatrice had not stirred; but Barry had left her for the moment, and she was alone. Her face, turned towards me, was so beautiful, so nobly expressive, that all my bitter resentment evaporated, and I acknowledged that Barry might be a better fellow than myself—nay, that he must be, if she thought him so. Children and angels have true intuitions. I approached, and said with forced self-possession,

A PALM HOUSE TETE-À-TETE.

"I take this opportunity of finding you alone to wish you good-bye, Miss Arne."

"Good-night," she said. "You are leaving early."

"Good-night and good-bye," I said. "On Monday I start for Colorado."

"Colorado!"

"Sir John and Lady Ogle, Miss Hale, and a few other scientific friends are making up a party to go and observe the total eclipse next month, visible from the Rocky Mountains. I have decided to join."

"Isn't it a sudden plan?" she said, surprised.

"Very sudden, but not the less irrevocable for being made but five minutes ago."

"I could not take such a sudden resolution without a strong motive," she said naïvely; "and I thought you did not care much for astronomy."

"I have a strong motive," I owned, "and it has nothing to do with the stars. Your friendship, Miss Arne, has made me very happy—too happy, it appears, for I feel as if I could not bear to stay and see your happiness with another."

I kept it up as well as I could, but my voice betrayed me. Looking into my eyes, Beatrice said, with the inimitable child-like gravity and impulsiveness that characterised her manner,

"Dear friend, did you think I could care for the man who was here just now."

"Everyone cares for him," I cried, stammering for the first time these three months.

"You are mistaken," she said. "No one ever will care very much. But it does not matter—he loves himself well enough for all."

"But he loves you, I know," I urged excitedly. "Do you mean to say he has not told you so?"

"I think he was going to," she said archly; "but the

Prince of Kleinstadt, whom he knows, passed by, and stern etiquette forced him to go and pay his respects."

"Where is he now?" I said, stepping into the place where I had seen him stand.

"With the Prince. Presently he will come back and apologise."

"Shall I go?" I whispered significantly. "There's not room here for us both."

"O no!" she murmured. "I don't want him *ever* to come back now."

"Beatrice," I said, overjoyed, clasping both her hands, "tell me you love me and will be my wife."

If a woman's first duty is obedience, Beatrice fulfilled it implicitly.

A torrent of playful recriminations followed. I taxed her with encouraging Barry. She protested that the idea that he could be in earnest never visited her brain till to-night—that she had not known how to shake him off, and I had never helped her. She confessed she had been jealous of Janie Somers and Mrs. Haller. Why had she gone to Ascot? I asked. Why should she not go to Ascot? she retorted. Had I never been to Ascot? Were people like ourselves, who enjoyed hours in a library, never to spend hours anywhere else? Why had I not brought her a single flower for her birthday? I told her about the squirrel's nest, and she made me promise to bring it next morning. Suddenly she whispered, "Here he comes!" and I saw Barry hastening towards her, looking extremely foolish. I beat a pretended retreat, and, screened by a palm, actually escaped his notice the first moment.

"I am so sorry," he began. "Could not possibly leave the Prince before. He was so affable, he would not let me go. Can you forgive me?"

" O, willingly," she said, with a spontaneity that took him aback.

" Then you will let me take you down to supper ?" he pursued.

But I had stepped forward to her side, and Beatrice, sliding her arm in mine, replied, with simplicity, but not without significance,

" I cannot—I am engaged."

I brought down the news to Richmond the next day. How express my gratitude to Miss Hale ? how discharge my unspeakable obligation to her, who had laid the corner-stone of my good fortune ? She had been the first to revive my expiring confidence in myself.

Never, so long as I live, will I allow a sneering word to be spoken in my presence against strong-minded women, against lady doctors, lawyers, orators, students of all sorts. I boldly affirm that their evolution has been a perfect godsend to a large proportion of mankind—diffident men like myself, whom fashionable mothers and coquettish daughters intimidate into agonies of self-distrust, fostering a shyness, awkwardness, and taciturnity that may become organic and incurable. Let not such luckless society lovers despair, since my example shows how the most complete social failure may sometimes be redeemed.

Beatrice, however, scouts the idea of my alleged natural deficiency in assurance or fluency of expression. Of shyness she declares she never saw a trace ; and when I persist, she quotes against me my proposal of marriage, which, for a shy lover, she maintains was the boldest ever made.

VENI, VIDI, VICI.

BY R. E. FRANCILLON.

ILLUSTRATED BY POWER WILSON.

—⁂—

"NO—I won't marry Sir Marmaduke Ireton.—Marmaduke!—Ireton!—They may say what they like, but I'll never be the wife of a man with a name like a Roundhead in 'Woodstock,' who squints, and drinks, and has red hair, and is hard to the poor, and likes billiards better than dancing, and hasn't a word to say. Maud Ashton told me what he's like—she met him in India—and I'll be bricked up in a convent wall before I'll let myself be taken down to dinner by Sir Marmaduke Ireton."

So said May Craven to Mrs. Arden, the mother of her old, or rather young, school-friend Grace. Mrs. Arden, that mirror of good-nature, looked down smilingly upon the bright, eager face of her little friend, and answered:

"Ah, the secret is out, then—that's why you were so bent on making a third in our little tour! Grace told me you had run away for fear of being married—what an idea! But of course, if you say so yourself, it's true. Is Sir Marmaduke Ireton an ogre? Has he proposed?"

"I should like to see him dare!"

"Isn't he rich, my dear?"

"Rich? Papa says he could buy up the county—so he's to begin with me."

"Well, you have all the luck, my dear. Believe an old *chaperon* when she tells you there's nothing one gets used to so soon as red hair, or even a squint, if the owner lends you his gold spectacles to look at him through. But how do you know he wants to buy you?"

May sighed. "Don't you know, mamma" (Grace being her sworn sister, Grace's mother was of course, "mamma")—"don't you know I've the bad luck to be heiress of Redlands? And that Redlands 'marches'—that's the word—with Whitelands, belonged to the Iretons ever since Sir Marmaduke's grandfather—his first ancestor—came over——"

"With the conqueror, of course?"

"No—from Sheffield. He didn't use swords, like a gentleman: he made knives. There's 'Ireton, Sheffield' on all our bluntest knives at home. Fancy a girl like me, that came over with Hengist and Horsa, marrying the grandson of a knife-grinder—and such a grandson! Yes, mamma, I've known from my cradle that Whitelands is to marry Redlands on the first opportunity. That's my doom; and now that horrid, grasping, squinting, red-haired, stupid, tipsy young man is coming home."

"Perhaps he won't ask you, my dear."

"Won't he!" and she glanced at the mirror which reflected the prettiest face that had been seen in Dinan, in Brittany—in all France, for many a long day. "And then—he will be asking Redlands, after all, not me. And I shall be seeing him every day; and I know what my own mamma meant by saying, 'May, Sir Marmaduke is coming home: we must make our welcome as warm as we can.'"

"And what did you say?"

"I said I'll make it *hot* for him! He shall go back to India to get cool again. And papa heard me say it. Oh, there was such a storm!"

Mrs. Arden looked grave. "You are a very silly girl. There are hundreds of girls that would jump at your chances. I wonder Mrs. Craven lets you join me and Grace. How came that, pray?"

"Because I chose. And with you and Grace I'll stay till mamma writes, like in the agony column of the 'Times,' 'May, all is forgiven: come back to your repentant parents, and they'll never do it again.'"

"You are a spoiled child, I'm afraid," said Mrs. Arden, shaking her head. "If you'd been one of ten, like Grace, you wouldn't have been able to come and go as you please." But she was not angry. Nobody was ever very angry with May.

"Of course I'm spoiled," said May. "And therefore I won't marry Sir Marmaduke Ireton—or anybody else, for that matter. I'm not going to honour and obey anybody but Miss May Craven. Ah, there's the bell for the *table d'hôte*—and here's Grace—come: I'm as hungry as a lion."

"Grace," whispered Mrs. Arden to her own fair-haired girl, as they followed May down stairs, "are you sure your mad little friend is fancy free? I'd no idea I was harbouring a domestic rebel."

"Have you noticed, mamma," said Grace demurely, "that no sooner were we in Jersey than we made the acquaintance of a certain young man with strange ease and quickness, considering that we are all English people? Did he not come to St. Malo by the next boat to ours? He's not smitten by me, I'm sure—and yet I shrewdly suspect we shan't be long in Dinan before we see him again."

"What! why, that poor travelling artist? Oh, Grace— and I'm her *chaperon!*"

"I've said nothing, mamma. Only keep your eyes open, that's all."

They followed May into the *salle à manger;* and Mrs. Arden

started. An overpowering steam of garlic saluted one set of nerves, and the sight of a quiet-looking young man, in grey clothes and with a thick brown beard, who was already seated at the table, overwhelmed another. Grace touched her significantly, and she saw a delicate, embarrassed rose-tint steal over the glowing face of May.

The young man rose and smiled brightly, and Mrs. Arden noticed that his chair was next to the three that were obviously reserved for her and hers.

"This is an unlooked-for pleasure!" said the young man, in a singularly pleasant voice. "We seem fated to meet——"

"So it seems, Mr. Brown," said the lady, coldly, arranging her party so that she might sit between him and May. "Where are you going when you leave Dinan?"

"I? Oh, I follow my whim. That's the only way to travel—to follow the attraction of the moment. May I ask your next destination? I know this country, and perhaps I might advise——"

"Ours? Oh, we follow our fancy. That is the best way to travel—to avoid everything that's tiresome as soon as it comes. Perhaps we shall remain here."

"You could not possibly do better. That's what I think of doing."

"Then that's settled," thought Mrs. Arden to herself. "To-morrow sees us back at St. Malo."

It was a dull dinner. May's lion hunger had left her. The young painter generally managed to amuse Mrs. Arden, who liked him for his own sake, but to-day he failed. She was transformed from the casual acquaintance into the *chaperon*.

"I don't like Dinan at all," she said to the girls, when they had left the table. "I'm poisoned already with their garlic—we'll go back to St. Malo to-morrow morning."

Grace smiled. "But we haven't done the place at all," said

May, opening her eyes wide, " and I know there's lots to be seen. However, even for the picturesque you mustn't be poisoned. Only, let's make the most of our time—let's take a walk somewhere—what do you say ? "

It was only the beginning of a lovely summer evening, and, as May was to be curbed in great things, it was fair to indulge her in small. As if it were not of the small things that life is made ! So, in an hour or so, the three travellers found themselves in the long avenue that leads to the ruined *château* of La Garaye—a foolish choice : for where but in that wilderness of massive foliage, in that tangled mass of vine leaves and ivy and crumbling grey stones, was it likely that a painter should be found ?

Behind the screen of green and grey they almost fell over the inevitable Mr. Brown, lazily seated on a fallen trunk under an apple tree, and smoking a cigar. Grace hid a laugh in her sleeve—Mrs. Arden could have killed the young man. May's large hazel eyes expressed just nothing at all ; but the young man's face, for a moment, reflected, let us say, the full hue of the setting sun. It is a rare sign of grace in these days for a strong young man to colour at the sight of a girl.

There was no help for the meeting ; and there was certainly no means of preventing his escorting them home. The only course open to Mrs. Arden was to prevent anything like pairing off. So she made up for her coldness at dinner by chaining Mr. Brown to her own side. He showed himself wise in his generation—woo the mother to win the daughter is a golden rule.

But the road was full of ruts and snags, the night was growing dark, and Grace Arden suddenly tripped, stumbled, and fell. It was a little odd that she fell just where there chanced to be no ruts or snags, but so it happened, and there she lay. Mr. Brown was at her side in a moment, and raised her as

lightly as if she had been made of gossamer. "Are you hurt?" he asked anxiously.

"I've only sprained my ankle. No—don't be afraid you'll have to carry me. I can walk home with mamma's arm—I only want mamma."

Mrs. Arden was really alarmed: her daughter's ankle was, after all, of more consequence than the heart of her daughter's friend. Grace did not limp very badly, but she was obliged to walk so slowly that the long legs of Mr. Brown, in spite of themselves, were forced inch by inch to widen the distance between Mrs. Arden and Grace, and himself and May.

The two in advance were both great talkers; and yet they went on for at least a hundred yards without a single word. Of course when the word came it was very commonplace indeed.

"So I hear," said he, "you are going to make some stay in Dinan? I'm so glad—it is a charming place—I expect to be here myself for I don't know how long."

"Indeed? Then you know more than I. So far from staying, we go back to St. Malo to-morrow. I don't exactly know why, seeing we only came here this morning; but mammas are a little whimsical sometimes."

"What!" he exclaimed in a voice of dismay, "you are going back to St. Malo?"

"Yes."

"You are not even going to stay a day?"

"No."

"Impossible—it is a sin—a shame. I hope it is not bad news?"

"Oh—no."

"Then I suppose that means—when I say good-night it must mean good-bye."

"Yes—I suppose so."

"Well—perhaps you are right after all—Dinan is simply the most hateful place in Europe. But St. Malo!—I've a good mind——"

"Why you are as fickle as mamma—I thought Dinan was so charming just now."

A turning of the road had separated them from their now distant companions. For the moment he was alone with May Craven in a beautiful world, under an orb who is responsible for much lunacy.

"I fickle?" he asked. "Would you call steel fickle because it moves from spot to spot at the bidding of the loadstone? Nothing is so easily moved, because nothing is so true."

"Don't you think we are leaving poor Grace rather far behind?"

"Oh, pray don't break the only chance I have of saying good-bye! There, we'll walk a little slower if you like——"

"The only chance! I thought you talked of going back——"

"That's the question. I'm thinking whether I will go back to St. Malo, or on—on—on—to nowhere. Which shall it be?"

She began to feel afraid, but not with an unpleasant sort of fear. She wished they were not quite so far from Grace and Mrs. Arden, but she would not have wished it if they had been nearer.

"Which shall it be?" she asked, trying to keep up her reputation for taking all things lightly. "I should say nowhere would be the most interesting——"

"May!"

All was said when he thus exclaimed "May!" He hurried on; for in one moment he had put his fate to the touch to win or lose all. "May, don't you understand? Shall I go on by myself, or back with you? Have you not guessed why I am here? I would follow you all over the world. For heaven's sake tell me I may still follow my loadstar—that I may still be as true as steel. Tell me, for if to-morrow comes and you go back—we have no time to lose—tell me now!"

They had indeed no time to lose. She once again heard "May!" but it was in the voice of Mrs. Arden. "There—we are called—we must go back——"

"Wait—May—wait—I will not go back a step till you have said if I may go back to-morrow—if you will have me—yes or no!"

There was no time to play with his heart or her own: it was now or never. "Yes, then," hurriedly whispered May Craven, who had always followed the first impulse of her heart ever since she was born, without thinking beyond the hour. He caught her hand for a moment, kissed it, and then let her run back in a panic to Mrs. Arden, following her more slowly, like one in a happy dream.

May was a wild bird, but she had been caught now, and by

one of whom she knew nothing except that he was a gentleman. She trusted because she loved: let us hope that the
love came partly because she trusted. But it was a wild plunge
into the unknown, all the same; and I feel a shadow already
falling over the bright life of May.

"Are you better, now, Grace, dear?" she asked, longing to
express sympathy with somebody or anybody.

Grace smiled. "You little hypocrite," she whispered,
"much you care. But if it's any comfort to you, I'll race you
all the way to Duguesclin's statue, and win."

There was no opportunity for explanation. Counsel must
be taken as to how and when the matter should be laid before
Mrs. Arden. So those whom it most concerned finished the
walk in silence, Grace and Mrs. Arden talking for all. But
May, though terribly frightened, was unutterably happy, even
in the face of the storm she foresaw at home. "Till to-
morrow darling," whispered the young painter as he pressed
her hand at the inn-door; and she answered him with her
eyes.

"To-morrow!" said Mrs. Arden to the two girls. "You'd
better pack now. I do hate tourists—it seems to me one only
leaves England to fall out of the Smiths into the Browns."

"Brown is an excellent name, mamma!" said she who had
turned up her nose at that of Ireton. "It's one of the oldest
of all—a grand old Saxon name."

"Oh, dear!" thought Mrs. Arden, "she's already reached
the point of reconciling herself to the sound of Mrs. Brown.
May, my dear—here's a letter for you."

May kissed Grace and Mrs. Arden more warmly than usual,
and escaped into her own room. As to the letter, she saw it
was only from home, and was in no hurry to open it. Her
own heart was full enough of news to need no more. But she
opened it at last, and read as follows :—

"My dearest May,—I don't know how to break the sad news. You must come home, *now*. Your father is *very* ill—how *shall* I write it? We are *ruined*. When I married, Redlands was what they call mortgaged *over and over*—and then there had to be borrowing—and that horrid county election—and of course we had to keep up the old position of the Cravens in the county, for *your* sake, my dear. So your father acted for the best—he tried to put things straight by investing in mines and things, and now it's *all* gone. We shall be *beggars*, and he will sink under the blow. My darling May, it depends upon *you* to save your father from ruin, from beggary, from a *broken mind*—perhaps from—I can't write the word. All the directors have turned out to be *cheats* and *swindlers*, and your father, who never knew anything about ledgers—how should he indeed, being a Craven of Redlands?—has got *mixed up with them*, and all because he tried to be a good father to you. I implore you, my darling, come back and be good—it is our only chance, May! Come back, and don't say a *word* to a *soul*—not even to Grace Arden.

"Your loving heart-broken

"MOTHER.

"P.S.—Sir Marmaduke Ireton is expected at Whitelands *any day*."

May let the letter fall. She had just engaged herself to a nobody—a wandering painter, whom she was learning to love with all her heart and soul—and now!——

Poor girl! She had faults enough and to spare, but none that were inconsistent with her bright, frank, honest eyes. Self-will does not of necessity mean selfishness, or waywardness in prosperity an incapacity for self-devotion in the hour of need. But there are limits to the endurance of a martyr. Had her mother's letter arrived a week ago, she might have made a face, and swallowed Whitelands, Sir Marmaduke and all: had it arrived an hour ago, she might have found it possible to crush her silent heart: but now her heart had spoken out: it was no longer her own to crush or resume. To sell herself—to be faithless to love—to revoke her promise

—to act like a jilt and a coquette—to set herself to snare the purse of a stranger, and to break the heart of him she loved—that was treason to her whole nature. But then to ruin those who had, as her own mother had told her, ruined themselves, and even incurred dishonour for her: to let the chance of an hour be the cause of their destruction: to let the faces of her father and mother upbraid her for her selfishness, all her days: to think of a new love before she thought of them—that was worse than mere treason to nature: it would be mean and vile. Even if this hateful Sir Marmaduke proved beyond the reach of her aim, she must not dream of the love of a poor man. She threw herself, undressed, upon her bed, and let opposing impulses fight over her, and draw her now this way, now that, while she was hardly conscious of the battle. At last her eyes closed in a miserable mockery of sleep: and when she woke, the tune of "Auld Robin Gray" was rambling in her brain.

Grace was by her bedside: and then the whole horror of the situation rose up before her. "Grace," she exclaimed, "I must go home at once—my father is very ill."

Which meant: "I must do what seems to be right, come what may. I should not deserve the love of a good man, if I sacrificed my father's welfare, his life, perhaps his good name, even for *him*." Mrs. Arden and Grace pressed her with sympathetic questions, but she would only answer, "My father is ill—I must go home."

She looked ill enough herself: but she would not delay her journey for an hour, nor would she let her friends see her back farther than St. Malo. But she managed to steal a last moment to scribble one little pencil note for the *garçon* to deliver to the man whose love she had accepted only a few hours—or was it years ?—ago.

"Please forgive me," she wrote: "don't think ill of me—since last night has happened what—I can't explain—must part us for ever. Forget me—you have not known me long—and I will try. God bless you and make you happy. May."

It was over—and she was on her way home to catch the owner of Whitelands. It was a horrible journey: it was like a long funeral, wherein she was following herself to the grave.

We may hope that she obtained a grain of comfort when, arrived at home, her mother embraced her warmly and said, "My darling May! You will save us still—I know you will!"

" And papa ? "

" He is better since we got your telegram, to say you were
coming home. But oh, how pale you look, May ! "

" I'm only tired. And——"

" Sir Marmaduke ? He comes home the day after to-
morrow, so the housekeeper says—I wrote to ask him to
dinner the day after."

Well, there was a reprieve. She learned the full misfortune
that had fallen on Redlands, and it was even worse than she
had already been told. She spent her days of grace in nerving
herself to the loss of her self-respect by preparing her eyes and
complexion for sale, and in burying what lay in the depth of
her heart, out of her own sight, and, so far as might be, out
of mind.

This was Wednesday. Thursday was passed in combating
" I hope that man will hate me," and the temptation " and I
will take good care that he shall." But she crushed the hope
and conquered the temptation. Friday came, and brought the
news, in the shape of an acceptance of " Mr. and Mrs. Craven's
kind invitation," that Sir Marmaduke Ireton was already at
Whitelands. Saturday came.

Six o'clock came : and she heard the sound of carriage-
wheels in the drive. Her heart grew heavy and cold as she
decked herself for the first interview with her intended victim.
It was with a bitter, involuntary pleasure, if there is room for
such a word, that her glass reflected pale cheeks and fevered
eyes. She knew not till then how far away her whole heart
had gone. Her mother came into her room.

" Go down now, May, if you are ready—yes, you want colour,
but you are looking very well, on the whole—I'm not quite
ready, and your father's behindhand of course, and it won't do
to let Sir Marmaduke find nobody to receive him."

" Oh please, mamma—let me wait for you ! "

"No my dear. I particularly wish you to go."

And so May, who had forgotten how to rebel, went down alone. Slowly she turned the handle of the door, and entered the drawing-room with downcast eyes. She knew that a man was leaning against the chimney-piece — that was all. So quietly had she entered that he did not hear her come in — at least he did not move. At last she dared look up, and saw the reflection of his face in the mirror. It was not Sir Marmaduke — she almost screamed below her breath as he turned round.

"May!"

Had her self-conquest sent her mad? Was she face-haunted?

He seemed more bewildered than she, but he recovered himself more quickly. "May—Miss Arden—I never dreamed of seeing you here—but you shall not break my heart without letting me know why."

"Oh, go, for heaven's sake—how dare you come here— and follow me——"

"How dare I? When Mrs. Craven asked me to come? But even if she had not, and I had known you were here, I should have dared——"

"What—mamma asked *you*?"

"No, Mrs. Craven asked me. And as I am here——"

"She never heard of you—and if she had—— She asked Sir Marmaduke Ireton."

"And I am Sir Marmaduke Ireton."

"Then—" She could not believe her senses, and it was well for her she could not: if she had, and if joy ever killed, she could almost have died of joy. Where were the squinting eyes and red hair? "I can't believe it ! You are Sir Marmaduke Ireton? You are not Mr. Brown?"

But his face fell. He had read the joy in her eyes—and he

MAY GOES UNWILLINGLY TO RECEIVE SIR MARMADUKE.

I. 116.

was not pleased to be thus welcomed as Sir Marmaduke who had been dismissed as Mr. Brown.

"That is my name, Miss Arden," he said coldly, but with a sigh.

"And I am not Miss Arden—I am May Craven. How strange," she went on, her eyes gradually waking up into their sun-like gleam, "that we should have—been together, and not have known our own names! Oh, why did you call yourself by a false name? What you might have spared me!"

"What!" he asked almost sternly: "should you not have written me that note at Dinan if you had known my real name?"

"No!"

"Good heaven—and you own it?"

I do not say that what May's impulse led her to do was either right or wise. I can only say that she could not bring herself to let her happiness slip from her again. Instead of answering, she drew forth her mother's letter, which she carried about with her as a talisman against temptation, and placed it in his hand: thus betraying the family skeleton to one whom she trusted only because she loved him, confessing that she was dowerless, and owning that she was trying to catch him because he was a rich man. It was frank and honest, but I doubt if any girl ever trusted any man so much before.

Nor do I say that he did what was wise—only that he looked from the letter into eyes that he seemed to read more plainly than words, and the cloud faded from his brow. For a moment he paused to read; and then, instead of being caught, he caught her—in his arms. "My poor May—I understand!"

All her life flowed back. "Can you ever forgive me? But oh, why did you trick me by calling yourself——"

"Brown? You must ask Mrs. Arden why she called out

"May" just at the unlucky moment when I was going to tell you all. When you are Lady Ireton you will find it pleasant sometimes to travel on foot, and call yourself Mrs. Brown. But I'm so glad all this happened—though you'll marry me because I'm rich, you told me you loved me when I was poor——"

"*Told* you, indeed! But oh, do you know Maud Ashton, who's in India, told me you are so stupid——"

"Quite right—so I am."

"And that you squint horribly—and have red hair——"

"And don't I ? And haven't I ?—By Jove, May! that was the late Sir Marmaduke—and a bad lot he was too, though he's dead, and was my own first cousin. He died in Calcutta a month ago. We're all Marmaduke, you know, either by first or second Christian name : that's the family tradition for—let me see—about thirty years. The baronet must always be a Marmaduke, and I'm Hugh Marmaduke Ireton."

"Then, please, I'll call you, Hugh. Do you mind ? "

"I'll be everything to you, darling, as long as you'll be May to me. And we'll pull your father through, never fear. I'm a purse-proud *nouveau riche*, you know, and Whitelands can pick up Redlands as easily as I could you, my own little May.—Ah ! "

"Ah," meant the sudden apparition of Mrs. Craven, whose amaze at finding the arm of Sir Marmaduke already round May's waist must be imagined, seeing that it cannot be described. But, under the circumstances, and knowing what he knew, it was not hard for him to put a good face on the matter.

"Mrs. Craven, may I introduce you to your future son-in-law ? "

"What ! all in five minutes ! " was all her wonder allowed her to say.

"I suppose you are thinking of *Veni, Vidi, Vici*," he said with a smile. "And you are right if you make them the words of May."

In five minutes more May was playing with a table-knife that bore the mark of "Ireton, Sheffield," on its blade, and thinking it the finest name in England. After all, she asked herself, what is in a name? But she was wrong, for there was much in taking upon herself the name of a gentleman. Nor does she repent of it, though Grace Arden teases her about it in amazingly long letters at least once in every seven days.

THE FAIR FACE IN THE YELLOW CHARIOT.

A Park Romance of the London Season.

I.

A BACHELOR still young and well-to-do is for obvious reasons an object of the deepest interest to his friends of the opposite sex. Lord Featherstone was as popular with ladies as if he had been a spirit-rapper, or a Hindoo potentate with diamonds to scatter broadcast and a suppressed begum in the background at home. They were always telling him that it was a sin and a shame the blinds in the town house should be constantly down; the hall filled only with shooting-parties; the jewels buried in the strong room at the bank.

And his heart! What a priceless jewel was that for some sweet maiden to win and wear! Scared affections? Ridiculous prudery! He had been a desperate flirt, no doubt; what matter? All men were flirts; many with less excuse than Lord Featherstone, who, as an excellent *parti*, like the Sovereign, could do no wrong. He had been wild, perhaps; but a man might be wild and yet not wicked; while for those who are their own fathers, enjoying their own titles and their own estates, the world makes ample concessions. When the time came for settling down, there would not be a happier or more fortunate girl in the three kingdoms than she whom the Marquis of Featherstone elected to make his wife.

Only he would not settle down. He meant to have his fling first; and probably it was his habit of throwing himself about that made him so difficult to catch. He was as wary as an old cockatoo; prompt to cut himself free from the most serious entanglements. After making hot love for a week during wet weather in a country house, papa and mamma heard that he had broken his leg in two places, or that typhoid fever had laid him low. His last affair was with a gay widow, who thought him safely hooked; but at the last moment he sent a postcard, conveying brief regrets, and sailed in his yacht for the South Seas.

He was absent after this for two or three years; but presently, wearying of the constant wandering to or fro, he returned, and took up the threads of his old life. The season was at its height, if a particularly lugubrious season can be said to have risen above a dead level of lugubrious dulness. The Marquis's friends said he was a fool to come back. Never had there been a season so " slow ; " nothing going on—not a creature in town.

" Looks like it ! " thought Lord Featherstone, as he tried to make his way through the serried ranks upon the stairs in a certain mansion in Grosvenor-square. The Duchess of Welshpool was "at home," and many of her guests wished they could say the same. In the entrance-hall men and women stood a dozen deep, pressing slowly towards the grand staircase, where two streams clashed together, flushed dancers coming down for cooling drinks, and the new arrivals eager to bow their bow, and in their turn come away. Now and again there was a positive dead lock. It was idle to say, " Excuse me," or " You are on a lady's dress," or " Would you allow me to pass ?" Until the wave surged onward every one was suspended, and held fast *in situ*, as if suddenly frozen cold. Not that the metaphor held good ; for the atmosphere reminded Featherstone of the tropics he had just left.

A crush of this kind is especially favourable for the minute observation of one's fellow creatures. Half a minute was enough to solve the mystery of Mrs. Chromer's yellow hair, and of the complexion people said was like milk. Little Penteagle's wig, again, could not be disguised, nor the high colour which old General Bawcock resolutely denied was *rouge*. But these sights, although curious, were not enthralling to a man who had just seen Fusiama and the Taj Mahal; and Lord Featherstone was on the point of turning tail and leaving the house when a bright face in the crowd arrested his attention, and he resolved to stay—at least until he could ascertain to whom it belonged.

It was quite a new face to him ; the face of a girl still fresh, and seemingly unaccustomed to the town. A merry *piquante* face, with small but perfect features, violet eyes, and a laughing mouth, showing often the whitest teeth. A face strikingly beautiful, but innocent and childish, just as the ways of its owner were unconventional and unconstrained. She laughed outright once; he could hear her quite plainly, and saw her shake out her curls in the plenitude of her merriment. A

most bewitching captivating young person, and Featherstone
was determined to find out who she was.   Surely some one
could introduce him.

He looked round in vain.   No one near at hand whom he
knew well enough to ask to do the needful.   Quite half an
hour elapsed before he caught Tommy Cutler, who knew all
the world, and then, going to where he had last seen the girl,
they found she had disappeared.

"Most provoking!" he said.   "Can't you tell me who she
is ?"

"Who's who in the present year!   Which who do you mean?
You must be more precise."

"She had gray—"

"Hair?   That's coming in.   I shall wear mine white soon;
it gives one an air of wisdom."

"You want it.   But there—there she goes!   Come on,
man !"

And he moved away rapidly when another voice, speaking
in soft, almost caressing, tones, stopped him.

"Lord Featherstone—back in civilization!   When did you
arrive ?"

"A few days ago," he replied nonchalantly, as he shook
hands.   "What a delightful dance!" and he proceeded to
hurry on in pursuit.

But Lady Carstairs was an old flame ; one who had helped
to bring him out as a lad, who had encouraged and petted
him, and, to tell the truth, flirted with him enough to make
Sir John jealous had he been a sillier man.   She did not
mean to be passed by now with a few words.

"Pray give me your arm, Lord Featherstone.   I should
like to hear some of your adventures.   I am not interfering,
I hope ?"

"I was going to dance—"

"You dance! What new miracle is this? Who is the charmer who has led you astray?"

"He's smitten," said Tommy Cutler. "All of a heap. Some new face."

"A new face is more attractive than an old friend," said Lady Carstairs rather bitterly.

"Old friends sometimes have new faces. Mrs. Chromer, for instance, who changes hers like the chameleon does his skin. But perhaps you can enlighten me—"

And he described the face which had so strongly attracted him.

"It won't do, Lord Featherstone. Very charming, I daresay, but conveys nothing to my mind. Golden hair, blue eyes, drab dress, and yellow trimmings—there are a dozen such here to-night. It was a pretty face, eh? Yes, that will be the end of it. You particular men, after years of the most fastidious fault-finding, surrender to some doll's face, merely pretty without expression. But after all, it's high time you took a wife ; it is, indeed."

"I nearly did abroad."

"A savage? a squaw?"

"Yes ; one of the carraway-seed Indians from the western slopes of the Alleghanies. She was very fashionable ; wore false hair—the scalps of her enemies inherited from her father."

"An heirloom, I suppose," said Lady Carstairs, who thought herself a wit.

"A very economical young person, who could dine off Brazil nuts, and who had no dressmaker's bill—to speak of."

"What a pity you did not bring her to Court! She would have made a sensation! But we could do better than this for you ; only you behave so badly to them all. There was Millicent—"

"No man likes to be told of his sins. Some day I will come and confess them, and you shall give me absolution. Now, I think I shall go to Pratt's."

They had walked through the rooms quite without success. The young lady of whom they were in search had doubtless left the ball. What matter? Next morning he would have forgotten this fair face altogether.

It was curious how quickly Lord Featherstone had resumed the old yoke. Not many weeks ago he was living a half-savage life in far-off wilds, hobnobbing with Red Indians, paddling his own canoe among the islands of the South Pacific, doing everywhere as the natives did; and now once more he became a fashionable Londoner, and did as everybody did in town. After breakfast a canter in the Park, meeting there friends, male and female, of whom the former offered him the odds, the latter carried him home to lunch; later, a look in at Hurlingham or at Lillie Bridge, back to some favourite boudoir for a quiet præcenal tea, a sumptuous dinner, a glimpse at the Opera or "the House," balls, drums, at home—anything that might be going, and the best of what there was.

"What a slave I am!" he was saying, as he jogged slowly towards the Row some days after the Duchess of Welshpool's ball. "I say each season shall be my last, but I cannot stay away from three in succession. Here am I at it again; sucked into the Maelström already, and swimming round like an empty hen-coop or a light-headed cork. But what else can I do? Politics—the game is not worth the candle; science—I'm not clever enough; art—I haven't the special gifts; travel—I've tried it; literature—every one—soldiers, shoeblacks, dowagers, and *dames de comptoir*—writes books; philanthropy—no faith, phil-womanthropy is more in my line. And yet I've never been really bitten yet. They're too eager, all of them; and the mothers force the running so. If I could only meet some simple little woman who'd take me for myself, and not because I was a good *parti*, I'd marry her out of hand, I would, and settle down. Marriage is a real solid occupation, and I'd like to try it, if I could only meet with the right sort of girl. But where is she to be found?"

He had been riding on at a sharp canter, which increased as he left the more frequented parts of the Row, to a hand-galop. So by the Serpentine, past the Magazine, round by the Upper Row, towards the Marble Arch, and he was galloping still as he turned southward meaning only to draw rein when he neared the Achilles statue and joined once more in the crowd.

But an unexpected vision suddenly arrested his course.

"By Jove! That face again!" Yes, the girl he had seen but a few nights since; the fair fresh young face which had taken his fancy by storm. She was alone, seated in a quaint old-fashioned yellow chariot, a ramshackle mediæval conveyance, probably as old as the hills. It hung on high springs of an antiquated pattern, its lining was of faded purple, its hammercloth had a fringe of tarnished gilding, its coachman was an aged retainer, with a mottled face, and livery that showed white at the seams; while the horses he drove were long past mark of teeth; a fossil carriage which had lain for centuries at rest, and which when dug up should have gone to a museum, and not, as now, into active life.

Strange contrast, this bright child; spring rose-buds on her cheeks and innocence in every line of her smiling face, alone in a vehicle better suited to a dowager or a duchess of the older school. A country-bred girl, of course; such fresh beauty is denied to Londoners. But where had she come from; who could she be?

He was determined to find out this time. With that idea

he turned his horse's head and gave immediate chase. The carriage would doubtless travel by the conventional route, across the Serpentine bridge, and back to the crowded Drive. There chance would certainly provide a friend to tell him what he wanted to know.

But, to his surprise, the chariot passed out at the Marble Arch, and left the Park. There was no time to lose. He pursued, promptly, along Oxford-street to the Circus, up Langham-place into Portland-place, sharp to the right by Weymouth-street into Albany-street, and so to Park-street. Here the coachman, as one not intimately acquainted with London, made, as it seemed, a false turn. He got into Gloucester-road, and at the end of it had to cross by the Chalk-farm Station, and back towards the Kentish Town-road. This regained he followed northward, and reaching the Hampstead road began to breast the hill.

What could have brought this young lady so far out of town? Business, pleasure, or mere desire for change of air and scene? While Featherstone was still debating, the carriage stopped short in front of a modest cottage. Presently an old gentleman issued forth and assisted the girl to alight. There was no footman, and as she went into the house she said loud enough for Featherstone to hear, "In an hour's time, Gregory;" then she disappeared. Under her arm was a portfolio, in the other hand an unmistakable colour-box. Of course, she had come out for a drawing-lesson; equally of course, when it was over, she would return to town.

Riding slowly to and fro, Featherstone waited while the time slipped by. The chariot, which had gone no further than a neighbouring "public," returned, and drew up in front of the cottage. Presently the young lady accompanied by her drawing-master came out, shook hands, jumped into the carriage, and was driven off.

Now, for the first time, Featherstone became aware that the coachman had been drinking, and was almost too unsteady to sit upon his box!

"The rascal! To take advantage of his young mistress being all by herself. She ought to be put upon her guard. Something's bound to happen. I really ought to look after her."

The coachman's erratic course soon proved that there was some ground for these forebodings. The pace at which he drove down the hill was break-neck, and his steering infamous. He had sea-room certainly, all the ample space of a wide suburban thoroughfare; but no road is wide enough to be traversed in long tacks, as if beating up against a head wind. Very soon too the coachman attracted attention and much derisive chaff. "Where's that garden rake?" "Who put you on the box, Mr. Bottlewasher?" "Why don't you buy a mangle or turn chimney sweep?" remarks calculated to raise the ire of the bibulous, and which our Jehu resented by glaring round in speechless semi-comical indignation, to the utter and more perilous neglect of his driving. Already by the merest shave he had weathered an apple-woman's stall; next he was nearly in collision with a light cart; then he was all but wrecked upon a heavy brewer's dray.

It was really time to interfere. Featherstone rode up rapidly.

"You're not fit to drive! You're endangering this lady's life. Here," he turned to the ubiquitous "Bobby" who had already cropped up as fast as does the mushroom in rank soil after rain—"I give this fellow into custody. Take him, carriage and all. My name is Lord Featherstone."

Policemen have immense respect for peers of the realm.

"Very good, my lord. But there ain't room for these horses and all in a police-cell."

"And pray what is to become of me?" said a small voice, a little tremulous in its tones, but not without asperity. "Am I to be given into custody too?"

Featherstone took off his hat.

"A thousand apologies. My interference would have been unpardonable but for the gravity of the situation. If you will but tell me what you wish——"

"To go home of course, as soon as possible. My aunt will be in terror."

"This rascal cannot drive you: he won't be fit, for hours."

"I certainly shall not wait hours. I must walk—or find another coachman.—O Gregory," she looked reproachfully at the old reprobate, "the last time you promised to take the pledge; and yet now——"

"O Miss Kiss," he spluttered out, as if quite alive to the enormity of his sins, "the brew was good, and I'd so long to wait——"

"If I might make so bold," said S 1002, "there's good livery stables at the Chequers. You might put the carriage up, or get another driver there."

A very sensible suggestion, adopted forthwith.

The chariot was conveyed thither in safety. Featherstone dismounted, then helped the young lady to descend.

"They will show you to a private sitting-room. You are not very much alarmed, I trust?"

"I ought not to be," she replied, hanging her head. "You are so kind. But how long shall I have to wait?"

"Not a second longer than I can help," he said gallantly.

Nor had she; the landlord produced a man in the conventional drab coat, warranted to drive a pair, and within ten minutes the chariot was ready to resume its journey.

Lord Featherstone went up to say so.

"I trust you will have no more *contretemps*." He spoke

gravely. "This new coachman is sober, but he is of course an utter stranger."

There was a shade of misgiving in his voice, which had the desired effect.

"Dear, dear, suppose he too should play some trick. I *ought not* to have come alone. Aunty said so. What shall I do now?"

"If you would accept me as an escort——"

How deep he was!

"Only too thankfully. But it would be trespassing too much upon your good-nature. You have been so kind already."

Such a sweet grateful little soul, with such a soft pleasing voice. She was absolutely charming.

"I must go back to town. If you would give me a seat——"

"But you have your horse. If you would only ride close behind, it would do."

"My horse has gone lame in two legs."

It was a wonder he hadn't developed navicular laminitis and farcy.

"Then I shall be doing you a service really?" she cried, with animation.

"Distinctly."

Then they got in together and drove off.

For a time neither spoke. Featherstone felt upon his good behaviour; he was disposed to be as deferential as to a royal princess. His companion was a little shy at first and tongue-tied, but this could not last. She was a chatterbox by nature, and soon broke the ice.

"Do you think he knows where to take us?" she asked.

"Not unless you've told him."

"Don't *you* know?"

"How should I? To London, I suppose."

"That's a wide address," and she laughed aloud. "No, Kensington-square; that's where we live, Lord Featherstone."

He started.

"You know my name, then?"

Artful young person, why did not she confess to this sooner?

"Of course; I heard you tell the policeman."

"That's well; now may I know yours?"

"Kiss."

Good heavens! Featherstone was near saying, "Kiss? Kiss whom? Kiss her?"

"Kiss Legh; that's my name. It's short——"

"And sweet." Featherstone could not check himself.

"Short," she went on, seemingly unconscious, "for Keziah. We come of an old Quaker stock on the borders, between Shropshire and Montgomeryshire. My father and mother are dead; all my people are dead. I went to school in France, and now I've come to London to be finished."

She prattled on now, frank, fluent, and unaffected.

"And how do you like it?"

"What? London?"

"No; being finished."

"I haven't got to the end yet. That'll be when I'm married. But there is not much chance of that, yet a while."

"Why not?" asked Featherstone, highly amused.

"I don't like anybody well enough."

"Perhaps nobody's asked you."

"Indeed, lots have. Herbert Fitzwygram—he is our cousin—he did, and Robert Fox did, and——" she guessed from his face that he was laughing at her, and she stopped abruptly.

"You are quite a stranger, Lord Featherstone, and you have no right to ask me such questions."

"Well, I won't; we'll talk about something different. We're getting into the streets. Do you know this part of London ? It's called Kentish Town, because it's in Middlesex."

She smiled. Evidently she was not one of those who bore malice long.

"I'm not well up in London geography. It's my first visit to town."

"I wish it was *my* last."

"Do you hate it so much ? "

"I'm tired to death of it. All the gaieties, the perpetual round of parties, balls——"

"O, I do love a ball ! I've only been to one."

"I saw you."

She turned her eyes on him, wide open, to see if he were telling the truth.

"But you didn't know me then. How could you tell ? And why weren't you introduced ? "

"Next time I will be. Will you give me a dance or two ? "

"A dozen if you like."

A very artless and original young lady, certainly.

But now they were once more in Oxford-street, and the job coachman headed, as in duty bound, by the shortest route for Kensington-square.

"He's taking us through the Park !" cried Featherstone, in some consternation.

"Yes ; why not ? I am glad of it. It's pleasanter than the streets."

" O, if you prefer it. Only——"

He was thinking that it was now well on in the afternoon, and the Park would be crammed. For the girl's sake, it would be better they should not be seen thus publicly together, and alone. For his own also ; few men like to be carted round the Drive in a carriage, least of all in such an antiquated conveyance as this old yellow chariot with its high springs.

" We'll go out at Hyde Park Corner then."

" No, no ; I love the Drive best.   Perhaps the Princess will be out ; and I like to see the other people, and you can tell me who they all are."

Like a martyr he succumbed.   It was best to put a good face on the matter.   Perhaps, too, he would not be observed, and with this idea he rather hung back in the carriage, and tried to hide behind his fair companion.

She on the other hand, was in the highest glee.   Chattering, criticising, laughing aloud as the chariot crawled slowly along with the stream : talking of bonnets and costumes; calling this a queer old woman and that a strange-looking thing ; continually asking questions, and insisting upon categorical replies.   Featherstone could not help himself.   He looked at the places she indicated, made out individuals, caught the amused glances and half " chaffy " nods of those who made him out in return, and by degrees realised that, for his sins, he had been recognised by at least half the fashionable world.   Before night it would be all over London that Beau Featherstone had turned into a chaperon for country cousins, or that he had been taken captive by a fair face in a yellow " shay."

II.

Lord Featherstone was inclined to be a little stiff and cold in his farewells spoken at the door in Kensington-square.   But then the pretty protestations of gratitude and thanks so volubly poured out by Miss Keziah Legh quite overcame him.   He actually promised to call the following day, although he felt it was much better he should not.   The temptation was, however, irresistible. She was so sweet and pleasant, so sympathetic, so unaffected, so unlike the other girls about, that he certainly must see her again. As he walked homewards, full of these thoughts, he ran up against Tommy Cutler near the Albert Hall.

"Halloa ! been to Kensington-square ?"

Featherstone visibly shuddered. Tommy Cutler knew all about it, then, already.

"Saw you in the Park, my lord. Understand now why you were so keen the other night about flaxen hair and bright-blue eyes, and only seventeen."

"Don't be an ass !" cried Featherstone angrily. "Here, hansom !" and his lordship drove on to Brooks's.

"Here is Featherstone himself," said a man, in the bay-window; "we'll ask him. I say, they're betting five to four you've started a yellow chariot, and were seen in it in the Park."

"Did you pick it up in Japan ?"

"Is it the coach Noah drove home in when he landed from the ark ?"

Featherstone abruptly left the room. The absurd story was evidently on the wing. More serious was the next onslaught.

"You ought not to have done it, Featherstone," said old Mr. Primrose, who had been his father's friend, and presumed therefore to give the son advice. "You have compromised the girl seriously; and she is such an absolute child."

"Excuse me ; I am not called upon to give account to you of all my actions."

"You ought not, I repeat, to have appeared with her thus publicly. It was bad enough to take her down to Richmond ; but to put your arm round her waist openly in the Park——"

"Really, Mr. Primrose !" Featherstone's face flushed, but he restrained himself.

He knew gossip grew like a rank weed, and he wished to root up this scandal at once and kill it outright.

"I may as well tell you at once: that young lady is about to become my wife. Under these circumstances, I presume no one can find fault with what happened this afternoon, which, nevertheless, is grossly exaggerated—that you must also allow me to say."

"Featherstone, I beg your pardon, and I give you joy. I knew something of these Leghs; not over-wealthy, but charming people. I am heartily glad to think this girl has done so well and so soon. Is it to be announced at once?"

"Well, not exactly at once," said Featherstone, thinking perhaps it would be as well to consult the young lady herself. Of course she would say "Yes;" but as a matter of form he ought to ask her.

There was another ordeal in store for him that same night. Lady Carstairs could not be silenced so easily as Mr. Primrose.

"Well," she said—it was at a reception at the Foreign Office—"the guile of modern girls passes all conception. If Mother Eve had lived in these times, the serpent would have had no chance."

"What new proof have we of the desperate wickedness of your sex?"

"I did not think you would fall so easily into the trap. But old campaigners think themselves armour-plated by experience; and it's a novel line of attack." He looked at her in amazement. "Fastness is no new trait in young ladies."

"Nor in old ones," put in Lord Featherstone.

"Thank you. But no woman of my time ever went to the length of compromising herself as the most effective method of hooking her man. This Miss Legh——"

"I beg you will not mention her name."

"This Miss Legh," went on Lady Carstairs, bitterly hostile

still, "although but a girl, might give lessons to all the veteran flirts in the kingdom. I've heard all about it."

"All, and probably more."

"Captain Cutler saw you leaving the Star and Garter together; I myself saw you in the Park. That any girl could allow herself to be thus affichée with a character like Lord Featherstone——"

"I'm obliged to you, Lady Carstairs, for your good opinion; but instead of defending myself, I'll take up the gauntlet for Miss Legh."

And he told the story exactly as it had occurred.

"She did it on purpose," Lady Carstairs said promptly.

"Came out on purpose to meet me in the Park? Made me follow her on purpose to Hampstead? Made her coachman drink too much beer on purpose, and pressed me to drive back with her to town?"

"Not quite all that, perhaps. But it would be her game to get you to go through the Park with her. Was it not at her express request—come now, confess—that you appeared with her in the most public place in the town?"

He did remember that Miss Legh had insisted upon going through the Park. Could it be that she wished to parade herself by his side, and be thus observed of all the world? Surely not; yet——

"You wrong her," he said chivalrously. Whatever he might suspect, he would make no admission that might do her harm. "All the blame in this matter is mine, and mine alone; and I am resolved to make her all the reparation in my power."

"What may that amount to?"

"To asking her in set form to become my wife."

"Lord Featherstone, you would never be so foolish! A more ridiculous notion I never heard."

"*Noblesse oblige.*"

"It's purely suicidal, uncalled for, unnecessary; you must not sacrifice yourself and your whole life."

"Perhaps it is no sacrifice."

"Am I to understand that you have fallen in love—at last? That this mere child, this chit out of the schoolroom, has brought you to her feet? I refuse to believe it."

"I am in earnest, I assure you. I shall marry her if she will only say 'Yes.'"

"Say, 'Yes!'" cried Lady Carstairs, with a scornful laugh; "what girl in her sober senses would refuse Lord Featherstone?"

Probably in his own heart he had little doubt that his offer would be well received. This rather increased a sentiment of self-glorification, which was taking possession of him as a reward for his disinterestedness. That he who might pick and choose where he pleased should throw himself away from a mere spasm of chivalrous generosity was perhaps more than was expected of him. Nevertheless, it was pleasant to do the right thing; and his satisfaction was increased as he pictured to himself this little Keziah, with her bright eyes and laughing mouth, full of grateful thanks for the honour he meant to do her.

It was quite with the air of a grand seigneur that he presented himself next day in Kensington-square. To his surprise he was not very well received.

There had been a scene between Keziah and her aunt directly the former reëntered the house on the previous evening. The girl, without attempting to withhold one iota of information, had given her aunt a full account of what had occurred—the coachman's misconduct, the danger only averted by the timely intervention of a strange gentleman, who had kindly escorted her home.

"His name was Lord Featherstone."

"That wretch!" instantly cried Miss Parker, an old maid, prim and precise in her appearance and in all her ways, yet not disinclined to listen to at least half the scandalous gossip in circulation through the world.

"Do you know him, Aunt Parker?"

"Who does not? He is a notoriously wicked man——"

She stopped short, feeling that the epithet could only be substantiated by details which it was better Keziah should not hear.

"I thought him very nice," Keziah spoke defiantly and very firmly in defence of her new friend.

"Of course you did. He can be most agreeable. I have heard that of him over and over again. That's the danger of him."

"He was so kind and obliging. He told me who everybody was in the Park——"

"Can it be possible that you were so mad as to go into the Park with him in the afternoon, when it was crowded, when hundreds must have seen you together?"

"Of course we came through the Park together; it was the shortest way home. I cannot see any great harm in that."

"It's not likely; you are so young and inexperienced; you can see no harm in anything. But he knew the mischief he was doing, only too well. The wretch, the wretch!" Mild Miss Parker would have been glad to see wild horses tear him limb from limb. "However," after a pause, "you must promise me faithfully that you will never speak to him again."

"He said he would call just to inquire how I was," Keziah said, in a low voice, which might easily have meant that she hoped he would not be told peremptorily to go away.

"*I* will see him if he comes," Aunt Parker finally replied.

"It is not fitting he should pursue his acquaintance with you, begun as it was under such questionable auspices."

And in this decision Keziah was forced to acquiesce.

When therefore, after some delay and demur, Lord Featherstone was admitted to Aunt Parker, her manner was perfectly arctic. She sat bolt upright, with a stony look in her eyes and only frigid monosyllables on her lips.

"I called," said his lordship, with much *aplomb*, "to see Miss Legh."

"Yes?" Aunt Parker asked, much as though Lord Featherstone was the boot-maker's man, or had come to take orders for a sewing-machine.

"My name is Lord Featherstone."

"Is it?" He might have been in the habit of assuming a dozen aliases every twenty-four hours, so utterly indifferent and incredulous was Aunt Parker's tone.

"It was my good fortune to be able to do Miss Legh a slight service yesterday," he went on, still unabashed.

"A service!" Miss Parker waxed indignant at once. "I call it an injury—a shameful, mischievous, unkind act; for which Lord Featherstone, although I apprehend it is not much in his line, should blush for very shame."

"Really, madam,"—he hardly knew whether to be annoyed or amused,—"I think you have been misinformed. Probably, but for me, Miss Legh's neck would have been broken."

"I know that, I know that, and I almost wish it had, sooner than that she should have so far forgotten herself." Miss Parker looked up suddenly and sharply, saying with much emphasis, "O Lord Featherstone, ask yourself—you are, or ought to be, a gentleman, at least you know the world by heart —was it right of you to take such an advantage? Did you think what incalculable harm this foolish thoughtless mistake

—which is certain to be magnified by malicious tongues—may work against an innocent guileless child ?"

"I know I was greatly to blame. I ought to have known better. But it was Miss Legh's own wish to go through the Park, and I gave way."

"How noble of you to shift the burden on to her shoulders! But we will not, if you please, try to apportion the blame. The mischief is done, and there is no more to be said, except to ask you to make us the only reparation in your power ?"

"And that is—?" he looked at her in surprise. She did not surely mean to forestall him, and demand that which he came to offer of his own accord ?

"To leave the house, and to spare us henceforth the high honour of your acquaintance."

"That I promise if you still insist after you have heard what I am going to say. I came to make reparation full and complete, but not in the way you suppose. I came to make Miss Legh—and if she and you, as her guardian, will deign to accept of it—an offer of my hand."

Little Miss Parker's face was an amusing study. Her lower lip dropped, her eyes opened till they looked like the round marbles on a solitaire-board.

"Lord Featherstone, you!"

"I trust you will not consider me ineligible ; that you have no objection to me personally, beyond a natural annoyance at this silly escapade."

"It is so sudden, so unexpected—so—so—" Poor Miss Parker was too much bewildered to find words, a thousand thoughts agitated her. This was a splendid offer, a princely offer. Match-maker by instinct, as is every woman in the world, she could not fail to perceive what dazzling prospects it opened up for her niece. But, then, could any happiness follow from such a hastily-concluded match? These latter, and better thoughts prevailed.

"Lord Featherstone, it is out of the question, or at least you must wait. Say a month or two, or till the end of the season."

"The engagement ought to be announced immediately to benefit Miss Legh."

"And that is your real reason for proposing? Lord Featherstone, I retract my harsh words; you shall not outdo us in generosity. We cannot accept your offer, although we appreciate the spirit in which it is made."

"I assure you, Miss Parker, I esteem Miss Legh most highly. I like her immensely; I am most anxious to marry her."

The bare possibility that he might be refused—he of all men in the world—gave a stronger insistence to his words.

Miss Parker shook her head.

"No good could come of such a marriage; you hardly know each other. You say you like her, perhaps so; but can you tell whether she likes you?"

"At least let me ask her? Do not deny me that. I will abide by her answer."

There was no resisting such pleading as this.

"I may prepare her for what she is to expect?" asked Aunt Parker, as she moved towards the door.

"No, no; please, do not. Let me speak my own way."

He did not distrust the old lady, but she might indoctrinate Keziah with her views, and prejudice her against him. It was becoming a point of honour with him to succeed, and he thought he could. He was no novice in these matters; ere now he had often held the victory in an issue more difficult than this in his grasp, and all he wanted now was a fair field and no favour.

"Aunt Parker said I was never to speak to you again," Kiss said, as she came into the room, with an air of extreme astonishment; "and now she sends me to you of her own accord! What does it mean?"

"It means that I have something very particular to say to you."

They had shaken hands, and she had taken her seat very demurely a little way off. Her eyes were, however, fixed on his in very steadfast inquiry. They were beautiful eyes, but as changeful as they were bright and sparkling. Now wide open with surprise like a child's, next half closed with roguishness, as though the whole world was an excellent joke, which she was enjoying all by herself. Again, on the minutest provocation they would fill and brim over with tears.

"This is delightful! You're better than a box from Mudie's. Is it a story, or a conundrum, or a joke? Go on, Lord Featherstone; do."

"You are no worse for your drive, I hope?"

"Is that all? Yes, I am ever so much worse—in temper. You should have heard Aunt Parker go on! Did anybody scold you?"

"I escaped any very serious rebuke—except from my conscience."

"Dear me, Lord Featherstone, you make me feel as though I were in church. Was it so very wicked, then, to help me in my distress? I thought it was *most* good of you."

This simple but italicised earnestness was very taking.

"No; but people are very censorious. They *will* talk. They are coupling our names together already."

"Does that annoy you?" Her air was candour itself. "Do you mind—very much?"

"Well, perhaps not very, very much. It can do *me* no harm."

" I am glad of that."

" But it may you, and it ought to be stopped."

" Of course ; but how ? "

" There is only one way that I can see. Let us have only one name between us. I cannot very well take yours. Will you take mine ? "

" Why—why—" A light seemed to break in on her all at once. " O, what a funny man you are ! That's just the same as an offer of marriage. You can't mean that, surely ? It would be too—quite too—absurd."

" I don't see the absurdity," said his lordship rather gruffly. Were well-meant overtures ever so shamefully scorned ?

" O, but I do ! " Keziah's little foot was playing with the fringe of the hearthrug. " I do. That is, if you are in earnest, which of course you're not."

" But I am in earnest. Why should you think I'm not ? "

" You don't know me ; you can't care for me. You never spoke to me till yesterday. You are only making fun, and it isn't fair. I wish you'd leave me alone."

Her eyes were full already.

" I am to go away, then ? That is your answer ? " She hid her face in her hands, and would not speak. " You will be sorry for this, perhaps, some day." She shook her head most vigorously. " Keziah Legh, you are the only woman I have ever asked to be my wife. I shall never ask another. Good-bye, and God bless you ! "

And Lord Featherstone, with a strange feeling of dejection and disappointment, left the room. He could not have believed that within this short space of time he could have been so irresistibly drawn towards any girl. Now he was grieving over his failure as though he were still in his teens.

Presently Aunt Parker came in, and found Keziah sobbing fit to break her heart.

"I don't want him! I don't want him! He can go away if he likes—to the other end of the world."

"Have you been ill-used, my sweet? What did he say to you?"

"He asked me to marry him," she said, with difficulty, between her sobs.

"Was that such a terrible insult, then?"

"He was only making fun. I don't like such fun. And I don't want to see him again, never, never, not as long as I live!"

"Kiss, you are right to consult your own feelings in this. But Lord Featherstone was in earnest, I think, and his intentions do him infinite credit."

Then she told her niece what had passed.

"Still, if you don't care for him, it is best as it is. Dry your tears, Kiss, and think no more about it."

"But I think I do care for him," she said, and began to cry again.

III.

LADY CARSTAIRS became very much exercised in spirit as the days passed, and yet nothing positive was known of Lord Featherstone's intentions towards Miss Keziah Legh. Old Primrose had not kept his own counsel, and rumours reached her therefore from without of the engagement. Yet no engagement was announced. She could not understand it at all. Then in the midst of her perplexity came Tommy Cutler with a startling piece of news.

"Have you heard Featherstone's last?" he asked, when he brought her his budget one afternoon.

"No; pray tell me!"

"He's off to Central Africa. Going to walk from Tunis or Tripoli to the Cape of Good Hope."

"Impossible! He's going to be married. At least, so every one says. He could never take a young wife on such a journey, and men only leave old ones unprotected at home."

"I have been telling everybody he was going to marry Kiss Legh," said Tommy, with an injured air, as though people were personally responsible to him for carrying out his gossip to the letter.

"I cannot understand it. I must know the rights of it. He is one of my oldest friends, and I cannot help taking an interest in him."

She made many futile efforts to meet him, then she called and sounded the ladies in Kensington-square with whom she was moderately intimate. They put back her cross-examination mildly but effectually. But at last she met Featherstone face to face and attacked him at once. "Your high-flown sense of honour did not bear practical test, then?"

"How so, Lady Carstairs?" His coolness was provoking.

"Why rush off to Central Africa, except to escape scandal?"

"Am I going to Central Africa? Perhaps I am. Why not?"

"Can it be possible that she refused you?"

"Who could refuse me, Lady Carstairs?"

"No; but do tell me, I am dying to know."

"You must find some one else to save your life, then."

"But, Lord Featherstone, we shall see you once more before you start? You will come and dine with us? Just to say good-bye."

"I will dine with you with pleasure, but not necessarily to say good-bye."

He could not well escape from an invitation so cordially

expressed, and the night was fixed. But he little thought what malice lurked beneath.

The party was a large one, and he as was often the case, very late. When he arrived, "a bad last," the other guests wore that despairing look of martyrdom which waits on extreme hunger and the exhaustion of every topic of talk. But he entered gaily, as if he had come a little too soon, shook hands with the hostess, bowed here and there, nodded to one friend and smiled at another, then, last of all and to his intense surprise, his eyes rested upon Kiss Legh.

Lady Carstairs had done it on purpose, of course; that was self-evident. Unkind, unfeeling, ungenerous woman! For himself he did not care, but it was cruel upon the timid birdling, so new and strange to the world. But fast as this conviction came upon him, yet faster came the resolve that Lady Carstairs should make nothing by the move. A thoroughly well-bred man is never taken aback, and Featherstone rose to the occasion. Without a moment's delay, before the faintest flush was hung out like a signal of distress upon Keziah's cheek, he had gone up to her, shaken hands, and spoken a few simple common-places which meant nothing, and yet set her quite at her ease.

"Miss Legh and I are very old friends," he said. "How do you do, Miss Parker? How is the coachman? Have you heard, Sir John, the Prince is expected next week? There will be great doings." And so on.

That little Kiss was grateful to him for his self-possession, was evident from the satisfaction which beamed in her eyes. O those tell-tale eyes!

Now Lady Carstairs brought up her reserves and fired another broadside.

"It is so good of you, Lord Featherstone, to come to us; and you have so few nights left."

“When do you go, Featherstone ? and where ?”

“Haven’t you heard ?   To Central Africa,” Lady Carstairs answered for him.

Can this be true ?   Keziah’s eyes asked him in mute but eloquent language, which sent a thrill through his heart.

“Where this story originated I cannot make out,” said Featherstone, slowly.   “I am not going to Central Africa. On the contrary, I have the very strongest reasons for staying at home.”

“And those reasons ?”

“Are best known to Miss Legh and myself.”

KISS AND TRY.

A Tale of St. Valentine.

By RICHARD JEFFERIES.

———•———

"I WON'T marry for money, and I won't be married for money, and I won't marry at all; and when I do, I'll please myself—so *there!* You are so stupid, Aunt Jane;" and the wilful little beauty stamped her foot, contradicting herself with a wrathful energy that would have done credit to an accomplished actress.

"My dear—"

"Don't ' my dear ' me! I'm not your *dear*. I can be *dear* to plenty of people if I choose."

"My dear, really you are so impetuous, you'll never be married."

"There it is again, that hateful topic. Can't you understand I don't want to? Why should I? I've got plenty of money; I've got a carriage, and two such pets of ponies, and a hunter, and a house in the country; what more do I want? I wish you would all let me alone. There's papa talking sorrowfully, silly old darling, about his declining years, and only me, and *me* not married; and if you are my aunt it's no reason you should worry me night and day. I *won't* have your lawyer if he's as rich as Crœsus—how much has he given you to plead his cause, eh?"

" You need not insult me, at all events. I counsel you for your own good. Miss Delaselle. Mr. Marshe is a most eligible person, most eligible. His father is in the front rank of his profession, and immensely rich ; your papa approves of his suit. There is a possibility of the dormant peerage being revived in the favour of that family : Mr. Marshe senior has rendered great services in high quarters."

" Thank you for your genealogical particulars. Now please tell me all about Captain Williams, and Theophilus Bishop, who will rise in the Church, and Sir Cornelius Wilkes, and Squire Thompson, and Mr. Burnaby, and Lieutenant Vane, and Lord Pauline, &c."

" Really, you may well pause ; the flirtations you carry on are beyond all belief. There were a dozen soldiers in the house yesterday."

" And there'll be two dozen to-night, and I shall have at least a hundred valentines to-morrow morning. Everybody likes me ; of course they do. All the men know I don't try to trap them into marrying me, like the other girls. Ah, there's a ring ; sure to be somebody to see me."

" Shameful ! " groaned Aunt Jane, composing herself to her work.

Marie glanced in the mirror over the mantelpiece, smiled, and adjusted a stray curl.

" Aunt, don't you think I look awfully nice this evening ? "

" Charming ! " said a gentleman's voice, as the door was thrown open, and Mr. Marshe was announced. " Pardon me, that dress is perfection."

" Sir, I do not like personal remarks ; they are extremely rude. However, your profession, I suppose, brings you into contact with vulgar people."

" Marie ! " reproachfully from Aunt Jane.

" Miss Delaselle is privileged," said Marshe, a dapper young man, not bad-looking, but obviously conceited. Marie said all little men were vain ; and as for lawyers they seemed to consider it the duty of heiresses to marry them.

"What divorce case are you engaged in now, sir ? " she asked.

"We do not undertake that class of work," said Marshe, loftily.

"Captain Williams—O, and Lord Pauline too ! I *am* delighted to see you. We have been so dull this evening, have we not, Aunt Jane ? "

These new-comers hardly acknowledged the lawyer, who on his part surveyed them with intense scorn. "Neither of them has a hundred pounds cash," thought he to himself, "and yet such airs."

Marie, however, was much more pleasant in her manner to them, which galled him extremely, yet he could not tear himself away ; and after twenty times resolving never to speak to her again, he had actually opened a tacit understanding with Mr. Delaselle.

She was, indeed, one of those girls of whom it may be justly said that there is no living with them nor without them.

He turned to pay court to Aunt Jane, when the Rev. Theophilus Bishop arrived. He was acting for the present as a curate in town, till a valuable living, in the gift of a relative, should become vacant by the decease of the aged incumbent.

"You cruel man ! " said Marie ; "I heard of your sermon ; so, if a poor lady is deserted by her husband and gets a divorce, she is not to marry again ? "

"We are opposed to such unions on the highest grounds, my dear Miss Delaselle. If we had only known that a divorcée was one of the contracting parties, we should have most certainly refused permission to use the sacred edifice."

"Well, it's very hard. Don't you think so, Mr. Marshe ? "

"To refuse would be illegal," said the lawyer, glad of a chance of putting down one of his rivals, "quite illegal, I feel sure, to say nothing of the bad taste."

"By the ecclesiastical law—" began the curate, firing up in a moment.

"It's a confounded shame," broke in Captain Williams.

"The ladies are deserving of every consideration," said Lord Pauline, an aged *beau*, but well preserved. "You may be sure the lady was the injured party."

"Ecclesiastical law—" repeated the curate.

"Suppose it was me," said Marie; "suppose I had a brute of a husband—of course I never mean to have one, that's understood."

"The premises are very lucid," said the lawyer sarcastically.

"And—and I was divorced. Mustn't *I*—have—well—"

"You of course would be an exception," said the curate; "but as a rule such marriages are even more sinful than those contracted simply with a view to filthy lucre."

This was a cut for Marshe.

"I hate women who marry for money," said Marie; "there's nothing so despicable."

"Nothing so despicable," echoed Captain Williams and Lord Pauline, neither of whom had a "dollar."

"Except a man's marrying a lady for her money," added the curate, who was well provided for as far "as the good things of this world went." "There should be a certain equality of position and of pecuniary means in order to insure mutual respect."

"Mutual respect be hanged!" muttered Captain Williams, in his beard.

"What did I hear?" said the curate; "the language of the barrack-room—"

"I say a girl that marries the man she loves is the truest

and the best," cried the captain loudly; "whether he's poor or rich doesn't matter. She's the girl for me."

To his surprise the captain caught Marie's eyes fixed on him with an expression of sympathy that made his heart give a thump of delight. Could she? He was not such a bad fellow, this captain, though a trifle outspoken.

"I differ from you entirely," said Lord Pauline. "I think nothing shows a more cowardly character than for a man without a penny and without social position"—this was a hint at his own title—"to attempt to obtain the affections of a lady who might engage herself to great advantage."

"Lord Pauline understands the world and human nature," said Aunt Jane. "His remarks are very just. O, good evening, sir;" with a marked emphasis on the "sir."

Marie merely bowed in a distant manner to the gentleman who had at that moment entered, and turned quickly towards the piano. They all crowded round her, and pressed her to play, scarcely deigning to exchange salutations with the new-comer, who was thus as it were excluded from the circle—except Captain Williams, who welcomed him cordially.

"'Tis poverty parts good company,'" whispered he, quoting the old song. "Never mind, old fellow; you're twenty times more a man than these miserable drumstick imitations. By Jove, what a chest you have!"

Thurstan Baynard was indeed "a man of inches," and broad in proportion—perhaps rather more than in proportion—though he had hardly yet reached his full development, being but twenty-six. A long silky black beard, thick curling moustaches, bright dark eyes, an open wide forehead, and rather massive head, gave him no inconsiderable claim to be called handsome. Thurstan was one of those men, sometimes met, who seem to possess every possible advantage except money. He was tall and strong, certainly good looking agreeable in manner, well read, and still better travelled—he had, for a time, carried despatches as a Queen's Messenger—full of animal health and naturally joyous temperament, saddened however, by the perpetual sense of impecuniosity and the pressure of petty debt. His family was well connected, of ancient descent, and yet practically he was a vagabond upon the face of the earth. The families of Baynard and Delaselle were branches of the same stock ; he and Marie had played together as children, and he was still free of the house ; but when growing years seemed to threaten the danger of an imprudent attachment, Mr. Delaselle spoke to him in private very seriously on the matter, " hoping that he would not take advantage of his position to compromise Marie's chances of an eligible match." This was extremely bitter to Thurstan, whose proud spirit was deeply wounded ; and henceforward he came rarely, and adopted a deferential distant manner.

Marie, on her part, scarcely noticed him now that they were arrived, he at manhood and she at womanhood. He thought it was pride ; still he felt constrained to call occasionally, for in truth he loved her beyond expression.

Nothing destroys a man's spirit like poverty, especially if he still by birth belongs to that class of whom it was said *noblesse oblige,* and cannot fully descend to the little meannesses too often compulsorily practised by those who earn their daily bread. There were as yet no lines upon his forehead, but there was an indescribable expression of subdued pain.

" I've come to say good-bye," said he to Captain Williams, as the two sat together in the background, while Marie played and sang gaily. Mr. Delaselle just nodded as he entered, and then devoted himself to Mr. Marshe.

" Where are you off to, then ? " asked the captain. " Why on earth don't you go into the army ? "

" Can't afford it—and can't live on thirteenpence a day

either. No; I'm going to China; you know I've studied fortification. I've an idea I could help them to fortify themselves against the Russians. They are much alarmed at Russian aggression eastwards. General Kauffman's guns easily smashed up the wretched walls and towers of the Central Asian Khans. I think China ought to pay well for instruction how to build redoubts *à la Vauban*."

" It's not a bad idea ; but how about leaving Miss Delaselle ? I thought you were— Well, no matter ; you're just the man for her. Yes, I'll say that even against my own interest. She'll be snapped up before you get back, man. Look at Marshe, and that prig the curate, and the old lord—pah ! Are you sure *she* doesn't care for you ? "

" She scarcely acknowledges me," said Thurstan. " And yet we used to— Still she has a right to do as she pleases. At all events I start to-morrow night for Southampton from Waterloo Station—"

" I'll see you off. By Jove, I'm sorry, deuced sorry ! The best fellows are always shoved into a corner. To-morrow night —it's St. Valentine's-day to-morrow, now I think of it."

Just then Marie's voice, blithe and rich in tone, began with an inimitable expression of innocent mischievousness, so to say, the old verse :

> " A' the lads they look at me,
> Coming through the rye."

"It's just like her," said the captain ; "and yet do you know, Thurstan, I believe there's something good in that girl despite all this frivolity. I wish you could have seen her just now when they were discussing marriages for money, and I said the best and truest girl was the one who married for love. There was a flash in her eye—I don't think she knows her own heart yet."

"Mr. Baynard," cried Marie suddenly, from her seat at the piano, "come and sing our old favourite, 'Annie Laurie.'"

The circle sneered at the mention of so simple a ballad. He hesitated; but she insisted, and finally he sang it—sang it as only a man could do who *felt* every line. It was true that she had never pledged her word, but she was indeed "all the world" to him. He had a beautiful voice, bell-like, yet liquid, and, to alter just one word of Byron,

> "Love hath not, in all his choice,
> An arrow for the heart like a sweet voice."

They were all silent when he ceased. Marie indeed seemed to recover herself with an effort, and thanked him gently, in a tone that nearly unmanned him.

"Dear me!" cried the lawyer; "I've forgotten I had a telegram to leave at the office. Excuse me. I'll return."

Mr. Delaselle accompanied him to the door.

"Something very despicable in business," said Lord Pauline.

"Very despicable, very," echoed the curate. "Contact with the coarser natures who seek the aid of the law must naturally react upon those who listen to their revelations."

"I believe there is a great fire," said Mr. Delaselle, re-entering; "let us go up to the high windows to see."

The gentlemen and Aunt Jane, who had a special horror of fire, followed him quickly; and Marie was moving in the same direction, when Thurstan, who had stood aside to let the others pass first, spoke her name gently.

She paused, and for the moment they were alone.

"Yes," she said kindly.

"I——I just called to say good-bye; I start for China to-morrow night——some years before I may see you again," said Thurstan, in a hurried and confused manner.

"Is this true?"

"It is indeed, quite true. You will remember me some-times, Marie?" he almost said "my darling," but his courage failed.

Her eyes fell; she flushed slightly.

"Yes, I shall remember you. Stay, let me think——hush! Is it a fire?" she added, in a different tone, hearing foot-steps.

"At a great distance; no danger," said Mr. Delaselle. Aunt Jane glanced suspiciously from Thurstan to Marie, and back again.

He felt that he was looked on as *de trop;* and confused, believing too that to stay longer would be simply to prolong his torture, wished them good-night, and left what he had almost nerved himself to say to Marie still unsaid, and now probably beyond his power to say.

A certain stiffness fell upon the party, and Marie seemed to have lost her gaiety, till in less than an hour Marshe returned, and she brightened up, to the great delight of Aunt Jane and Mr. Delaselle, who saw in this a sign of affection for him, and were reassured.

Marshe was very lively. The fact was he thought he had done a clever thing.

It was this. Driving to the office of the firm, Marshe, Marshe, and Copp, he recollected that he had a valentine in the pocket of his overcoat. It was a very expensive one, which he had selected with much care, containing a few love verses of the approved order, surrounded with a gorgeous design, and perfumed. He argued with himself *pro* and *con*, after the manner of the judicial mind, as he drove along, whether he should address the envelope himself in his own proper handwriting, or whether he should disguise his style, or get someone else to assist him. This highly important question has agitated the hearts of valentine senders ever since the graceful old custom began.

Clearly, if directed in his own handwriting, Marie, who knew it well, would recognise the sender immediately; of mystery there would be none, and the fun would be lost.

If the address was written by a stranger it was ten chances to one that she would never fix upon him, in which case the valentine might as well be thrown in the fire at once. What was to be done? A Frenchman would say that the answer to this apparently trifling question decided his destiny. It was still open when he reached the offices of the great firm, in which his part was really merely nominal. In these vast businesses each partner has one department to himself, and perhaps scarcely ever hears the name of the clients of the others: this young man, pert and fashionable in his ways, thought no more of his profession than was absolutely forced upon him. They were working very late that night; his father was sitting still, getting up a matter for a parliamentary committee—the telegram he had forgotten referred to this.

"Ah, Jones," said he to a confidential clerk who had a room to himself, a kind of antechamber to the great man's, "just put this letter in a large envelope, one with the firm's initials on,—only the initials, mind,—and direct it with the type-writer to Miss Delaselle, —— Street, Mayfair. Have it ready for me."

In this way he thought he had conquered the difficulty. The writing machine really prints exactly like type; but the initials would leave a clue to guess by. Clever young man!

Jones, so soon as his back was turned, smiled, and smelt the letter. "Aha!" thought he, "I'll have a look; it's a valentine; I can smell the perfume."

The envelope was but just stuck; he loosened it, and pulled

out the valentine, laying it on a long letter he had just finished
with the machine.   Hardly had he taken a peep when the door
opened again, and Marshe stood in the opening—still, however,
with his back turned—talking to the principal.   In an awful
fright, Jones upset all his papers, crammed the valentine and
the long letter hastily into envelopes, and wrote the directions
like lightning.

"That will do——capital!" said Marshe, taking the
valentine.   "It's rather an awkward looking parcel, though.
Give me that other letter; I'll send them both to post by the
boy as I go down-stairs."

He dashed back rapidly to Marie, who, as soon as he arrived,
became as merry as ever, and raised his hopes exceeding high.
When the evening closed, Marshe thought to himself, "She
has evidently come round.   I'll strike while the iron is hot,
and put the question to-morrow night.   By the bye, that ill-
favoured Thurstan I hear is off to Hong-Kong.   Glad of it;
always had a lurking suspicion there was something between
them."

Who, in all great London, should have been so happy as
Marie that night?   Rich, fêted, with crowds of admirers, and
sure to have a hundred valentines next morning!

Would any one have believed that she never slept all night,
but passed the weary hours, thinking, thinking, thinking, and frequently shedding tears.   Till Thurstan was about to leave her, in
all human probability for ever, she had never known how much
she loved him.   Indeed, she had hardly ever felt that she had a
heart; life had been one long round of joyous frivolity.   Now
she knew the utter nothingness of all the nicknacks of wealth.
Of what use were dozens of admirers if *he* was not there?
She remembered Captain Williams's blunt declaration that the
best and truest woman was the one who married for love.   Poor
Thurstan had not a penny.   Some of these men who courted

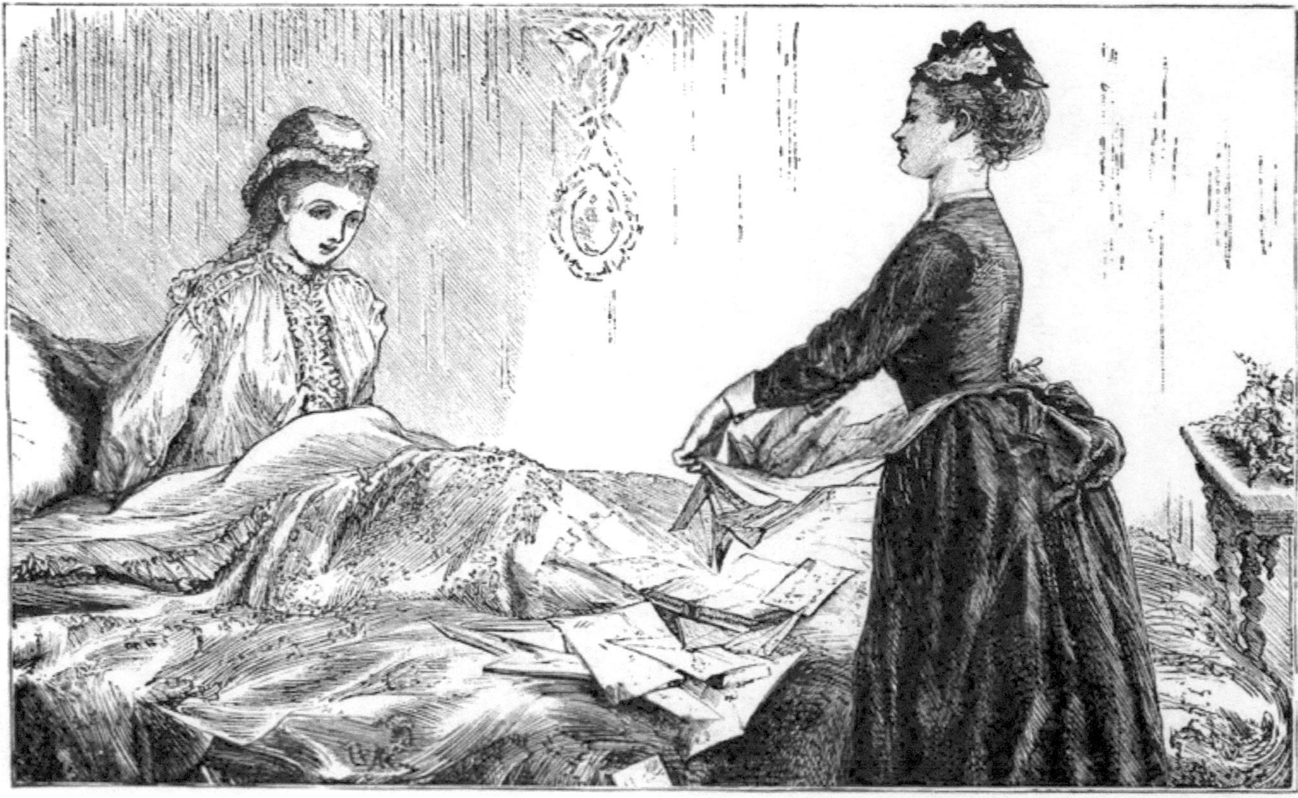

"HERE WERE THE HUNDRED VALENTINES."

I. 159.

her had shown such bad taste as to describe the shifts he was sometimes put to ; instinctively they felt he was a dangerous rival, and thought to hold him up to contempt.

"I *know* he loves me," she said to herself; "why has he never said so ? It is this money; he is too proud to have me think he woos me for my money. To-morrow I shall lose him for ever."

From sheer exhaustion she fell asleep at last, and was awakened by her maid, who had brought to her bedside a perfect heap of letters. Here were the hundred valentines !

Scarcely twenty hours before she had looked forward to this moment with delight ; now she pushed the heap away as a vanity and vexation of spirit.

"Perhaps Thurstan has sent one," she thought presently, and turned them over, seeking the well-remembered hand-writing. "No, not even a valentine ; very likely he is too poor to buy one that he thinks good enough for me. What is this thick letter ? What curious writing ! It's printing, I think."

Curiosity impelled her to open it. She read and read, and a colour rose in her cheeks.

"Is it possible !" she cried, and sprang up. "I'll do it! I *will !* I don't care !"

Hurriedly she wrote a note, and despatched it to Thurstan's chambers. A bold thing, doubtless : but reflect, they had been playmates. It ran thus :

"Miss Delaselle and Mr. Delaselle would like to see Mr. Baynard early in the day, that they may wish him farewell. They will feel much hurt if he does not come."

"Good heavens !" she thought, "if it should not reach him ; if he should not come."

Thurstan, indeed, did hesitate, feeling that to see her again would be a severe trial. But love, all-powerful love, would

not be denied. He went. She had so arranged that he found
her alone in her boudoir.

"It's extremely rude of you, sir, to force me to write to
you." Now he was there, she could not resist the temptation
to play with the mouse she had caught. "Why did you not
tell me before that you were going?"

Thurstan, unhappy and down-hearted, could not meet her
light tone with answering raillery. He stammered some excuse.

"And *why* are you going, sir?"

"I must obtain a living somewhere."

"Why not in England?"

"The competition is so great. And everybody despises me
because I am poor."

"Stanny," said she, using an old familiar abbreviation, and
placing her little hand on his broad shoulder, "Stanny,"
you're a big man—a giant—and O, so strong; can't you push
your way in the crowd?"

"I've tried," said he simply.

"No, you haven't. I tell you what, Stan—I'm not afraid of
you, though you are so big—*you're a coward!* There—O,
don't flash your eyes at me! You're afraid, and so you are
running away. You'll cry next, I suppose" (this was very
cruel, Marie, bitterly cruel). "You're not half so brave as I
am. Men are not half so brave as women" (her voice sank
lower, and she looked at him, and her eyes suddenly filled with
tears, though he, gazing away, did not see it). "Do you know
what I should do if I were in your place?"

Something in her tone made him glance at her with a strange
sensation in his throat.

"What would you do if you were me?" he said.

"Kiss and try," she whispered softly, letting her head droop
against his shoulder.

He did it. There are no words by which so sudden a revul-

"STANNY, YOU'RE A BIG MAN; CAN'T YOU PUSH YOUR WAY IN
THE CROWD?"

II. 160.

sion of feeling can be described. The half-hour that followed was the happiest in his life. Suddenly he remembered himself.

"I am so poor," he said. "Forgive me—they will say it was your money."

"Are you sure you are so poor ?" she said archly.

"Quite sure."

"Then read that ; " and she put Marshe's valentine into his hand.

He tried to, but he could not take his gaze from her; and the letters seemed confused.

"Listen," she said, and read it. Slowly the truth dawned upon him. Jones, the clerk, in his hurry, fearing to be caught peeping, had put the letter and the valentine in the wrong envelopes, or rather confused the addresses. Marie got, instead of a valentine, a long letter from Copp, the second principal of the firm, which had been really meant for Thurstan. The valentine went heaven knows where. Of course, how it happened was not found out till afterwards, but there was no mistaking the contents of the letter.

Copp in formal phrase informed Mr. Thurstan Baynard that by the terms of the will of General Sir Frederick Baynard, just deceased—a distant relation who had never previously owned him—he was entitled to a very large sum in consols, and still more valuable estates ; *provided*—ah, whenever was there a blessing without a black side (?)—provided that within the space of twelve months he married a lady possessed of not less than a given amount, upon whose children the whole was to be settled. The old man was a miser, and it had been the work of his life to rehabilitate the fallen fortunes of the family. Casting about for a means of keeping the money he had painfully amassed in the family, he had hit upon this odd, but not unreasonable idea.

" So you see," said Marie, " you're richer than I am. Perhaps you won't have me now ?"

His answer was a fresh embrace.

" Ah," she said, mocking his previously mournful tone, " I'm so poor now compared to you, you'll think it was your money."

" Incorrigible," said he, kissing her.

" Incorrigible, indeed," cried Aunt Jane, who had entered unseen. " This really is shameful—most ungentlemanly."

" He is richer than—everybody," said Marie, laughing. " This is the most beautiful valentine I ever had."

" And this is the most beautiful one _I_ ever had, or ever shall have," said he, laying his hand on her shoulder with an air of possession that horrified Aunt Jane.

Matters, however, were soon explained, and her objections melted away, as did Mr. Delaselle's.

They were married early in May, Captain Williams being Thurstan's best man.

" I was certain she loved you," he said. " I can understand now what she meant on St. Valentine's eve when she looked at me so meaningly, when I said the best and truest woman was the one that married for love. She loved you when you were poor. You ought to be grateful to St. Valentine all your life ! "

MISS MONKTON'S MARRIAGE.

By the Author of "A FRENCH HEIRESS IN HER OWN CHATEAU."

I.

LETITIA.

"SHALL I tell you what I mean to do, cousin Florinda?" said Miss Monkton, as she sat over the fire one evening in Christmas week.

"If you please, my dear."

"I mean to marry an officer. Then I shall move about with the army in spite of papa. I have some thoughts of Crosby, his own aide-de-camp. What would he say to that, now? I can tell you I have a prodigious fancy for Crosby."

"*Captain* Crosby," said Mrs. Bushe, in the tone of mild remonstrance which was all she ever ventured on with her charge Letitia.

She had been wandering softly round the room in the fire-light, putting the books straight on the table, restoring the contents of Letitia's workbox, which lay tumbled in a confused heap on the sofa. Now she moved forward and stood on the hearthrug, a pale slender woman in a black satin gown, with light hair put plainly back, and worn delicate features, with enough beauty lingering about them to show that twenty years ago she might have been as lovely as Letitia was now.

Crosby, or any other aide-de-camp, ought to have felt himself honoured by Miss Monkton's fancy. She was "fair as the day," as her nurse said, with an old-fashioned bloom of roses in her cheeks, laughing eyes, brown hair with gold threads in it, which she wore gathered up into a mass of short curls, and a grace of movement and attitude which was not affected even by the oddly hideous short-waisted gowns of the time. Mrs. Bushe and she had lived together in this old house, thirty miles from London, for the last ten years, while Sir George Monkton, her father, a distinguished general officer, had been with the army. They had only seen him twice during that time; but he wrote constantly to them both, and ordered every little thing about their household as if he had been living a mile off. Now, at the end of December 1815, they were expecting him to pay them a visit. He had come over from France two or three weeks ago; but with Sir George business always took precedence of pleasure, and other people's business of his own, so that there were all sorts of military affairs to be settled in London before he could take a few weeks' rest and see his daughter.

"Pray don't scorch your face, Letitia," said Mrs. Bushe, moving her slow pensive eyes from the fire to those rosy cheeks in the full glow of it. "I wish your papa to find you looking well."

"Never mind," said Letitia, smiling. "He won't bring Crosby with him."

"You astonish me."

"Well now, cousin Florinda, it is all his own doing. He began three years ago, 'A fine young fellow, Crosby by name, has joined the regiment lately. He is Irish, and I know nothing of his antecedents; but he will make a smart officer.' And you know it has gone on ever since. Crosby here, Crosby there, distinguishing himself over and over again. I know

papa was only too glad to have him for his aide-de-camp when
poor Captain Smith was killed last June. Since then he has
been his right-hand man completely; has even addressed his
letters sometimes—and very well he writes, too."

"All that may be very true," said Mrs. Bushe, looking
down with the faintest smile of amusement, which Letitia did
not see. "But you don't seem to be aware that you are
talking of this gentleman in a very extraordinary way. Let
me assure you that he himself would not be flattered by it, and
your papa would be horrified."

"O, but he would be flattered. Haven't I heard you say
that men are the vainest creatures on earth? Especially
officers. You detest officers, don't you?"

"I think they are not always to be trusted," said cousin
Florinda gravely and coldly. "Before I was married—at
your age—I thought very much as you do."

"Then you can't blame me," said Letitia, who was leaning
her chin on her hands and staring into the fire.

"Dear child," replied cousin Florinda after a moment's
pause, "I trust these ideas of yours may never lead you into
unhappiness like mine."

"O, no," said Letitia, and then she checked herself.
Major Bushe had been the most worthless of men; had
treated his wife unkindly, spent all her money, and left her,
without a farthing, on the charity of her relations. Still his
widow, having loved him in her young days, would not hear
anything said against him now; and Letitia, being given to
thoughtless chattering, often found silence the best refuge
from an almost forbidden subject. She believed in her heart
that poor, pretty, gentle, old cousin Florinda would have
talked a great deal about her past troubles if she had been
encouraged. But Letitia hated feelings, and any talk that was

likely to bring them uppermost; it therefore suited her best to suppose that cousin Florinda preferred living in the present.

They were presently disturbed by a great tramping and rattling outside, and the pealing of a loud bell. Sir George's carriage had driven into the yard. They knew him well enough not to rush out to meet him. Letitia pirouetted round the room; but was standing quite still near the door in her white dress, composed, but with scarlet cheeks and slightly disordered curls, when Sir George walked firmly and quickly up the stone passage, and came into the room.

He was a slight active-looking man of middle height, with gray hair cut close, and a dark reddish complexion. He had taken off his greatcoat, and walked in like anybody else, as if he had been in the house for a week.

"How d'ye do, Florinda?" he said, shaking hands with Mrs. Bushe. "You are very well, I hope. Letty, how d'ye do?"

"How d'ye do, papa?" said Letitia, coming forward with small sliding steps. Her father kissed her, then held her hands and looked at her for a moment.

"You have been roasting your face. A bad thing, especially in cold weather."

"You have had a very cold drive, papa?"

"Nothing worth complaining of," said Sir George.

He sat down, declining the arm-chair that Letitia pushed forward, and taking a high one by the table. Since he had come in, the night somehow seemed much colder; yet they both knew that it was only manner, and that Sir George was really the best man in the world. He talked politics, and told them what he had been doing in London.

"Dinner is waiting, I think," said Mrs. Bushe presently. "I thought you would like to have it as soon as you came in."

"Thank you. Quite unnecessary. I dined in town three

hours ago. But pray don't let me keep you from your dinner," said Sir George, getting up and walking towards the door.

"O no, Sir George. I daresay it is not ready; and in fact Letitia and I have dined. We want nothing more," said Mrs. Bushe, rising too in a flutter, "thank you. If you will excuse me, I'll speak to the servants."

She glided out, full of natural feeling for the cook, who had been doing her very best to welcome the hungry traveller. Last time he had arrived unexpectedly, and dinner had had to be cooked in a hurry at eight o'clock at night. Sir George was one of those men, now and then to be met with, who make no fuss about themselves, and yet give the greatest trouble to everybody.

"Florinda seems rather nervous this evening," said Sir George, looking approvingly at his daughter, who was quietly embroidering a workbag, and did not seem at all disturbed by household cares. "She looks thin. How do you agree?"

"Very well indeed, papa. We never quarrel."

"You obey, do you? Submit to rules? I believe many young women of your age think themselves independent."

"So I am—tolerably independent. I do whatever I please."

"Whatever you please! You are more fortunate than most people, then," said Sir George, smiling for the first time. "And you wish for no change? You told me in a letter last year that this place in winter was a living sepulchre."

"Did I? I forget; but I must have been in a bad temper that day," said Letitia. "The place is not gay, of course; but no, I wish for no change, papa, thank you. Unless——"

"Well!"

"Unless I could go about with you."

"That has been impossible. Now that we have peace, I may take you to Paris next summer."

"O, delightful!" said Letitia, clapping her hands.

"But there is an 'unless' in the case there too."

"What can that be, papa?"

"I shall not explain myself at present. Do you see much of your neighbours at the Castle?"

"We see them occasionally," said Letitia. "But cousin Florinda does not care much for their society—neither do I."

"That is prejudice," says Sir George decisively. "They are excellent people, an old and wealthy family, nothing to be said against them."

"I have nothing to say, except that they are countrified and dull. I assure you, papa, Mrs. Barrett and her daughters think of nothing but making jam and knitting stockings. Mr. Barrett sleeps in his chair all day long, and young Mr. Barrett shoots rabbits."

"Prejudice," says Sir George again. "They are most worthy people."

"Don't you think that worthy and stupid are often only two words for the same thing, papa?" said Miss Monkton, with a mischievous glance of her bright eyes.

Sir George moved from one stiff attitude to another, and frowned.

"Where did you get these ideas? Florinda Bushe is not a fit person to have charge of you."

"O, don't blame her, papa, pray. She is always being shocked, and scolding me. I am very sorry; but I see most of the Barretts over the top of the pew in church, and that makes one feel ill-tempered, you know. They wear such ugly bonnets; but I daresay they may be good. And young Mr. Barrett stares rather."

The General's face softened.

"I have not much acquaintance with the ladies of the family," he said, "but Humphrey Barrett is an excellent fellow. I saw him in town last week; he came very civilly to call upon me. You are quite mistaken, if you think his soul is in his rabbits. And, by the bye, he hopes to have the honour of dancing with you next Wednesday night."

"At their ball," said Letitia.

"Exactly. Are you fond of dancing?"

"O papa, amazingly!"

"You told Humphrey Barrett so one day, when he walked down the road from church with you and Florinda."

"I believe I did."

"Then this will at least show you that he is a good-natured fellow. This ball is given in consequence of that remark of yours. So let me hear no more ungracious speeches about the Barrett family."

Letitia smiled, but without feeling particularly pleased. No arguments, she was sure, could make her think young Barrett anything but an awkward lout. And she did not believe this about the ball, for she felt sure that Mrs. Barrett had mentioned it to cousin Florinda before that Sunday.

The dinner mistake was not the only one made by Mrs. Bushe and her servants that night. The best and largest bedroom in the house had been prepared for Sir George. He had made up his mind that it would be much more convenient to everybody if he slept in a little room near the hall-door, which was at present filled up with old books, boxes, and lumber. It was therefore cleared out and made ready for him. Then when it was finished, and Sir George walked in to look at it, he immediately ordered out the fire and the carpet. His habits were simple, he said. He did not wish to accustom himself to luxuries, or to give any unnecessary trouble.

All being at last arranged, Letitia and her cousin wished Sir George good-night and went upstairs together. Before going on into her own room, which was inside Florinda's, the girl stopped to kiss her and say good-night. Mrs. Bushe was a good deal taller than Letitia. She held her in her arms, and looked down into the bright face with tired loving eyes.

"Cousin Florinda, you look worn out," said Letitia. "Now listen to me. Don't get up to-morrow morning. I will give papa his breakfast."

"I could not desert my post, my dear, thank you."

"O, well, you need not blame me for being obstinate. What plagues men are! Don't you think papa must drive his aide-de-camp quite mad? And who do you suppose he has made into a hero now?"

"I can't guess, indeed," said Mrs. Bushe.

"That stupid heavy fellow, Humphrey Barrett. He saw him in town last week. And what do you think? He told him that this ball of theirs is given in compliment to me. Because I told Humphrey I was fond of dancing. That must be a story, you know. Mrs. Barrett told you of it before."

"She did," said Florinda, colouring. "But to do them justice, her chief idea seemed to be that it would please you."

"O!" said Letitia.

Perhaps Florinda Bushe was scarcely a fit person to have the care of her, for she never could help telling her the truth. Under Letitia's smiling penetrating gaze, no plot, no secret, was safe with her cousin. She looked away, she tried to move aside, but Letitia took hold of her arms and held her fast.

"There is some plot, I see," she said. "And you seem to be in it. You, the Barretts, and papa. What does it all mean?"

"A plot, my dear!" said Florinda. "I can't understand you. You are talking nonsense."

Letitia's laughing face grew graver and more determined.

"A plain question, then—and I'll have a plain answer.

Have you all taken it into your heads that I am to marry young Barrett? Tell me the truth, pray!"

"Letitia, have I ever deceived you?"

"Cousin Florinda, if you ever tried, you never succeeded. Come, you must not be angry. You love me, I know; you don't wish to make me miserable, and the less you say, the more I shall suspect. Unless you tell me the whole truth at once, I won't go to the ball. I'll fall down-stairs and break my leg."

"A sprained ankle would answer the purpose, and be well sooner," said Florinda, smiling faintly. "Well I'll trust to your honour to behave like a gentlewoman. Mrs. Barrett has taken it into her head, certainly; she has hinted as much to me several times. And I suppose her son has too. It seems from what you say that he has made some advances to Sir George, which have not been unfavourably received."

"And they all forget that there is one other person to be consulted," cried Letitia, stamping her foot. "What have I done to be given away to a lout like that! I hate and detest him! How can papa—how can *you* think such a thing possible!"

"He is heir, you see, to a fine property. There is some talk of his standing for the county. His politics and your papa's are the same; and no one has a word to say against his character."

"Ugly wretch!" said Letitia. "I hate these old country families. Their brains are as thick as the mud in their fields. When I want to bury myself alive, I'll do it under pleasanter circumstances. *You* never thought I would marry him, surely?"

Her eyes sparkled indignantly as she looked at her cousin. Florinda kissed her flushed forehead, and answered quietly,

"I hardly thought you would be pleased with the idea.

Now go to bed, my dear child, and to sleep. Of course your own wishes will be consulted."

"I should think so!" said Letitia, beginning to laugh.

Two hours later, Mrs. Bushe stole into her charge's room. Letitia was sleeping like a child, though there was a damp look about the long eyelashes that lay on her rosy cheeks. She moved and smiled as her cousin bent over her. Was she dreaming of the ball?

II.

A HERO IN THE SNOW.

WHEN they came down next morning, it was snowing thickly. Sir George sat in the coldest corner of the library, writing letters, and grumbling about something that Crosby had forgotten. Presently he called Letitia to copy some papers for him, and she set to work at once, writing a neat little hand which satisfied her father. They sat at each end of a table in front of the window, which looked out on a square grass-plot bounded by an ivy-wall. Masses of snow already hung on the ivy, and the north wind had blown a great drift into a corner. It was snowing still, and one or two bold but shivering robins came hopping on the window-sill.

"Poor little things! I'll fetch you some crumbs," said Letitia, who had quite recovered her usual good temper. The idea of Humphrey Barrett was too absurdly impossible to bear the light of day.

"Keep to your writing for the present," said Sir George. "I want those copies as soon as possible."

Presently, having finished another letter, he laid his pen down and leaned back for a minute.

"Imagine a military secretary, or an aide-de-camp, leaving his work to feed robin-redbreasts!" he said, with a good-humoured smile.

"I don't believe that women do their work less well than men, because they are a little soft-hearted and can't endure to see birds starving in the cold," said Letitia.

"There is a time for everything," answered Sir George.

"It must seem rather strange to you, papa, to have me working with you instead of Captain Crosby," said Letitia, after a few minutes of diligent scratching.

"I feel like a man who has lost his right arm," said Sir George thoughtfully. "Very grateful for your help, Letty, all the same."

"You like him very much, then, papa?"

"He has been extremely useful to me. He has a head, which is more than can be said for most young fellows. He will get on. The Duke has noticed him several times. Yes, I value Crosby in spite of his faults."

"What are his faults?"

"Being an Irish adventurer, with all the absurdities of his nation, and nothing in the world but his pay."

"O!" said Letitia, with a slight tone of satisfaction, which Sir George did not notice. If it had struck him, and roused any train of thought, this story would most likely never have been written.

"He is the most hasty-tempered fellow I ever met with," he went on. "A few weeks ago, he turned off a man for robbing him, without any evidence of the fact. All he told me was, that the rascal had a villanous face, and he could believe anything of him. Now that is not justice, and I told Crosby so."

"I should have agreed with him, most likely," said Letitia. "People's faces generally tell the truth."

"That is a very juvenile doctrine," said Sir George smiling.

After another short silence Letitia looked up again.

"Where is Captain Crosby now, papa? In London?"

"Yes; I left him at the hotel."

"Was he going home for New Year's-day?"

"Home, home!" repeated Sir George, with a letter in his hand. "Crosby? Why no. He has no home, I suppose. He is an Irishman."

"But he has a home in Ireland?"

"I never heard of it. He appears to have no relations or connections of any kind. An adventurer—he has to carve his fortunes for himself."

"Poor man!" said Letitia. "And yet he is a gentleman?"

"To be sure," said Sir George.

For the last few minutes his manner had been very absent, and now he began to frown, to mutter, and to twist the letter he held backwards and forwards.

"This must be explained. I have certainly mislaid his last letter. Confound it! what is the use of trying to do business without Crosby! The communication was made to him, too. This is most vexatious!"

"What is it, papa?"

"Business connected with the regiment."

Sir George gave no further explanation, but got up, pushing his chair back so hurriedly that the robins flew away in a fright. He walked once or twice up and down the room, and then stopped by the table.

"Mind, Letitia, I will have no unnecessary fuss. But tell me honestly, would it be great disturbance to Florinda to have a bed made up in some small room for Crosby? He is a soldier, like myself; he wants no luxuries. But I cannot settle this affair without him."

Letitia answered gravely that she had no doubt cousin Florinda would be happy to receive Captain Crosby, or any friend of her papa's.

"Very well," said Sir George. "No extra trouble must be given in the house. I will write to Crosby at once, and send the letter by an express messenger. He will be here to-morrow."

He sat down again at the table.

"Papa," said Letitia, when the letter was half written, "excuse me, shall you take him to the ball? If so, you had better tell him to bring his uniform."

"I suppose they will be glad to see him?" said Sir George doubtfully.

"O, fancy the delight of the Miss Barretts! A new partner, and an officer too!"

"Very true, poor girls. And Crosby is an agreeable fellow," said Sir George, so unsuspiciously that Letitia was ashamed of herself.

A man and horse were sent off to London through the snow.

Miss Monkton, in high spirits, tried on her dress and ornaments, and figured before the glass in her own room, till Mrs. Bushe, who was looking on, gave a little sigh.

"What is the matter?" said Letitia, looking round.

"Nothing, my dear. Only I should like to feel that your thoughts sometimes travelled beyond your own amusement."

"And don't they?" said Letitia. "I expect to amuse many people besides myself, and among them—hush! This ball of Humphrey Barrett's will not be so bad after all."

Mrs. Bushe, in spite of her gentle good-nature, could not bring herself to rejoice in Captain Crosby's coming. Considering Letitia's excitability, and the fancy she had already taken to the young officer, she thought it a serious risk. She debated with herself whether she ought to have warned Sir George of this before the messenger started : but Sir George had said so firmly that it was a matter of necessity, and whatever nonsense Letitia might talk, there could be no doubt of the real dignity and honourableness of her nature. Still she was a very head-strong girl, as no one knew better than Florinda.

Miss Monkton was a little vexed by her cousin's want of sympathy. She took off all her finery and wrapped herself up in a scarlet cloak and hood, looking like winter in its prettiest form. Then she went out and walked about the garden, dis-daining to stay in the paths that had been swept for her, and wandering away into the shrubberies. There she walked under the trees, which now and then played at snow-balling, dropping soft white lumps from their heavy-laden twigs upon her cloak.

It was a pleasant afternoon, not very cold. All the clouds had cleared away, and the yellow sun, hanging low in the south-west, shone softly in a pale-blue sky. The shrubbery, along which Letitia was walking, bordered the road for some distance : this was to her left. To her right, beyond the belt of trees and bushes, a little river moved slowly, black by con-trast with its glistening white banks, and the great field that stretched away in front of the house and garden. At the farthest end of the shrubbery, which she presently reached, a light wooden bridge crossed the river, leading into the field, and some rather crazy wooden palings and a shallow backwater, partly frozen over, divided her from the road. Letitia stood still a moment looking about her, and was rather startled in that quiet place by hearing voices on the road a little way off.

In those terrible times of distress the roads to London were full of tramps and beggars of every kind, and Letitia was never allowed to walk out by herself beyond the grounds. Even here in the shrubbery any determined beggar might reach her very easily, and she was a long way from the house. But that certainly was not the voice of a beggar. Letitia stepped from the path, and made her way through the snowy bushes till she could see down the road. A postchaise was stopping there, with a pair of tired-looking horses. The driver was busy examining the feet of one of them, and the passenger was standing by him on the snowy road, a good deal interested in what was going on.

"Have you never been on this road before then?" Letitia heard him say, in a clear, pleasant, impatient voice.

The driver grumbled something in answer.

"What a fool you were, then, not to ask your way in that last village we passed through! We may have miles further to go, and the horse is dead lame. Your looking at his feet will do no good. I see a house through the trees up there. I shall go on and ask the way."

He acted so instantly on this determination, that before Letitia had quite retired into the shrubbery he had caught a glimpse of her red cloak. He came close to the water's edge and stopped. Some instinct made her stop too.

"Will you do me a great favour?" he said, in so courteous and agreeable a voice that Letitia came quite frankly forward to the palings, and made him a polite bow. Seeing this little picture of a lady smiling in her scarlet hood among the snow, he took off his hat with almost the air of a Frenchman, and looked at her for an instant in silence.

Letitia afterwards remembered an unpleasant thought that came over her just then.

"O dear! I hoped Crosby might be something like this, and there certainly can't be two of them."

The hero of the post-chaise was a tall young man, with

decided and handsome features, a charming smile, and black hair curling closely. There was something slightly foreign about him, a lively eagerness of manner, which showed itself in the first moment of acquaintance. In his talk, too, there was a little accent of some kind; Letitia hardly knew what. Her imagination had no time to work; the stranger revealed himself so soon.

"I shall be happy to do anything I can," said Letitia sweetly.

"A thousand thanks. Can you tell me how far I am from Sir George Monkton's?"

"O, what fun! Is it possible!" thought Letitia, opening her eyes. She smiled as she answered,

"You are there already. The house is at the end of this shrubbery; you see it through the trees."

"I had no idea I was so fortunate. Is it possible, then, that I have the honour of speaking to Miss Monkton?"

Letitia graciously smiled her assent.

"Allow me to introduce myself. You may have heard my name—Crosby."

"O yes. Papa often talks of you."

"Does he, indeed! May I send the chaise on to the house? I will be with you directly."

Letitia stood still in her snowy corner, in quite a whirl of delighted amusement. This was better than ten balls. Captain Crosby rushed down the road, and returned the next moment with a roll of papers in his hand.

"How will you get across the water?" said Letitia, seeing that he quite meant to join her in the shrubbery.

"Water! O, here are stepping stones."

Letitia was not aware of their existence; but somehow, with one or two splashes, and a hand on the fence, Captain Crosby was by her side.

"You have chosen a snowy walk," he said.

"The snow comes so seldom that I quite enjoy it," said Letitia.

They turned into the path, and walked slowly back towards the house. Captain Crosby's business with his chief did not seem to be anything very urgent, but presently he remembered that his appearance might as well be accounted for.

"I must explain my sudden arrival," he said. "Sir George does not expect me, I know."

"You did not meet his messenger?" said Letitia, looking up.

"His messenger!"

"He found this morning that he could not do without you, and sent off a man to ask you to come down at once and bring some papers that he wanted. So we expected you to-morrow, though not to-day."

"You have told me the only thing I wanted to make me perfectly happy. Those very papers are in this packet. I have information for Sir George, too, which I should not have cared to send by letter."

There was a moment's silence. Letitia was aware by this time that Captain Crosby had beautiful dark-blue eyes, and certainly a most graceful and charming manner. She was also aware that he expressed, without words, a deep admiration for herself. All this was very delightful, and the least bit confusing. She walked along, looking down at the snow. Captain Crosby looked at her.

"I hardly know how I shall get back to town to-night," he said. "One of my horses has fallen lame, most fortunately— I beg your pardon a thousand times. You may be of a different opinion."

Letitia was too truthful to be a flirt, and had had no experience.

"To-night! I should think not!" she said. "We are going to-morrow to Mrs. Barrett's ball, and papa said you would go with us."

"I am immensely pleased to hear it," said Captain Crosby.

His want of home and connections did not seem to have any effect on his spirits; there was a free frank light-heartedness about him which made it quite impossible to treat him with any stiffness. A dangerous adventurer, certainly, as Mrs. Bushe had feared, and she, with her larger experience of men, might not have felt Letitia's ready trust in him.

Mrs. Barrett's ball was an amusing subject to talk about. By the time they reached the house the General's daughter and his aide-de-camp were on a footing of intimate acquaintance that Humphrey Barrett might in vain have hoped to reach with Miss Monkton.

Sir George was very glad to see Crosby, told him so, and sent off another messenger after the first for his baggage. Crosby himself was all that everyone could wish : devoted to business with his chief; full of polite attention to Mrs. Bushe, who had to confess that he was very agreeable. And as to Letitia, when she saw what was so plain, that evening and the next day, that he belonged to her all the time, and watched for every opportunity of being near her and talking to her, she felt happy and a little frightened, and did not quite know what to make of this almost magical fulfilment of her wish.

III.

MRS. BARRETT'S BALL.

Sir George Monkton's carriage and horses had a hard task in ploughing through the snow in the hilly lanes that led up to the Castle. The drive was twice as long as usual, but the people in the carriage bore it patiently enough. Even Letitia did not complain.

Captain Crosby, though perhaps he hardly told himself so, would have been quite happy to sit opposite her for any number of hours, as long as the lamplight just shone on her face in such a perfectly becoming manner. He had admired her very much from the first, but to-night she was lovelier than ever. Crosby considered himself a great critic, and when she had come down into the drawing-room before they started, he had been at once struck by the good taste which had dressed her simply in white, with quiet little ornaments that any girl might have worn. Crosby was one of those Irishmen who know the right thing instinctively when they see it, without any theories to found their knowledge on. But people were not so much bothered with theories in those days; they liked and disliked by instinct or tradition. In some way Crosby was satisfied, and made up his mind, perhaps presumptuously, when one considers all the facts of the case. He was turning over different plans in his head as they sat in the carriage, and was therefore a little more silent than he had been before.

Letitia herself seemed to be in a wonderful state of happy excitement. She chattered away almost faster and more freely than Sir George approved; but even he could not find it in his heart to check her. So they all arrived very cheerfully at the Castle.

This was a large square house, built on the top of a hill. The present Squire Barrett's great-grandfather had lived in the remains of an old castle on the same site; but his son, a man of more enlightened mind, not being able to put up with the ghosts, rats, and other inconveniences that he found there, pulled it down and did away with it altogether, and built a most satisfactory family mansion in its place. One might have hunted England over before one found anything much squarer, uglier, or more prosaic; but the Barretts were a good sensible old family, and their motto had always been " use before ornament." So the present generation never complained of their house, or did anything but honour their grandfather for having built it.

The carriage drew up at a broad flight of steps, covered with an awning. Sir George and his aide-de-camp got out at once. At Mrs. Barrett's request they were both in uniform, and very well they looked. Sir George gave his arm to Mrs. Bushe, and took her into the house. Captain Crosby had the happiness of following with Letitia.

" Do you mean to enjoy the evening ? " he said to her.

" O yes, indeed.   I do love a ball."

" You will give me the honour of the first dance ? "

" Certainly, with pleasure."

" I'd have gone a thousand miles, of course, with this at the end of it; but on the whole I believe I have no passion for balls.   It is a moral defect, I know; you need not tell me so. I am very much ashamed."

" Ah," said Letitia, " but you have been to so many, no doubt.   This is only the fourth in my life."

" I wish it was only the fourth in mine, or the first, for that matter," said Captain Crosby.   " There was one other, though, that interested me, in a different way.   The Duchess of Richmond's ball at Brussels, the night before Quatre Bras."

" Ah, you were there ! "

The deep enthusiastic interest in Letitia's eyes, as she lifted them to his face, would have been too much for any soldier.

" Yes. It has been described to you often, no doubt, by Sir George and everybody else."

" People have told me about it, but I should like to hear again. How splendid and how awful it must have been, the distant cannon breaking in upon the music ! " said Letitia, in a low voice.

" Yes ; even to those who expected it, as many of us did. I remember poor Smith—my predecessor, you know. He told me, before we went to the ball, of his engagement to a girl we all admired prodigiously. There he was, of course, dancing with her, she looking more beautiful, more happy than any one in the room, and he such a fine manly fellow. I caught sight of her at midnight, when they had just parted ; it was indeed a change ; she never saw him again, you know. For- give me ; I have no right to sadden you like this. For Heaven's sake, smile ! Such things must happen in time of war, and if a man dies a death that his friends need not be ashamed of, why, then—How could I be such a fool ! "

Letitia had hung down her head, her cheeks had lost all their pretty colour, and her eyes had filled with tears. They were slowly crossing the wide hall, on their way to the drawing- room, where their party had just been announced. Captain Crosby bent towards his companion with a smile of tender interest and admiration, and slightly pressed the hand that lay on his arm. At the moment Letitia could not speak, but she recovered herself almost directly.

Near the drawing-room door several servants were standing Captain Crosby stared so hard at one of them that the man bowed to him. He frowned, and returned the salute slightly. Then he and Letitia, following Sir George and Mrs. Bushe,

found themselves being received by Mrs. Barrett in the drawing-
room.

She was a short, plain, sensible-looking woman, and seemed
the brightest of the family, though her manner was provokingly
downright, and devoid of any kind of "nonsense." Her two
daughters were large fair girls, who looked meek and suppressed,
as if all the nonsense had been crushed out of them from
childhood. Her husband was tall, square, and heavy, and had
not much to say. Her only son, the Humphrey of Letitia's
aversion, was a tall fellow too, very like his father, but with
more life and quickness in his eyes, and a truly English
haughtiness of manner, with something of the bully in it
towards people he chose to consider beneath him. He wore
his scarlet hunting-coat, and looked well enough, but could
not get rid of a countrified air, which was very evident in
contrast with Captain Crosby's elegance.

Nearly everybody in the county was assembled in the Castle
drawing-room that evening. Music was just beginning to
strike up in the adjoining ballroom. Great fires were blazing;
Christmas wreaths hung about in all directions. The peace
with France had raised everybody's spirits, and it seemed quite
right to welcome in the new year with music and dancing.

Humphrey Barrett walked up to Miss Monkton, as she sat
by Mrs. Bushe, Sir George having taken Crosby away to
introduce him to some of the gentlemen, and asked her for the
first dance with a confident air; he evidently thought it nothing
but his right.

"Thank you," said Letitia; "but I have promised it to
Captain Crosby."

"That's too bad," said Humphrey, trying to hide his disgust
under a joke. "You should not have let a stranger forestall
your neighbours."

Letitia raised her eyebrows and smiled slightly, but gave no answer to this ill-mannered speech. Humphrey saw that he had made a bad beginning. He asked her for the next dance, which she was obliged to promise him, and then stood by her, talking rather tiresomely about the weather, till Captain Crosby came to carry his partner away.

The ball went on like other balls. Letitia danced several times with Crosby, and several times with Humphrey Barrett, and once or twice with other gentlemen. She was the beauty of the evening, and many people would have been only too glad to dance with her, if they had seen any chance for themselves. Perhaps some of the humbler ones were dissuaded by the scowls of young Barrett, who stood by the wall during two or three of her dances with Crosby, and glowered after them in a way that even shocked his mother, who came up and begged him to dance with Miss So-and-so.

Crosby behaved much more philosophically; perhaps one can understand that. If his chief admiration was for Miss Monkton, his politeness, his pleasant talk and perfect dancing were quite at the service of any young lady to whom he was introduced. He made the Miss Barretts smile and blush, brightened the shy and stiff, laughed with the lively. If it was true that he did not care for balls, no one there, at least, seemed to find more enjoyment in this one.

Sir George sat down to play whist with some of the elder people. Mrs. Bushe sat with some of the other ladies, and watched the dancing. They did not find her very sociable, for her eyes and thoughts were following Letitia, who came back to her now and then looking more happy and brilliant than ever.

Once Letitia was sitting down by her cousin, and Captain Crosby was standing by, waiting for one of their dances. They were rather silent at the moment, for the continual chatter of the rest of the room did not seem to be necessary here. Letitia was leaning back fanning herself, and Crosby was looking at her, and talking in a rather broken way to Mrs. Bushe, who answered him absently. Humphrey Barrett, who had been watching them from a distance, came up and stood by them. The slightest smile curled Crosby's lips as he turned to speak to him.

"I saw a man among your servants in the hall," he said, "who was with me not long ago."

"With you!" said Humphrey.

"Yes. Roger Vance."

"His last place was with Major Clark. I had his character from him. He is my own man."

"Do you like him?"

"Capital fellow—can do anything."

"So he can," said Crosby. "He was with me six months, though, after he left Major Clark; but I suppose he thought it not worth while to apply to me."

"Major Clark gave me a very satisfactory account of him," said Humphrey, with some stiffness.

Crosby took no further notice of him, but turned to Miss Monkton, and led her away to the dance. As they walked along the room, he said to her:

"Mr. Barrett seems completely satisfied with that man of his, but I could tell him that he is a rascal. I turned him off for theft. And in my opinion his character is written on his face."

"Why did you not say so?"

"One has to consider before one takes a fellow's character away. It would deprive him, you see, of all chance in life. You can see the justice of that, I am quite sure. He will perhaps keep honest now, for his own sake."

It appeared to Letitia that her hero was as perfect in justice and mercy as in more showy virtues.

Meanwhile, Humphrey sat down by Mrs. Bushe, and began to entertain her.

"Which do you like best now, soldiers or civilians? Of course soldiers are the most attractive. I may wear a red coat, but never so smart a one as his."

"The coat has not much to do with it, I should think," said Mrs. Bushe, smiling.

"O, I beg your pardon, but it has, in most ladies' eyes. They seldom look beyond the outside of a man—more's the pity. But you have not answered my question."

"I have been connected with soldiers all my life," said Mrs. Bushe, in a low voice. "It is quite natural that I should prefer them, is it not?"

"Well, I don't know. Now I should have thought that the more you saw of all that glitter, the more you would despise it."

"That," said Mrs. Bushe, "is taking for granted that because a gentleman serves the king, and wears a handsome uniform, he must wear under it a bad heart and a weak mind. And that is—well, it is not generally the case, I think, Mr. Barrett."

Humphrey looked at her doubtfully, but did not speak.

"A gentleman is a gentleman, and a good man is a good man," she went on, rather prosaically, "whether he wears a red coat or a black one. I do not see why we should set soldiers on one side, as people do, and civilians on the other. There is no real reason for it."

"Except that it is the fashion, and that rules everybody," said Humphrey.

Then after a minute's pause he asked her abruptly who Captain Crosby was.

"I can tell you nothing about his family, for I know nothing," said Mrs. Bushe. "He is an Irishman, and a good officer."

" Sir George, I suppose, knows more ? "

" At any rate he knows enough to satisfy him," said Mrs. Bushe gravely. " If you feel interested in Captain Crosby you can inquire of him."

" Well, I don't know about that. He must know of course, or he would not let him dance all night with his daughter."

" An aide-de-camp is like the son of the house," said Mrs. Bushe. " There is nothing remarkable in that."

" Ah, but you may nurse a serpent that will sting you," answered Humphrey solemnly.

" That is a very disagreeable notion."

" It is. Confoundedly disagreeable. But you can't deny that it's true."

Humphrey now seemed to have exhausted his powers of conversation. He got up and walked off along the room, as if the sight of the dancers was too much for a reasonable being.

Mrs. Bushe could not feel sorry for Humphrey, but one must confess that she felt anxious about Letitia, and watched her and Crosby together as nervously as he did. Letitia's happiness, and Crosby's devotion, could hardly escape the blindest eyes. However, Sir George presently came back into the ball room, and Mrs. Bushe was glad that he should see for himself; she could not make up her mind to speak to him, to bring poor dear Letitia into a scrape. One ought not to be surprised if girls were a little thoughtless and gave themselves up to the pleasure of the moment, without considering possible consequences.

Everybody agreed that it was a delightful ball, though the drive home was rather more silent than the drive there had been.

Letitia took off her wraps, and came and stood by her cousin's fire, gazing into it for a minute or two rather dreamily.

It was so unusual for her to look thoughtful that Mrs. Bushe was rather alarmed.

" Are you tired, Letitia ? " she said.

" No.   Cousin Florinda, I think Humphrey Barrett is without exception the most odious man——"

" My dear, after all their hospitality ! "

" Well, I cannot help it.   A man must be odious who sees you don't like him, and yet plagues and torments you with his politeness.   I hope I shall never go to the house again."

Mrs. Bushe was silent, and only hoped that this violent hatred of Humphrey Barrett did not mean an opposite feeling for somebody else.

" Well, poor man," she said at last, as Letitia also remained silent, " it is a pity that he troubled himself to be attentive to you.   He meant well, no doubt."

" He certainly is the most disagreeable person I ever met," said Letitia.   " Just look at the contrast between him and Captain Crosby."

" My dear, such remarks on gentlemen do not come well from a young girl like you."

Mrs. Bushe spoke very gravely and gently.   Letitia coloured, but looked up with her fearless open eyes.

" You think I don't know what I am talking about, and am only fanciful," she said.   " But I have good reason, I can tell you.   Did you see that little affair at the cloak-room door ? "

" No ; what was it ? " said Florinda, instantly interested, and forgetting her function of reprover.

" Well, you had gone on with Mr. Barrett.   Humphrey, I declare to you, was nowhere to be seen.   Papa was in the middle of the hall, talking to that old Admiral.   Captain Crosby had my shawl in his hand, and was just going to put it over my shoulders, when Humphrey started round some corner and literally snatched it from him. 'That is my business, sir,' he said in the voice of an old bear. O, cousin Florinda, Captain Crosby behaved so well. I was in a horrid fright, as you may suppose. I turned round and looked at them, and even thought of crossing over at once to papa, for their faces were as red as fire. But he saw that I was frightened, and he said in the coolest quietest way, ' Pardon me, sir. I was not aware that you were close by.' Humphrey did not say a word; but the scowl on his face was too hideous and dreadful. I was obliged to take his arm, and to let him bring me down the steps, but I assure you I could hardly say good-night civilly. My dear, it was plain to me that Humphrey Barrett wanted to pick a quarrel with Captain Crosby; and he would have succeeded, too, if I had not been there."

"I am glad Captain Crosby behaved so well—so like a gentleman."

" I wonder if he will say anything about it to papa ? "

" I think not. No; he will probably never mention it again. I am very sorry, my dear, that you should have been so upset. Mr. Humphrey Barrett will be sorry too, I daresay, to-morrow."

" Not he ; it was just like him," said Letitia. " Tell me, cousin Florinda,"—laughing a little,—" is that a usual way of —of—trying to make oneself agreeable to a lady ? "

" Not if one thinks about it, I imagine. But there are things, you know, which put people out of sorts and make them forget themselves. Probably the poor young man did not enjoy the ball quite so much as he expected."

" Then I am sure he was very selfish," said Letitia. Her good spirits seemed to have returned ; she smiled sweetly, and kissed her cousin in a sudden little overflow of happiness and affection. " Good-night. I'm going to bed," said she ; " but I can't feel sure about sleeping."

Mrs. Bushe would not keep her, and dared not ask any more questions about her enjoyment of the ball. But she stole into the inner room on her nightly visit an hour later, and found her dear charge sleeping peacefully.

IV.

CROSBY IN DIFFICULTIES.

SIR GEORGE and his aide-de-camp sat together next morning in the library, writing letters. The sun was shining outside and Letitia in her scarlet cloak passed like a winter fairy up and down the white paths. Once she came so near the windows that Crosby's eyes met hers, and they both smiled and coloured a little at the happy accident. Sir George, who with all his quick sight in military matters—perhaps because of it—was wonderfully blind in such things as these, went on writing large and black and saw nothing. Presently he folded his last letter, addressed and sealed it, got up, walked along the room and back again.

"You had a pleasant evening, Crosby ?" he said. "I did not know you were so much of a dancing man."

There was some consciousness in Crosby's bright blue eyes as he looked up at his chief.

"Well, sir, it was a very pleasant party," he said, smiling. " At these country houses one does not always meet so many pretty and well-dressed people. The ladies were very agreeable too, and drew one out in spite of oneself."

" Don't make excuses. I was glad to see that you entered into it heartily. What did you think of the Barretts themselves ?

My own opinion of them is pretty decided; but I should be glad to hear yours."

"They seem to be—excellent people," said Crosby.

"You are not so foolish as my daughter is—to be influenced by looks, and so on."

"Looks!" said Crosby, more cheerfully. "The young ladies are very good-looking, and Mrs. Barrett has no doubt been handsome. Good forehead, good nose, some character in her face."

Sir George smiled.

"Poor Mrs. Barrett! Don't know about that. But the girls certainly have good figures and good complexions. And Barrett told me they would have seven or eight hundred a year each. Not a bad recommendation. If it was not so very much better for young men in our profession to be unmarried, I should say you could not do a wiser thing."

"Good heavens, sir!" muttered Crosby.

"That had not occurred to you? Well, perhaps you are right. Did you make much acquaintance with young Barrett?"

"Not very much."

Sir George was marching slowly up and down a small space between the table and the fire. Crosby in his place at the other side of the table, leaned his head on his hand, and stared half in amusement, half in alarm, at his chief's straight tight figure, at the sharply cut mouth from which such strange things came out. Marry one of the Miss Barretts! Was Sir George really so blind? Or—horrid thought suddenly flashing in—was Letitia's fate in any fearful way decided already? He must know that at all costs; and then—Crosby against the world!

"Young Barrett won't set the Thames on fire, I suspect," he said presently.

"Now, there I believe you to be mistaken," said Sir George, suddenly turning upon him. "These hasty judgments generally are. I don't mean to say that there are not many cleverer men in England than Humphrey Barrett. You yourself have much more brilliancy, quickness, that kind of thing. But for sound sense, Crosby, for knowing the right thing and doing it, for resolution and independence of character, for making his way— and that's a talent in itself—I would back Humphrey against you."

"I am sorry you think me such a fool, sir," said Crosby, smiling.

"You know what I think of you well enough. We won't argue that point. All I say is that Humphrey has the talents most useful to himself. You, my dear Crosby, have those that are pleasantest to me. I should be confoundedly sorry to have an obstinate dog like Humphrey for my aide-de-camp."

"I am obliged to you," said Crosby, quite touched ; for this was a great deal from Sir George.

"These Barretts are an old family," the General went on. "And in one thing they are very different from most old families : they have always been careful people, and every generation is richer than the one before it. When Humphrey marries, his father means to allow him five thousand a year."

"Very handsome," said Crosby, as Sir George paused. "And being such a prudent fellow he won't spend it foolishly."

"No."

Sir George poked the fire, and stood looking into it as he went on talking.

"I had a good deal of talk with Mr. Barrett last night on these matters. He broached the subject himself. You know me well enough to be aware that I am not a rich man, Crosby, and that it is—a—advisable that Letitia should marry well. She has no idea of household management; it is not in her character, and Mrs. Bushe has not succeeded in doing her much good in that way. Now this is a very good match for her. It has been laid before me in the most open and honourable way, both by Humphrey Barrett and his father. Their ideas are most liberal—"

Crosby jumped up, and interrupted his chief with an exclamation,

"Humphrey Barrett marry Miss Monkton!"

"Why not?" said Sir George.

"Forgive me, sir. One sometimes feels surprise without being able to give a reason. It seemed somehow incongruous," said the young man.

"Incongruous or not—I don't understand your modern phraseology; and what you mean by 'incongruous' is a mystery to me—however it may strike you, it is very nearly a settled thing. I expect Humphrey here this afternoon, and I hope at least, from my long knowledge of Mrs. Bushe, that she has brought Letitia up to consider obedience a duty. Old-fashioned, I know; but I am not aware that the Ten Commandents have yet been done away with. Perhaps you are surprised at my mentioning them in common life. Incongruous, is it?"

"Not at all, sir. You are very good to place so much confidence in me. I can only hope that Miss Monkton will be as happy as—she deserves to be."

After this Captain Crosby escaped from the library, and went for a walk to cool his brain and decide what was to be done.

He did not believe for an instant that a spirited girl like Letitia would let herself be married to a clodhopping lout like Humphrey Barrett; but there was no knowing to what lengths Sir George, with his military ideas, would carry parental authority, and Mrs. Bushe was too timid to interfere.

" My lovely darling, there is only me to save to you," Crosby soliloquised; " and by heaven it shall be done! O, if it were but six weeks hence! The three years will be over then, and I shall defy Humphrey Barrett and all his advantages! But what is to be done now? I must wait a little. I must see the turn things are taking—how she likes the lout's visit this afternoon—she hated him cordially enough last night, thick-headed clown! I wish I had been hanged twenty times before I laid that wager. I might have known it would bring me into some fool's scrape like this. But after all it is worth any trouble to win such a sweet angel as this. My wit against Barrett's not a bad encounter for me."

It seemed as if Captain Crosby had not a bad opinion of himself. Perhaps a little boastfulness is among the faults of his charming race; but in a perfect gentleman like him it never could offend anyone, and was only in fact a happy courage and confidence in himself.

He took a very long walk, thinking that he might as well be out of the way in the afternoon. Humphrey Barrett and himself would be better apart. So, having started before one o'clock, he wandered all round the country, very much to the surprise of those country-folks who met him making his way through their snowy lanes.

He had to ask his way several times, but did not get much information from the shy stolid people. One friend he made however, a sturdy old farmer, who overtook him driving home from market in his smart gig, drawn by a strong handsome horse which Crosby noticed and admired. In reply to his question about the way, the farmer told him to jump up; and for four miles or so they drove together, talking in the most friendly manner, till they came near a picturesque mass of stone farmhouse and buildings, with a square garden bordered by clipped yew-trees. It was already almost dusk, and the cheerfullest firelight gleamed out from the large kitchen window across the yard.

" Yon's my house," said the farmer. " My old woman will be glad to see ye, sir, if you'll turn in with me and have something to warm ye before you go on further."

" No, thank you, not to-day," said Crosby. " It is getting late, and I must go on, though I feel very much tempted to accept your kindness."

" Well, sir, if you're in this country again, and will give us a look any day, we shall be right glad to see you and talk a bit more over the war. I'm Farmer Pratt, and my house is called Jack's Croft."

" Thank you, Farmer Pratt," said Crosby. " I shall be glad to renew my acquaintance with you, and with this capital horse of yours too."

As he walked on down the road, while the farmer turned into his yard, he could not help looking back at the homestead as it lay there among its fields with a few thatched cottages near it, all, for that time and that county, so tidy and comfortable. In contrast, at least, with certain farms that this young Irishman had in his mind's eye.

The white smoke curled so slowly and contentedly up into the soft gray air ; the windows glowed red ; the old dog had come out wagging his tail to welcome his master home, and now stood looking after the stranger who had gone on his way ; the great army of brown stacks defended the house on one side, the garden-walls and trees on the other ; all was safe and strong and peaceful. Crosby looked, and then turned and walked on with long quick steps towards the chief object of his thoughts. What was she doing now ?

V.

CROSBY'S CONFIDANTE.

THERE was something electric in the atmosphere of Sir George Monkton's household that evening. A storm was brewing, Crosby perceived, if it had not already begun. Sir George himself was silent and sulky; Letitia was sulky too and miserable; Mrs. Bushe was in a state of distress, casting anxious imploring looks from one to the other. Crosby talked, and she did her best to answer him, though feebly and absently. Letitia would not look up or speak.

After dinner Sir George had nothing to say; but leaned back in a chair by the fire and closed his eyes, a wonderful proceeding for any one so upright and lively. Crosby presently went into the drawing-room, and found Mrs. Bushe there alone. She glanced up rather nervously when he came in, and went on with her knitting.

"Sir George is not sociable this evening," he said presently; "so I have left him to his thoughts."

"Ah—yes—so I see," said Mrs. Bushe.

A silence of several minutes. Then Crosby, who was standing by the chimneypiece, bent towards his companion with a sudden gravity and earnestness of manner.

"Mrs. Bushe, may I confide in you?"

"I think you had better not, indeed, Captain Crosby." Florinda coloured, and answered hastily. But something in the young man's face seemed to appeal to her better feelings, and she went on, "For heaven's sake oblige me by avoiding these subjects! Say nothing. You can only make us all more unhappy than we are."

"That would grieve me indeed. I do not quite agree with

you; but I will be silent as to myself, if you wish it, for the present. I'll only ask you—what is it all about?"

"O, you know very well," said Mrs. Bushe.

"Was young Barrett here this afternoon?"

Mrs. Bushe nodded.

"Sir George told me this morning that he was coming. And Miss Monkton? You are too kind to keep me in a state of uncertainty."

"I really don't know, Captain Crosby. However, if Sir George told you so much—well, poor Letitia is not in good spirits, as you saw at dinner. She cannot bring herself to agree with her father in this affair. She is not so submissive, poor dear girl, as—Sir George is inclined to be angry with her. I am most deeply grieved. I can't think that he will insist."

"No, he will never do anything quite so barbarous; it is impossible," said Crosby. "Now, I entreat you, listen to me. You understand *my* detestation of this young Barrett. Do you think Sir George's opinion of me is good enough to let me also come forward—to let his daughter choose between us?"

Mrs. Bushe lifted her eyes slowly, looked at him, smiled, and shook her head. Poor dear Letitia, the choice would be only too easily made! Crosby, with every movement full of grace and distinction, with his handsome face full of eager generous excitement, his eyes bright with the true spirit of a lover in the olden times, ready to go through any danger for his lady's sake, to fight single-handed with a thousand men. Florinda was very sentimental, and of course he had all her feelings on his side.

"I know quite well," she said, "how highly Sir George thinks of you. If it was *only* personal! But you see there are so many things to be considered."

"To be sure," said Crosby. "But you don't think all the

advantages are on one side ? You think there would be a chance for me ? "

"Now you want me to pay you a compliment," said Florinda. "It is not a good thing; but I will say that I really wish you were Mr. Barrett, because I fear he will succeed in the end."

"He will not, he shall not, Mrs. Bushe!" answered Crosby. "Thank you; but indeed I would not change places with Barrett if he were three times as rich as he is. It would not answer at all. You don't understand me now, but you will some day. And you really think Sir George has made up his mind so strongly? There are other minds besides Sir George's. And if I chose I could make him change his."

"Then I wonder that you don't," said Mrs. Bushe, justly regarding this as a piece of Irish bravado. "Seriously, though, I do feel very friendly towards you, and I think it is a sad pity that you have set your heart on this. You astonish me a little too. For surely it would hardly be prudent in you to think of marrying—a girl like dear Letitia, too, who has no idea of the value of money, or anything else. I know what it is to be young and romantic," Florinda went on, slightly bending her head. "No one can enter into the feelings of young people more than I do, or know better how the wildest foolishness seems the only good and right and necessary thing. I have been afraid of this—your allowing yourself to become attached to Letitia. Sir George, I think, ought to have considered it too. Nothing so natural; yet unfortunately, you see, nothing so hopeless. Unless by some magic art you could, as you say, make Sir George change his mind."

"Ah, well," said Crosby, who had listened to her soft voice very patiently, "I am not at liberty to say much, but this I will say. I shall never ask a lady to do anything wild or foolish in marrying me. Could this Barrett affair be put a stop to for six weeks or so, do you think ? "

Mrs. Bushe was slightly startled by his manner in asking the last question: he looked up so suddenly, as if a new idea had flashed across him. She thought the poor young man was a little touched in his brain by the imminent loss of Letitia.

"I hardly see how it could be," she said. "What good would that do, except putting things off a little?"

Crosby did not answer this.

"What would Miss Monkton herself say to me, do you think?" he asked presently, with another quick look.

"Dear me," said Florinda, colouring, "I really can't answer that question."

"But everything depends on that, you know," said Crosby. "I know at least from you, and from herself last night, what she thinks of Barrett. Now what does she think of me?"

As Crosby's good angel—I think it was he—would have it, the drawing-room door was just then opened rather quickly, and Letitia herself came in. All her brightness had deserted her. She walked across the room, with heavy eyelids lowered, took up a screen, and sat down by the fire.

"What were you talking about?" she said, as the two who were there already fell into a rather awkward silence.

"I will tell you," said Crosby, his voice trembling a little. "I was asking Mrs. Bushe for a little encouragement, which she has hardly given me; yet I can't keep silence for want of it. I was asking her what you thought of me. Now I ask you."

"Captain Crosby, for shame!" murmured Florinda.

It is doubtful whether either of them heard her.

"What I think of you!" said Letitia, looking up at him as he stood beside her, with the smile that had faded alive again in her eyes. "I think you—hardly need ask that. We are very good friends, are we not?"

"I hope so," said Crosby. "But I want something more.

LETITIA INTERRUPTS AN INTERESTING CONVERSATION.

I can't talk of being 'good friends' with the star that must
rule my whole life, when I see its light on the point of being
extinguished for ever for me. Will you let me tell you how I
admire, adore you, and what agony it gives me to hear of such
plans for you ? "

He spoke low and very earnestly. Poor dear Letitia, wildly
conscious of a happiness almost too great for her, and at the
same time of the deep black gulf of impossibility between her
and it, rose up from her chair with a little cry, knelt down by
Florinda, and hid her face in her lap. To Mrs. Bushe the
moment was agonising ; her duty to Sir George in conflict
with her sympathy for these two, touched beyond expression
by Letitia's movement, by Crosby's appealing eyes.

"Will you not give me any answer ? " he said, after one
long minute of silence, during which Florinda bent over the
girl with her arms clasped round her.

"O, what am I to say ? " whispered Letitia ; but to this
Mrs. Bushe could give no response.

Crosby waited a moment, and then said,

"As to what you will say to me, I must leave that to yourself. I should like you to say to your father, 'I cannot make
this marriage you have planned for me ; you must let me
marry the man I love—Gerald Crosby.'"

Letitia lifted up her lovely face then, and, still holding her
cousin with one hand, gave the other to him with a look that
told him all he wanted to know.

"Yes," she said.

The person who seems most to deserve one's sympathy at
that moment is Mrs. Bushe. What ought she to have done ?

VI.

AN AWKWARD SECRET.

CROSBY would have found it a much easier business to storm a dozen French batteries one by one than to go to Sir George, against all the opposing circumstances, and ask him for his daughter. He had to do it, however, and he did it the next morning in the library. He told Sir George that ever since he had first had the honour of meeting Miss Monkton his affection had been unalterably hers. He talked rather grandly, while Sir George sat gravely listening to him, and ended by saying that he had the happiness of knowing that his affection was returned. Sir George was never violent; but this was a little too much for him. He used a few strong words, and asked whether Captain Crosby considered this the conduct of a gentleman.

"Indeed, that I do, sir," answered Crosby promptly, with all the air of his country. "Was I to stand by and see a lovely young lady sacrificed in a match that she abhors? That is asking too much of human nature."

"And I suppose it would equally have been asking too much to ask you, in your position of confidence and with your doubtful prospects, not to fall in love with my daughter, or at least to hold your tongue upon it," said Sir George.

"I should have been silent for some time longer," said Crosby, "had it not been for this Barrett affair, which made all my hopes depend on speaking at once."

Sir George was silent for a minute or two. He was evidently very much vexed; but Crosby thought that on the whole there was no danger of being turned out of the house. His chief, in fact, was as fond of him as he could be of anybody; and all his vexation was not owing to the danger of his own pet plans. He stroked his face, he walked up and down, and grunted several times.

"Sit down, Crosby," he said at last, "and let us talk this over seriously. Why, what do you mean by 'some time longer'? Do you expect to come into a fortune?"

"Not exactly, sir. Things may look better."

"The army is a splendid profession," said Sir George. "But I am a poorer man than I was when I entered it; and your experience will probably be the same. You will get steps in rank, though that is a slow business now that the war is over; but your expenses will rise at the same time. And you want to marry Letitia! Confound it, how can you be such a fool!"

Sir George was in a better temper now.

"Certainly," said Crosby, "my prospects in life don't look so well as Barrett's. But I feel convinced that you would never repent of giving your daughter to me."

"Unfortunately I can't feel the same conviction," said Sir George. "You Irishmen are the most presuming fellows. Why, how could you keep a wife like Letitia? I should hear of nothing but debts."

"You would hear of no debts, sir."

"Upon my word, sir, you are amazingly confident. I am very angry with you, don't forget that. You have put this into Letitia's head, and I shall have more trouble with her than ever."

Crosby smiled; he did not much care for that.

"No laughing matter, I can tell you," said Sir George. "Listen to me. We have always agreed very well, and if you could succeed in convincing me that you have anything to live on, I might think this over. Young people always do get their own way by sheer obstinacy, I believe. But if you don't succeed in satisfying me, the marriage with Humphrey Barrett shall go on.   Letitia's objections to it are all nonsense. They are excellent people.   She will get used to them and be very happy."

Crosby looked rather thoughtfully into the fire.   The smile had died away, and the brightness was gone from his face; he found himself close upon a serious difficulty, into which his chief's next words plunged him headlong.

"Perhaps you forget that we know nothing about you, your father, your family, and so on.   I forgot it myself, to tell the truth.   But under these circumstances I must ask you to give me a full account of yourself."

Sir George had been talking lately in the business-like tone he generally used, with more and more good nature in it as he went on, and realised how much he liked Crosby.   But the young man's manner now brought a sudden sharpness into his eyes.   He frowned suspiciously as Crosby stared into the fire, flushing slowly redder and redder.   Suddenly he looked up.   The expression of Sir George's face was not very re-assuring; but there seemed to Crosby to be only one way out of his dilemma.

"You have known me long enough, Sir George," he said, "to trust my word.   You have placed great confidence in me for months past, though for all you knew of him my father might have been a tinker."

"Well, go on.   Is he a tinker?" said Sir George.   "His son does him credit."

Crosby smiled rather gravely.

"I lost my father some years ago," he said; then there was another pause.

"Hang the fellow!" exclaimed Sir George with an im-patient movement.   "What's the meaning of all this!   You are going quite the wrong way to work.   I like truth and openness. If you are ashamed of your relations, say so, and don't beat about the bush. What you mean by these proposals of yours, if you can't even give a straightforward account of your own family, is a puzzle to me indeed."

"My greatest wish is to be candid with you," declared Crosby. "I am in a difficulty, and you will be generous enough to consider it. Circumstances make it almost impossible for me to say anything about my family at present. Six weeks hence I'll gladly tell you anything you may wish to know. At present will you take my word for it that my position and prospects in life are better than Barrett's; that, so far from being ashamed of my relations, I have every reason to be proud of them ; and that these things only have made me bold enough to ask your daughter to be my wife ? "

Sir George could not help being struck by the strength of truth and earnestness in Crosby's manner. But the absurdity and unreasonableness of what he said was still more striking.

"That is all very well," said the General rather coldly. "But you cannot expect me to consider it enough. I do not see what 'circumstances' have to do with it. I must have the truth sir, or hear no more of this. If there is any secret in the matter you can trust me."

At this moment the butler opened the door and announced Mr. Humphrey Barrett.

VII.

THE TAILOR'S SON.

THE glances bestowed by the two young men on each other were anything but friendly. Crosby got up, bowed stiffly to Humphrey, and stood with his arms folded and his head slightly bent. Humphrey stared, frowned, took the nearest chair, and sat flicking his boots with his riding-whip. He looked a fine broad-shouldered fellow, with a ruddy healthy colour from his ride in the cold. His first greeting of Sir George had been rather eager, with a sort of cordial respect in it; but a cloud immediately came over his face at the confused air of the two men who received him; for Sir George felt himself in a false position, and in consequence of this his manner was both awkward and dry. There was a minute of total silence.

"You did me the honour of saying that I might call on you to-day," said Humphrey at last.

"I did," answered Sir George.

Humphrey looked at him, and then at Crosby, with rising anger. What did Sir George mean by letting that insolent ass of an aide-de-camp stay in the room at such an interview as this, when he was to have Letitia's answer? Well, whatever it meant, he could soon have his revenge.

"Should I offend you, sir," he said, "by asking for a few minutes of private conversation? We shall discuss our business better without a third person—if Captain Crosby will pardon the remark."

As he spoke he gave Crosby a look which was quite insulting in its haughty dislike.

"Mr. Humphrey Barrett is under a slight mistake," said

Crosby quietly, though his eyes flashed. "Would it not be best, sir, that he should know the whole truth?"

"No quarrelling, gentlemen," said Sir George, "or I shall know how to settle the affair at once, without regard to either of you. Now we had better talk this over in a friendly spirit. Since I saw you yesterday, Mr. Barrett, I have made a discovery—not altogether a pleasant one to you or to me. You have done me the honour to make proposals for my daughter. I have to tell you that she does not receive them very favourably; and I find that the reason of this is an attachment between her and Captain Crosby."

"An acquaintance of three days!" said Humphrey, colouring crimson, with an attempt at a smile. "Let me offer my congratulations, Sir George. Your son-in-law would be an ornament to any family. Pity his own is not more worthy of him —and of such a marriage."

"Sir!" exclaimed Crosby, with a sudden step forward.

Humphrey got up, and turned towards the door. He was smiling more, while Crosby looked furious.

"You will answer this insult to me," said the young officer.

"By no means," said Humphrey. "I only fight with gentlemen."

Sir George listened to this out-burst with consternation in his face.

Just then there was a little noise in the hall outside.

"I will, then. You may come too if you like," said Letitia; and she opened the library-door, and walked in, followed with some hesitation by Mrs. Bushe, flushed and tearful.

Everybody was silent when she came in. Crosby's face softened; Humphrey's smile died away, and a look of deep anger and disappointment succeeded it. Sir George came forward, took his daughter's hand, and held it with unusual kindness of manner.

"Are these gentlemen quarrelling, papa?" said Letitia, looking round with her bright blue eyes.

"Do you think yourself a small treasure, to be given up without a word?" said Humphrey, with such fierce meaning in his eyes as they met hers that she was obliged to look away. The shrinking dislike, so evident in her manner, brought a sudden look of rage into his face.

Then Captain Crosby came forward gravely, and said,

"In the presence of these ladies, sir, will you be good enough to explain your words just now?"

"What is all this?" said Letitia, again speaking to her father.

"Mr. Barrett has implied that Captain Crosby is not by birth a gentleman," replied Sir George very dryly. "I myself should be glad to know what he means—Crosby knows why. These things should be clear and above board. I hate mysteries."

"But you told me yourself that he was a gentleman. And certainly no one need ask," said Letitia, in her clear voice.

Crosby bowed his thanks.

"I had every reason to think so; but there seems some difficulty in the way of his giving an account of himself," said Sir George.

"Why don't you tell papa all about it?" said Letitia. "I —we all want to know—" and then she blushed and stopped suddenly.

"Can I ask you to trust me so far as to remain in ignorance of my true birth a little longer, without any change in your opinion of me?" said Crosby, looking at her earnestly.

"As long as you please," answered Letitia. "Say so too, papa. He has some good reason."

"There you are right, Miss Monkton. He has a very good reason," said Humphrey.

"Then pray tell us what it is," said Letitia, quite ready in her lover's defence to look him fearlessly in the face.

"Yes; for heaven's sake let us know what you mean?" said Crosby.

His proud bearing as he stood there not far from Letitia would not have suggested that he had anything to be ashamed of. Mrs. Bushe, who had been feeling very anxious, saw it with pleasure, and remembered the mysterious things he had said the day before. Perhaps he was a prince in disguise—but who? On the whole, for dear Letitia's sake, considering the Royal Marriage Act, she hoped not.

Humphrey Barrett looked slowly round at them all, and the unpleasant smile curled his lips again as he said,

"Well, you bear me witness that I am asked to say what I know. If Captain Crosby had been more courteous I might have kept it to myself; but 'tis the kindest thing, after all, to open Sir George's eyes. He may brave it out as he likes, standing there, but I have it on good authority. His father lives in Cork; he is old Mat Crosby the tailor. Everybody in the south of Ireland knows him well."

This announcement had its differing effect on the group that stood round. Mrs. Bushe turned pale and caught her breath with a horrified gasp. Sir George frowned, became extremely red, dropped his daughter's hand, and turned to look at Crosby. Letitia began to laugh. As for Crosby, a sort of spasm passed over his face; what it meant nobody could say for certain, but to Sir George it was as good as a confession. Especially as, after one glance at Letitia, he made no attempt to contradict Humphrey, but stood grave and silent, as if waiting for somebody else to speak. Humphrey's face slowly brightened and became triumphant, as Sir George's darkened more and more.

"If this is believed," he said to Crosby, "you have only yourself to thank for it. Your authority, Mr. Barrett?"

"A man who was his servant till lately—Roger Vance."

"The fellow he turned off," said Sir George. "There is something queer about this affair altogether. Crosby, I have liked you, as you know. If you will at once tell us frankly who you are, I will believe your word against Roger Vance's."

"I thank you, Sir George," said Crosby, with the faintest smile. "I have already asked you to trust me. I told you that I could not say anything about my family at present. I can only repeat what I said then."

"You will not even say that the fellow's story is a lie?"

"I decline to enter any further into the subject."

Mrs. Bushe sighed. Letitia was listening almost breathlessly. Sir George looked completely puzzled for a moment, and then burst into a rage.

"Then you are the son of this tailor, sir! And for all this time past you have acted a lie, have pushed yourself into the society of gentlemen, have wormed your way into my confidence! Do you suppose I should have made a tailor's son my aide-de-camp, have invited him to my house, and then to be subjected to such unheard-of insolence?"

"I can bear a good deal from you, sir," said Crosby. "But if an honest tailor's son has wit enough to pass for a gentleman, I do not see why he should be so heavily handicapped. In the English army the way is open to merit, and you cannot say that I have not done my duty as an officer."

"It is perfectly impossible!" said Mrs. Bushe, no longer able to contain herself. "Look at him, Sir George. A tailor's son!"

Crosby's elegance and distinction, as he stood there so calmly in the midst of the storm, were perhaps more likely to influence women than men. But Sir George himself could not look at him without feeling of some sort.

"Come now, Crosby," he said, "I hate all this tragical

nonsense. Tell me in plain words that you are not this tailor's son, and I'll believe you. I will, upon my honour."

Crosby looked at Sir George for a moment, and then turned towards Letitia.

"What do you wish me to do?" he said. "I have very urgent reasons for not answering any question whatever about myself at present; still, if I am to lose you by my silence, these reasons must of course give way. I only care for your opinion. Does my being called a tailor's son make any difference to you?"

"Difference, sir!" broke in Sir George. "It makes this difference, that you will never see or speak to my daughter again. Leave the room, Letitia."

"Directly, papa," said Letitia. She was quite pale, but she looked so resolute, as she walked across to where Crosby was standing, that nobody moved a finger to stop her. She stood still before him, and put both her hands into his.

"Don't answer any questions for me," she said. "I do not care who your father is. It will never make the smallest difference to me."

For a minute there was a dead silence. Crosby looked down into the true sweet eyes that were raised to his, and very gently and reverently kissed her hand. Then Letitia walked out of the room, and Mrs. Bushe followed her.

"You will oblige me, Captain Crosby," said Sir George, in his driest and coldest manner, "by leaving this house at your earliest convenience, and by keeping up no sort of communication with me or any member of my family."

Crosby bowed, and left the room without making any answer.

Then Sir George went up to Humphrey Barrett, who had been watching this scene with a mixture of rage and satisfaction, and shook him very kindly by the hand.

"These family troubles are awkward things," he said. "Come and see us again soon. I hope your next visit will be a pleasanter one."

"Is there any hope of that, sir?" said Humphrey, in a downcast way.

"Of course. I shall settle that for you. I am master in my own family," said Sir George.

VIII.

THE WEDDING-GOWN.

THE following days were days of great unhappiness to Letitia and Mrs. Bushe. Sir George, perhaps embittered by his disappointment in Crosby, became quite unbearably tyrannical. He went so far as to vow that before he went back to town Letitia should be married to Humphrey Barrett. Letitia, losing something of her brave spirit since Crosby had disappeared and nothing more was heard of him, spent most of her time in tears, which did not soften Sir George at all, and spoiled her eyes and complexion sadly.

About three weeks had passed in this disagreeable way, and Letitia was getting tired of crying, and beginning to wonder whether Crosby had forgotten her, when one evening things came to a crisis.

The weather had changed and grown warmer; the snow had all melted away by degrees, and everything was enjoying itself under soft blue sky and sunlight; there was a sweet smell of spring in the wind that blew freshly across the green meadows and lanes.

Mrs. Barrett and her daughters took advantage of this fine weather to walk down one day in thick boots and warm shawls from the Castle, and pay a visit to Letitia. The young lady appeared, after a good deal of persuasion from Mrs. Bushe, and even her stony heart was melted a little by their extreme friendliness. The girls looked so simple and good; Mrs. Barrett talked in a sensible downright kindly way, and did not mention Humphrey's name. Letitia was obliged to be polite, for, after all, Mrs. Barrett's dance was a pleasant recollection; her spirits were elastic, and she was a little tired and even ashamed of crying so much. When they went away, however, Mrs. Barrett lost her advantage by kissing Letitia, and saying with oppressive motherliness, "My dear, we are very happy. We are all so fond of you."

Letitia did not quite see the meaning of this, for it had never entered into her head, whatever her father might say, that she was to marry Humphrey whether she liked it or not. She thought Mrs. Barrett was a stupid woman, but submitted to be kissed in silence. The girls seemed half inclined to follow their mother's example; but Letitia held out her hand in a way that admitted of no question at all; she had no notion of being on such terms with the whole Barrett family. Mrs. Bushe looked on in melancholy silence; her spirits had become lower in these last few days, as Letitia's had risen a little. Some awful secret seemed to be weighing on her mind.

When Letitia went up-stairs to dress for dinner she was surprised to find Florinda in her room, consulting with her maid and a London workwoman over endless yards of white satin and a large box full of feathers and flowers. Florinda looked round with startled eyes at the girl as she came in; she had not expected her quite so soon. Letitia stared at these preparations.

"What is all that? A new gown of yours?" she said to her cousin.

"Have you seen your papa, my dear, since our visitors went?" said Mrs. Bushe.

"No; how should I?" answered Letitia.

After several stormy interviews with his daughter, Sir George had ended by leaving her to herself, and as far as possible ignoring her existence; for the last week they had scarcely exchanged a word.

"He had something to tell you—I thought he would have told you," said Mrs. Bushe, rather confused.

"I have not seen him. What beautiful satin! It looks like somebody's wedding-gown."

Letitia took hold of the satin and shook it out on the floor, holding it against her own pretty figure. "There, Atkins, pick up my train. Don't you see I'm going to Court?" she said, laughing, to the maid.

"Miss Monkton will look beautiful, ma'am," said the work-woman, a person they often employed, turning to Mrs. Bushe for sympathy.

But in Florinda's face there was nothing but the deepest sadness.

"Mrs. Bushe hates these vanities," said Letitia. "You will be splendid for once, though, cousin Florinda. What a pity you did not get it in time for that ball!"

"Come into your room, dear child. I must speak to you," said Mrs. Bushe. "Do not mind these things now, Atkins; we will see them another time. I will ring when I want you."

"Well, what is the matter? Anything new?" said Letitia.

There was a straight hard little sofa at the foot of the bed, on which Mrs. Bushe sat down, while the girl stood in front of her.

"O Letitia," said Mrs. Bushe, "your father is very cruel. It is wrong of me to say it, I know, but I must. Is it possible that you are still the only one in this house, or even in this neighbourhood, who does not know what is to happen next Thursday?"

In days long after, when Letitia told the story of her life, she never could remember that moment without shivering. It was so cold, so sudden, the feeling of absolute loneliness, and then the almost passion of self-reliance which followed it. She was never the same again; that evening ended her childhood. It was a woman, cruelly hurt, but not in the least subdued, that stood before Mrs. Bushe and gazed at her silently. Florinda was by far the most agitated of the two. She had expected a stormy scene with Letitia, but this stoniness was much more dreadful.

"My dear," she said, "sit down here. Speak to me!"

"I cannot conceive what you mean," said Letitia, quietly. "You are talking riddles, and I hate them as much as papa does. What is to happen next Thursday?"

"O Letitia, you are so unlike yourself!" said Mrs. Bushe, beginning to cry.

"For heaven's sake don't do that! Be reasonable," said Letitia. "I ask you a simple question; but I can answer it myself, for I understand now. You and papa are wonderful people indeed. Next Thursday is my wedding-day, when you mean to marry me to Humphrey Barrett. Everybody is charmed, with one exception; and that fine satin gown is expected to keep *her* quiet. Very clever indeed."

"Letitia, you will break my heart!" sighed Mrs. Bushe.

"You are doing your best to break mine; but fortunately it is not so fragile."

"What could I do? I was forced to obey Sir George. I thought he would have told you himself before this."

"I should like to understand the why and the wherefore of it all," said Letitia, coolly.

"Your papa thought that if you found everything was finally settled with the Barretts, you would be more likely to submit quietly," said Mrs. Bushe. "He is going abroad again very soon, and he thought, considering all the circumstances, it would be best to leave you safely married. They are really very good people, and admire you so much."

Florinda spoke faintly and wistfully. Letitia listened with her eyes on the ground. There were no tears, no exclamations; she did not even change colour. After a little pause she turned away from her cousin, and walked up to the table.

"We shall be late for dinner," she said. "You had better go and dress."

Florinda left her silently. This new mood of Letitia's, the cold indifference of her manner, was harder to bear than anything that had gone before. She longed to put her arms round the girl, to weep with her, to comfort her, to be reproached and scolded, if only she might give her love and sympathy. If there had been any wild despair in Letitia's manner, such as she had read of in romances, she would have been frightened. There was none, and yet she was frightened.

What made it still stranger and more unnatural was, that Letitia talked all through dinner to Sir George with a pleasantness which astonished him. She had lately taken some interest in poultry, had been feeding the chickens and the ducks herself, and she wanted to know something about foreign fowls—how they were managed and fed, and what were the best breeds. Sir George knew nothing, but tried to say something. He also was uncomfortably conscious of the change in Letitia—that she had grown up in this one afternoon, that her heart was no longer in her face. He wondered what it meant. After dinner, when Mrs. Bushe got up to go into the drawing-room, Letitia remained a moment standing, with her hands on the back of her chair, facing her father as he walked across to the door.

"Papa," she said, while both Sir George and Florinda hesitated between the table and the door, "I have to thank you for my beautiful wedding-gown."

Sir George tried to speak and to smile, stammered frightfully, and grunted out,

"Glad you are pleased with it."

"I should have liked longer notice," said Letitia, with a coolness which struck Mrs. Bushe as quite awful. "But I suppose it was not convenient to you. There is one thing I must ask, however."

"What is it? Anything I can do—" said Sir George, beginning to feel great relief and pride in the success of his plan.

"I think you forget how little I know of Mr. Humphrey Barrett. We really ought to make more acquaintance. I wish you would ask him to dine with us to-morrow."

"With the greatest pleasure, Letty. My dear girl, you little know how gratified I am," said Sir George, earnestly. "Now mind, you must ask me for anything you want—anything that money can buy. No reward can be too great for dutifulness."

He came forward, as if he meant to kiss his daughter; but she did not seem to see this, and went quietly out of the room after her cousin. Sir George, very much pleased, sat down to finish his port. It was evident that he, at least, knew how to manage a refractory young woman.

Presently Mrs. Bushe opened the door softly, came in, and sat down near him a little way from the table. Sir George looked up, and wondered what was the matter with her. He did not quite see why Florinda should choose to put on such a solemn face, when everything was going well, when Letitia had made up her mind to submit, and had lifted such a weight of anxiety off her friends' shoulders.

"You don't look well, Florinda," said Sir George amiably. "You took nothing at dinner. Let me give you a glass of port."

Florinda thanked him, and declined this decidedly.

"I am obliged to you," she said; "I am perfectly well."

"Ah, glad to hear it," said Sir George. "Well, is it some clever management of yours that has brought Letty to her senses? I give you great credit. I am most agreeably surprised."

"O, I don't want you to deceive yourself," said Mrs. Bushe, her voice trembling. "I am in great alarm about Letitia. She saw the white satin gown, and I was obliged to break it to her suddenly. I never saw anything so extraordinary as her manner. She is not submissive, Sir George. She is in despair."

"Despair! absurdity! Does it look like despair, begging me to ask Barrett to dinner? You are too sensitive and fanciful, Florinda, to understand a girl of Letty's character. She has a great power of accommodating herself to circumstances, of making up her mind strongly on any one point. She inherits it from me. A power of self-conquest, in which you may, perhaps, be rather deficient. No reproach to you. It belongs to the natural character. Letitia is only behaving as I confidently expected her to behave. She has been too much indulged. As soon as she finds that I am seriously in earnest, she submits with a good grace. Despair! you have been reading too many novels."

Florinda had a dim idea that she could not trust her own senses, and therefore she quietly accepted Sir George's contradictions. First he was agreeably surprised; then it was what he had confidently expected. After all, it did not matter much what his feelings were. She sighed and got up.

"I can only tell you my impressions," she said. "Letitia's manner to me is a new thing. She is reserved, cold, abrupt. She sits buried in thought, or talks in a strained unnatural way. She is not herself. I believe that if by any means she can escape this marriage, she will. And I must say, Sir George, at the risk of offending you, that in my opinion, by forcing her into it, you are doing a great cruelty to your only child."

"My esteem for you is very great," Sir George replied gravely. "But on this subject we differ, and must continue to do so. I am satisfied with my arrangements for Letitia, and with her acceptance of them. At present I desire to look no further."

He had his hand on the handle of the door, ready to open it.

"I wonder where Captain Crosby is," said Mrs. Bushe.

"Why should you vex me by mentioning his name?"

"I do not believe a word of that story about his birth."

"He may not be a tailor's son," said Sir George, "but he is an adventurer of some kind, of course. Otherwise he would have made no mystery about his family. Cannot you understand, Florinda, what I explained to you the other day—that it is specially to save Letitia from any consequences of an absurd fancy for him, that I have hastened on this marriage? A year or two hence you will do me justice. You will not talk of my cruelty, but of my wisdom."

Sir George bowed his cousin out of the room and went back to his port, very much satisfied with himself. He was glad he had kept his temper with poor Florinda, provoking as she might be; of course all she said was dictated by sincere affection for Letitia and himself. Still the *rôle* of Cassandra, was a very tiresome one, and he wondered she had not the tact and good sense to avoid it.

IX.

A FORLORN HOPE.

LETITIA began the next day by being measured for her satin gown. She went through this without showing much interest; but also without any appearance of disgust. Afterwards she put on her red cloak and went out to feed the chickens.

There was a large paved yard behind the house, with stables and coach-houses and dog-kennels all round, and a wooden granary in the middle, built on posts several feet above the ground. On the steep steps of this granary Letitia stood with her bag of grain, and at the sound of her voice the feathered creatures ran and flew from every corner of the place. White pigeons came fluttering down from the roofs and chimneys, and perched about her; cocks strutted, hens cackled and quarrelled; the little lady was in the midst of a noisy greedy crowd, over which she poured showers of yellow grain. While she was doing this the yard-gate opened, and a tall young woman came in with a basket of eggs on her arm. She half paused at the sight of Letitia, standing there in the sun. Then she curtsied and came towards her, stepping carefully among the chickens.

Miss Monkton looked rather curiously at her bright rosy face, at the clear dark eyes which were watching her so anxiously, and glancing round now and then as she came, as if to make sure that there was nobody within sight or hearing. All the doors were shut; the men were busy or away; only one old dog looked out of his kennel, wagged his tail, and went back again.

"Pray, ma'am, do you remember me?" said the young

woman with the eggs, standing at the foot of the steps, and dropping another curtsey.

There was no peasant shyness in her manner, but the well-bred fearless ease of a yeoman's daughter. She was well dressed, too, and carried her basket gracefully. And there was a kindliness in her smile which made Letitia smile too as she answered her,

"I am sure I have seen you before."

"I have brought eggs and butter to the house many a time. I've got some eggs here now; but I came to-day on purpose to see you, ma'am. I am Kitty Pratt, of Jack's Croft."

"Can I do anything for you?" said Letitia.

"Will you kindly read this, ma'am, and give me an answer to take back?"

A small sealed note appeared from under the folds of Kitty's shawl. Letitia felt almost dizzy as she took it; the writing was familiar to her. She turned away to read it. Kitty quietly set down her basket, took the bag of grain, and went on feeding the impatient fowls.

"The bearer of this can be trusted. Will you send me word by her whether the terrible report I hear is true? I am not far from you, but dare not compromise you by appearing. Tell me that if it is true, it is against your will, and it shall never happen."

Letitia read this three or four times over. Then she turned quite calmly to Kitty Pratt.

"This note tells me you are to be trusted," she said.

Kitty's eyes met hers with a smile that was nothing but truth.

"I see you are," said Letitia. "The gentleman who sent it, is he at your house?"

"Yes," said Kitty. "He came two days ago, and asked my father to take him in. He wished to be in this neighbourhood without any one knowing. He has not told us his name. We call him the Captain."

"Tell him to wait till to-morrow," said Letitia. "He shall have an answer to-morrow, do you understand? Tell him there is one chance to be tried; but it may fail. Will you remember that?"

Kitty nodded.

"Have not you butter or eggs, or something to bring here to-morrow?"

"I could bring two pound of butter, if Mrs. Bushe liked to order it."

"I order it. Bring it to the house about this time to-morrow, and, as you go back, look for me outside the gates, under the trees yonder: you can carry my answer. Thank you. Now take your eggs to the house."

Kitty curtsied and went, without another word.

All that day Letitia was a great trial to her affectionate cousin. When she answered or spoke to her, there was a studied carelessness in her manner, an abruptness that was almost rude, and quite silenced gentle Mrs. Bushe. She also felt that the girl avoided her as much as possible.

Towards evening Letitia seemed a little excited; her cheeks were very pink, and her eyes brighter than usual. She did not put on one of her prettiest gowns to receive young Barrett; but in spite of that, Mrs. Bushe though she had seldom looked prettier. It was a painful prettiness, though, to any one who knew Letitia well. As to Humphrey, his position seemed quite to puzzle him. He was rather grave and silent all through dinner, though Sir George did his best to draw him out. Certainly no stranger looking in upon them, would have guessed that the two young people were to be married to each other in a week. They sat on opposite sides of the table, and hardly exchanged a word.

After dinner, in the drawing-room, Letitia said to Mrs Bushe,

"Will you do me one more favour?"

"One more, my dear?" said Florinda wonderingly.

"Will you let me be alone with Humphrey, when he comes in? Pray don't hesitate. It is the only chance of our understanding each other, and I suppose you think that desirable."

"O Letitia, you puzzle me completely. If you knew what I feel!" sighed Florinda.

Letitia smiled coldly.

"My dear, do you hate this man?"

"What a strange question! Hate him! O no, I am not so uncharitable. All men are our brothers, you know, so it would be wicked to hate one of them. But don't look agonised, for I really have seen him much worse than he is to-night. The idea of marrying me seems to have tamed him; he is quite awed and downcast. I shall have to tell him not to be afraid of me."

"Letitia," said Mrs. Bushe very gravely, "this whole business distresses me more than I can say. But to hear you speak in this terrible, unnatural, almost unwomanly way, is the worst part of it all. I will go, for I cannot bear to be with you. Why did you not say at once to your father that you would not and could not marry this man?"

"Papa has a bad ally in you, cousin Florinda,' answered Letitia, quietly. "And it is the last thing I should have expected of you, to advise disobedience. But when one is driven to the end of one's resources, and is without friends or help, one must fight people with their own weapons. A hateful thing to do, but sometimes the only thing. You must hope, now, that Humphrey Barrett and I may agree."

"I don't in the least understand you," said Mrs. Bushe. "I think I shall go mad, if I talk to you any longer."

" Then pray go and rest in your own room," said Letitia.

Mrs. Bushe went. Letitia walked restlessly up and down the room till she heard the distant opening of a door, and a heavy step coming along the hall. Then she sat down by the fire with a screen in her hand, to receive Humphrey.

He was rather startled by finding her alone. All his bullying self-assertion seemed to have left him ; he was tamed, as she said, by this swift and strange realisation of his wishes. He drew a chair near her, sat down, and looked at her. Letitia glanced at him over her screen, and said the evening was rather cold.

" Is it ? I have not felt it so," said Humphrey.

Then they were both silent for a minute or two. Humphrey was angry with himself for being such an ass as to have nothing to say to this lovely girl, who had actually consented to be his wife—so her father assured him ; but even to his dim perceptions she was wrapped in an icy mist, beyond his power of penetrating. At last, rather bluntly, he put some of his thoughts into words.

" Is it not strange to think what will have happened, this time next week ! Can you imagine it at all ? I can't."

" O, perfectly," said Letitia ; " I have heard so much about it, to-day and yesterday."

" Well, I'm very glad to hear that," said Humphrey. " I really was in despair ; and you don't know what it is to me to have it all settled like this. My people admire you, and all that, as much as I do. We none of us thought that you would ever bring your mind to it ; but you shall never regret it, I promise you that."

Heavens ! what sort of love-making was this ! Even in her desperate position Letitia felt as if she must laugh. She did smile, and this had the effect of cheering and emboldening Humphrey.

"Letitia—I don't know a prettier name," he said. "I've been told that it means 'joy,' and if so it suits you well. One never could be dismal with you."

"I am glad you think so," said Letitia, "though I am afraid you are mistaken. I wish I knew you a little better, Mr. Barrett."

"Well, you will soon do that. But call me Humphrey, if you please," said the young squire, pulling his chair a little nearer.

Letitia, however, did not look encouraging, and this was his furthest advance.

"I want to tell you something, and to ask you something," she said, "and I wish I knew how you are likely to answer me."

"How do you think, now?"

"Kindly and generously, I *hope*," said Letitia, in a low voice.

"I'm glad you do me so much justice," said Humphrey. "Always be true and open with me; you will find it your best policy. You don't understand what I feel for you, I see that. Come, then, try how far you can trust an Englishman."

Letitia changed colour slightly at this last word.

"You know," she said, "that all this arrangement for next week was made by papa without any knowledge or consent of mine. I only heard of it when everything was finally settled. I might have made a great fuss, but I am tired—I have had trouble and vexation enough lately, and I thought that my best way was to speak to you."

"We have all had vexation enough, and from the same cause," said Humphrey, as she stopped for a moment.

"Then you understand me. I have only to tell you that I meant what I said that day. It is dreadful for me to say this to you, but this treatment has driven me to forget that I am a young girl. Nobody will tell you if I don't."

Letitia turned her face towards him. All the pretty colour had been driven from it by strong feeling; she was white and like a statue, except her deep blue eyes. But all the sweetness was gone from them; they gazed at Humphrey with a sad wild sternness. Most men would have felt a little nervous at the idea of marrying the owner of them. Humphrey scowled jealously, as he had so often done before.

"What! you are still thinking about that impostor fellow?"

"Wait; you have not heard all yet," said Letitia hastily. She felt that in another minute or two it would be impossible to speak to him.

She got up, and Humphrey did the same; they stood two or three yards apart in front of the fire.

"I want to appeal to you," Letitia said. "If you are kind and generous, I must tell you what you will do now. It is for your own advantage as well as mine. Do you want to marry a woman who will make your life miserable?"

"I certainly shall not do that," said Humphrey.

"Ah, well, if you wish to avoid it, you will set me free. Tell papa we have agreed that we don't understand each other, that we could never make each other happy. I will tell him so too. Let me go."

"Here is a fine position for a man," said Humphrey—"to be thrown aside like an old glove, because of a mad fancy for a fellow no better than an Irish beggar! I'll wager anything you like you will never see or hear of him again. He has played his game and lost it."

"Perhaps I never may see him again," said Letitia. "That has nothing to do with what I ask you: will you release me from this engagement, that was made without my knowledge?"

"Now I call that asking too much," said Humphrey. "All my friends know I am going to be married; I've asked them to the wedding. My father has made law arrangements for me—everything has been settled. A fine fool I should look if it was broken off now. And you can't ask it—you can't expect it; I who have loved you so long and so faithfully, and was so happy at the thoughts of your having given in at last. Sir George so pleased too—everybody satisfied—and you must needs go and upset it all."

There was something so grotesquely peevish in Humphrey's indignation, that Letitia began to feel a sort of contemptuous pity for him. It was impossible to carry on any tragical pleading with a man like this.

"There's nothing in any of those reasons," she said, "to compare with a life of misery."

"But it will not be that. As soon as you get used to it, you will be happy and thankful," Humphrey persisted.

Letitia shook her head.

"It is no use arguing the matter," she said. "I hear papa coming. Once for all, will you release me or not?"

"No, that I won't," answered Humphrey decidedly.

Letitia left the room instantly, gliding past Sir George in the passage, and springing up-stairs so quickly that he had not time to speak to her. Mrs. Bushe, going down presently, found that she was fled; and was not much surprised that she did not appear again that night. Humphrey went away soon after, without mentioning the trying scene he had gone through.

When Mrs. Bushe went up-stairs to bed, she ventured to look into Letitia's room. The girl was sitting in her dressing-gown by the fire.

"Come in and say good-night," she said, in a voice that went to her cousin's heart; it was the old Letitia come back again, only with a new tenderness of manner. "I love you, because you are the only one of them all that loves me. Don't break your heart about me, dear Florinda."

She held out her arms. Mrs. Bushe laid her head on her shoulder and cried, while Letitia kissed and soothed her gently ; there were no tears in her eyes.

"There, don't be unhappy," said Letitia. "It will all be right in the end. It is no use fighting against Fate you know. Good-night. Go to bed now, and don't think about me any more."

Mrs. Bushe, however, lay awake all that night. Once she felt obliged to go and see what Letitia was doing, whether she was able to forget her trouble in sleep. But the door between the rooms was locked ; and to her cousin's tender inquiries in the morning Letitia would only answer, "Why shouldn't I sleep ?"

X.

JACK'S CROFT.

THE kitchen at Jack's Croft was a great picturesque room, with an enormous fire-place and seats in the chimney-corner. A broad staircase went up on one side. The furniture was heavy and old, all in the dark oak, worn by constant use and polishing, which one finds still in some out-of-the-way farm-houses. There was handsome old blue china on the dresser, and the rough beams of the ceiling were a hanging forest of bacon and dried herbs. Before the fire, which had a blazing log on it, stood Mrs. Pratt, bright and picturesque as her house, tall and sturdily built, with dark eyes and rosy cheeks, like her daughter Kitty's. Kitty, the only child and heiress of Jack's Croft, stood leaning against the table, with a basket in her hand, and a shawl thrown over her arm.

LETITIA AT JACK'S CROFT

I. 229.

"Mercy on us!" said Mrs. Pratt. "And where is she now?"

"I left her in the garden with him," answered Kitty, smiling, "He was looking out for me, you see, and he met us at the gate. I never saw such a look on a man's face, mother. How he does worship her, to be sure!"

"Well, Kitty, it's the queerest affair altogether as ever I heard tell of. She can't stay here, you know. You'll have to take her back, or perhaps father'll drive her in the gig. It's a long way for a girl that isn't used to trudging, like you are. She had no business to have come at all, and that's the long and short of it. You oughtn't to have brought her."

"You'd have done the same, mother, if she'd looked up in your face and said, ' My whole happiness depends on seeing that gentleman at once. Let me go home with you.' You couldn't have set yourself against her, sweet pretty creature."

As Kitty spoke Crosby and Letitia came in together. Mrs. Pratt curtsied, and hastened to set a chair for the young lady. However shocked the good woman might be, she could not forget her manners.

"No, thank you. I cannot sit down," said Letitia quickly. "O Mrs. Pratt, I hear you are very kind-hearted. I have so much to ask you."

"Mrs. Pratt is the very best woman in the world," said Crosby. "The most generous and the noblest. That is lucky for us, as our whole future depends upon her."

"Law, sir, I don't understand you," said Mrs. Pratt.

"My dear friend," said Crosby, with the greatest earnestness, "let me explain to you. When I accepted your hospitality, and that of your good husband, I told you that private affairs of my own, about which I was very anxious, might keep me for a few days in this neighbourhood. Now you see the explanation. I need not say any more, need I?"

Mrs. Pratt looked from one charming young face to the other. She could not help smiling; but she bit her lips and shook her head.

"Why, sir, I don't clearly see what you are driving at," she said. "And if you want my opinion, it is that this lady had better go quietly home again."

"Don't be so cruel and severe, Mrs. Pratt. You are giving her quite a false idea of you," said Crosby.

"Well, sir," said Mrs. Pratt, with firmness, "if our Kitty was to run off to somebody else's house to meet a young man without our approval, I know very well what her father and me would say to her."

"But Kitty would never be so cruelly treated as I have been, so driven to extremity," said Letitia. "For no reason my father turned him out of the house, and means to force me to marry another man. All depends on my escaping. I must escape, Mrs. Pratt, you will help us?"

Letitia came forward and took one of the good woman's strong brown hands, holding it tight between her own, and looking up with eyes that might have softened a millstone.

"My dear," said the farmer's wife tenderly, "do just consider what a foolish thing you are doing. Leaving your home and everything just because a handsome young gentleman asks you. There ain't one among them, my dear, that's worth it. If I was to do my duty I should just have the horse put in, and get the master to drive you back home this minute. I never heard such madness in my life. As for you, sir, you ought to be ashamed of yourself. Pray how do you expect me to help you?"

"Perhaps your friendliness made me expect too much," said Crosby. "But since I received this lady just now at the garden-gate, I have thought that you would persuade your husband to lend me his gig and that strong horse I admire so highly. Then I should drive to London, where discovery is almost impossible. It also seemed to me likely that you might allow your daughter to accompany us. I would see to her safe return."

At these demands Mrs. Pratt lost patience, and observed very sharply that gentlefolks thought the world was made for them. She begged the Captain to give her no more of his nonsense. She would not listen to another word. Kitty go with them, indeed! Kitty was a respectable young woman, who had never been in London in her life, and never should go to such a wicked place with her mother's good will.

At the end of all this, which sounded rather hopeless, Letitia sank into a chair and hid her face in her hands. Captain Crosby frowned as he stood beside her.

"Are you ill, dear madam?" said Kitty, going up to Letitia.

"Yes. I am very tired and miserable," sighed Letitia.

"Bless her dear heart, I daresay she is," said Mrs. Pratt, all her natural kindness returning. "Come, then, my pretty one, go up-stairs and rest in Kitty's room for a while. Then you shall go quietly home. They're all wild after you already."

"I shall never go home," said Letitia.

"Well, anyhow, go and rest yourself a bit. You're that excited, you don't know what you're saying. That's right; lean on Kitty, my dear."

Crosby stood and saw his lady-love conveyed away up the dark old staircase. It was true that the painful excitement she had gone through lately, added to the fatigue of that morning's walk, had been almost too much for Letitia. He was almost wild, between anxiety for her, and the difficulty of getting out of this new scrape with success and honour.

"You will do a very cruel and very foolish thing, Mrs. Pratt," he said, " if you refuse to help us in such an emergency as this."

" Sir," said Mrs. Pratt, " I'm sorry to disagree with a gentleman like you. But your own conscience tells you that it's a cruel and a foolish thing *you're* wanting to do. No good ever came of a young lady's going against the will of her family."

" Confound her family ! "

" I won't be sworn at in my own kitchen, sir, if you please," said Mrs. Pratt.

" I beg your pardon," said Crosby, bowing. " I am a good deal irritated just now, and with reason."

He walked out through a door that led into the garden. Mrs. Pratt looked after him.

" I never did see a pleasanter young man, nor a handsomer," she soliloquised. " But the impudence of these here officers ! Our best horse, and Kitty into the bargain ! What'll he want next, I wonder ? That young lady goes back to Sir George's this very day, as soon as Pratt comes in, or I'm not mistress in my own house. I'll have no such doings here."

Crosby was mooning about up and down the tidy garden-walks, almost at his wits' end what to do with his treasure, now that he had it, when Kitty Pratt came carefully creeping down in the shadow of a hedge, beckoning to him. He joined her, and they had a long confidential talk in an arbour, where her father smoked his pipe on summer evenings. Then Kitty went back in the same cautious manner to the house again.

That was a strange day at the farm—it was very still, the sun was shining, and the hours crawled on slowly—to Mrs. Pratt, vexed and anxious, as she waited for her husband to come in ; to Letitia, following Kitty's advice by staying in her room ; to Kitty herself, with all her resolution and cleverness ; to Crosby, as he wandered about outside, uneasy, in spite of his faith in Kitty, and not caring to go in and encounter her mother.

Towards one o'clock a message came in from the farmer, saying that there was no need to wait dinner for him. A friend of his, ten miles off, had sent to say that some of his most valuable cows were ill, and he should be glad to see him and hear his opinion of them. So he had ridden off at once from the field, and very likely would not be back till late at night.

Mrs. Pratt and Kitty and Crosby dined together rather silently at the great kitchen-table, the servants dining in the back kitchen beyond. Letitia did not come down. After dinner Mrs. Pratt retired into the parlour, and seated herself in her own large armchair, quite determined, with such dangerous people in the house, not to go to sleep as usual. But nature and habit were too much for her, and perhaps she slept with unusual soundness, after her agitation in the morning.

Crosby went out into the garden, and Kitty into the yard, where everything was very quiet. There was always a lull in the farm-work in the middle of the day, and just now not a man was to be seen about the premises; possibly one or two were resting themselves in a warm corner of the barn. Kitty went to the yard-gate, and looked up and down the road; not a creature to be seen. Yes! there was a horse trotting up the lane. In another minute he had stopped at the gate.

"Good-day," said Kitty, perceiving at once that the rider was one of Sir George's men.

"Good-day, missus. We are in sad trouble down at Sir George Monkton's. Our young lady's gone, and we are searching for her all over the country. You haven't seen nothing of her?"

"If I had," said Kitty, "don't you think I'd have brought her back by now? She's not a young lady to be wandering about by herself."

"'That she ain't. Well, I wonder where she can be gone.
There was that Irish gentleman, Captain Crosby, as they say
is a tailor's son. Sir George thinks she's run off with him,
perhaps to London."

"Mark my words," said Kitty; "if she's gone with him,
they'd never do such a blundering thing as go to London.
Why, it's full of Sir George's friends, surely. They'd find
them in a minute. No, they'd have gone straight off to Ireland. No doubt about it. That's the road you ought to take,
young man, if you want to catch them."

"Ireland! Well, and I shouldn't wonder if you was right,
missus," said the man; and he touched his hat and rode off.

"Crosby—a tailor's son!" repeated Kitty to herself as she
turned from the gate. "Anyhow I must help them. I wonder
if she knows it, though, throwing of herself away like that.
Well, it's time for me to harness Boney."

Fortunately for Kitty's designs, the stable where her father's
best horses lived, and the place where the gig was kept, were
in a quiet corner of the premises, with their backs turned to
the large yard, and opening on a little grass yard of their own,
only commanded from the house by Kitty's own window. From
this small court there were two gates, one into the large yard,
the other into a large field with a grass road across it, so that
a carriage could drive away from Jack's Croft quite silently.

Just as Kitty was buckling her last strap, Captain Crosby
appeared at the stable-door.

"Doing it yourself?" he said.

"The fewer we trust, the safer we are, sir," replied Kitty.

"It is early for you to have come to that conclusion," said
Crosby, hardly noticing the coolness of Kitty's manner towards
himself.

"Well, sir, if you'll put him into the gig," said Kitty, "I'll
fetch the young lady."

"Kitty, one moment; are you repenting of your goodness to us?"

"Repent!" said Kitty scornfully. She hesitated a moment, and then went on, speaking very quickly: "There was one of Sir George's men at the gate just now, asking for her. I sent him off pretty quick. But he told me something about you."

"What was it, now? That my father was a tailor?"

His laughing eyes were almost too much for Kitty; she turned away from them.

"Well, if he was, you're not good enough for Miss Monkton; you know you're not. And I suppose she knows nothing about it?"

"Ask her. Say anything you like to her. I give you free permission," said Crosby.

"I might do it without that," muttered Kitty as she walked away.

She found Letitia in a state of feverish impatience waiting for her. She had been looking out of the window into the little yard, had seen Crosby standing at the stable-door laughing, and wondered why in the world he was wasting time so. Kitty looked rather grave as she came into the room.

"Before we go down, ma'am, may I say a word to you?" she said.

"O yes; to tell me to walk softly. Of course I will," said Letitia.

"Yes; but there's something else. I've promised to serve you, and I mean to keep my word; but I've heard just now something about the Captain, from one who came asking after you. They say he's a tailor's son, and I thought you ought to know it."

"Why, Kitty," exclaimed Letitia, turning round in a sudden fire of indignation, "am I to be tormented with this by you, too? I neither know nor care whose son he is. If he was your lover, would you care whether his father was a king, or a tailor, or something much lower still—a beggar in the streets, if you like? Wouldn't you trust him?"

"I don't know about that, ma'am," said Kitty. "And I shouldn't like either a king or beggar; one's own station is best."

"O, plague on all your prudence and wisdom!" cried Letitia. "There, he has got the horse in. Lead the way now. I'll follow you like a mouse."

Three minutes later, Captain Crosby, Miss Monkton, and the generous but undutiful Kitty were seated in Farmer Pratt's gig, and his good horse Boney was trotting swiftly and silently across the grass-road towards the labyrinth of cross-country lanes, through which, under Kitty's guidance, they meant to make a bold dash for London.

———

XI.

THE LONDON CHURCH.

If Letitia had once called her country home a living sepulchre, the London house in which she now found herself deserved that title much more. It was in a narrow street of tall dark old houses like itself, with no thoroughfare, so that nobody ever came down it who had not some business at the houses themselves. Even then these houses, though they were close to a busy part of the City, were deserted by the people for whom their fine broad staircases had been built, their large rooms floored with oak, their panellings and balusters carved handsomely. But no wonder, for they were terribly dark and dismal. Letitia could not help feeling this, though the woman to whom the house seemed to belong—a wild, untidy, warm-hearted Mrs. O'Brien—had received the runaways as if they were a prince and princess, had almost gone down on her knees to adore Letitia, and had raved about her beauty till Letitia was obliged to beg her to stop. At last leaving Mrs. O'Brien to Kitty, she found herself standing with Crosby in one of the windows of the drawing-room, which smelt rather musty in spite of its large fire, and the magnificence of all its yellow brocade and carving and mirrors.

"O Gerald, what a strange house!" said Letitia; "and who is that funny woman?"

"She is a countrywoman of mine, the best and faithfullest creature," said Crosby. "She was in our service, and then married Lord Killarney's butler; and they took this house with all its old furniture, as you see, and let lodgings. I trust you won't dislike her?"

"O, no, not if she is a friend of yours," said Letitia.

It struck her directly that by a question to Mrs. O'Brien she could probably hear the whole truth as to Crosby's parentage; but this was a temptation easily conquered.

"I shall not ask her who you are," she said, smiling at him.

"As to that, my darling, please yourself," answered Crosby.

Letitia shook her head, and the subject was not again alluded to between them.

Kitty was not so delicate-minded. She asked Mrs. O'Brien a whole string of questions, and apparently had satisfactory answers, for her spirits rose, while those of Letitia flagged a little. They remained quietly in the lodging for a week or more. Crosby, who was staying somewhere else, came to see them every day, and often had to spend most of his time in consoling Letitia, who was seized with fits of home-sickness and self-reproach.

"At any rate, my dearest angel," Crosby remonstrated, "your father brought it all on himself. If he had not treated you with such tyranny, you would have been at home at this moment, and we should have waited patiently for better times. But we had no alternative."

"Ah, yes, I know. But I am so sorry about Florinda. She is such a dear creature, and loves me so sincerely. My happiness was everything to her, and papa made her completely miserable. What must she be feeling now?"

"We will make it all up to her, one of these days," said Crosby. "Her home shall be with us; will that please you my Letitia?"

"Yes, indeed; you are very good."

Somehow the clouds soon passed away, and the future shone out very brightly again. The mystery of it was only like a soft golden haze, which made it more attractive and delightful. No matter whose son Crosby might turn out to be, he must always be himself, and he was perfection. At last came a morning when through a thick yellow fog, lighted by link-boys along the streets, a small party of people went from Mrs. O'Brien's house to the very dismallest of City churches, with pews and galleries, stuffy moth-eaten curtains and hangings, a few dim candles lighted about the east-end, a fat old clerk with spectacles and a bad cough, a vague dreamy clergyman with a pale face and a mass of grey hair. What a strange wedding for the heiress of Sir George Monkton! Perhaps such things had often happened in that church before, for both parson and clerk seemed to take it as a matter of course; and there was no awaking of interest or curiosity in either pair of eyes, at the sight of this elegant young gentleman and lady in travelling dress, with their two incongruous witnesses, Kitty Pratt, and Mrs. O'Brien. The clerk gave away the bride as if it was part of his day's work, and he had given away hundreds before.

The solemn words of the service, gabbled as they were, had a great effect on Letitia; when it was over, she was crying so much that she could hardly see to write her name in the register, and neither saw nor thought of the name that was written above. Kitty did, however, and smiled as she scratched her own.

Gerald Crosby led his wife down the damp old passage between the pews, and out at the side-door of the church into a street where a post-chaise was waiting. He and Letitia were inside it, and the horses were moving, before she realised what had happened.

"O, good-bye—good-bye, Kitty!" she cried starting forward.

Kitty curtsied, and waved her hand.

"Good bless and prosper ye, my—" screamed Mrs. O'Brien; the end of her sentence was lost in the rattle of the wheels.

Two days later, Kitty returned to Jack's Croft in her father's gig, drawn by Boney, and driven by Mrs. O'Brien's respectable husband. She brought back with her two or three fashionable gowns and bonnets, a shawl for her mother, a silver-mounted hunting-whip for her father, and a hundred-pound note, which Captain Crosby had left in her hand with a very hearty squeeze, just before he got into the carriage.

After being well scolded and forgiven, Kitty set off to relieve the minds of Letitia's relations. Fortunately, perhaps, for her, Sir George was in London, searching for the runaways.

Mrs. Bushe never dreamed of reproaching Kitty for her part in the matter. It was too delightful to have her mind so entirely set at rest. She cried first; but soon dried her tears, kissed and thanked Kitty, and rejoiced with all her heart.

XII.

LADY FITZPATRICK.

THERE was a fashionable place in those days, not a hundred miles from London, which shall be called Gaytown-by-the-Sea. London people who had any reason for disliking Brighton, and yet liked sea air combined with dancing and card-playing, went there a good deal. There were Assembly Rooms, a high promenade overlooking the sea, a few good shops, and a comfortable hotel. The climate was supposed to be very mild, and so it was in the first fortnight of Letitia's married life, which she spent there. She and her husband, however, did not take much part in the gaieties of the place, neither did they walk up and down the promenade. They spent most of their days away on the shore, enjoying the green tumbling sea and the fantastic forms of the yellow cliffs, picking up shells and sea-weed like two happy children. Crosby sketched, and Letitia suggested and admired. People at Gaytown wondered who they were and what they were doing, this young couple who somehow looked more fitted for society than for roughing it as they did, making friends with the fishermen and venturing out in boats on this winter sea with the most surprising boldness. Yet nobody who thought the thing strange knew how strange it really was, and that the young bride herself often wondered who she and her husband were. She had married him in full faith and trust. At the moment when the mystery might have been cleared up to her by a glance at the register, her mind had been confused and her eyes blinded by tears. Since then Crosby had told her nothing, and she had not chosen to ask him; yet at times, now that the first excitement was over, she felt quite wild with curiosity. Nobody knew where they were, for Crosby would not let her write. Kitty's revelations had been quite enough, he thought, to set Sir George's and everybody's mind at rest. He told Letitia that they knew everything, and were quite happy about her. Letitia smiled, as she thought, "Then you can't be a tailor's son;" but she asked no questions, though she wondered how they knew. Crosby saw the wonder in her eyes, and answered it:

"Molly O'Brien was a traitor, and told Kitty all sorts of things."

"If they all know, why shouldn't I?" thought Letitia, but she did not say it.

One evening as they walked back along the sands, Crosby said to her,

"This is rather an important day to me, and it is our last but one at Gaytown, unless you wish to stay longer. But you shall decide that to-morrow before I order the horses."

"As you please," said Letitia. "I like the place amazingly. Perhaps we may be here again some day."

"Yes; for certainly no place can be associated with more charming recollections."

"No, indeed. But what is it that makes this an important day to you?"

"It is three years to-night since I laid a wager, which I have won. And after all it was not such a foolish one," said Crosby.

The morning of that next day broke with furious showers of hail, and Letitia, who had been looking forward to a last walk, stood at the window rather disappointed. Her husband, however, was in the highest spirits. He had not told her anything yet, and, now that the suspense was just over, it is sad to have to say that Letitia's happy faith began to flag a little. She was tired, perhaps; at any rate, she thought that secrets and wagers and all such things were tiresome and ridiculous, and that it did not much signify after all whether her father-in-law —he was dead, too—had been an Irish tailor or an Irish squire. But she was ashamed of her ill-temper all the time, and looked up smiling when her husband pointed out a ray of sunshine shooting from under a flying cloud, and said that the weather was clearing off, and they might as well take a turn on the promenade.

"To tell you the truth, my dear Letty," he said, "I promised to meet a friend there. So pray put your bonnet on, and let us go at once."

"O yes! What friend is it?" asked Letitia. "I had no notion that you knew any one here."

"He arrived from town last night," said Crosby; and with this Letitia had to be satisfied.

By the time they reached the promenade the sun had fairly chased the clouds away, and was shining out quite warmly and pleasantly. The sea was covered with white horses frisking, and made a great noise as it came thundering on the rocks down below. There was a fresh wind still blowing, and people who ventured on the promenade could hardly keep their feet at first. In consequence of this it was almost deserted. But at the further end of it there was a quiet place sheltered by a wall of cliff; and here, long before they reached it, Letitia saw a lady and gentleman standing.

"Are those your friends, Gerald?" she said.

"Yes, dearest," he answered, pressing her arm, and looking down with a bright triumphant smile.

The rude wind had disarranged his wife's bonnet a little, and had blown some curls over her face. But he thought she had never looked more lovely than she did that morning by the sea, as he led her on to meet those two who were waiting for them in the shadow of the rock.

As for those two, the lady was middle-aged and the gentleman young. As Letitia came nearer to him, she saw in their smiling dark eyes, their graceful figures, their whole air and appearance, such a wonderful likeness to Crosby, that she half stopped and clung to him.

"O Gerald, who are they?"

He did not answer; for, seeing her movement, the lady came quickly forward.

"Mother, this is my wife," said Gerald, gently.

"My sweet girl!" said the lady, embracing Letitia, who felt as if she was in a dream.

"Will Lady Fitzpatrick spare a word to her brother Denis?" said the young man after a moment; and Letitia turned round to shake hands with the strongest possible likeness of her husband. Only Denis was rather shorter, and not quite so ornamental.

"Ah, now tell me who he is?" said Letitia, looking up at Gerald's mother with all the earnestness of an Irish girl.

"Do you mean to say he has not told you? You poor dear heroic creature!"

"Why, my lady, of course he has not told her!" exclaimed Denis, laughing. "He would have lost that wager of ours, which I have regretted so bitterly ever since. However, my five thousand pounds won't go out of the family, that is some comfort. Now, Fitzpatrick, I hope you mean to pay your debts. By the bye, all is smooth for you with Sir George Monkton. We met him in town the day before yesterday. He attacked me like a raging lion, actually mistaking me for you—that's a compliment for you. I could not have pacified him, but her ladyship took him in hand and brought him to reason."

"Hush, Denis; remember who you are talking of," said his mother. "Come, dear Letitia, I'll walk with you to your lodging, and we will leave these two rattlepates to settle their own affairs. I am afraid this distracted wager of theirs has cost you a good deal of suffering."

" O no," said Letitia, as the lady took her arm, and walked with her towards the town. " I could not have been happier. But pray tell me who he is, and all about it."

" My dear, I can't understand your not knowing. He is Lord Fitzpatrick, of course. Only an Irish peerage, people will tell you; but for my part I think we are as good as the English. As to this wager, he began by spending great sums on building and improving, and a great deal of nonsense. He went beyond his income and got into difficulties. Then he resolved to volunteer into the army. His brother said to him very naturally, that no doubt his name would get him a commission at once. This hurt Fitzpatrick's foolish pride. He told Denis he would lay him a wager of five thousand pounds that he would keep his name and birth a profound secret for three years, be known as nothing but an adventurer, and yet get on in the army as well as any other man. He even said that if any stories were invented as to his birth, he would not contradict them. We never thought such a mad idea could be carried out for three years. He has done it, however, and has contrived to win you too, by far the gayest feather in his cap. I am obliged to respect him now."

Lady Fitzpatrick talked a good deal more about her sons and their wager; but this was all that Letitia cared much to hear. Except that she was glad to find the dear name Crosby not quite an imagination; it was his mother's name. And Gerald was really his own.

The story of Miss Monkton's marriage may as well end here. One has the satisfaction of knowing that Letitia never regretted her trust in the Irish adventurer.

Sir George was angry for some time, and did not finally forgive them till Humphrey Barrett, having married a rich brewer's daughter, deserted his political colours, and came in for the county on the wrong side, which was his father-in-law's. After this Sir George repented, and was very civil to Lord Fitzpatrick.

Mrs. Bushe took up her abode with Letitia, and lived on the most affectionate terms with her and her husband. Letitia's children grew up to love her and tyrannise over her, as their mother had done before them.

But I will not say anything about Letitia's children, charmingly agreeable people as they are. I can only think of their mother as almost a child herself, dancing round the room in a white frock, all her curls shaking, or trotting smilingly along the snowy shrubbery, wrapped in scarlet, to her first meeting with the hero of her dreams.

THE STORY OF A RETURN-TICKET.

AT last I had arranged everything for a good long holiday.
I really wanted it very much. I may also state—and I
desire to do so in a modest sort of way—that I really think I
deserved one. I had been working very hard. I had been
working in an East-end parish, where we are really made to
understand what work means, as a curate, on a hundred a
year. I lived in one of the best houses of the parish, which
was nevertheless a mean little house; and if I left my study-
window open, and I always drew as near as I could towards
the light, some of my beloved parishioners would not mind
sweeping anything they could off my study-table. I had only

one friend, the son of a peer, who had taken similar lodgings in a similar street with a view of studying the great question of the condition of the people. A brief residence satisfied him respecting the problems of this great question, and he cleared out in the direction of Belgravia.

My rector was then the only gentleman and man of education in the neighbourhood. He suffered greatly, however, from Population on the Brain. He was always talking, thinking, dreaming, writing, working, about the population of his parish. He was constantly writing to School Boards, to the Ecclesiastical Commissioners, to charitable societies, to charitable individuals, about his population, which seemed to be always increasing, according to the Malthusian theory, in a geometrical ratio. I think, however, that I had the largest part of the work to do among the population, so far as the arrivals, junctions, and departures of the said population were concerned. Having had no holiday for a couple of years, I was not surprised that my rector volunteered at last that I should take one; telling me, however, that the Population would be glad to see me back on my earliest convenience. I stood out, however, for six weeks, and made up my mind that I would not open any letter or telegram which my rector might send me till the six weeks were over. Only I did.

I was taking fifty pounds with me for the expenses of those six weeks. This was the amount of one whole half-year of my annual stipend. Of course I should not be able to spare all this out of my salary. But fortunately I had an aunt, one of the right sort, who hadn't much money, indeed, but who did more good with her little than most people by their abundance. She it was who, when my parents wanted me to enter the Law, told me, if I so preferred, to take the Gospel instead; and when my friends considerately informed me that I was dooming myself to poverty and obscurity, said that, as far as her narrow means went, she would back me up. Her means were but small, but her hearty sympathy and occasional cheque eked out my narrow stipend, and enabled me to grapple with that hydra-headed population.

"Tommy," she said to me one day, "you don't look at all the thing. You are sallow and flabby in the cheeks, and hollow below the eyes."

The account of my personal appearance was not flattering, but it was correct.

"So I shall trot you off to the Continent, my dear boy, as soon as the rector will give you a holiday; and I shall give you a cheque for fifty pounds to pay your expenses."

I faltered my acknowledgments.

"But remember, Thomas, that you can't both have your cake and eat it. I shall have very few fifties to leave you, my dear boy, but I do not like you to wait for them until I am gone. Fifty pounds may do you more good now than it might by-and-by. I should like to see you as strong as when you went to the East-end. Only you will be fifty pounds poorer than would otherwise be the case by-and-by."

I did not argue the matter with my good aunt. Fifty pounds of her little stock meant a diminution of her annual income to the extent of some thirty or forty shillings, and I knew that this could be spared and be a real luxury to her to invest it in my health and welfare. I therefore very cheerfully allowed her to add this to many other kindnesses, and took myself to the delightful employment of settling my plans.

I set about these plans in a very systematic manner. I studied maps with the voracity of a uhlan. I invested in a *Bradshaw*, and in *Murrays* to any extent you like. Day by day I went by the "Underground" to the British Museum to look at maps, pictures, books. I wrote to all my travelled friends to glean all the experience I could. Instead of one tour, I was qualifying myself for a dozen. I could have electrified an examiner by my knowledge of the map of Europe. I was always covering half-sheets of note-paper with skeleton tours. My only embarrassment arose from the endeavour to bring my tour within reasonable limits of time and money. On the whole, I thought I would go through Switzerland and the Italian lakes, then to Venice, and back through the Tyrol. Only when at Venice one really must go on to Florence, and to Rome, and to Naples. Then it would be so pleasant to run on to Cyprus—everybody just then was going on to Cyprus; and then it would be only a few days to Egypt, to Palestine, to the isles of Greece. Ah, delusive visions, too fond, too vain! I little thought that they were all to end in the bathos of a return-ticket.

The night came when I started by the mail-train to make the night passage between Dover and Calais. Of course I was going to Paris. Nearly every journey in the world leads through Paris, just as all roads went to Rome. As I paced the railway-platform I observed a gentleman also pacing the platform. He was a good-looking man, and also he looked good; two things which do not always go together. He had fine clear-cut features and dreamy smiling eyes. I was glad to find myself seated opposite to him in a smoking-carriage. Not that I really cared anything about smoking, but I thought that to light up a cigar would be an appropriate prelude to my extensive travels.

It was very remarkable how pleasantly that fellow and I got on. With some fellows you do get on; with other fellows you can never get on at all. You vote them cads from the very commencement. I expect that there are such things as elective affinities between men and men. Now this young fellow was one of the frankest and most unreserved men whom I had ever met. He spoke " with effusion." He seemed to be incapable of anything like reticence. In reality he was not a young man; but though there were a few touches of gray in his hair, his mien and manners were young, with a most engaging simplicity; and once or twice a suspicion crossed my mind that he might be just a shade stupid. He told me his little history. It is very odd how often in railway-carriages I have met with people who insist on telling me their little histories and mysteries—who hold me, like that Ancient Mariner, with their "glittering eye."

His history was very simple. He was a clerk in one of the higher ranges of the Civil Service. He was nobody, but his father had been the younger son of an honourable, and the honourable had been the younger son of a lord, and the lord had been the eldest son of an earl. All semblance of a title had been absorbed; but still he belonged to a great house; and the head of the house, recognising his family duties, had got him a nomination to a good appointment; and he had had to "swot" with a crammer, and at last got through. He had never quite paid off all his Oxford debts from that day to this; and this third cousin, the earl, kept a very tight hand on him, and he had to pay so much away every quarter from his stipend, and to insure his life, and to report himself regularly to his august relative. Still he did happen to find himself in possession of a surplus fifty-pound note, and had obtained his relative's permission to spend his holiday on the Continent.

It really seemed not improbable that I and this agreeable new acquaintance should see a good deal of each other. We had the same amount of tether in the way both of coin and furlough. We had each taken a ticket to Paris. From Paris the whole world lay before us, to roam where we listed. He really was a very kind-hearted man. A little incident revealed this to me. When we got to Dover we found that the storm-

signals were up; and one weather-beaten tar, whose opinion
we consulted, said that it would take three men to hold the
captain's hat on. However, we determined to go on; but "the
silver streak" showed itself in a very turbulent mood. One
old gentlemen observed to me that he had been to the West
Indies and back, and had never suffered so much. Mr. Wyvill
had descended into the cabin to fortify himself with brandy-
and-water, while I had taken my seat on the open deck and
stared intently at the funnel, which I was told was an infallible
specific against sea-sickness. Just as I was about to try this
truly scientific experiment, a big wave swept over the deck and
completely enveloped me in a sheet of water. I was drenched
through and through; not a thread or shred was dry.

"Well, old man"—it is astonishing how quickly a traveller's
intimacy progresses—"how are you getting on?"

I explained that I wasn't getting on at all. I was wet through
and through.

"O, sea-water never hurts a fellow; you never catch cold
from sea-water."

This is, I know, a prevalent opinion; but it is as "the
Pelagians do vainly talk." All I can say is, let a man sit
thoroughly wet through for a couple of hours, with the additional advantage of a keen night wind cutting through him,
and he will stand as good a chance of a cold as any lunatic
could desire. What I know is, that when we arrived at Calais
I found myself unable to proceed. The train in correspon-
dence with the boat was starting almost at once, and there was
neither time nor opportunity to change one's clothes properly.
I determined to stop that night at Calais. I urged my good-
natured companion not to lose any time, but to go on with the
train; but he obstinately refused to separate his travelling fortunes from my own.

It was really very good of him. The journey and the

wetting had upset the British parson much more than he had felt disposed to show. So we had a quiet day at Calais, which is just the sort of place for a quiet day; went to the church, and saw some of the cannon-balls which the English had thrown in; paced along the endless tree-planted walks; fraternised with the great Gallic nation at various *cafés*; revived our recollections of Beau Brummell; made part of a prolonged *table d'hôte*; and got very comfortably into Paris next day. We did not intend to do very much at Paris. Three days were all that we allowed ourselves. For, as we acutely argued, a man can run over at any time to Paris; but we cannot very often make a prolonged tour, and we must make the best of the opportunity. Certainly the companionship of such a docile good-natured fellow was, up to the present time, a decided help to me.

But the morning after our arrival in Paris he came into my bedroom, next his own, in a most melancholy and distracted manner. It was just the woebegone expression of the man who came into Priam's bedchamber at the dead of night, and told him that half his Troy was burned. He was utterly disconcerted; and although his manner was to treat a thing lightly, and pass it off, I saw that he was disconcerted.

"It's all u-p with me, old man."

"What's the row now?"

"Lost all my money, that's all."

"That's beastly hard lines."

"I should think so, slightly."

"What do you mean to do now?"

"I am sure I don't know. I am cleaned out, and can't go on. I hardly know if I have got enough money to go home with."

"How do you suppose it happened?"

"I really can't tell. I put my fifty-pounds—a five-pound

note and a *rouleau* of napoleons, which I was told were the proper things to take with me—in my pocket-book, and the pocket-book itself into a coat-pocket. I had enough money in my purse to carry me as far as Paris; and going to get my money just now, I found that it was all gone."

"Could you have left it at home or at the money-changer's?"

"I don't think so. I felt the pocket-book all safe when I was in the train."

"I thought there were one or two queer fellows in the railway-carriage."

"Yes; and so there were in the steamboat. And, for the matter of that, I did not at all like the appearance of the cad who sat next to me at the *table d'hôte* at Calais."

"And you'll have to give up the idea of Milan and Florence and Venice?"

"Yes; and the Tyrol and Cyprus and Constantinople, and what not."

"What a grind!"

"What a grind!"

"Well, we had better have a cup of coffee. Then we'll go and have our *déjeuner* on the Boulevard des Italiens, and see something of Paris; and we will settle next day what is to be done."

So we went about; and for a man who was demi-semi-ruined he certainly took life cheerfully, and made a very good breakfast. We did some of the sights, and had a drive in the Bois, and dined, and heard some good and cheap music in the evening. The very soil and air of France make people light-hearted. But the last thing at night he looked horribly grave, and said that he was very sorry that he could not go on to Switzerland with me.

How could I help this nice pleasant fellow—so gentlemanly, so kind, so helpless? It at once came into my mind that I

really must help him if I possibly could, but it was so difficult
to see how. I had so little money, and I wanted it all for myself. My professional means were practically mortgaged to
my tradesmen, and I had only my aunt's *douceur*. I had
once been greatly impressed with a motto which ran thus:
Do all the good you can, in all the ways you can, to all the
people you can. Sympathy I had in abundance with my new-
found friend; but I was ashamed to give a mere expression of
sympathy unless I could accompany it with something sub-
stantial. I offered all the condolence I could, and then took
my bed-candle and went up-stairs.

But somehow I could not rest. Wyvill was such a good
fellow evidently. No mistake about him. It was so hard
that he should lose both his money and his holiday. Of
course I called him an ass for his stupidity in losing that
pocket-book; but I instantly retracted the derogatory expression. There was something about Wyvill which quite
released him from the category of asses.

Somehow or other a thought had been working in my mind
for a little while; a new intention began slowly to evolve itself.

"Now, Jones, my boy," I said to myself, in the remons-
trating style of soliloquy, in which I sometimes indulged,
"you have got an opportunity, if you will only cast about for
the ways and means, of doing a real kindness once in your life.
It may be many years before you have such another chance.
Put your best foot forward and try what you can do."

The idea which occurred to me was that I might take a
return-ticket. I had noticed the advertisement of return-
tickets to Switzerland in that morning's *Galignani*. What I
had originally intended and plotted out, as has been set forth,
was to take a regular little tour. How many hours had I
spent enjoyably over *Bradshaw* and *Murray*! I suppose that
the fruition of enjoyment could hardly equal the felicity of

planning. And now that ominous and ever-recurring slip was to come off betwixt the cup and my lip. My original intention had been to go to Switzerland by way of Paris, and return by the Rhine, or else take a wider sweep and come back through Germany. Now if I drew in my wings and took things on a diminished scale, I certainly might be able to save some twenty pounds. The great expense in travelling is, of course, the locomotion. If I took a return-ticket I should have less ground to travel over, and might also economise money by staying *en pension* instead of staying at a series of hotels. It would be at least twenty pounds saved; and twenty pounds would enable this honest fellow to have his holiday, and save him from returning home in discomfort and disappointment.

I had been feeling rather feverish and upset, partly from the Channel wetting and partly with this question, which had been opened up to me; but directly I had settled it I sweetly slept the sleep of the just.

I had made up my mind, in the case of this man, to do as I would be done by. "But though on pleasure I was bent, I had a frugal mind." If any of his relatives liked to help him out of the bog, such a relative would be welcome to my share of moral satisfaction arising from a virtuous action.

"Don't you think your great friend, that lord of a cousin, would help you if you were to write or telegraph to him?"

"Old man," returned Wyvill, an absurd way of addressing his junior which I could never persuade him to leave off, "I wouldn't have him know it for all the world. I should never hear the last of it. It is the sort of thing which he could never forgive. We should quarrel for life."

Then I made my proposition to him. I can really claim no merit for making it. It seemed to me as easy and natural as possible. I was only doing for him what I felt sure he would do for me under similar circumstances.

"Look here, Mr. Wyvill," I said, "I have just got fifty pounds. I'll lend you half of it with pleasure: and we will continue our journey as long as our money holds out."

I was a perfect master of all the pecuniary calculations of a tour. I was brimful of information. Tap me, and a pellucid stream of fiscal information on tourist subjects would flow out.

"We could run about Switzerland a good deal," I continued. "It is not a big country, after all, and the railways are all cheap and handy. And then we can go and live *en pension* for a few weeks, if we want to economise, and spin out the time very well."

I will not say how much Mr. Wyvill thanked me. But he did thank me a great deal, a great deal more than was necessary. He explained his position to me, which was quite unnecessary, and made it clear that my little loan would be returned by Christmas.

So the train took us through the flat country of France, until, high in the air, like light clouds, we saw the snowy summits of distant mountains. We really saw a good deal of Switzerland, boated on lakes and climbed up mountains. Remembering that we were not so rich as we thought ourselves a little while back, we did a great deal more walking than we should otherwise have done, which was, of course, all the better for us. I remember especially that, having gone up to Righi one day, we sailed in the sunset along the Lake of Lucerne, and stopped to sleep at Fluellen. Next day we walked through the St. Gothard Pass, and got as far as Bellinzona, looking down upon the wondrous opening view of the soft Italian country; and so on through chestnut woods, with the sound of waterfalls in our ears. Then we came to an exquisite lake set, gem-like, amid the mountains. It was a kind of enchanted land. There was an hotel on the borders of the lake which had once been a monastery, and it had now its cool corridors and arcades. The living rooms were vast; and so skilful were the contrivances for modifying the heat, that, though that summer was a hot one, we were cool enough, especially with the assistance of unlimited iced lemonade.

It seemed to me that this lonely region was just the place where we could most happily while away our holiday, and that we could hardly light upon better quarters than where we were. Our bill for two days was rather stiff. I went to the landlord of the hotel, whom I found a most intelligent and civil fellow, and told him that we meant to stay for some little time, and that if he were willing to take us on *pension* terms instead of hotel terms, we were very content to stay with him. A very reasonable agreement was soon arrived at, and the mention of this circumstance may perhaps put some of my readers up to a wrinkle if they have " outrun the constable " on their travels. Neither did the reduced terms imply any reduced fare. At the *table d'hôte* we had all things in common, and very good commons they were.

I really believe that this particular way of spending a holiday was much better for me than the plan which I had originally proposed to myself. Of course it would be more ambitious to climb Mont Blanc or Monte Rosa, and it would be very nice to go out to Cyprus or Roumelia. But all this implied activity and not rest, and rest was what I wanted. There was something heavenly in those sapphire skies, in the lemon-groves, in the brooding mountain shadows cast over the lake. It was Mignon's country. Let me quote Dr. Shuldham's translation of Goethe's song :

> " Know'st thou the land where the spiced citron blows ?
> In foliage dark the golden orange glows.
> A gentle wind breathes from the deep-blue sky,
> The myrtle stands so still, the laurel-branch so high.

Know'st thou it well?   O there with thee
Would I, my heart's beloved, gladly flee.

"Know'st thou the house, with pillared porches tall;
Glitters each room, and broadly gleams the hall :
Where sculptured statues meet with stony stare
Thy gaze?   Who caused thy tears, O child of care?
Know'st thou it well?   O, there with thee
Would I, my strong protector, gladly flee.

"The mountain-path in cloudland dost thou know,
Where seeks the mule his footing in the snow?
There dwells in caves the dragon's ancient brood;
There leans the rock, and o'er it leaps the flood.
Know'st thou it well?   There, there with thee,
O guide my footsteps!   Father, come with me!"

Dear Wilhelm Meister!   Reading that enchanted page I would gladly renew the possibilities of adventurous youth.   I thought that life's romance was all over for the drone of an East-end curate.   But it was not so to be.

One afternoon, coming back from an excursion from some "mountain-path in cloudland," we saw signs of some extra bit of business and excitement about our hotel.   There was a crowd about the archway that led into the central court of our hotel.   In the court there was a large travelling carriage, about which groups and hangers-on were clustered admiringly; and we were told that an English *milor* and some gracious ladies had arrived that day.

By and by Wyvill came into my room in a state of considerable excitement.   It was a very pleasant room with an outlook on the lake, which seemed like a gorgeous picture set in a frame. My little iron bed was stowed away in a corner, and across it a curtain, which being drawn converted my room into a snuggery, if we wished to retreat from the vast public rooms.   Here we drank the wine of the country—very pleasant and cheap— and smoked mild cigarettes.   Here Wyvill found me, breaking in somewhat impetuously for a man of his languid nature.

" Who on earth do you think has come in that travelling carriage ? "

" Not knowing, can't say."

" It's my cousin, Lord Dash ! "

" You don't mean it ! That earl who looks so sharp after you ? "

" The same. Isn't it a nuisance ? "

" An awful nuisance."

And yet it seemed to me rather hard that the Earl of Dash should be voted a nuisance. The helpless cousin, Frederick Wyvill, was all the better for this great connection, and the supervision which this great connection was kind enough to exercise over him. Wyvill's great anxiety evidently was that the earl, being on the spot, was bound to find out all about the important loss of that fifty pounds. I represented to him that this accident was really no particular business of Lord Dash's ; that Lord Dash could not know it unless he chose to tell him, and he was under no necessity of telling him if he did not choose.

" But you don't know that man's powers of wigging ; you don't know that man's powers of wigging," he kept on saying ; " and he's sure to get it out of me, quite sure."

He felt himself powerless to conceal anything from the basilisk eyes of the lordly Dash. He was sure " it would all come out." Wyvill was a sort of man who always wanted some other sort of man to exercise an ascendency over him. His notion was that he had better cut and run for it. But the earl might have already detected his presence. Besides, he had no money to enable him to run away.

That afternoon I had a distant view of the noble lord extending three patronising fingers to Wyvill, who received them in a bashful and penitential manner. I wondered whether he and his daughters would make their appearance at the *table d'hôte.* But such a great man as the earl of course thought fit to dine in his own private apartments, and Wyvill had to dine with them. He did not have half so good a dinner, or half so lively a dinner, as we had in the *salle-à-manger;* and he had to pay four or five times as much for it. Thus it happens in this world that one man's impecuniosity is balanced by another's abundance. Our landlord was kind to us, but he took it out of the noble lord.

We discussed matters over some *Asti spumante.* Wyvill told me that the dinner was dull, and that his noble relative felt it dull, and intended to grace the *table d'hôte* with his right honourable presence next day. So he came in on the morrow with his daughters, two bright, pleasant, unaffected girls. Wyvill introduced me to them and to the earl. The noble lord was a very shrewd old man; he evidently looked upon his cousin as being partially imbecile, and there was a good deal of satire mixed up with any remarks which he addressed to him. The earl was full of anecdotes and observation; evidently a man who was painfully anxious to do right, benevolent and high-principled. He came as little near the idea of a bloated aristocrat as any man whom I had ever seen.

It so happened that I saw a good deal of Lord Dash and his people. There is no place like an hotel by an Italian lake for getting up intimacies. You take your meals together, you sit in the drawing-room together, you climb the hills and boat on the lake together. I really was very much interested and amused by the earl's remarks. He noticed this, and gave me plenty of them. As for Wyvill he evidently shirked his noble relative. He did not care for autobiographical remarks of an improving tendency. He had the bad taste not to care for his cousinesses, if I may coin a word which is much wanted in the language. He was long and lazy. He would go in a boat if he was not required to pull; or climb a mountain if he could

THE ARRIVAL OF LORD DASH AND HIS DAUGHTERS.

260.

do it on a mule's back. *Voilà tout.* So he took heavily to smoking and billiards, while I escorted the young ladies, with or without their noble sire, over the lake or up the heights.

Lady Gertrude and Lady Alice had been travelling for some time. I soon saw how much ground they had travelled, and they must also have seen how little I had done myself. These young ladies nicely balanced each other. Each supplied a counteractive principle to the other; and if I flirted with the Gertrude I was recalled to my senses by the Alice. Fortunately I had read travel-books so extensively that I was able to hold my own when we discussed matters. Only I confess that when I heard their description of regions which I longed to traverse, which I had studied in my waking hours, had pictured in my dreams, with a sense of irritation I started impatiently to my feet, and remembered remorselessly that I was bound in the fetters of a return-ticket, and that any progress was barred by my inexorable fate.

I often vengefully contemplated that obnoxious little document; I execrated it, I shook my fist at it, once I stamped it vindictively under foot, and was only restrained by prudential motives from altogether destroying it. It needed a frequent glance at Wyvill's placid happy countenance, drinking in the beauty and freshness of the heavens and the earth, to reconcile me to the painful limits imposed on me by the return-ticket. Under the melancholy circumstances I felt myself in some sort of way a ticket-of-leave man.

Before the full term of my holiday was over I was summoned home by my rector, who explained as an excuse that the population was growing with a rapidity which was simply frightful. Not content with an extraordinary average of births, the parish had imported a mighty influx of labourers for dock extension or something of that sort. The rector wrote in an agitated frame of mind, and evidently in a state of collapse. It was very hard lines; but the recall was peremptory, and, to say the truth, in spite of that admirable system of balances and compensations, Lady Gertrude was beginning seriously to assail my peace of mind. When I announced my intention of a speedy return—through the same flat French country, through the same inevitable Paris—that good fellow Wyvill said that he must accompany me. As he had another ten days to run, I would not allow this, and left him pathetically lamenting that when he no longer had me to back him up he was sure that "the murder would out."

I reached home, and resumed the heavy routine of my East-end duties. Sometimes I thought of those days by the enchanted lake; but it was a kind of reverie in which I hardly dared to indulge for long. One day, however, ten months afterwards, when that pleasant interlude was almost vanishing from my memory, I received the following letter from my Lord Dash :

"Dashwood Park, May 1.

"My dear Mr. Jones,

"The living of Dashwood in my gift is just vacant, and I give myself the pleasure of offering it to you. In value it is close on nine hundred a year, and the grounds adjoin my own. Of course it is a great point with us to have a pleasant neighbour, which will be insured in your case. But I must tell you that this is not the real reason which induces me to offer you preferment. I have been informed by my excellent but careless kinsman, Frederick Wyvill, of your most kind and generous behaviour to him, for which I thank you very much, and which we both thoroughly appreciate. I hope you will write very soon, and tell me that you accept.

"Yours very faithfully,

"DASH."

The offer was too good to be refused. The aunt who

thought that I had hardly seen the value of my money was delighted when I told the story to her, and I am sure that she would tell me in any case that I had done the right thing.

Wyvill and I used to interchange occasional letters, and in more than one he hinted at our resuming, under happier auspices, that abridged journey to foreign parts. At last there came a time when I wrote to him to say that I really was going to undertake something approximating to the "grand tour." I added that I should be favoured with a companion who was at once handsomer and more helpless than himself; but that for such a rare combination I should be obliged to have recourse to one of the opposite sex. In fact, Lady Gertrude and I were about to make a honeymoon tour.

But thinking of good old Wyvill, I have written a sermon on this text : "Be not forgetful to entertain strangers, for thereby some have entertained angels unawares."

KITES AND PIGEONS.

By JOSEPH HATTON.

ILLUSTRATED BY LINLEY
SAMBOURNE.

I.

CONSPIRATORS.

"I HAVE given my word to marry you to one of our guests within a month, have I not?" said Colonel Tippits, of the First Poppleton Militia, to his daughter, Clementina.

"You have, papa! And I am sure you will keep your word," said the lady, rolling a pair of full grey eyes with a languishing air, which she had practised for five-and-twenty years.

"As the daughter of your widowed mother, introduced into this sublunary sphere long before I had the pleasure of knowing the dear departed, society may not consider that I have any special duty to perform in your case; but I have—yes I have, Clementina, and that duty shall be done."

"Thanks, thanks, dear papa; as you were saying over your first cup of coffee, the property of Mr. Thornton's uncle joins your estate, and it certainly would be an advantage if I formed a matrimonial alliance with that gentleman."

“You are a dutiful girl, Clementina. If such a union could be negociated, I know you would do what is right. I have brought the gentleman here under your own immediate influence. I leave the rest to you.”

“The only unfortunate incident in the business is Miss Austin’s return,” said Clementina, toying pathetically with an empty egg-shell. “Your ward, sir, is always in my way. Why the London season could not have lasted another week I cannot think.”

“Another week, and to-morrow is the 1st of September, the glorious first, as they call it. What are you talking of, my dear? It would be an utter impossibility. London could never think of committing such an offence against the social laws. The season last another week, bless the child!”

The child was a gushing young thing of five-and-forty, a plump, round, enthusiastic heap of womanhood, with an armful of false hair hanging down her back, a pair of cheeks that would insist on being red, despite powder and other appliances, and two big grey eyes that rolled, and languished, and searched for a husband. The papa was a tall, weak-headed gentleman, who had made his way from a lowly position to one of comparative affluence. No one ever knew what the colonel’s origin was, and no one inquired. He had been a well-to-do man for more than fifteen years, during five of which he had lived at Tinsell Hall, where our story opens.

“You need not fear Miss Austin, love,” said the Colonel, passing his hand carefully through his scanty hair, and looking at himself in a conveniently-placed mirror. “You need not fear poor Miss Austin.”

“Poor Miss Austin! I do not understand you,” said Clementina. “I only know I hate the minx because she is not poor.”

“Hate her no longer, child of my heart—no I didn’t exactly

mean that, rather let me say, child of my widowered years. She is not the heiress you imagine. I have sworn to marry you; and, in order to do it, I have taken the jewel out of the Austin diadem."

"You are too clever for me, you dear old thing," said Miss Tippits, getting up, and kissing her papa-in-law on the forehead.

"There, no demonstration, love. Save your kisses for Mr. Thornton, or Mr. Pigeon junior. These are the two chances I give you this week. One bird is in the house now; the other is on his way. If you do not bag one of them, it will not be my fault."

"Nor mine, sir," said Miss Tippits, surveying her back hair furtively by the aid of a pier glass and mirror.

"We must not finish breakfast before Mr. Thornton comes down," said the Colonel. "I told him we should not wait for him. These young swells like that sort of thing. It is familiar, and makes them at home; and is, I believe, the correct thing in the very best society."

"Yes, papa dear; but you were going to say something about Miss Austin."

"There are no secrets between us, Clementina," said the Colonel, putting a heavy gold-rimmed glass in his eye, and balancing it there with difficulty. "You have played a daughter's part towards me in the most dutiful and affectionate manner; you have kept my house economically, and looked after my accounts as faithfully as one could possibly expect in a woman, and I reciprocate."

"Yes," said Miss Tippits, impatiently; "yes. Go on."

"Miss Austin, as my ward, possessed a large estate in India. Miss A. came of age a month ago. I have relieved her of the bother of an uncertain kind of property, you know, by settling upon her one thousand a year, in return for which she gives up to Colonel Tippits, of Tinsell Hall, the whole of her lands, tenements, hereditaments, and property whatsoever, and her reversionary interest in old Twizall's will; so we are now worth, my child, something like eight thousand a year more than we possessed a month ago, and your rival is not anheiress."

"Oh, you dear papa! oh, you love!"

"Don't gush; it is not polite," said the Colonel.

"Oh, if you could only make her ten years older, and take away her complexion, I would back myself to beat her in a canter. And you, dear Colonel, you my dear second father, my papa, and mother, and friend all in one, you now will be able to go into parliament."

"Ah, there you hit me, Clementina," said the Colonel, rising to his feet, and striking an attitude suggestive of walking into parliament at the head of the poll. "When I received the colonelship of my regiment at Inglenook, I said—you remember the vow—my next step is a greater one still. 'Gentlemen, brother electors, freemen of the glorious borough of Inglenook, the time has now arrived when you are once more called upon to exercise the highest privilege of Englishmen.'"

"Hear, hear," said Miss Tippits, not, however, without a pang of regret for having led the conversation into a channel which always became tedious.

"'The time, I say, has now arrived," continued the Colonel, addressing the breakfast-table, and scowling at Miss Tippits; "the time has now arrived when, according to the laws of your great though unhappy country, you may make your voices heard in the Senate of the land by electing to that assembly a man of your own choice."

Miss Tippits again exclaimed, "Hear, hear!" and as she did so, there entered upon the scene Mr. Thornton, a young man of good family, and, what Society would call, excellent prospects. There was, however, a feud between himself and his uncle. Happily this would not prevent Thornton from coming in for his uncle's property some day, seeing that the estate could not be left to any one else. Mr. Thornton liked going down to shoot at Tinsell Hall, because it joined the property to which he was the rightful heir, and he could inspect it from Colonel Tippits's stubbles.

"Ah, Colonel, rehearsing your hustings' speech?" said Mr. Thornton. "Good morning, Miss Tippits. I hope I have not kept breakfast waiting."

"No, Mr. Thornton; papa said we were to treat you as one of the family, and thus try to make you feel quite at home. Do you take tea or coffee?"

"You are very good," said Mr. Thornton; "I will take coffee."

"No, did not wait, you see, Thornton; make you quite one of ourselves; no stranger, as I shall say to my constituents— true friendship means familiarity."

"But familiarity breeds contempt, they say. You must correct your little speech, sir. Eh, Miss Tippits?"

"Oh, certainly; yes, by all means," said Clementina.

"Happy thought! Thank you, Mr. Thornton. It would never do to lay oneself open to the opposition by a slip of that kind. Two heads are better than one," said the Colonel.

"Oh, yes!" said Miss T.

"If they are only sheep's heads, as the proverb hath it," responded Thornton.

"He means that for a dig at me," thought the Colonel. "No matter, I'll be even with him; I'll marry him to Clementina."

"Proverbs are stupid things as a rule," said the Colonel. "What do you propose to do this morning, Mr. Thornton?"

"I am going to give Miss Tippits a lesson in billiards, if she will permit me; and then I propose to reconnoitre three or four coveys of birds, so that I may know exactly where they lie in the morning."

"That is very kind of you," said Miss Tippits.

At this moment a servant announced that Miss Austin had arrived. Miss Tippits only said, "Indeed!"

Mr. Thornton looked curiously at his host.

"Excuse me," he said, "did your servant say Miss Austin? Pray excuse me as one of the family; the name interests me much."

"The servant did say Miss Austin," Colonel Tippits replied.

"Is her name Kate?" asked Mr. Thornton, laying down his knife and fork, and wiping his hands with a napkin, "daughter of an old Indian heiress, staying in Belgrave Square with her Aunt?"

"Yes," said Miss Tippits, gasping out the words in an agony of jealous apprehension; "my papa's ward."

"Bless my soul!" exclaimed Mr. Thornton, unable to control his feelings. "This is a pleasure!"

Miss Tippits and the Colonel exchanged looks of chagrin, just as Miss Kate Austin entered the room.

"Back again, you see, Colonel," said Kate.

"Welcome to Tinsell Hall," exclaimed the Colonel, taking Miss Austin's hand.

"Mr. Thornton!" said Miss Austin, suddenly seeing the Colonel's guest. "This is a surprise!"

"It is indeed," said Thornton, shaking her hand with an enthusiasm which was a little foreign to his nature. "Colonel Tippits, you have no idea what a surprise this is. Would you believe it, Miss Tippits, I began to fear I should never see Miss Austin again. I met her at a ball last season. I have hunted after her everywhere this year, and have never been able to find her."

"How singular!" said Miss Tippits.

"Infernally singular," said the Colonel to himself. "Have you breakfasted, Miss Austin?"

"Yes, thank you; an hour ago," Miss Austin replied. "I came from town exactly in forty minutes."

"For my part," said Miss Tippits, "I wonder how any one can exist in town at this time of the year."

"The season has appeared a long one to me, I confess," said Kate; "I was heartily tired of it."

"When my dear papa got his colonelcy a month ago, and his regiment was up for a month's training at Inglenook, and he had to leave town in consequence, I came with him at once, though it was at the sacrifice of a Frogmore garden party."

"A good fib well told," the Colonel thought.

"I am rejoiced to hear you were glad to get into the country," said Mr. Thornton; "London is a wicked place."

"Is it not?" said Clementina, rolling her eyes at Mr.

Thornton, and making up her mind to run Miss Austin hard for the hand of her friend.

Here the servant entered with a letter, which the Colonel looked at several times through his eye-glass, and then, with due apology, read, giving the breakfast-room the full benefit of its contents.

"Oh, indeed; ah, very good. Mr. Tom Pigeon junior, and Mr. Theophilus Pigeon senior, will arrive at the Inglenook Hotel to-day. Dear me; very good. We must call upon them, Miss Tippits. They are a strange pair, Mr. Thornton."

"The Pigeons?" said Mr. Thornton.

"Yes. Ah, very good, Mr. Thornton—pair of pigeons; pardonable joke; retired merchants, sir; met them in London the other day."

"Now, Mr. Thornton, I am ready for my lesson at billiards, if you have really finished breakfast," said Miss Tippits, interrupting something the guest was saying in an undertone to Kate.

"Certainly," said Mr. Thornton, offering his arm to the buxom coquette of forty-five. "Miss Austin, will you join us? We are going into the billiard-room."

"No, thank you," said the lady; "I must assist my maid to unpack presently. Meanwhile I will stay with the Colonel."

Miss Tippits congratulated herself that she had made the first score. As she left the room she rolled her eyes significantly at the Colonel; but she did not see the disappointed expression on Mr. Thornton's face as he glanced reproachfully at Kate Austin.

II.

ARRIVALS AT THE GREEN DRAGON.

Two voices; the first a husky, panting voice, struggling under a burden; the second a sharp ringing cockney voice, making its way from the hotel yard and through several passages into the best ground-floor private sitting-room.

"I'm blowed if ever I see such a gent in all my life," said the first voice, which was the voice of the Green Dragon boots, " and I've seen a few in my time."

"I say, hi, there! You there!" exclaimed the second voice in the hotel yard; "will you fetch this luggage, or will you not? it is not much I ask; will you or won't you?"

" Coming, sir," said the boots, bundling an armful of bags and wrappers upon the floor.

" Will you or won't you?" said the voice from without.

" Coming, sir," said the boots from within.

" Coming; so is the end of the world—never saw such management," answered the cockney in the yard.

At this moment the landlord was heard introducing himself to the noisy visitor, and the voice became more conciliatory; you heard it saying, "Very well, very well; it is not much I ask; if the luggage will be taken in soon, all right."

At the end of the coffee-room, exactly opposite the door leading into the hall and yard, there enters a tall, gaunt figure.

" Who are these new arrivals? fancy I know the voice."

" Oh, how do you do, Mr. Kite; beg pardon for not seeing you. The governor's got him in tow now, thank goodness; they're father and son from London, sir—by morning mail—

the young un is like the gent with the cork leg ; never saw his equal."

"Ah! yes," says Mr. Kite, aloud, supplementing the remark with a private communication to himself; "my old master, the rich tailor of Bond Street, and his harem scarem son. I'll step inside and reconnoitre."

"Oh, you think you've got all, do you," says the voice from without, evidently following a second porter laden with luggage. "Wonderful! you shall have a medal for thinking, you shall."

With which remark, Mr. Tom Pigeon enters the best private sitting-room.

"Never saw such a set of slow coaches," he continues, as he contemplates the boots and his assistants. "Pity the Green Dragon himself don't turn up ; he'd keep you alive."

"Shouldn't want no Green Dragon to do that if you was here, sir," said boots.

"Hollo! where's the governor?" exclaims Mr. Tom Pigeon, feeling in his pockets as if he expected to find him there ; and then suddenly disappearing in the hall and returning with an elderly gentleman.

"Come along, governor, come along—keep moving—the family motto, you know," says Mr. Tom Pigeon.

"Moving," says the governor, who was no other than Tom's respected father. "Keep moving; why, I am worn out already; my appointment with Colonel Tippits is not until one o'clock, and I shall have to sit here and bite my nails for the next two hours."

"Bite your nails!" exclaims the younger traveller; "nothing of the sort."

"I shall not stir from here until the time," says old Pigeon, carefully seating himself on an old-fashioned sofa.

"All right," replies his son. Rings the bell. "Waiter!"

"Yes, sir," responds the chief waiter of the Dragon.

" Where's Miller's farm ? "

" Who's Miller ? " asks Mr. Pigeon senior.

" Never mind who Miller is," responds the son, " that's my
affair—that's my secret, guv.   You have your secrets, I have
mine ;—that's fair, eh ?   But you shall see my secret, dad,
nevertheless.   Waiter, why don't you tell me how far it is to
Miller's farm ?   Say you will or you won't—that is all I ask—
you will or you won't ? "

" You never give me time, sir," says the waiter.

" Time, sir ! " exclaims Tom ; " give you time.   Time is not
to be given away, waiter; take it by the forelock and keep
moving; that's the way to deal with time."

" Two mile, sir—that's the distance."

" Right you are; when you have anything to say, say it
qiuckly and at once.   What can we have for dinner ? "

" But, sir," began the waiter.

" Don't but me," says Tom, familiarly pushing the waiter out of the room. " Be off and see what there is for dinner; and order a four-wheeler to take me to Mr. Miller's farm."

" For shame, Tommy; you should not be so impestuous," says Mr. Pigeon senior, who, instead of stopping the torrent only increased its velocity.

" There you are again," says Tom; "now didn't I tell you not to call me Tommy—did I or did I not?—here we are a-going into Society, and you are a Tommying me just as if we were on the shop-board. And what do you mean by im-pestuous?—I never heard of such a word—you will have to go to a School Board and be polished, governor. Now it is not much a doating son asks of a doating father: will you drop the Tommy, the shop, and the tailor?"

" All right, Tommy," says the father, sinning again in his very promise of amendment. " Oh, lor, Tom—I mean, my dear Tom."

" There, that will do," says Tom, patting Mr. Pigeon senior affectionately on the back. " Now will you tell me your busi-ness with this swell at Tinsell Castle. Secret for secret, eh?"

" No, Tom, I will not."

" You won't."

" No."

" That's just what I like," says Tom. " Smart and to the point."

" It's only an old bill for liveries."

" Governor—governor, that's a fib."

" Well, look here, Tom, my boy," says the father, preparing to make a statement; "look here, now——"

" No, no, Theophilus Pigeon, Esq., keep your secret; tell no fibs."

" Well then, Tommy——" begins the father.

"Tommy again—hang Tommy! Can't you say Tom or Thomas or Jackass, or anything but Tommy? What is the good of our going into Society if it is always Tommy?"

"Well, then, Tom; for jackass you are not."

"Sir to you," says Tom.

"Well, then—— "

"You've said that before; don't say it again."

"No, I will not," says Mr. Pigeon senior, getting up from his seat a little angrily; "no, I will not. Remain in the dark."

"In the dark be it," says Tom, nothing disconcerted; "anything, so that it is decisive."

"Oh, I am so tired," says Mr. Pigeon senior.

"Then go to sleep, dear old boy," says his son, promptly. "There, tuck up your legs, and have a nap—a little drop of something short and an hour's nap."

Tom's prescription was accepted. The reader would have been agreeably surprised could he have seen how affectionately Tom covered his father over with a travelling-rug, and made the sofa comfortable. If the son had no reverence for the author of his being he was not devoid of affection; though it tried his patience greatly that his father did not acquire with more rapidity what Tom considered the true habits and manners of Society.

<hr>

III.

TOM DISCOVERS HIS FATHER'S SECRET.

Mr. Tom Pigeon, having seen his father comfortably asleep, resolved to sit down quietly for a moment and reflect upon the situation. Miller's farm contained one of the prettiest and roundest little girls that the Cattle Show had ever brought to London with an English farmer. Tom was thinking that he would like to have driven tandem to Jessie Miller's home.

"That would have been the style," he said to himself, imitating, as he sat in his chair, the action of driving a pair of restive horses. "Dashing leader prancing through the town, cantering through the lanes—pull up at the farm—out runs Jessie to meet me—farmer wondering at the turn-out, and pretty little Jessie. Hollo!"

The exclamation was one of pain. Tom had been sitting on his father's over-coat.

"Hollo! Oh, jemminy! Scissors and paving-stones! A needle a yard long! What the deuce does the governor do with needles in his pocket now that we have retired from the profession and are going into Society."

Examining old Mr. Pigeon's coat, Tom discovered a needle-case and thimble.

"He promised me faithfully that he would drop the shop, and go into Society with me like a gentleman; and here he is going on worse than that fellow Kite, who used to be his head cutter-out."

While Tom was discussing his father's shortcomings there fell out of the old man's coat a letter. It was addressed to Theophilus Pigeon, Esquire.

"Oh! oh! *Esquire,* eh? That means a hand in the governor's pocket, I'll swear," said Tom, alternately glancing at his father asleep and the letter. "We must read this, Thomas Pigeon junior, only son and heir of your father; we must not allow our dear father to be swindled; no. Here we go, then."

"Col. Tippits will be glad to extend the mortgage to £25,000, and hopes to see Mr. Pigeon on the first of September; and Col. Tippits further hopes that Mr. Pigeon will introduce his interesting son at Tinsell Castle on the first opportunity.

"TINSELL CASTLE, *Aug.* 20."

Tom made a variety of significant gestures signifying surprise and delight. He shook his fist affectionately at the old man asleep on the sofa, and laughed silently all over his face. It was an expressive face, full of humour and intelligence. The mouth was large and flexible. It worked in comic sympathy with a peculiar wink with which Tom kept in good-humour persons with whom he pretended to be very angry.

"That's the dear old governor's secret," he said. "He's worth twenty thousand pounds more than I thought, and, I dare say, another five-and-twenty thou to boot. Bravo, dad! Bravo, Theophilus Pigeon, Esquire! Bravo, Pigeon and Son!"

"Thought I'd remind you of the fly, sir," said the waiter, entering just upon the consummation of Tom's discovery.

"Fly, sir. What do you mean?"

"The four-wheeler, sir?"

"Four-wheeler," said Mr. Pigeon junior, remembering, for the first time since his arrival at the Dragon, that he had brought an eye-glass to accompany him into Society. "Fly, four-wheeler—what do you mean?"

"The fly you ordered," said the waiter.

"Some mistake," said Mr. Pigeon junior, remembering that, with the eye-glass, he intended to revise his mode of speech. "Ah, waiter; ah, some mistake. If I did order a fly it must have been months ago. I have found five-and-twenty thousand pounds since then. Make it a carriage and four, waiter. Yas, yas."

The waiter disappeared, with a puzzled air; while Mr. Pigeon senior slept on, unconscious of the additional fillip which had been given to his son's ambitious views in regard to Society.

"Yas," said Tom, waving his hand to himself in a misty glass over the mantle-shelf. "Yas, this is the happiest day of my life. For a slow coach, the governor has kept moving, after all. Go into Society! I should think we would—rather! See life! Just so. Motto, still keep moving."

Mr. Kite, who had by this time sufficiently remembered his old friend, now entered the room.

"How do you do?" he said. "Who would have thought to find you in Inglenook?"

"Eh?" said Mr. Pigeon junior, critically examining Mr. Kite's boots and cravat through his glass.

"I asked after your health, sir," said Kite, drawing himself up to his full height, and looking down upon his friend.

"Indeed," said young Pigeon. "Yas, yas."

"Don't you know me?" asked Mr. Kite.

"Never saw you in my life before—never—assure you," said Tom.

"Not remember your father's shopman?"

"Father never had a shop; therefore never had a shopman, d'ye see. Father's son don't know shops or shopmen. See?"

"Yes, I see. Very good; I see," said Mr. Kite. "My name ain't Kite. I never was a shopman, nor a cutter, nor anything of the sort. I am a gentleman; so are you, sir, I perceive. Mr. Pigeon, sir, I hope I have the pleasure of seeing you well."

"Very well, indeed, thank you—" said Tom. "Are you in Society, Kite?"

"I should think I was," said Mr. Kite, stretching out first his right arm and then his left, and pulling down a pair of white shirt-cuffs over a pair of faultlessly gloved hands. "Should think I was in Society."

"Ah, father and I are just going in," said Tom, as if Society were an exhibition for which he had secured reserved seats.

"Indeed; Mr. Pigeon, I am delighted; we shall often meet. I am down here professionally, preparing the way for return of Colonel Tippits as a member of Parliament."

"Ah, yes; we know Tippits," said Mr. Pigeon. "How is Tippits?"

"Very well indeed," said Kite; "charming thing your knowing Tippits; he is the *ton* here. I am his agent, accredited to the house of Topham and Downham, Bribem Court, E.C."

"Just so. Very glad to hear it, Kite," said Tom, trying to find his eye-glass, and pulling out his watch by mistake.

"Glass is in your left hand."

"Thanks," said Pigeon, evidently a little nettled that Kite had noticed his confusion. "Now look here, Kite, no more nonsense; let us understand each other: it is agreed that we drop the shop."

"Certainly."

"The Pigeons of Belgrave Square are worth a hundred thousand pounds if they are worth a penny; the Pigeons are now seeking change of air; the Pigeons are on their travels; they are going into Society; it is not much they ask, but that much they mean to have, you understand."

Mr. Kite assured his friend that he perfectly understood him, and hoped to call him friend for many a long year to come. He said he was going to call at the Castle, and offered to leave the cards of Pigeon and Son with his own, whereupon Tom broke out into a towering passion.

"You have just promised me, in the most solemn manner, that you would sink the shop, and you talk of cards. I tell you we have neither cards nor patterns; Pigeon and Son have retired for ever; Pigeon and Son are gentlemen residing at the family mansion in Belgrave Square, and anything to the contrary from you, Kite, will simply get you kicked out of Society straight, in addition to being cut off with a shilling by your old master."

"My dear sir," said Kite, "you do not understand. In Society gentlemen have address cards—private affairs which they call pasteboard—you will know all about it by-and-bye; you may trust Charlie Kite; he will be true to himself and to his honourable friends the Pigeons."

With which grandiloquent assurance of friendship and protection, Mr. Kite bowed profoundly to his friend and withdrew.

"Now to wake the governor," said Tom, shaking old Pigeon by the collar.

"What is it?" grumbled the old man.

"Wake up; I've found a letter with five-and-twenty thousand pounds in it."

"Where, Tommy, where?" The old man was wide awake now.

"Here, here," Tom replied, flourishing the letter of Colonel Tippits.

"Oh, you rascal!" exclaimed Mr. Pigeon senior, trying to snatch the letter from his son.

"Why, you rich old Belgravian swell, you are worth a hundred thou—something like a secret—oh you Crœsus, you Rothschild, you Bank of England—a hundred thousand; and still you are not happy."

"Yes I am, my boy—I am indeed," said old Pigeon; for he knew nothing of Aladdin the Second and the Tycoon.

"I repeat," said young Pigeon, throwing his head back and jerking out his chin. "And still you are not happy?"

"Yes, dear boy, I am," said Mr. Pigeon senior, putting his hand on Tom's shoulder; "but money has its cares, Tommy—I mean Tom or Thomas."

"Go on, guv, I forgive you; you can call me Tommy now and then, when nobody's near, you know; it is only in the presence of other people that it makes me so wild to hear you sinking dignity and high life."

"Very good, dear Tom, I will remember; but as I was a saying, my old partner used to hobserve, Ah, Pigeon, my friend, he used to say—ah, Pigeon, you are a lucky dog—your needle is always sticking in the right place."

"Blow your needle," said Tom, rubbing his back. "I differ with your old partner; but tell me, sir, tell your son and heir, who only lives to make you happy, tell Thomas Pigeon, Esquire, junior, how much you are really worth."

Old Pigeon listened cautiously, and looked to see that nobody was within hearing near door or window.

"What do you say to a plum, Tommy?" he whispered.

"Tommy again—never mind, the plum makes up for it," said young Pigeon. "It's enough to drive a fellow mad, governor. A plum—a plummy plum plum! Now look here, my dear old friend and father, Theophilus Pigeon, of Belgrave Square, plumber;—no, I don't mean that; I'm a little off my head, you see, what with plums, and Kites, and castles. Henceforth we are in Society. From this moment we are swells; we must dress better than this (looking at his trousers and examining his father's coat); we must give some rascally tailor an order at once; blow him up, and do the haw-haw business, and wink at his daughter if he has one, and swear politely, and smoke shilling cigars."

"No, Tommy, if we are going to be gentlemen let us behave as such; that is my motto."

"Come in," bawled the younger Pigeon, in reply to a knock at the door.

"Will you please to order dinner, sir," asked the waiter, entering.

"Yas," said Mr. Pigeon junior, "yas, we'll have everything you've got."

"Yes, sir. And please, sir, the carriage is waiting."

"Dismiss it," said the rich young man; "we shall delay our visit to the farmer's; we are expecting a call from the Castle."

"Yes, sir."

"And, waiter."

"Yes, sir."

"Are there any rascally tailors in this place?"

"Yes, sir."

"How many rascally tailors?"

"Two, sir."

"Tell them to send me half a dozen suits of clothes, morning and dress."

"I suppose you are another candidate for the borough, sir. Yes, sir."

"Don't tell me what you suppose; tell the rascally tailors what you please."

"Yes, sir; when shall they call to measure you, sir?"

"Measure me," said Tom, with well-feigned bewilderment. "Oh, ah, yas, of course, true—true; they measure you" (imitating the operation of measuring)—"I remember; we will be measured, waiter, we will be measured."

"Yes, sir; I will order the rascally tailors at once," said the waiter, leaving the room.

"The impudent puppy," said old Pigeon, when the door was shut. "Tommy, I don't like this new-fangled manner of yours; tone it down, dear boy; tone it down. I never knew a real gentleman as had that style; it ain't true breeding."

"Nonsense, governor; you don't understand the laws of fashionable life. It's no good a fellow wearing an eye-glass, and being a swell unless he has eye-glass on the brain," said

Tom, making a great show of polishing his glass, fixing it in his eye, and trying to let it fall suddenly from its position while he was speaking.

"I differ with you, Tommy, but I'm willing to let you have your fling. You know I love you with all my heart; my fortune is yours. Spend the money honourably and fairly; if you could spend it without going into Society, as you calls it, I should be all the better pleased."

"All right, dad; rely on me. I'll do nothing to disgrace the name of Pigeon; but Society's a *siny quy non*. I only ask you to sink the shop and keep moving—onward, and keep moving."

"Well, I shouldn't mind, Tom, if we moved a little now. Couldn't we take a bit of a walk together until the Colonel comes?"

"A bit of a walk!" Tom exclaimed, seizing his father by the arm.   "Hang it, governor, we'll have a gallop together."

With which remark Tom ran his father gaily into the hotel passage; then into the yard; and, finally, into the High Street, where the shopkeepers seemed to have considerable business on their doorsteps. The majority of the Inglenook tradesmen, or their assistants, were standing at their doors on this Feast of St. Partridge. Some of them were out in the adjacent meadows; you could almost hear their guns going off in the stubbles. The sportsmen who were left behind consoled themselves with the thought that the bags would be smaller on account of their absence.

IV.

WINNING A WAGER THAT NEVER WAS MADE.

Mr. Pigeon senior soon tired of Tom's gallop, and returned to the hotel, while Tom tried to visit Miller's farm by a short cut across the fields.

"Who are the Millers, in this neighbourhood?" old Pigeon asked the waiter.

"The farmer, you means?" asked the waiter.

"Yes, my son spoke of Miller, the farmer."

"Well, he was warmish once," said the waiter. "A snug farm, and first-rate land; but the Colonel's been and had him, sir; had him at 'oss-racing, I think; and he's going to leave the farm."

"Lost all his money on the turf, eh?"

"Yes, money and turf too," said the waiter; "for he's got to turn out of the farm; and that's a fact as will go again the Colonel a good deal when the election comes on."

Further conversation was interrupted by the entrance of a messenger with a letter for Theophilus Pigeon, Esquire.

"Thank you, young man," said Mr. Pigeon, with the practised obsequiousness of half a century.

"Thank you, sir," said the messenger.

"My respects to your master," said the old man, opening the letter—"proud to serve him."

"Yes, sir."

"No, no, I don't mean that," said Mr. Pigeon—"proud to see him."

"Is that the answer, sir?"

"Yes, that's exactly it," said old Pigeon, wishing with all his heart that Tom would return.

The truth was Mr. Pigeon had only met Colonel Tippits

once, and that was prior to the retirement of Pigeon and Son to the classic regions of Belgrave Square. He had no difficulty in meeting the Colonel then; but since the Pigeons had become gentlemen, the head of that illustrious house of tailors felt that he had all the manners and habits of his life to re-learn. During the first few months of his residence in Belgrave Square he had been caught in the act of touching his hat to some of the inhabitants of the locality, and twice had been seen shaking hands with a valet.

"Look out and see if my son's a-coming, will you, waiter; there's a good fellow," said the old man.

Tom rushed into the room as the waiter was leaving it, much to the physical discomfort of both, seeing that they came into violent collision. When Tom had sufficiently recovered from the shock to call the waiter a "stoopid ass," he pro-ceeded to take off his coat, which was covered with mud.

"Why, what have you been doing?" asked his father.

"Getting through a hedge. I didn't know there was a ditch in the way. Not much damage done. Only torn a hole in my favourite coat. Mud will brush off—hole will mend."

"Why, the Colonel and his daughter will be here directly," said the father, taking Tom's coat and examining the torn sleeve.

"The deuce!" said Tom.

"In a quarter of an hour," said the old man, fumbling in his overcoat.

"By Jove! What's to be done? I can't go into Society with a hole in my coat."

"I always carry a needle and thimble," said the old man, cheerfully.

Tom shrugged his shoulders, and said he knew it.

The implements of his craft were speedily produced, and old Pigeon was preparing to commence work. The old man's face lighted up with pleasure at the thought of plying his needle once more.

"It's many a long year," he said, "since I really did a stitch, but——"

"And it will be many a long year before you do another," exclaimed Tom, taking the torn coat away from his father. "What! do you think I would permit the wealthy progenitor of my being to mend my coat. Never! I will do it myself."

The old man was more delighted at the thought of Tom "doing a bit of tailoring," than if he had been permitted to mend the coat himself.

"Ah, that will gladden my old eyes, Tommy," he said, stooping down, the better to take in the full picture of Tom at work.

"Will it; then they shall be gladdened with a last final grand exhibition." With which remark, Tom leaped upon the table and seated himself cross legged, at which old Pigeon roared with laughter and stamped his feet with delight.

"Never was so glad in all my life. Well done, Tommy; ah, your heart's in the right place, after all."

Tommy stitched away and nodded at his father, while the old man laughed and danced, and declared Tom was his own son, and an honour to his family.

"I am like the picture of old Penn Holder in the play now; but look here, governor, keep your eye on the window; it would be an awful sell if the Colonel turned up," said Tom.

"All right, I'm looking—not such long stitches, Tommy— not so long," said the father, watching Tom's work with critical carefulness.

"Oh, bother! they're splendid stitches; hanged if I don't enjoy the work myself," said Tom, drawing his arm to and fro briskly, and bending his head to the garment on his knee.

"Bless you, my boy; if you spends all the money we can soon earn some more."

"Now, look here," said Tom, suddenly stopping and contemplating his enraptured parent; "no vulgar memories on account of the treat I am giving you; forget it the moment it's over."

"All right, Tommy," said the old man; "all right, my boy; I'll never disgrace you."

"If the Colonel and his daughter only saw us now," said Tom.

The old man went into fits of laughter at the idea.

"What would Society say?" gasped the old man between his loud guffaws.

Tom laughed heartily, too, but stopped all in a moment. He was sitting nearly facing the door; and he saw behind his father a tall, pompous gentleman, in a light overcoat, with a lady on his arm, standing in the doorway.

"Why, Tommy, what's the matter?—what are you staring at?" exclaimed the father, in the midst of what otherwise would have been a tremendous peal of laughter.

Tom making no reply, it naturally occurred to the old man to turn round and judge for himself of the nature of the sight which had startled his son. Meanwhile, Tom Pigeon carefully drew up his legs and slipped from the table.

"Gentlemen," said Colonel Tippits, in a round, unctuous voice, and smiling blandly, "I and my daughter, Miss Tippits, have done ourselves the honour of calling upon you; but we beg that we may not disturb your amusement."

Tom Pigeon took the Colonel's cue in an instant; leaping to his feet, and bowing to the lady, he began to laugh.

"I beg you will excuse us, miss," said Tom, feeling for his eye-glass; "must keep moving, you see—it is our family motto; I apologise most humbly, yas."

Then turning to his father, he exclaimed, "I have won, sir; I have won, Mr. Pigeon."

Old Pigeon looked at the Colonel, then at Tom, and, finally, at Miss Tippits for an explanation.

"He says he has won," observed Miss Tippits.

"Oh!" said old Pigeon, staring at Tom, who had meanwhile slipped on his coat; "he has won, has he?"

"Yes, I have won," said Tom; "ha, ha! he, he!"

The Colonel laughed as heartily as Tom, who, while laughing at one side of his mouth, on the other side, in stage whispers, was urging his father to laugh. "Why don't you laugh, governor?"

Old Pigeon, thinking that, by some canon of Society, it was necessary to laugh, made an effort to comply with Tom's urgent request; but he made a melancholy failure of it.

"Couldn't do it to save my life," said the old man.

"You see, Miss Tippits," said Tom, "I had torn my coat; so I said, Mr. Pigeon senior, I will bet you my opera box against your drag that I mend it in five minutes—I, who never had a needle in my hand—I, your son, will mend that coat in five minutes."

Here old Pigeon put his head into a cupboard, and began to have a violent fit of laughter.

"Did it within the time—won the wager easily."

"Capital idea—very good indeed," said the Colonel, looking at his daughter for approving recognition.

"How very droll," said Miss Tippits.

"Yes, life is droll—everything is droll in its way," said Tom, "yas, yas."

Then he thought Miss Tippits was a very fine woman; and so she was. She wore a light Dolly-Varden costume, which set off to perfection her wealth of golden hair from Vigo Street.

By this time old Pigeon had come out of the cupboard and out of his fit, too; and Colonel Tippits, making a great show of his respect for the old man, said how gratifying it was to himself and Miss Tippits that his son had consented to accompany him. Old Pigeon said Tom had some business of his own in the neighbourhood; but Tom immediately assured his father that this was only his fun, and the Colonel suggested that they should now adjourn to the Castle.

"Mr. Pigeon junior, will you take my daughter to the carriage?"

"With great pleasure—yas," said Tom, stretching out his left arm, pulling down his cuffs, and offering his right arm to the lady.

Miss Tippits accepted the escort with a simper, and Tom was more and more convinced, that she was a very fine woman indeed. For the time being she completely eclipsed poor little Jessie Miller, who had made such a deep impression upon Tom's heart during the Cattle Show week nearly a year ago.

Mr. Pigeon took the Colonel's arm, and presently the whole party were rolling gaily along the highway towards Tinsell Castle.

V.

IN THE TOILS.

TINSELL CASTLE was a bran new house of a mixed order of architecture. It had been built chiefly from the design of Colonel Tippits himself. The Blue wags of Inglenook, who were opposed to the Colonel's candidature for the borough, called the house Inglenook Gaol. A commercial traveller once told the boots at the Dragon that he had mistaken it for the Little Tinsell railway station. The castle was, indeed, the subject of much humorous criticism, and not without reason. It was suggestive of prisons, railway stations, almshouses, and model cottages; though it did not look unpicturesque on the bright September day through the elms which had not been erected by the Colonel. The old trees, with their leaves slightly browned by the first tints of autumn, tried to shut out the great staring brick and glass house; but the castellated towers and the curious gables obtruded themselves here and there; and thus it was that the castle looked far more picturesque and imposing than it had any right to do.

The interior of Colonel Tippits' residence had had a narrow escape from insufferable vulgarity. When the Colonel commenced to furnish it Lord Verrier died, and there was a sale by auction at the Hall. The Colonel bought many of the principal articles of furniture; and it was easy to see where the taste of the nobleman had neutralized the assumption of the sham aristocrat.

Seated at the piano in the drawing-room, on the morning after the arrival of the Pigeons, was a pretty young lady in a light morning dress. She was playing the accompaniment of a new song, and wishing herself a hundred miles away from Tinsell Castle. Instead of humming the words of the song, she was saying to herself that she envied the independence of cooks and housemaids. She was wishing, in her poor little heart, that her father had never sent her to school. "If he had not," she said, almost aloud, "I should now be a happy cook or kitchen-maid, instead of a stupid, unhappy companion to a stuck-up nobody."

This was Jessie Miller, a fair example of the modern farmer's daughter of this age of pianos and accomplishments. The English agriculturist always grumbled at the weather and market prices ever since the world began. In the present day he sends his sons to public schools, has French governesses for his daughters, indulges himself in all kinds of modern luxuries, and still grumbles on. George Eliot's Hetty Sorrel has long ceased to exist. She has converted Mrs. Poyser's dairy into a drawing-room, learnt French, donned a chignon and dress-improver, and openly set her Dolly-Varden cap at the young squire. Bless her heart, why should she not? Show me a fairer face, a brighter eye, or rounder arms!

How it was that Jessie Miller fell in love with Tom Pigeon is a mystery which the writer of this veritable history will not attempt to solve, any more than he will attempt to explain why so many pretty girls are married to ugly and commonplace men. Titania is not the only woman who has not seen the asses' ears; not that Tom Pigeon was an ass. If he had been educated, and had lived in good society, he might have been a dashing, clever fellow; but he was a tailor. Though he always vowed he had a soul above buttons, you could see he was a tailor. He walked like a tailor, swaggered like a tailor, and had a tailor's notions of Society. Let it not be thought that I am girding at a useful and respectable class of industrial artists. I have reason to respect the craft. They are patient, long-suffering; and I know members of the profession who are gentlemanlike and full of noble ambition. But Tom Pigeon was no more worthy of Jessie Miller than that scheming Miss Tippits was worthy of Tom Pigeon; and yet Jessie Miller had given her heart to the vulgar, though generous, little tailor who would go into Society.

"Well, Jessie, have you learnt that accompaniment?" asked Miss Tippits, breaking rudely in upon Jessie's thoughts.

"Yes, miss," said Jessie.

"Can you play it perfectly? We have more company at the Castle to-day, and I wish to sing that song this evening."

"I can play it, Miss Tippits," said Jessie.

"Sit down, then, and let us try it."

Jessie's round dimpled little fingers wandered over the keyboard, and Miss Tippits commenced to sing one of the pretty sugar-and-water ballads of Virginia Gabriel. In a voice of remarkable power she requested an evidently stubborn exile to . "Come back to Erin," promising him on his return that Killarney should ring with the mirth of a large party of friends and relatives. Jessie followed up the invitation in loud chords and rattling octaves. The exile, however, was deaf to the charmers. Miss Tippits was not pleased with her own share in the performance, and requested Jessie to sing the song herself, which she did, in a sweet, sympathetic voice that would most assuredly have melted the exile's heart if he could only have been brought within the magic influence of the pretty little vocalist.

"Charmingly sung, Miss Miller," said Miss Austin, entering the room as Jessie was finishing the ballad. "You are quite an artist."

"It is a good thing she is," said Miss Tippits. "What would the poor thing do if she had no accomplishments? Ah, education is a great blessing!"

"It is, indeed," said Miss Austin. "These Pigeons do not seem to have had much acquaintance with the schoolmaster."

Jessie started at the name of Pigeon.

"They can do without the schoolmaster," said Miss Tippits, scornfully. "They keep a banker."

"I understand they are very rich," said Miss Austin.

"Rich! They roll in wealth," said Miss Tippits.

"As the Colonel's pigs roll in dirt," said Miss Austin; "and with about as much grace."

"What a coarse expression, Miss Austin!" exclaimed Miss Tippits.

"An appropriate simile," said Miss Austin; and she walked to the window as old Pigeon entered the room.

Miss Tippits was right, nevertheless, in characterising Miss Austin's remark as somewhat coarse. It was coarse, though it did not sound objectionable, coming from Miss Austin, whose ladylike manner and musical voice would have sanctified almost any expression in the language.

Immediately on being discovered Mr. Pigeon senior said, " Oh ! my son is not here—beg your pardon, ladies."

"Pray do not go away, Mr. Pigeon," said Miss Tippits, bouncing up to the old man with a loud demonstration of hospitality. " I am sure we hope you will make yourself quite at home."

"Certainly ; thank you, miss," said the old man, looking straight at Jessie Miller, who, at a distance, was betraying an especial interest in Mr. Pigeon.

" Have you been introduced to Miss Austin?" asked Miss Tippits.

" The lady in the window—had the pleasure of meeting her on the stairs," said the old man nervously.

Miss Austin bowed.

" This is Miss Jessie Miller, my companion," said Miss Tippits, waving her arm in the direction of the farmer's pretty daughter.

" And a very nice companion, too, if I may make bold to say so," said old Pigeon. " I think that is the young lady as my son was running after before breakfast this morning."

" Eh ? what ? " exclaimed Miss Tippits. " Jessie, Jessie, what is the meaning of this ? "

" Some mistake, sir," said Jessie, haughtily. " A ridiculous mistake."

"Well, maybe it is. Beg pardon, I'm sure ; mistakes will occur in the best regulated establishments ; you can't always ensure a good fit ; I mean, that you do not know when— Excuse me, Miss Tippits ; I will go and see after my son."

" Ah ! Mr. Pigeon," said Mr. Thornton, entering the room at this moment ; " you do not take long to dress."

"No, thank you," said old Pigeon; "I was wondering where my son is."

"He said I was to take care of you until he came," said Thornton; "but you are in excellent hands, I see."

"We were talking about riches shortly before you came down, Mr. Thornton," said Miss Tippits, posing herself on an ottoman in the centre of the room.

"Pitying the wealthy, I suppose," said Thornton, smiling significantly at Miss Austin, whose face beamed with good-humour the moment Mr. Thornton entered the room.

"No, the poor," said Miss Tippits.

"Mistake, Miss Tippits," said Mr. Thornton. "The rich alone are entitled to pity. They are always in a fume and fret about their money; don't know where to invest it, or how; always dreaming they have lost it; never know when it is safe; banks break, companies wind up, stocks fluctuate—if they don't, investors are always afraid they will. Very miserable people, believe me, rich people. Then they want to go into Society, the vulgar rich. Society snubs them, looks down upon them, will have nothing to do with them. An unhappy lot, depend upon it, the rich."

Mr. Thornton was a fine, handsome fellow, a man of education, and a man of position. He was a member of several leading clubs in town, and had seen the world.

"You are quite right, sir," said Mr. Pigeon, in a grovelling, humble way, as if he felt that he had no right to be standing on the same carpet with a Thornton. "I say it humbly, and with deference, but I agree with you."

"Here comes Kite, the politician, Kite, the free-lance; we will hear what he says," remarked Mr. Thornton, as the voice of Kite came into the room, heralding himself and young Pigeon.

Mr. Kite bowed solemnly and low to ladies and gentlemen;

Mr. Pigeon junior was imitating the bend and manner of Kite most successfully just as old Pigeon rushed up to his son.

"O, Tommy, I'm so glad you have come!" exclaimed the old man.

"Go away, go away," said Tom, in a whisper; "it is not much I ask. Do behave yourself."

The old man, who had been pining for Tom's presence as though the young fellow had been on a long journey, shrank back abashed, and pretended to examine a water-colour, supposed to be a genuine Turner.

"Miss Tippits, I have been inspecting the Castle," said Tom, approaching the lady of the house in his grandest manner. "Yas; and a very fine castle it is."

Miss Austin and Miss Miller were engaged in an interesting conversation near the piano.

"I am glad you like the house," said Miss Tippits.

"Yas, I assure you, very much," said Tom. "Excuse me examining the pictures." And he lounged towards a showy piece over the mantelshelf, stumbling awkwardly over an ottoman, and only being saved from an ugly fall by the ready arm of Kite, who kept a watchful eye upon his young patron.

"Are you fond of pictures?" asked Miss Tippits.

"I doat on them," said Tom; "I am always buying pictures; my father has a very fine collection."

"Yes, miss," said old Pigeon, who had recovered from his son's rebuff. "The Paris fashions for the last thirty years; a very fine——"

"Yas," said Tom, frowning at his father, and stamping on his foot; "yas, works of French masters very curious."

It was lucky for Tom that Mr. Thornton had joined the two ladies near the piano.

"Yes, I have seen them," said Mr. Kite. "The grouping

of the figures is charming, the accessories wonderfully put in, the colouring superb."

" True, quite true," said Tom, feeling for his shirt-cuffs, and bringing them down upon his hands in the most approved style of the West-end; "we are both fond of collecting pictures."

" And accounts," whispered Kite to old Pigeon. " Wonderful hand at that."

Old Pigeon chuckled.

" Did you speak?" asked Tom, quickly.

" Beg pardon," said Kite.

" Just so," said Tom. " As I was saying, Miss Tippits, to the Colonel half an hour ago, there is nothing better than country life. It is altogether so jolly; so much fresh air, such a flavour of turnips about, that one ceases to remember the stifling air of West-end parlours."

" Saloons," whispered Kite.

" Just so," said Tom.

" I am so glad you like the country," said Miss Tippits, rolling her eyes at Tom, and settling down into the ottoman cushions in a fond, languishing manner, calculated to impress any beholder with the kitten-like innocence of her nature.

" The country," exclaimed the Colonel, arriving magnificently upon the scene, " the country, Mr. Pigeon, is England's glory. But for the country, this degenerate nation would sink to the deepest depths of poverty and crime; and it is for a constituency which is about to exercise the noblest privilege of Englishmen, to pause in their wild career before they give their votes to any person who is not imbued with a sense of what is due to the country, to his constituents, and to that grand *rôle* in the play of nations which England is destined to fill, and always will fill, and must fill—I say, and must fill—to the last syllable of recorded time!"

Mr. Thornton said, " Hear, hear ! " and continued his description of the absurdities of the last new play, which entertained Miss Austin immensely, and astonished in an equal degree the unsophisticated Jessie, who could not understand the meaning of a bad play, the theatre, in her small experience, being always delightful and exciting in the highest degree.

Tom Pigeon tried to fix the Colonel with his eye-glass. Failing by that means to bring the candidate's oration to an end, he began talking to Mr. Kite ; but the Colonel went on until he was pulled up by an overwhelming roar of laughter from old Pigeon. The Colonel had expressed a hope that he should meet his young friend, Mr. Tom Pigeon, as a brother-member in the Commons House of Parliament.

Fortunately for the Pigeons, two new arrivals were announced at this juncture. Miss Tippits, with as grand a Society air as she could achieve, came forward to meet the new comers, who were evidently persons of some distinction. Presently the company was increased by several other visitors. A general ripple of small talk commenced, turning chiefly upon the weather, the shooting season, the scarcity of birds, autumn tints, the large crop of wheat, and the latest novel. The Colonel availed himself of this opportunity to get Tom Pigeon into a corner, and follow up an interesting conversation which he had initiated in the Castle gardens.

" And you think you could be happy with my daughter, you sly dog," said the Colonel, beaming with generosity. " Too bad to commence a siege upon her heart within the first four-and-twenty hours of meeting her ; but youth is hot and head-strong. Well, I like you, Mr. Pigeon—I like you. We have a distinguished party here to night—all the *élite* of the county. It would be pardonable on such an occasion to introduce your health in a few words after dinner, alluding to our probable new relationship—Beauty and Fashion going into Society with Wealth and Intellect, and all that sort of thing."

"Yas, yas," said Tom, overcome by the Colonel's condescension, and dazzled with the splendour of Miss Tippit's blue satin dress and golden hair. "I'm not a man to do things by halves. No, sir, 'Onward!' is my motto. Your daughter, Colonel, is a very fine woman, and, as you say, in Society to begin with; knows what Society is, and could sit beside a fellow in the Park, four-in-hand, and all that, and preside at one's table. That's my style. I mean to see life, and I mean to go into Society with a dashing woman. Miss Tippits is all that; Miss Tippits took my eye the moment I saw her; and if Miss Tippits will say the same of me, why, I'm on, Colonel, and ready to say the word at once."

As the last words escaped his lips, Tom started from his seat as quickly as he had sprung from his father's overcoat at the hotel.

"Who is that young lady?" he asked, seizing the Colonel's arm, and fixing his eyes on Jessie Miller.

"Which, sir, which?" asked the Colonel, slowly raising his eye-glass.

"In the white dress."

"Near my daughter?"

"Yes, yes. Can't you tell me at once? It is not much I ask."

"Oh, that is Jessie Miller, my daughter's companion," said the Colonel, as if he thought it almost necessary to apologize for the very existence of so ordinary a person.

"Companion?" repeated Tom, looking vaguely at the Colonel.

"Yes; a sort of menial, a dependant, whom Miss Tippits has taken pity upon. Her father has come to grief. Miss Tippits would not allow the girl to become a common servant,

and has, in the kindest and handsomest way, taken her in the position of companion."

"Ah, I see," said Tom.   "She's not in Society, eh?"

"Oh dear, no!" said the Colonel, scandalized at the very idea of such a possibility.

"I like your daughter for taking pity on her," said Tom, gravely.

"My dear Mr. Pigeon, you are a kind, humane man," said the Colonel.

"By Jove, sir!" said Tom, raising his voice, "I like your daughter more for being kind to that poor girl than for any thing she could have done."

Tom was very much in earnest, and seemed inclined to go and speak to Jessie; but the Colonel detained him.

"You have met that poor girl before, eh?"

"Yas," said Tom, a little awkwardly; "yas, once, some months ago."

"Ah, you sly dog! you sly dog!" said the Colonel, taking Tom's arm, and walking with him as far away from Jessie as possible. "Just like you young sprigs of fashion. A pretty girl is not safe—companions, barmaids, nurse-girls, anything if it has a pretty face. Well, well, that is excusable in you young millionaires. The canons of Society do not forbid it."

There was consummate skill in the Colonel's coupling of companions, barmaids, and nurse-girls; it put Jessie Miller at once out of the pale of Tom's consideration, and the "sly-dog" compliment just suited his present mood and temper.

"Yas, yas, Colonel," said Tom; "I flatter myself I know a little of the world. It is not much I ask—a pretty girl, a good cigar, and let me have my sherry dry."

"Good, good!" exclaimed the Colonel. "Society will open her arms wide to a man of your mettle."

Dinner was announced as the Colonel was introducing Mr. Pigeon junior to the Rev. the Vicar of Inglenook.

"Dinner is on the table," said six feet of plush and buttons, with the solemnity of a mute.

"Best news I've heard to-day," said old Pigeon to Kite.

"There he goes again," said Tom Pigeon to himself. "Nothing will polish the governor."

"Mr. Pigeon junior, will you take in my daughter?" said the Colonel.

"With pleasure," said Tom.

"Mrs. de Smythers, may I have the honour?" said the Colonel, offering his arm to an Indian widow, at the same time firing off a series of suggestions and commands for pairing the remainder of the guests.

Old Pigeon had been duly considered by the host; but the-scene altogether had been too much for him. The lady assigned to his care had found some more gallant gentleman, and Pigeon was left to bring up the rear, muttering to himself as he did so, " Well, I never see such a fuss! They might be going to a dance instead of a dinner."

VI.

BETWEEN THE ACTS.

TINSELL CASTLE had dined. The ladies were in the drawing-room; the gentlemen were discussing politics over old port and new filberts. Colonel Tippits had made several efforts to throw off a score or two of his choicest platitudes; but he had found Mr. Thornton a stiff and uncompromising opponent.

The dining-room opened conveniently upon a conservatory; and old Pigeon was the first to avail himself of the Colonel's permission to go outside and have a cigar prior to joining the ladies in the drawing-room.

Old Pigeon was heartily tired of Society. The Colonel might have heard him saying so as he tried to light a cigar in a shady corner of the lawn. It was a fine, clear, moonlight night, the weather almost as warm as July.

"I'm blowed if I ain't precious sick of this," grumbled old Pigeon. "What with the Colonel's speeches and Tommy a-losing that bet of a cool two hundred, as the Colonel called it—well, I says, says I, ‘ Let me go outside and smoke a quiet cigar.’ Says Mr. Thornton, ‘ We must join the ladies.’ ‘ By all means,’ I says, and I slips out ; and I only wish I was in the train a-going back to London.”

“ Hullo, governor ! you’ve come out for a breather, eh ? ” said Tom Pigeon, with a half-burnt cigar in his mouth, and the ashes of it on his waistcoat. “ Well, how do you like being in Society and in a castle ? ”

“ Well, Tommy,” said old Pigeon, “ if I may be allowed to give my opinion, I’d sooner be at the Elephant and Castle, having a quiet pipe.”

“ Ah, governor,” said Tom, “ you are too old to get out of vulgar habits ; you’ll never alter.”

“ I don’t want to,” said the old man.

“ I feel a bit of a squeamishness here,” said Tom, laying his hand on his heart, “ a sort of a no-howish feeling. Thornton says it is a regular out-and-out Society pain—a sort of a fashionable pain—a twinge of the *blazzy*, Kite calls it.”

“ I don’t like that Kite, Tommy,” said the old man. “ He ain’t no good.”

“ Oh he is not a bad sort,” said Tom.

“ He knew you was a going to lose that bet,” said the old man, pushing his penknife through the end of his cigar, and wishing he had a pipe.

“ Never mind the bet, father,” said Tom. “ It will come right if you will only be a little careful ; but what with your talking of giving an inch and taking an ell, your Tooley Street joke, and the Paris fashions, you do make it hard for a fellow to keep his equilibrium.”

“ What’s that, Tommy ? ”

“ Never mind what it is, dear old boy. It is not much I ask—sink the shop, and consider our new positions.”

"Why, Tommy, there's a petticoat! It's that pretty little girl, the companion," said old Pigeon.

Tom intercepted the young lady.

She had a basket of flowers in her hand.

"Why, Jessie," he said, familiarly and heartlessly, "I thought you were inside yonder."

"Sir," said Jessie, "allow me to pass."

"How distant we are," said Tom. "Where have you been?"

"To say good-bye to my father, you mean, unkind thing," said Jessie.

"Gone on a journey, has he?" Tom asked, trying to maintain an air of nonchalant indifference.

"Yes. Allow me to pass, sir."

"Those are pretty flowers. Are they out of the Colonel's garden?"

"They are the last flowers from the farm which my father is leaving for ever. There! Now I hope you are satisfied," said Jessie, beginning to cry.

"Tom, you are a brute!" the old man exclaimed.

"Don't be angry, Jessie," said Tom.

"Angry? Pooh!" said Jessie, between crying and sobbing. " I would scorn to be angry with such a person as you."

"Person!" said Tom. "Ain't I as good as anybody else?"

"Write to me and say you are coming to see me, and then never to come near me ; and when you see me accidentally dare not speak to me because Colonel Tippits says it is contrary to the rules of Society to pay attention to a companion. Tom Pigeon, you are a donkey and a cruel man."

Tom put out his hand to take Jessie's arm.

"If you touch me I'll scream," said Jessie. "I have said what I wished to say, and now I am going inside there, as you call it."

Jessie swept by Tom and his father, as she spoke.

"Very well," said Tom, sticking his glass in his eye. "Depart, Miss Miller, depart!"

"Oh, you silly, stupid, stuck-up ungrateful thing!" she said, scornfully turning round to fire off this last volley as she entered the Castle.

"That's one for you, Tommy," said old Pigeon.

"Yas, yas," said Tom, staring at the door, which Jessie had closed behind her. "Yas, that's my secret—governor—that pert party in petticoats. I said I would show you my secret. Before destiny called us to fame—before we vowed to go into Society—I loved that young woman. Yas, governor, your son was in love, and coming down here to pay a clandestine visit to his sweetheart, when you asked me to accompany you in the same direction."

" Lor ! " said the old man.   " What a curious thing ! "

" The Colonel says," continued Tom, " if a young gent of fashion was to marry a companion, it would be death to him."

" You don't say so, Tommy ! " exclaimed old Pigeon.

" Death," said Tom, solemnly.   " But say no more about it; here comes Mr. Thornton, who is a real swell bred and born."

" I am sent to bring in the Pigeons," said Mr. Thornton. " Messieurs the Pigeons, come in and be plucked.   We are going to play loo."

" Now, none of your larks, Thornton," said Tom.   " Larks, d'y'see ?—play upon the word."

" Never mind playing upon the word, sir," said Thornton. " Come and be played upon."

" Mr. Thornton, let me ask you a question—won't detain you a moment.   Have you a peculiar pain here " (pointing to the region of the heart)—" a sort of a dull kind of a pain ? "

" No ; can't say that I have," Mr. Thornton replied.

" How long have you been in Society ? " asked Tom, pathetically.

" Well, I hardly know—always," said Mr. Thornton, ejaculating, inwardly, " Poor, miserable Pigeon ! "

" Ah, then you have got used to it—most extraordinary thing ! " said Tom.

" You will get used to it also," said Thornton.   " Eels get used to skinning, pigeons to plucking."

" Now look here," exclaimed Tom, letting his eye-glass fall, and throwing aside a fresh-lighted cigar, " I don't like that sort of remark.   You know the rules of Society better than I do, and perhaps you are within those rules now, otherwise, Mr. Thornton, I would punch your head—I would, 'pon my soul ! so there ! "

" Bravo, Pigeon ! " said Thornton, coolly patting the little fellow's back. " Give me your hand, Pigeon. I had no idea you were so plucky ; we will be staunch friends."

Thornton took Tom's hand in his big, manly palm, and shook old Pigeon's son and heir until his teeth chattered.

" That's right," said the old man, " that's right. I hate quarrelling."

" And I hate humbug," said Tom. " ' Onward and over-board ' is my sentiment ; and a man with a hundred thousand at his banker's is not going to stand anybody's humbug—that's the way to say it."

" Quite right," said Mr. Thornton, planting himself between the two Pigeons, and taking an arm of each, " quite right. You are in the way to get a splendid lesson on humbug. Come along, gentlemen, come along."

<hr>

VII.

A STORM IN SOCIETY.

If this were a drama instead of a mere story the last chapter would have been called, in the technical language of the practical dramatist, a carpenter's scene. It would have given reasonable time for the next set, a return to the drawing-room —an interior with which the reader is already acquainted.

Let the faithful historian present the scene as though the equally faithful reader sat by his side in the first row of the stalls and saw it.

Miss Tippits sits at the piano, with her foot on the soft pedal, playing a new set of waltzes *pianissimo*, that no one may be disturbed by the music, and, also, that her mistakes may be less noticeable than they would be under the influence of the *forte* pedal. She is bending her head sentimentally to the music, as if her soul were communing with the spirit of the sublime composer (a bandmaster in one of the line regiments), or the less ethereal part of her nature were threading the figures of the dreamy waltz in the arms of Mr. Tom Pigeon, Mr. Thornton, or whomsoever else may be destined to call her his own.

At a card table, placed in the furthest corner of the room, sit Kite and the Rector of Fullpark, playing a harmless game of cribbage. Down near the footlights are Miss Austin, the Colonel, and several guests seated upon ottomans, and lolling in easy chairs, talking in a miscellaneous fashion upon a variety of questions, the whole of which the Colonel vainly endeavours to turn to political account, being invariably interrupted just as he is about to rehearse his hustings speech.

Presently there enter from the carpenter's scene—or, rather, speaking as historian, not as dramatist—from the garden, where that interesting incident of the last chapter has just taken place—presently, I say, there enter Mr. Thornton, Mr. Pigeon senior, and Mr. Pigeon junior. As they appear, it suddenly occurs to the Colonel to ask Miss Tippits to sing " that little song."

" Do, my dear Clementina, sing that little song," says the Colonel.

" Papa, dear, don't ask me," says Miss Tippits.

" Yes ; do sing," say several voices all at once.

" Do oblige us," says Mr. Tom Pigeon.

" Then Jessie must accompany me," says Miss Tippits, taking up a bundle of music, and beginning to search for " that little song."

" Where is Jessie Miller ? " says the Colonel, looking round the room, and searching every corner through his eye-glass.

No one answers the question ; but Jessie glides out of some

unsuspected corner, and takes her seat at the piano to play the accompaniment to the song which Miss Clementina Tippits was practising when this story opened.

"Generous creature, to allow little Miller to accompany her —to share the honours of the evening—eh?" says the Colonel, in a low voice, to Tom.

"Yas, yas," Tom replies.

While the song is being sung, and the accompaniment is being played, the Colonel, listening attentively to both all the time, motions Tom Pigeon to a card table, at which both seat themselves, opposite Kite and a solicitor of Inglenook, who has taken the Rector's place.

Everybody applauds the song, and the card players cut for deal.

Old Pigeon thereupon remarks that his son Tom sings a good song.

"Mr. Pigeon junior is engaged," says the Colonel.

"But you have not commenced the game," says Thornton; "let us have Mr. Pigeon's song first."

"O yes, certainly," say several voices.

"Yas," observes Tom; "anything to oblige, as Mr. Ketch said. Is it the wish of the company that I should sing?"

"Vulgar person," says the Rector, aside to his neighbour.

"Certainly," says Mr. Thornton; "we are waiting."

"And so are we," says Kite, with the faintest indication of a wink at the Inglenook lawyer, who is shuffling a pack of cards, and mentally calculating the amount that may be dragged out of a young, vulgar, wealthy cockney in two hours.

"Perhaps it would not be out of the rules of Society if the companion," says old Pigeon, "was just to—" (imitates, in dumb show, the act of playing an accompaniment on the piano).

"Look after the governor," says Tom to Mr. Thornton; "I'm afraid the wine is getting into his head."

"Certainly," says the Colonel. "Miss Jessie Miller, will you kindly accompany Mr. Pigeon's song ? "

Jessie says nothing, but sits down, determined to accompany him in half a dozen keys.

" Miss Jessie Miller will oblige," says old Pigeon, in a maudlin way, half aloud ; "number ninety in the books."

" Governor, governor," remonstrates young Pigeon, in an aside whisper, "will you or won't you ? "

"What do you wish me to play ?" asks Jessie, when Tom walks up to the piano.

" Don't be so hard on me," Tom says, quietly.

"I don't know it," says Jessie.

"This is the tune," says Tom, in desperation, humming a few bars of an impossible melody.

Jessie follows him on the instrument, and then asks if he is ready.

"Yes," he says he is ; and in evidence thereof he breaks out into the following new and original ballad :—

> " A toast !   To our darlings at home—
>   Our wives and children dear ;
>   Here's a health to those that we love,
>   Let us drink the toast with a cheer ! "

"If I might be allowed," says Tom, "I would ask ladies and gentlemen to join in the chorus."

"Very good," says the Colonel, smiling ; " charming—so very natural."

" We will take the lead from you, Mr. Pigeon," says Thornton ; whereupon Tom repeats the verse as a chorus, and the Colonel's guests think it a very humorous thing to "join in," which they do quite pleasantly.

Tom continues the song with renewed vigour, his father nodding and beating time to the tune.

> " When the world is frowning and dark,
>   And friends grow fickle and cold,
>   Her fond smile shall brighten the clouds,
>   And tinge them with colours of gold."

" Admirable sentiment, charming moral," says the Colonel, inviting old Pigeon, by an easy gesture, to join the card table, to which Mr. Pigeon senior responds.

Everybody intimates that the song has charmed them very much. Colonel Tippits takes Tom's arm, compliments him upon his vocal powers, and conducts him to the card tables, where cutting in and cutting out goes on at once to the evident satisfaction of all the parties concerned.

" Happy pair the Pigeons," says Mr. Thornton to Miss Tippits, who is rolling her languishing eyes at a young curate, supposed to have great influence with the bishop.

" Yes, very," says Miss Tippits.

" Eccentric," continues Mr. Thornton ; " very odd there should be a Kite in the same company."

Thornton glances at the card tables as he makes the remark.

" I do not think it at all singular," says Miss Tippits; "there is a Mr. Green and also a Miss White here."

" Yes, true, true," says Thornton ; " you do not object to the name of Pigeon now, Miss Tippits."

" You are always facetious, Mr. Thornton. I suppose Miss Austin does not object to the name of Thornton," says Miss Tippits, withdrawing her eyes from the curate and rolling them upon Mr. Thornton.

" She has just done me the honour to say that she does not," replies Thornton, accepting the optical charge with remarkable coolness.

Miss Austin, who has been discussing the relative powers of Browning and Tennyson with a gentleman (he has heard "The Brook " sung at a Penny Reading, and been advised to get up

"How they Brought the Good News to Ghent"), comes to Miss Tippits' ottoman at this moment, and asks her friend what Harry is so earnest about.

"About you," says Miss Tippits; "he was asking me to be one of the bridesmaids."

"Harry!" exclaims Miss Austin, in a pretty confusion.

Thornton is rather taken aback at the unexpected smartness of Miss Tippits.

"I congratulate you both," says that lady, with as little asperity as she can put into her voice.

Miss Austin bows. Mr. Thornton is about to make a suitable reply, when the conversation is interrupted by high words at one of the card tables.

"Hallo! what is this!" says Mr. Thornton; "a storm in Society."

"I saw you do it," says young Pigeon, in loud angry tones; "you are a cheat."

He is addressing Kite, who rises from the table.

" Gentlemen, gentlemen," remonstrates the Colonel, in his blandest manner.

The whole company rise from their seats in various parts of the room.

" An infernal cheat ! " exclaims Pigeon.

" Before ladies, too," says the Colonel, attempting to take Tom's arm.

" You son of a tailor," shouts Kite, beginning a withering reply to Tom, who immediately upsets the table, and seizing Kite by the throat, gasps out, " Ladies or no ladies—tailors or no tailors—you shall give up that card."

The ladies hurriedly leave the room ; the gentlemen throng round Pigeon and Kite, just in time to see Mr. Pigeon junior fling his adversary, and pull out of Kite's coat-pocket an ace of spades.

Tableau and end of scene to turbulent music.

VIII.

AFTER THE STORM.

In one of his " Roundabout Papers," or somewhere else, Thackeray promised to write a story that should be all dialogue. He never did it. The idea has borne fruit in this poor narrative of Tom Pigeon's expedition into Society. I have eschewed description. I leave the actors in this little drama to play their own parts in their own way. The reader has formed her own idea (I say *her* own idea, for what *he* is capable of such a formation) of the character, manner, and appearance of every individual visitor at Tinsell Castle. She also knows exactly what would be said about the disgraceful scene at the Castle. It is not necessary to tell her how the few good people who had been got there by misrepresentations concerning whom they would meet considered themselves insulted and defrauded. She knows all about persons of the Tippits character, who try to thrust themselves into Society. She has never met them, of course; but she has heard of them and read of them in books. The Pigeons are mysteries to her, perhaps, but she can easily imagine what sort of a figure Mr. Shoddy, who made her last riding-habit, would cut with a house in Belgrave Square, and a vulgar son dreaming of Society. Why should I, the humble reporter of these few insignificant scenes in the insignificant lives of the Kites and Pigeons, trespass upon the intellectual and indulgent reader with my own views? The very thought is presumptuous. I return to the dialogue, with a humble apology for this almost unpardonable reference to my own existence. I will only venture to say that we are back again in the drawing-room of Tinsell Castle on the day after the storm. Kite and Mr. Thornton are in the room.

"I assure you," says Kite, "it was quite a mistake—I assure you, on my honour."

"Appearances were against you," says Thornton.

"By all that is good I swear to you it was a mistake; you must prevent scandal, Mr. Thornton, or the Colonel's chances of election for Inglenook are at an end."

"I don't think there is any danger of Tippits ever being a member of parliament, even for Inglenook," says Thornton.

"You are wrong, sir, believe me," says Kite; "but, no matter, whether right or wrong, sir, you must use your influence with Mr. Pigeon. Pray do, sir; he respects you."

"You called him a son of a tailor," says Thornton.

"I did not mean it personally—it was only figurative; just as you say a son of a gun. I meant no harm, Mr. Thornton, I assure you; the term might even be construed into one of endearment."

At this moment there enters Mr. Thomas Pigeon, at sight of whom there disappears with almost miraculous rapidity his old friend Kite. Young Pigeon has been going about the house, asking nearly every person he meets if he experiences any pain in the region of the heart. Mr. Thomas Pigeon has had a severe and continuous attack of that peculiarly uncomfortable pain, which he was told on the previous day belonged to Society. It had attacked him most seriously on hearing that Miss Jessie Miller had made up her mind to leave the Castle, and more particularly since she had met him on the stairs and insisted upon cutting him dead. The pain had been so intense during the morning, that Tom began to wonder whether his father was not quite right in attributing it to what he was pleased to call this new-fangled humbug of being in Society, and doing everything that you didn't want to do and pretending that you liked it. Tom had been closeted with Colonel Tippits; he had also had a serious conversation with Mr. Thornton; Miss Miller had looked prettier than ever she had done, as if only for the purpose of cutting him; his father had solemnly warned him that he was being swindled, bought and sold, and made mincemeat of; so that altogether Mr. Pigeon junior may be said to have had anything but a lively time of it during the last twenty-four hours.

"Ah, Mr. Thornton," he said, on entering the drawing-room, from which Kite had just disappeared, "how are you sir—how are you?"

"Well, thank you, very well," said Thornton, thrusting his hands into the pockets of a loose morning coat, and surveying the odd figure of the ambitious young merchant tailor, formerly of Bond Street.

"Got no pain here?" Tom asked, ruefully planting his left

hand upon that part of his light waistcoat which covered his heart.

"No, no," said Thornton, laughing.

"Ah, I have—a confounded pain, sir!" said Tom. "I don't think being in Society, as you call it, is good for me."

"Society! My poor, dear young friend, you have never been there yet. But is there no other reason for your heartache? I saw you watching that pretty Jessie Miller this morning, when you were dressing. I saw you, sir; I saw you looking out of your bed-room window."

"Well, I did not say that you did not see me."

"Don't be angry."

"I am not angry."

"You are blushing, then."

"I beg your pardon, I am not," Tom said, turning his head away from Mr. Thornton, and trying to hide his face behind his eye-glass.

"Mr. Kite is anxious to have your forgiveness," said Thornton, considerately changing the subject: "he declares that the whole thing was a mistake; he vows it upon his honour."

"Upon what?"

"His honour."

"Don't like the guarantee. The Colonel assured me he had kicked the brute out of doors."

"He may have done so," said Thornton; "but Kite is one of those persons who, being kicked out at the front door, come in at the back."

"Why, he had the audacity to call me the——"

"Yes, yes," said Thornton, before Tom could finish the sentence; "he says that was not meant personally: in fact, that it was more in the light of a term of endearment, just as you say a son of a gun—do you see?"

"Yas, yas," said Tom, promptly, and with evident relief, "very good; I thought that was all he meant, after all. He is a clever fellow."

"You knew him, then, before you met him down here?"

"Slightly, yas, yas," said Tom, plucking up his collar and his courage at the same time. "I gave him a wonner, eh? It astonished him rather, and the Castle too. By Jove! I almost forgive him for falling so cleanly when I hit out from the shoulder. It was as good as a play."

"Yes, no doubt," said Mr. Thornton. "Now look here, Mr. Pigeon junior, I know all about that pain of yours. You don't care for Miss Tippits. Don't frown, my friend, don't frown. You would rather be out of the bargain. Forgive Kite; he is no worse than his friends, between ourselves. Let us go into the garden and have a chat."

Mr. Thornton had a way of making people do what he wished, and he found no difficulty in persuading Mr. Pigeon to act upon some very wholesome advice which he gave him under a tree on Colonel Tippits' lawn.

Meanwhile Mr. Theophilus Pigeon had encountered Miss Jessie Miller in the breakfast-room, and had, in the frankest way possible, obtruded himself upon her confidence. He admired her morning dress; he expressed his great regret that Miss Miller was going to leave the Castle; he candidly told her that he neither cared for the Castle nor its society, and he was sure in his heart of hearts that his son Tom was of the same opinion.

"I don't want to hear anything about your son Tom," said Jessie, impatiently stamping her pretty right foot upon a full-blown rose in the Brussels carpet.

"Ah, you once thought differently," said old Pigeon, coaxingly.

"Perhaps I did."

" You liked him once."

" Perhaps I did."

" Why don't you now ? "

" Because he doesn't care for me."

" How do you know he don't ? "

" What a silly question, begging your pardon. It would not be right to care for a poor farmer's daughter now he's in Society."

Jessie emphasised the last two words, and tossed up her head with an air of defiance and contempt.

" Hang Society ! blow Society ! " said old Pigeon. " Don't be angry with me, Miss Jessie, because I love you already as a father might, and I want to know all about this affair between you and Tom.   How long have you known my son ? "

" A year," said Jessie, looking upon the ground, and sighing. " He came to the hotel with father from the Cattle Show, and we all went to the theatre."

" The sly dog ! I remember him saying he had met some very nice people at the show."

" And he came and had tea with us," continued Jessie ; " and we have written to each other ever since ; and the other day my father had to leave the farm, because he lost his money horse-racing."

" Oh ! that was it," said old Pigeon ; " and the Colonel was your father's landlord. Between ourselves, Miss Jessie, I don't think much of this Mister Colonel. What do you say ? "

" Nothing," said Jessie.

" You are mum, as they say."

" Yes."

" Jessie ! Jessie ! " called the unmistakable voice of Miss Tippits at this period of the conversation ; " where are you ? "

"But if Tommy was to ask you to be his wife?" said old Pigeon, hurriedly, determined to make the most of his time.

"Tommy," exclaimed Jessie, snapping her pretty fingers, "I would not have him if his hair was hung with diamonds."

Then saying, "I am coming, Miss Tippits," she darted out of the room, and left old Pigeon to his own reflections.

"Not if his hair was hung with diamonds!" said old Pigeon, looking at the door which Jessie banged as she fled; "that's one for Tommy."

It is impossible to say how many times Mr. Pigeon would have repeated Jessie's words had he not been interrupted by Colonel Tippits, who, having searched the house for his friend, had found him at last, mentally staggering under the startling rebuff of Miss Jessie Miller.

"My dear Mr. Pigeon," said the Colonel, in his loud, pompous voice, "I have been looking for you everywhere."

"Indeed!" said Mr. Pigeon; "well, if you repeat the same exercise to-morrow you'll have to go further afield to look for me."

"Why, sir, why?" asked the Colonel.

"'Cos I means to cut this, sir; if not to-day, by the first train in the morning. I'm too plain a man for this sort of thing. I've never been in a castle before."

"Every Englishman's home is his castle," said the Colonel, majestically.

"No, not exactly," said Mr. Pigeon senior; "every Englishman's home is not a castle, sir, begging your pardon; and a good thing too, Colonel. But we will not argue the point; let us come to business. About that mortgage; I'm willing to renew it, as you know, but on one condition."

"Name it," said the Colonel, promptly, prepared to concede much.

"You must let my son off this bargain, sir, about Miss Tippits."

The Colonel started and looked fixedly at old Pigeon.

"It's very kind of you," said Mr. Pigeon, undaunted—"it's very kind, and a great honour—we know that; but it's a mistake altogether. We Pigeons are only humble birds; and it's like mating one of us to a pheasant, or a peacock, or a n-ostrich—it ain't natural, Colonel; and it will never do."

While the Colonel is endeavouring to explain to Mr. Pigeon that the intermarrying of the middle with the upper classes of Society is acknowledged to be an important element in the social system, let us look in upon Miss Tippits and Mr. Kite, who are playing out an interesting little scene in the library.

"I have told you before," says Miss Tippits, "that your suit is hopeless in both cases. I decline your hand again, as I have previously done. You know my reasons."

"That contemptible Pigeon is one of your reasons," says Kite.

"You had my answer before I ever heard of or saw Mr. Tom Pigeon," says Miss Tippits; "and I will not stay in the room, sir, to hear papa's guests spoken of with rudeness."

"Stay, stay, Clementina!" says Kite, seizing her hand.

"You cannot hope to have last night's affair overlooked," continues Miss Tippits, allowing Mr. Kite to retain her hand, as though his ecstatic seizure of it were a very ordinary occurrence.

"It was quite accidental, that mistake of the card—on my honour. Miss Tippits, once for all I now lay my life and fortune at your feet. For three long years I have loved you; it is only that passion which has induced me to work and slave, day and night, in your father's political interest. It is now impossible that he can do without me."

"That is no concern of mine," says Miss Tippits.

" It is—it is, Clementina ! Let us be a happy family; say what your heart prompts you to say—that you do not love this Pigeon—that you will now reward the love and faithful service of a true, devoted heart ! "

Miss Tippits, looking into the garden, sees Tom Pigeon and Jessie in close conversation ; she knows that Thornton is beyond her reach. Taking her cue from fate, without a moment's hesitation, she returns Kite's pressure of her hand.

" There is some one coming, Mr. Kite," she says ; " take me into the drawing-room."

Kite at once takes the blooming husband-huntress under his

arm, kisses her fat and rosy fingers, and disappears with her just as the Colonel and old Pigeon enter the room.

"We shall be alone here, sir," says the Colonel. "Pray be seated."

"Thank you, Colonel!" says old Pigeon, determined not to be influenced by the largest possible amount of politeness.

"Now, Mr. Pigeon, you do not surely mean to say you are serious?" begins the Colonel.

"I am, sir."

"Think of the honour and the position which your son would obtain by such a marriage."

A knock at the door interrupts the Colonel's speech.

"Confound the people! why cannot they leave us alone? Come in!" he exclaims.

"It is only me," says Tom Pigeon, entering and looking at his father with a peculiarly satisfied smile.

"We were just talking about you, Tommy," says old Pigeon.

"Yes; I know all about it," says Tom. "It's all right. I've got rid of that infernal pain I had—got rid of it and all other pains too. Don't be surprised, Colonel; nothing ought to surprise nobody in these days. Now look here—I'm plain and aboveboard, father, and I ain't up to this kind of life; and, what's more, without meaning to be offensive, you've been playing a sort of come-into-my-parlour-said-the-spider game, and——"

"Sir!" exclaimed the Colonel, "I do not understand you."

"No; but you will," says Tom.

"I do," says old Pigeon. "My dear boy you have come to your senses, that's it—ain't it?"

"Right you are, governor," says Tom.

"I await an explanation," says the Colonel, taking up a dignified position upon the hearth-rug and looking as calmly as he could, first at Tom, and then at old Pigeon.

" If you will come into the drawing-room, where several friends are now assembled, and request the presence of Miss Tippits and Mr. Kite, I shall give you a full and complete explanation," says Tom, taking his father's arm and leading the astonished old man from the room.

We leave him standing in the doorway and telling the Colonel that " No offence is intended, Colonel Tippits—only we all means business, and that business is to be settled at once, sir, with all respect, in the drawing-room of this noble Castle."

The prompter—who, in this case, is the story-teller—proceeds to ring up the drawing-room scene accordingly.

IX.

AND LAST.

THE change which had come over Tom Pigeon during the last few hours was almost as remarkable as the transformation of that extraordinary creature which would " split " in presence of Kingsley's wonderful water baby. Mr. Thornton had been talking to Tom about a variety of subjects, and the Colonel unfortunately for himself, had explained to his expected son-in-law the reason why he was enabled to give Miss Tippits so handsome a dowry. Moreover, Tom had met Jessie Miller in a shady walk, outside the lawn, and had there and then confessed himself an ass and a coward. Miss Austin had followed this up by a judicious word or two concerning Mr. Thornton's expectations and the Society which Tom might yet see if he played a manly part, as he had been advised to do, at the Castle, on this last day of his father's visit; for old Pigeon had packed up, and was determined to go to London without further delay. Tom must indeed have been a booby if the events of the previous four-and-twenty hours had not convinced him of the excellence of Mr. Thornton's advice to break the Tippit bondage, and be free. Besides, Thornton had placed such excellent cards in his hands, that the most unskilful player in the world's game could not fail to make every trick. Tom was, therefore, master of the situation when the family and guests assembled in the drawing-room.

"Now let me arrange your places," said Tom when all were assembled. "It is not much I ask, Colonel, and I have nothing to say or do that can be objectionable, you know."

The Colonel said Mr. Pigeon had only to say what he wished to secure his utmost desires at Tinsell Castle.

"Ah, Kite ! I did not see you for the moment," exclaimed Tom, rushing up to Kite and shaking him by the hand. "We are going to have a family and general explanation—just as they do at the theatres you know, Kite. Now look here, Kite, and Miss Tippits, will you kindly sit here, on this ottoman ? There—thank you—that will be excellent."

Old Pigeon looked on in amazement.

"And, Mr. Thornton, will you sit here on my left—thank you, near Miss Austin—yes, that will do capitally. Miss Miller, you shall sit near me ; and Mr. Theophilus Pigeon, you shall sit where you please."

'Thank you, Tommy," said old Pigeon.

"This is very amusing—very," said the Colonel somewhat contemptuously.

"Glad you think so," said Tom, taking the eye-glass from his neck and putting it in his pocket. "Colonel Tippits, ladies and gentlemen, Mr. Thornton has done me the honour to allow me to be his spokesman on this interesting and important occasion ; Miss Austin ditto ; likewise Miss Jessie. Kite, shall I speak for you ?"

"Tom Pigeon, you are a good fellow at heart—I will trust you," said Kite: "though I am not clear about what you mean."

"Shall I add your name, Miss Tippits," said Tom: "may I represent your interests in the family settlement? The cards are all in my hands; and as I am about to retire from Society, I know what I am doing. Yes or no: it is not much I ask?"

"I shall remain a spectator, sir," said Miss Tippits.

"Very good," said Tom—"Colonel, what can I do for you?"

"Sir," said the Colonel, "as head of this establishment, and in the capacity of——"

"Yes, yes," said Tom, interrupting the speaker; "we know all that, and we intend to come to the hustings to hear you speak. Meanwhile capital, you know—capital must have its due weight. The Pigeons will foreclose, unless—you know what I mean."

"I submit, for the present at all events," said the Colonel.

"Mr. Thornton's solicitor and a friend are at the Green Dragon. They are not quite satisfied with Colonel Tippits's papers in the matter of Miss Austin's guardianship. Put that little matter right, Colonel, and the lady shall settle her present annuity upon you."

"How dare you, sir!" exclaimed the Colonel, rising to his feet and confronting Tom, his face scarlet with indignation and fear.

"Don't interrupt, Colonel," said Tom, nodding at Thornton, to reassure that gentleman, who seemed, for the moment, to fear that Tom was not playing his cards discreetly.

"Your conduct, sir, is disgraceful," said the Colonel.

"No: quite a mistake. Not mine," said Tom. "Pray be calm: it is all for your own good, I assure you."

The Colonel walked about the room impatiently, and old Pigeon did nothing but stare at his son.

"Miss Tippits," continued Tom, "finding that she really does not care for Tom Pigeon, who is only a tailor's son, and not in Society——"

"Well done, Tommy; I knew your heart was in the right place," said old Pigeon, unable to remain quiet any longer.

"As I was saying," continued Tom, "before Mr. Pigeon senior interrupted me, Miss Tippits, having reconsidered the state of her affections, accepts one thousand a year, which I shall settle upon her, and with it the hand of my old friend, Charley Kite."

"Bless you, Pigeon! Bless you!" exclaimed Kite, looking a world of admiration at Miss Tippits, and everlasting gratitude at Tom.

"The Colonel, wishing to be at peace with all men," went on the calm dispenser of Fate, "restores Mr. Miller to his farm; and Thomas Pigeon, selfishly desirous of being happy for life, asks Jessie Miller, before this noble company, if she will have old Pigeon's harum-scarum son for better for worse, &c., with an understanding that going into Society is not his game in future."

Then turning to the young lady on his right, Tom, raising his voice, said, "Jessie, I love you, and confess it."

"Don't be foolish, Tom," was all Jessie said in reply.

"I will not be foolish any more," said Tom. "But I put the question now, once for all: Will you, or won't you?"

"I will," said Jessie, blushing and looking steadfastly upon the floor.

"Hooray!" exclaimed old Pigeon. "Hooray! and many of them."

"Don't anticipate events," said Tom, looking at his father and waiving his hand for silence. "Is it agreed, Colonel Tippits? Mortgage renewed for any length of time you like. A thousand a year for Miss Tippits—Mrs. Kite I hope to say ere long. No law-suit about Miss Austin's property, and a splendiferous present from old Pigeon into the bargain. Miss Austin's annuity, you know, settled on yourself. Everybody happy, and no troublesome consciences, eh? No opposition at Inglenook?"

"You tempt me, Mr. Pigeon—my instincts are naturally social and liberal," said the Colonel, who had been carefully calculating the chances in a law-suit, and the inconvenience of foreclosing the mortgage on Tinsell Castle.

"Say yes," said Tom.

The Colonel crossed over to old Pigeon. "How much?" he said, in a loud whisper.

Mr. Pigeon senior took the Colonel, and whispered something in his ear.

"I knew I should settle it, Mr. Thornton," said Tom; "it has all come as it ought; we are all sorted as right as nine-pence, just like a play, and it might be called Birds of a Feather! Here, for instance, here are we the humble but happy Pigeons——"

"Tailor birds," whispered Thornton to Miss Austin.

"Did anyone speak?" asked Tom, immediately. "Yes or no? it is not much I ask. To proceed, as I was saying—here we are, the Pigeons, the Kites, and——"

"The love birds," said Thornton.

"I shall call you the magpies, presently," said Tom, laughing and shaking his fist at Thornton. "Shall I go on or not?"

"Hear him, hear him!" exclaimed the Colonel: "that is what I shall demand for my honourable opponents on the hustings."

"Hustings!" exclaimed young Pigeon. "Happy thought! This is the only hustings worth appearing upon; you ladies and gentlemen the only electors worth appealing to! Ladies and gentlemen, free and independent——"

"I protest!" said the Colonel. "I only have a right to make an election speech here."

"Ladies and gentlemen, I will only say, Vote for the Pigeons!" said Tom.

"And the Kites," said Miss Tippits' intended.

"That will do," said old Pigeon. "Let us all shake hands, and be friends!"

"With all my heart," said the Colonel. "I don't know what I lose by the transaction, but this is the happiest day of my life."

"And mine," said Kite, kissing Miss Tippits.

"And mine," said Tom, putting his arm round Jessie.

"And mine," said Thornton, pressing Miss Austin's hand.

"And mine," said old Pigeon, taking both the Colonel's hands in his, and shaking them until the two old old boys were quite red in the face.

If this were really a play (instead of being just like one, as Tom Pigeon puts it), the whole of the company would waltz prettily to the tune of Tom Pigeon's chorus, and the curtain would go down amidst, I hope, a round of applause. But not being a play, the story ends with the explanation that the Pigeons did not leave the Castle until after the celebration of a triple wedding at Inglenook, the gorgeous celebration of which obtained for the Colonel so much *kudos* that his election for the borough is a matter of dead certainty. Mr. and Mrs. Tom Pigeon are at the present moment on their wedding tour at Margate; Mr. and Mrs. Thornton are similarly engaged at Nice; Mr. and Mrs. Kite are amusing themselves at Hamburgh; old Pigeon is having a quiet pipe in his favourite bar parlour; and Col. Tippits is only waiting for that peculiar combination of parties which is to bring about the next general election.

HOW WE GOT MARRIED.

IT is curious to reflect how the majority of married couples may be said to have *drifted* into the wedded state. Some chance meeting, some trifling circumstance, is in many cases the commencement of an acquaintance that ripens into a life-long union.

"That not impossible she
Who shall command my heart and me"

is rarely (save in France) introduced to us in orthodox form as our future wife. We stumble on our fate unexpectedly in nine cases out of ten: a visit to a country-house; a shower of rain, which induces us to lend our umbrella to a stranger; a journey by a public conveyance,—all these may be the first steps on the road that leads us into the proverbial "lane which has no turning."

We sheltered a young lady from a shower of hail at a flower-show, and little thought *then* that she was the future Mrs. Brown. When we assisted that old gentleman and his daughter at the railway station, nothing was further from our thoughts than matrimony; yet in another twelve months that young lady was standing beside us in the full glory of white satin and orange-blossoms.   As for accidents, if ever I met with one by road or rail, and was conveyed to a private house for recovery (people always are, in novels), I should, if a single man, fully expect that a beautiful daughter of the house would undertake the post of sick-nurse, and eventually become my wife.

After all, it was through an accident that I did get married. Not the orthodox fall from a horse, or injury in a train ; but an accident of another kind.   Some years ago when I went to my first curacy—I had never left home before, except for my school and university careers—I found Martin-on-Sands terribly lonely at first.   It was a dull respectable little watering-place, on the east coast ; with the usual row of white houses with green blinds facing the sea ; the usual "esplanade ; " the usual little shops where shell ornaments were sold.   It was an intensely quiet place ; its inhabitants proudly boasted that "no excursionists ever came there," and indeed there was nothing to attract them.   There are two types of English seaside resorts : the gay and noisy, where donkeys, bands, and niggers

flourish; and the quiet spots like Martin-on-Sands, where existence is peaceful, not to say stagnant.

People with large families came to us during the summer and autumn, lodgings and provisions being reasonable, and the sands affording capital play-grounds for the children; but the town was not a lively residence at the best of times. The vicar was an old man greatly afflicted with gout, and the chief work of the parish devolved on his curate; but there was not very arduous toil for either of us. Most of the townspeople had realised the Wise Man's wish, and possessed " neither poverty nor riches." Except season visitors we had few gentry among us; small lodging-house keepers, shop-keepers, and fisher-folk making up the bulk of our population. At the same time we had hardly any actual poor. The fishers were, as a class, quiet hard-working people, and seemed able to earn enough to keep themselves and families in fair comfort.

Of course there was the usual routine of parish work, church services and school, sick and aged people to visit; but I found my time certainly not too well filled. Mr. Gray, the incumbent, disliked anything new, and would not have permitted any additions to the usual round of my parochial labours; so I found plenty of leisure in which to be dull. We were a large merry family at home; and sometimes, sitting by myself in my lodgings, evening after evening, time went slowly enough. A few months after my instalment in my new post, I succeeded in persuading a married sister to come to Martin-on-Sands with her children. This was, indeed, a pleasant change for me, and nearly every evening I used to go round to her lodgings to enjoy a chat with her and a romp with the children, with whom I was a great favourite.

One dark autumn evening I had started out later than usual —a visit to a sick man had detained me; but I was anxious not to omit my usual call, as Helen was to return to London the next day. I hurried along the neat row of houses which formed the aristocratic quarter of our town, and rapped at the well-known door. "You need not announce me," I said, passing the neat maid-servant; "I am expected;" and I hurried upstairs. Just outside the drawing-room door lay a large black-fur rug, which I had never observed before. As I looked at it the idea struck me that I might make a brilliant entrance into the room on this farewell visit. It was past seven o'clock; all the children would be assembled in the drawing-room after their tea. I would enter in the character of a bear. Wrapping myself in the rug, I opened the door and crawled in on all-fours, emitting sundry growling sounds. A scream greeted me—that was to be expected; but in place of the laughter that ought to have succeeded it, I was terrified to hear a shrill female voice, certainly not Helen's, exclaiming, "Thieves! Murder! Rose, Maria! help, help!"

Stunned for a moment, I hastily began to disengage the bear-dress; and when I got the length of my knees with my head free, to my dismay, found myself in a strange room, with two strange ladies standing opposite; one young and very pretty, the other a much older one, who stood intrenched behind a chair, in which she had doubtless been peacefully dozing until disturbed by my abrupt entry. It must have been a shock to her to be awoke from tranquil repose by the sight of a strange animal crawling in at the door, nor was the discovery that the animal was a strange man likely to reassure her.

As for myself—a German author has noted in his diary that at a certain date he "behaved as a fool"—I certainly passed a similar mental verdict on myself. I had evidently entered a wrong house by mistake, and played what looked like a practical joke on an entire stranger. It was a dignified and pleasant position for the curate of the parish to find himself

A NEW WAY OF ENTERING A DRAWING ROOM.

in! If the story spread to the rector's ears! Mr. Gray was a starched specimen of the old school of frigid politeness, who abominated levity of demeanour, and I am sure would not have crawled on all-fours had his life depended upon it. I was young and shy, and my absurd position was really no joke to me. As soon as I could find breath I essayed to explain matters to the frightened and irate old lady. I apologised most humbly for my intrusion, explained my mistake; but my efforts were ill received. I found an ally, however, in the shape of the sweet-looking girl, who endeavoured to mollify the old lady's wrath, accepted my apologies smilingly, and joined me in every possible way in trying to sooth her angry relative.

"It's all a mistake, auntie," she whispered. "Don't you see it's Mr. Morley, our curate?"

"And more shame for him to play such a vulgar ungentlemanly trick!" retorted the old dame, not to be so easily mollified.

"Madam, you cannot think I intended to alarm you thus," I stammered, wishing I could sink into the floor. "I unfortunately mistook the house; I was intending to make a little diversion for my nephews and nieces."

"Is there not a number on my door, sir? Could you not have ascertained that you had entered the right house before commencing this buffoonery? Very unbecoming for a clergyman in any case, in my judgment."

"O auntie!" whispered the young lady, her face flushing. Then turning to me, she said gently, "My aunt is not strong, and this has startled her; but I am sure the mistake was quite accidental on your part."

How grateful I felt to her for those kind words!

"Sir," said the old lady, eyeing me severely through her spectacles, "as my niece appears to know you, and states that you are the curate of this parish, I suppose I am bound to acquit you of intentions of robbery, which your extraordinary conduct at first suggested. At the same time it is difficult to understand any gentleman in your position exhibiting himself, even to juvenile relatives, in the foolish, the undignified manner in which you entered this room. I should have imagined that Mr. Gray would have selected an assistant of less levity of character. My nerves have received a severe shock, and as you are now aware that this is not the house you intended to visit, perhaps you will leave us."

I blundered through a few more apologies, and went out terribly crestfallen, though the young lady bowed and smiled as we parted. Evidently *she* was not offended.

Helen received the news of my adventure with peals of laughter.

"Charlie, Charlie! that you should have selected old Mrs. Piggot of all people to play this trick upon! You are an unlucky fellow!"

"Do you know the old lady, then?"

"Only by repute. She comes here every year, and has often lodged with my landlady. She is really a kind-hearted old soul, I believe, but has a very crusty temper."

"I can vouch for that," I answered ruefully.

"O, if I had only been there!" cried Helen, going off into fresh peals of laughter. "Poor dear Charlie crawling in, and old Mrs. Piggot's wrath—what an introduction to one of your parishioners! I wonder if the old lady will ever forgive you."

She did one day. Probably the reader guesses the sequel of my story. I made Helen call on the offended dame next day, and she succeeded in making my peace so well that I was allowed to present my apologies in person afterwards.

Then I called occasionally; of course on each occasion seeing Miss Rose, the old lady's niece. Then, as Fate willed it, Mrs. Piggot fell ill, and took a fancy to winter at Martin-on-Sands. Of course Miss Rose and I met frequently during these months. A friendship grew up between us; friendship often ripens into a deeper feeling. Just a year after my abrupt entrance into Mrs. Piggot's drawing-room, I married my Rose. The old lady agreed at last—I think she had her doubts about my "steadiness of conduct;" but although only a curate I had a comfortable private income to offer Rose, who had hitherto been a pensioner on her aunt, and this circumstance may have weighed in my favour.

It is some years since our wedding-day; but as I look back I feel grateful to the accident which was instrumental in bestowing on me the sweetest and dearest wife that ever blessed a man's home.

At the same time I would not advise my readers to enter strange houses wrapped in rugs, on the chance of finding another Rose.

BRADBURY, AGNEW, & CO., PRINTERS, WHITEFRIARS.

www.ingramcontent.com/pod-product-compliance
Lightning Source LLC
Chambersburg PA
CBHW051114120726
47905CB00005B/1271